To Isabel

MW01393628

I hope you enjoy!

NEVES

A novel by

CARLOS R SAVOURNIN

Carlos R Savournin

Copyright © 2008 by Carlos R Savournin
All Rights Reserved

This book is a work of fiction. Names, characters, businesses, organizations, places, events, and incidents either are the product of the author's imagination or are used fictitiously. Any resemblance to actual persons, living or dead, events or locales is entirely coincidental.

Library of Congress Cataloging-in-Publication Data
Savournin, Carlos R.
NEVES / Carlos R Savournin. – 1st ed.
ISBN: 978-1-4357-0900-3

Printed in the USA

For too many people to mention

(You all know who you are)

For my family.

Thank you for your undying support.

For those who believe, no explanation is necessary.
For those who do not, no explanation will suffice.
- Angela Ortega

Chapter One

The deaths that stained her memory and infected her mind were still with her though the war was over. They would be with her until she exorcised them. There were those who would not believe her stories of the war, but that was of no concern to her. First, she needed to find refuge; a place where her mind would settle and her body would rest.

What if Death followed me? she wondered as she entered the hotel's lobby.

The automatic doors slid to a close, sealing out the night's storm. The stale air of the building hit her at once, her breath falling short at the sudden claustrophobia, and she gripped the handles of the plastic bags in her hand tighter on reflex alone. A hotel, she thought, would be the safest place to hide; once she was in her room, alone, away from anyone and everyone who posed a threat. But the moment she stepped foot in the lobby, she second guessed herself. Could it be she just walked into another trap?

She glanced over her shoulder to make sure her car was visible before taking count of the people in the lobby. There was a young couple waiting for the elevator, a mother and child near the souvenir boutique, and an elderly woman at the check-in desk attended by a young man. None of them noticed her enter, but Cynthia knew that each of them were a threat. Her death could be *inside* one of them.

Stepping onto the cheap carpeting, she hissed when a jolt of pain ricocheted from her right calf and settled around her waist. The wound was bandaged with a piece of torn cloth wearing heavy with the mixture of rain and blood. It served its purpose and stopped the bleeding, but the pain was a different story. She prepared herself for another jolt, taking a slow step forward, keeping a steady eye on the check-in desk.

The elderly woman turned toward the lobby's doors giving Cynthia nothing more than a passing glance, and for that, she was thankful.

She moved slowly toward the check-in clerk, a young man dressed in a burgundy uniform that seemed out-dated. Avoiding eye contact with him, her eyes went to the nametag on his lapel.

Danny.

"One room, please," she said, making sure no one else could hear her.

He smiled then began pecking away at the computer's keyboard.

She could feel his eyes studying her as he checked the vacancy, and the voice in her head began with yet another prayer.

Please don't recognize me, please…

"Aren't you Cynthia Grazer?" he asked. "The writer?"

Defeated, Cynthia took quick glances around the lobby. It was empty.

Vocally, she didn't answer, but the look on her face was more than a whisper of confirmation. She looked at his face for a second and found his young eyes focused on her. Cynthia saw his face had yet to meet a wrinkle or seemingly feel the steel of a razorblade. She quickly estimated his age to be, at most, twenty.

"I've read all your books," he said. "I'm a big fan."

They were the same words she heard from her fans many times before, but their delivery was different. Most fans smiled, even laughed when meeting her, but Danny seemed concerned.

And why wouldn't he be? Beside the fact that she was limping the entire way to the check-in desk, Cynthia knew she didn't look like the publicity photos on the backs of her novels. He had every right to be concerned after seeing her limp and discovering the bruises on her face's delicate skin.

Cynthia kicked herself for not thinking of being less conspicuous, but she couldn't think right about anything at all. Still, she forced a smile as she readjusted her hair in the messy bun above her head, inadvertently revealing the bruised tear on the center of her forehead. She combed her hair back over it, praying Danny didn't notice.

But he stared directly at it then frowned at her. "Are you okay?" he asked.

"I'm fine," she said. "One room please."

He didn't continue to pry.

"The length of your stay?" he asked, trying hard not to stare.

"One night," she answered immediately.

Danny pecked some more and the printer beside his computer erupted to life. He took a key card and swiped it in a reader much like a credit card machine and a wave of relief fell over Cynthia. He found a room for her – hopefully on a floor that was otherwise empty.

"Danny," she said softly. "Can I ask you a favor?"

His eyes widened, obviously surprised by her voice. He nodded, meeting the writer's green eyes for the first time that night.

"No one is to know I am here," she told him. "Please don't tell *anyone* that you've seen me, and if anyone calls for me, tell them that you've never heard of me, you've never read one of my books, you don't know me. Can you do that?"

Danny nodded still in obvious surprise.

"Thank you."

She paid for the room in cash, and when he handed her the key card, his eyes widened again. She knew at once that he noticed her hands. Both sets of knuckles were bruised, the skin healing from numerous wounds as though they were forced through a cheese grater. His grip on the key tightened.

When she was unable to pry it from his hand, she looked back at him in surprise.

"Are you okay?" he repeated, demanding it the way she demanded her orders.

Cynthia sighed and looked away. "Send up a first-aid kit, please," she told him, his finger gently touching hers across the key card. The touch of the stranger felt somewhat comfortable to her, unexpectedly relaxing her. She met his eyes again and forced a thankful smile. "I'll be okay."

Danny released the key. "Seventh floor," he said. "Room 77." He watched as she limped towards the elevators weaving the plastic bag's handles between her thin, damaged hands.

*

The elevator doors opened on the seventh floor revealing a long, lonely corridor. It was dimly lit; small light fixtures were set between each wooden door on both sides of the hall. She studied the beige walls and matching carpeting until the hall turned left and out of her sight. The rattling of a distant ice machine filled the air, but beyond that, there was complete silence.

She stepped off the elevator cautiously, the doors sliding closed behind her, trapping her in the hall. The first door to her right was marked with a golden *70*, the door to her left was tagged *71*.

Room 77, Danny's voice echoed in her head.

She could see her number on the fourth door to the left.

Fifteen paces…I can do this.

She began her descent, limping toward the door without looking away from it. Seek your goal and aim to achieve it, her therapist told her a hundred times before, and as Cynthia passed the door marked *73*, the motivation began to set in. Though she only took a few steps, she was that much closer to her room and that much closer to her salvation.

The bell that echoed suddenly throughout the hall was not loud, but it was enough to bring Cynthia to near panic. It came from behind her, and she immediately realized she heard the same bell moments before.

The elevator…

She stopped, her heart pounding relentlessly in her chest as the doors slid open behind her. She felt the burn of a stare, sending her body into tremors. Death followed her after all.

It was in Danny…

She wasn't ready to face her enemy. Not again. Still, she strained her neck to turn just her head, keeping her body facing forward in case she would have to sprint away. She could barely walk, let alone run, yet recent experience taught her that when the body soared with adrenaline, amazing things happened. A mere flesh wound would not keep her from saving her own life.

The light fixtures began to flicker on and off before she had a full view of the elevator, but they remained burning at full power. Cynthia wanted to believe that it was due to the storm, but she knew that if Death *had* arrived, they might have flickered from Its presence. She saw stranger things in the past week.

But the elevator was empty. The bell was still ringing in her ears as she scanned the small lift. There was no room for anyone to hide in its corners, nor had there been enough time for someone to have stepped off and into one of the rooms behind her. It was as if the elevator opened on its own.

She rushed to the door marked *77* and quickly unlocked it, not daring to look over her shoulder. The door opened inward into an abyss of darkness and Cynthia cursed her luck. Her hands felt for the light switch on the walls before she entered, and when she found it, she quickly flipped it upward. Just as the soft light filled the room, she entered swiftly and slammed the door behind her. Turning the bolt above the knob, she locked herself into the room before inspecting it.

One lock, she reluctantly thought. She would have felt better if there were a second.

The room was as small and simple as the hallway. The carpet and walls were matching beige, and there were several landscape paintings hung in no particular fashion. A television set atop a small dresser was a short distance from the foot of the queen-sized bed, and as Cynthia looked to the opposite wall, she froze.

She caught her own reflection on the sliding glass door amidst the night's sky. It led to a small balcony where the beach's shores could be seen just beyond the parking lot below. Tossing the plastic bags onto the bed, Cynthia crossed the room and pulled the verticals closed in a hurry. The blinds would remain closed that night.

The door tucked in the east corner of the room led to the bathroom. A single bulb hanging from a fixture in the ceiling nearly blinded Cynthia when she flipped it on, revealing the room's contents. A stand-up shower stall, a toilet bowl set beside it, and a small sink next to a rack stocked with clean, fresh towels. Without a second's thought on how small the room was, she turned on the sink's faucet, and splashed her face with cold water.

It felt amazing; her skin, dried by the recent sweat and tears, absorbed the water like arid soil. It was complete rejuvenation, though a careless scrub of the abrasion on her forehead proved quite displeasing. Avoiding her reflection in the mirror above the sink, she reached for a towel and walked out of the bathroom, promising herself a full shower when she was done with what she planned to do, even if it meant waiting until sunrise.

After adjusting the pillows by propping them onto the headboard, Cynthia slowly brought her tired body down, becoming weak the moment she felt the softness beneath her. Her head pounded with exhaustion and her blood shot eyes grew dry and heavy as the thought of undisturbed slumber entered her mind. She wanted to give in, but she couldn't because sleeping was out of the question.

Slowly, she brought her legs upward onto the bed then unlaced her sneakers. After reaching for one of the plastic bags at her feet, she sat back on the fluffed headboard and allowed a moment to recoup.

She emptied the bag, spilling its contents onto the bed; three spiral bound notebooks and a five pack of pens with foam grips. She stacked the items neatly, deciding to make immediate use of the contents that were the last to fall out; a pack of menthol cigarettes and a brand new disposable lighter.

She didn't ask Danny for a smoker's room and, frankly, she didn't care whether she was in one or not. A quick glance at the night table beside the bed told her that her luck was improving; between the lamp and the telephone, and beside the alarm clock was an ashtray. Without another second passing, Cynthia placed a cigarette between her dry, pale lips and lit it.

She listened to the sound of its burn as she puffed it slowly taking a deep breath to inhale the sweet poisons. Cynthia's head fell backwards onto the board, and she closed her eyes. It was her first cigarette in nearly twenty years. She admitted missing it, and remembered how much she loved it. She puckered her lips and exhaled, watching the gray smoke dance around her until it vanished. Her shoulders relaxed, *slumped* in fact, as though the tension was lifted.

The pack would probably be emptied before sun-up.

She glanced at the alarm clock; the red digital numbers reading 9:07 P.M. After taking another puff, Cynthia placed the cigarette onto the ashtray and one of the notebooks on her lap.

Each notebook contained 150 college ruled pages, and she wondered if it would be enough to tell her story. She had not written an entire novel on notebook paper since her first, but it was not a novel she intended on writing.

It would be her first deviation from fiction, and she would be criticized for it. Not because it was nonfiction, but because of its contents. She wasn't discouraged, though. In fact, it was quite the opposite.

She opened the notebook to the first blank page then opened the pack of pens.

Cynthia Grazer was the first thing she wrote. She stared at her handwriting at the top of the page, and as though she were dissatisfied with it, she wrote her name again…

Cynthia Grazer

…and once again…

Cynthia Grazer

Satisfied, she closed her eyes and took a breath delving into the memories so fresh in her brain. Her mind ran through the events of her life that she wanted to put on paper, but Cynthia was uncertain as to whether or not she was ready to relive it. It was a story that she deemed necessary to tell, not only for herself, but also for those who would believe. It was the story of the events that led her to the hotel on that very night.

She thought of beginning with a formal introduction; expressive words explaining her deviation from fiction to a story of her life. She wondered if she should elaborate on the fact that she was risking her career and reputation by swearing to a story that many people wouldn't believe. Knowing that some of her peers would call her story nothing more than a publicity stunt, she considered insisting that her story was true. But just as those thoughts entered her head, she shook them away. An introduction was not necessary to begin her story.

She puffed her cigarette once more, deciding that the best place, the only place, to start her story was obvious; at the beginning.

The Beginning: June 6th; Eighteen Years Ago

We were just kids then - teenagers in the midst of summer vacation and without a care in the world. Freed from the tediousness of school, we were only concerned about how we could make the time pass. But time proved to be our enemy as the events that changed our lives began to unfold, and there was nothing we could do to stop it.

I remember mom and Aunt Mayra were up worried early that morning. The sun was barely over the Miami skies, and the sounds of their worried voices woke me. When I walked into the dining room, I knew something was wrong because Aunt Mayra was smoking, a habit my mother and father despised. Mom was pacing in the kitchen, a phone attached to her ear and a look of concern across her face. She slammed the receiver onto the unit and slapped her thighs in desperation.

"I'm sure he's fine," my Aunt Mayra told her, "he's a good detective."

Then it hit me; Dad had not come home from work. He was usually in before we were sleeping, but Mom said he was working on a big case and he'd be running late. Though he had been late before…

"He always calls," Mom told her sister, then picked the phone up and punched numbers.

"Try Hector," I said from the entrance of the dining room. My dad's partner on the force, Hector Corona, was always by his side. If one couldn't be reached, it was only natural the other was tried.

"We already have," Mom said. "We can't reach him either." There were tears in her eyes, and she was trembling. Countless times, she told my father to leave the force. She was terrified that one day she would receive the dreaded phone call, but Dad assured her it would never happen. It was for that very reason that Dad never told us about his cases, insisting it was better we didn't know so we wouldn't worry. Still Mom had his badge number memorized for such an occasion.

"What's going on?" Luis asked from behind me. "What's wrong with Dad?"

My brother was only fifteen at the time, two years younger than myself, and I couldn't stand him. I didn't *hate* him, but like every other family of siblings, our rivalry was very much alive. I treated him the way an older sister should treat her dorky brother.

"Nothing's wrong," I said to him, sneering over my shoulder. "Go back to bed."

"Shut up."

"This is *not* the time, you two," Mom warned us. "Both of you go back to your rooms."

We didn't move. Luis and I just exchanged glances then looked to Aunt Mayra for her rescue. She didn't give.

"*Now!*" Mom yelled.

We each bolted toward the staircase before Mom let out another anger filled yell.

"It's your fault," Luis whispered from behind me as we reached the second floor, clear of Mom's super ears. "Stupid Cyn's gotta ruin it for all of us."

"Shut up."

"What am I supposed to do now?" he whined. "I'm wide awake, thanks to you."

"I don't care what you do so long as you leave me alone." Before he could respond, I turned from the hall into my room and swiftly closed the door before him.

Leaving him to find a locked doorknob, I glanced to my cousin sprawled on my bedroom floor. She and I spent most of our childhood years together and lived like sisters. Two years before, my Uncle George landed an accounting job in a prestigious New York firm, packed up the car and moved, taking my Aunt Mayra and cousin Rebecca with him. A few days after we were released from the prison of school, Aunt Mayra informed my mother that she and Uncle George separated, and she wanted to stay with us for the summer. Despite the news, I was excited to have my cousin back.

Luis was not too happy about it. It was like having two older sisters instead of just me.

She was awake when I walked into the room. Her eyes were open, but she was still on her back, staring up at the ceiling.

The night before, after everyone was asleep, Rebecca stole a few cigarettes from her mother's purse and we smoked them out of my bedroom window. Like adults, we spoke of the daily dilemmas in our lives while we puffed away until three in the morning. It was barely seven when I walked back into the room, and I could see Rebecca was not pleased at the fact that she too had been awakened.

"Dad still hasn't come home," I said to her as I crossed the room toward my bed. "Mom's freaking out downstairs."

"Do you think he's okay?" she asked.

Sitting on my bed, hearing those words, I assured myself that he was. Aunt Mayra was right when she said Dad was a good detective. A well-respected man, my dad's name was known by officials across Dade County. If something happened to him, someone would have certainly informed us of it.

"He's fine," I finally said.

The doorbell rang and I froze, my blood pressure rising instantly.

Rebecca and I exchanged glances while I quietly said a little prayer. Despite my confidence in Dad, I knew he wouldn't ring the doorbell to enter his own home, and visitors were rare at such an early hour.

Unless they had bad news to accompany them.

Luis was already in the hall by the time I opened my bedroom door. We headed to the top of the staircase and leaned over the balcony for a clear view of the front door below.

Mom approached the door slowly, snuggling the top of her robe to keep it closed. Aunt Mayra followed closely behind, cigarette in hand.

"Who is it?" Luis whispered.

I didn't answer. I was still praying.

"Where the *hell* have you been?" Mom asked after she opened the door.

A handful of roses were held up to her face, shortly followed by another hand holding a bottle of champagne. My father stepped into the house, the top buttons of his dress shirt undone, and his tie and suit jacket slung over his right arm. He looked tired, exhausted in fact, but it didn't keep him from smiling.

"What is this?" Mom asked him, looking from the roses to the bottle.

There was a glisten in his dark brown eyes that morning; I noticed it from the second floor. Either he won the lottery and spent the night celebrating, or he closed the case he lost many nights of sleep over. My guess was the latter.

"We put the son of a bitch away," he said to her in a whisper then repeated it, loud enough to scare Rebecca into full consciousness. After putting Mom's gifts on the floor, he swept her off her feet in a massive hug.

My mother was probably confused, yet she could do nothing but laugh. She hadn't been given the chance to ring his ear about not calling, but I knew she would save it for later.

*

Mason Bayer was the son of a bitch that he put away. The house was suddenly alive when Dad began telling us the story of his pursuit. Mom put on a fresh pot of coffee, Aunt Mayra lit another cigarette, and Rebecca joined us as Dad took his seat at the table.

But his stories were never as exciting as we hoped. He would tell us very little of the suspect and moved directly to the tedious process in which he and his team captured the bad guy. From identifying just what kind of person they were dealing with, to the matter in which he was tracked, the story was always the same. What interested me were the details; the "trophy" the killer took from his victims, the careless clues he would leave behind, the forensics.

We learned that Mason Bayer was a serial killer and, somewhere in his story, Dad mentioned the trademark. Using any flat surface around his victim's body, Mason numbered his kill in backward English using their own blood for his art. Dad said Mason got as far as *XIS* before he was captured. It was a job well done.

Most of his colleagues felt the same way, apparently. Before Mr. Coffee finished the brew, the now famous Detective Todd Grazer received a phone call from the Mayor himself, congratulating him. Shortly after, the Chief of Police granted my father the rest of the week paid vacation. Before eight o'clock that morning, my father had gone from missing, to the most popular man in the city.

It was an exciting time for him, and Dad insisted we celebrate. The day was young, the weather was just above eighty-five degrees, and the pool out back was begging to be used. He excitedly suggested a bar-b-cue then insisted we invite a few friends. This was a happy day, he said, and happy days are celebrated.

*

When Luis told me that the Sheyers were to arrive before noon, I nearly fainted. Noon was less than an hour away, and I hadn't even showered! The Sheyers and my parents became friends when we moved to the neighborhood nearly ten years before. Their younger son, Logan, and I attended the same class, and by next summer, we would graduate high school together. His older brother, Nick, graduated the year before, and he was the reason I nearly passed out.

I was secretly in love with Nick. Well, it wasn't a secret, really. Everybody knew it; except Nick, and he wouldn't know as long as I lived, I was convinced. He was a varsity football player, and I was in the book club – happily ever after just didn't seem like a reality. Either way, I hurried into the bathroom and prepared myself for his visit.

At five minutes before noon, I was in the back yard with the adults, grabbing a can of cola from the cooler as Dad began setting the coal for the grill. Nick would arrive at any moment with his family, and I was prepared.

They were late, or so I assumed. I later discovered my despicable brother thought it would be funny to lie about the time the Sheyers were arriving, just so he could squeal with delight when he saw me in a panic to prepare. They didn't arrive until 1:30 that afternoon, and beside the fact that my makeup was now smudged, my hair was a frizzed mess and the empty can I was holding to appear casual was beginning to irritate me. Luis would pay for this, I told myself.

Mr. Sheyer stepped out into the back yard first and I stood to my feet, my eyes instantly searching behind him for Nick. Mrs. Sheyer stepped out second, followed by their son, but not the one I was hoping for.

Logan was the last one out. As each of them greeted my parents, I stared at the house, hoping Nick was just lagging behind.

"I don't think he's here," I said to Rebecca, almost in a whisper as the Sheyers were just meters from us. I didn't want them to hear.

"Oh yeah, I forgot," Luis said from somewhere behind us. "Nick said he wasn't coming."

I could have *killed* him, but he was already greeting the Sheyers, and I had no choice but to remain composed. I smiled as I welcomed each of them with a hug; except Logan. I found him as repulsive as I did Luis. They were the best of friends, and anyone who was a friend of Luis' earned the same treatment I gave him. They even *looked* alike. Both were tall and lanky and both forever in blue jeans and tee shirts. The only difference was that Luis, like me, was dark haired and Logan, like Nick, was blond.

Only it looked better on Nick.

So while they were off doing whatever it is that little brothers do, Rebecca and I took advantage of the sun and sat on the pool deck for another hour or so before Dad's next guests arrived. Detective Hector Corona, my father's partner, was joined by his daughter, Joanna, and another expensive bottle of champagne. Both he and Dad expressed their joy with a strong hug and heart-filled laughter while Joanna greeted everyone else then joined the rest of us on the pool deck.

"I'll never understand how two people can be so happy at one man's misfortune," she said to us as she sat on the deck.

"Hello to you, too, Jo," Rebecca followed.

"I mean, really," she continued, "I hope they don't act like this at their office."

She was eighteen years old, going on thirty. Growing up with Jo, I learned a lot. I looked up to her; considered her somewhat of a mentor. While most of us were excited to be free of school work, Jo kept her head straight and kept us out of trouble. "You're not old enough to smoke," she would tell us when the cigarettes were lit, and when that didn't work, she resorted to "Smoking is a terrible habit."

There wasn't a Mrs. Corona. A terrible divorce drove her to California to live with her parents, and Jo usually visited her every summer. That year, she stayed because she wanted to look into a few colleges before the school year gave out.

"Where's Nick?" she asked me after inspecting the yard and finding only Logan and Luis tossing a football back and forth.

I gave her the depressing news; that he wouldn't be joining in our festivities, but she shrugged and turned her attention to the boys again. "Well, at least I have Logan to keep me company," she said. "He's such a cutie."

"That's gross," I said.

And the day progressed as such. After devouring the hamburgers, hot dogs, potato salad and gallons of cola, the adults moved into the house for conversation and alcohol. The rest of us enjoyed the clear skies and summer sun until the last minute. Before long, night began to fall, and we retired to the house as well.

*

Before midnight, all the adults were drunk. Mr. Sheyer insisted that his wife drive home, but she slurred in response and they busted into a rowdy laugh. Both Dad and Hector were still reminiscing on the fact that Mason Bayer was behind bars, each taking a swift gulp from the second bottle of champagne. Mom and Aunt Mayra weren't sober either, but they were too busy cleaning up the table to notice.

There conversations shifted to the amazing way they saved the city by catching Mason Bayer to planning a fishing trip the following weekend. It would never happen. The amount of plans that were left as nothing more than spoken words always flowed across the table come drink time, and that was a clear signal of their intoxication. Fishing? My father never even touched a fishing pole in his life – but it was better than hearing the name Mason Bayer ever five minutes.

"Look at them," Jo said, staring at the entrance of the dining room. "They're like a bunch of drunken teenagers."

The rest of us were sprawled around the living room. Luis and Logan obediently remained on their side, behind an imaginary line Rebecca drew to split the living quarter in two. Still, all we did was talk, mostly about the adults.

"I guess we'll be staying here for the night," Logan said.

"I don't think so," I shot back. "There's no room."

Then, as if on cue, my father stood dramatically from his chair, nearly knocking it backwards into Mrs. Sheyer. "No one is driving home tonight," he announced in a deep rumbling voice, then pounded on his burly chest before letting out a belch. "You're too drunk!"

"You're the one who's drunk!" Hector replied.

"Told you," Logan said. "It happened last Christmas, remember?"

"How can I forget? There's still fungus on my pillow."

"There's plenty of space!" Mom yelled excitedly. "We'll let the kids stay in the pool house for the night, and everyone can use their rooms…"

She continued talking, but her words drifted when my brain registered what she said. Mom and Dad never let us have the pool house for the night! The instant she said it, all of us were exchanging excited looks as though we were awarded a grand prize.

"Is she kidding?" Rebecca asked, her words low as though should our parents hear her, they would change their minds.

"I hope not," Luis answered.

Dad walked into the room, his large face filled with euphoric joy. "Kids," he roared, "you're staying at the pool house." And just like that, it was settled.

We could have started jumping for joy like Dad and Hector were earlier, but we hid it from the adults until they were clear out of sight. Instantly, we were putting our shoes back on, barely able to stand the excitement.

Every time we asked them if we could have the pool house, they would shoot us down before we could word the question. Eventually, we stopped asking all together, knowing that one day, they would allow us to do so. The day had come, and I could only think of one thing that would make the night grander than it already was.

"It's too bad Nick isn't here," I said as casually as I could. "Wait until he finds out we had the pool house to ourselves."

Three knocks on the front door were followed by the turn of the doorknob. All of us turned to the foyer of the large living room and stared at the door as it opened inward slowly.

"Hello," the voice called from outside, instantly melting my skin.

Nick walked in.

The night was in my favor.

The Fallen Mighty

The pool house was set on the east side of the yard, at least fifteen feet from the back porch of the main house. It was normally used as a guest room for out of town visitors, and for just such occasions. Large enough to accommodate four adults for day-to-day living, it was fully equipped with a private bathroom, a small kitchenette and a plush sofa bed. A retractable bed that slept two was tucked in the corner, as were the sleeping bags from last summer's camping trip.

It was decided that the men would use the floor for the night so the girls could rest comfortably on the beds. However, sleep was not our priority.

Rebecca managed to steal a box of cigarettes from her mother's carton and distributed them evenly amongst the rest of us; except to Jo.

Within minutes of our being there, the house was filled with second hand smoke, and Luis opened the window to a view of the pool for ventilation. The house, where all the adults were presumably ready for bed, was just beyond the pool. From our view, all the lights on the first and second floors were already turned off.

"They can't already be asleep," Luis said, watching the house.

"No way," Nick replied. "Just be patient."

Patient? "For what?" I asked, remembering how long the three boys were talking together before Luis moved to the window.

"When they're all asleep," Logan began, "Nick and I are going on a beer run."

"You can't buy beer," Jo said in a whisper, as though anyone outside the house could hear her. "You're not old enough."

Nick shook his head, "I'm not going to buy it. I'm going to go inside and grab some from the cooler."

She was shocked at his plan, gasping then insisting he forget about it. What if they notice the beer was gone in the morning?

"They're drunk, Jo," Rebecca said, finding the idea splendid. "They won't know where they are in the morning, let alone how many beers were left. Besides, there's like three untouched cases in the kitchen."

The debate didn't continue much longer afterwards. Despite what Jo said, Nick ordered Logan to lace his sneakers and they both left for the run a little over half an hour later.

I sighed in admiration. *He's so brave…*

Moments later, four teenagers were lined up at the window, watching their friends slowly creeping toward the house. Nick was in the lead, but Logan followed closely behind. They slowly opened the sliding glass door leading to the dining room beyond a curtain of darkness, and for what felt like an eternity, we waited for them to reappear. When they did, we silently cheered amongst ourselves. They ran back to the pool house after sliding the door to a close, and we greeted them eagerly.

"Piece of cake," Nick said between breaths, our eyes moving directly passed him to the dripping six-pack in his hand.

Since Jo wasn't going to drink, she sat on the couch and watched us spread around the room, smoking, drinking, and enjoying every minute of it.

As the time passed, we found ourselves much like the adults were earlier; different conversations were flowing back and forth between the beers. I found myself in a conversation with Nick for more than fifteen minutes, and I didn't once made a fool of myself by stumbling over my words and blushing as I usually do. No doubt the liquor contributed to my new found confidence.

"What has your dad told you about him, anyway?" he asked me after taking a sip from the can.

"About who?"

"Mason Bayer, the guy they put away."

I shrugged, and told him what I knew; nothing beside the fact that he numbered his victims in backwards English.

"In their blood," Jo added from behind me.

"Strange," Nick said with a frown. "I never heard anything about it on the news."

"You don't even watch the news," Logan followed.

"I wonder why they're so secretive about their work," Luis said, proceeded by a thunderous belch.

Logan took a deep breath in the direction of the belch. "Good one," he said to Luis. "I could smell your dinner in that one."

Jo rolled her eyes in disgust and Rebecca laughed.

"Because they have to be," I answered Nick. "I don't think I'd like to know about some dyslexic psycho killer then go to sleep knowing my dad's looking for him."

"But if there's a killer out there, wouldn't it be better to keep us all informed?"

Jo shook her head. "Serial killers, like Mason, tend to have a plan. They don't normally kill people at random, there's always a pattern. Dad told me this guy acted on vengeance, so no one outside his circle was in any danger at all. That's probably why it was never on the news."

Her father was not as strict on the secrecy as my dad was. Whenever they worked a case together, we usually turned to Jo for the gory details.

"How many more people did he plan to kill before he was caught?" Rebecca asked her.

She shook her head. "I'm not sure. Six was all he did in."

"They'll execute him, no doubt," Nick said.

"I don't think so. Not yet, anyway. Dad told me that he and Todd escorted Bayer to some high security mental hospital under the supervision of one of their men. They want to evaluate him."

"What for?" Luis asked.

Again, Jo shook her head. "I don't know. They'll probably start studying him like some lab-rat." Her tone suggested that it was inhumane to do so.

"Good," Rebecca said. "That scum deserves whatever they do to him. I'm glad Uncle Todd and Hector put him there."

"Enough with the boring shit," Logan ordered, pointing at us with an empty can. "I want more beer."

"Who's next?" Nick asked.

"For what?" Rebecca followed.

"The next run. Logan and I went last, it's someone else's turn."

Luis lit a cigarette then said, "Not me. I don't think I can walk."

"I think Cynthia should go," Rebecca suggested. "It's her house."

"Yeah Cyn," my brother added. "You go."

I frowned and declined their nomination. "What if Dad catches me?"

"Fine," Nick said, standing from the floor. "If you're going to waste time arguing about it, then I'll go again. But somebody's gotta come with me. Who's it going to be?"

I bolted from the floor faster than anyone could take a breath. "Me!" I announced, rather loudly.

"You just said you didn't want to!" Luis said, finding he could use the situation to his disposal.

I warned him not to proceed with a single glare and shoved Nick toward the door.

*

The thick air was a clear warning for a rainstorm even if the skies were cloudless. The moon was full, and as though it were biased, its vast light fell directly over Nick and I as we walked slowly toward the house.

"Okay," he said, his hands in the pockets of his jeans. "Jo's dad is asleep on the couch, you'll hear his snoring as soon as we walk into the house."

I giggled, flinging my hair behind my shoulder.

"The cooler is in the kitchen next to the refrigerator. It's dark in there, but we'll find it once our eyes adjust."

"Is Hector the only one in the living room?" I asked. We were about half way to the house, and the thought of breaking in was beginning to work on my nerve. I tried not to let it show.

"I didn't look, but I doubt anyone else could sleep with him. I'm telling you, he sounds like a beast."

I giggled again, but softly this time.

"Just remember to be absolutely quiet. He probably has his gun on him and God forbid he mistakes us for burglars."

"My dad sleeps with his gun under his bed. If he hears a shot fired in the house, he'll go for his, I'm sure."

"That's all we need."

We reached the sliding glass door that led into the dining room, so the talking ceased. I cupped my hands on the glass and peered in.

He was wrong about the darkness, the living room was partially lit by the pale light of the moon. I slid the door open carefully and allowed Nick to step in before me.

He was wrong about the snoring, too. Amidst the light of the living room, there was silence, instantly making me feel like we walked into a trap.

Hector's awake…

I wanted to tell Nick it was a bad idea, to forget the beer and return to the pool house without looking back, but he was already sliding the door to a slow close behind me.

"I'll go get them," he whispered. "Stay here and watch for anyone."

"What do you want me…"

"*Shh.* I know where the beer is, so just stay here, and be quiet."

Before I could argue any further, he was half way to the kitchen and out of whispering range.

Defeated, I slowly worked my way toward the living room, my eyes locked onto the shadows cascading across the floor in the moonlight. It was a sight barely seen in my house come nightfall; Mom made certain that each drape was drawn to a close come bedtime. Either she forgot to do so, or Hector preferred to sleep with the night exposed.

A hollow noise stopped me in my tracks half way to the living room. My heartbeat jumped and I tried to identify the sound. It came from the second floor; a *thump* that indicated the tumbling of a heavy object. From the noise's positioning, to the east of the house, it was coming from my bedroom.

Someone's awake. Get out now!

I glanced at the kitchen, praying Nick would hurry, and scared to take another step. I was convinced that at any moment, one of the adults would turn the corner and find me lingering in the dining room.

The sounds of the vertical blinds crashing together stripped me of my paralyzed fear, only to fill me with a genuine concern. It came from the picture window in the living room, the same one the moonlight found its way through. It was open. Slowly, I stepped toward the opening of the living room for a view of the couch where Hector slept, and of the window just opposite of him.

The staircase remained empty as far as I could see, so I scanned the room at length.

The vertical shades were swaying from left to right in a methodical motion before the open window and the moonlight was strong enough to light the couch almost entirely. I could see Hector resting comfortably, covered in a dark quilt across his torso, and his…

Oh my God…

I gasped on pure reflex when my eyes went to the wall above the couch. I took a step back, feeling the panic at my fingertips, and I lost my breath reading the word over and over again in a disbelieving stupor.

NEVES

It was written across the white wall from left to right and ran the length of the couch. It looked like black paint, drops leaving a thick trail from the turn in every letter. When I looked back at Hector, I realized that it was the same black that was stretched across his torso. It wasn't a quilt at all, nor was it paint. Hector had been killed and numbered in his own blood.

I screamed, or started to when someone cupped a hand over my mouth from behind me. I screamed louder when I was pulled back, away from the living room.

"It's me!" Nick whispered in my ear. "Calm down!"

I kicked and fought for my footing as he quickly dragged me backwards, refusing to let me go.

"Shut up!" he ordered once we reached the far end of the kitchen, away from sight of the living room, just before the utility closet. He spun me around and grabbed my shoulders. "I think someone is in the house," he said then pointed to the ground.

Still fighting for my breath, I nervously looked to what he was showing me; muddy footprints. They led into the kitchen from the dining room, no doubt originating from the couch.

It's not mud…blood.

"It's him," I said, as softly as I could. "It's Mason Bayer."

"What? Are you sure?"

I nodded quickly, biting my lip so that not to cry out loud. "I think he's upstairs. I heard him."

Without responding, he ran to the phone on the kitchen wall and dialed a few numbers before frowning. "It's dead."

"Nick," I said, fearing the same of my parents. "Mom and Dad are…"

"*Shh…*" he ordered again.

I took a breath, realizing that my fear raised the volume of my voice, but that wasn't why Nick demanded the silence.

His eyes narrowed and he remained still, analyzing the sound that now echoed into the kitchen. It was hollow, like the one before, but it was a descending beat that was obvious the moment we heard it clearly; someone was coming down the stairs.

"Oh my God," I whispered, my body trembling with the idea that Mason Bayer knew we were inside the house.

Moving swiftly, Nick slid to the utility closet and opened the door. Without a word, he demanded I enter the small room. He followed, bringing the door to a near close behind us, but leaving it open enough for a peek through.

I stood behind him, breathing heavily and sweating. Praying that my parents, our parents, were still alive was all I could do while worrying that the killer would find us in the small room. If he did, there was nowhere for us to go. Our hiding place was a trap all the same.

Nick's head was bobbing up and down like a bird's for a full view of the kitchen. Suddenly, he froze, took a deep breath, and then slowly turned back for a glance at me.

The fear in his eyes confirmed my suspicion. Mason Bayer was standing in my kitchen. He heard us, *smelled* us, something that we did caught his attention. He was looking for us.

Nick continued to look through the gap in the door, and I continued to pray. Only now, I was praying that my father would run down the stairs with his gun in hand to blow the intruder away.

The rumbling sound of the sliding glass door opening filled the room, and Nick's back stiffened. Either Mason was working his way to the pool house, or worse, one of the others had come, wondering why Nick and I were taking so long.

"What is it?" I whispered.

He didn't answer immediately. After a few seconds, he threw the door open and rushed out of the room.

"Nick, no!" It was a full scream.

The killer was standing at the kitchen's entrance, staring out into the dining room, and he didn't notice us until I screamed. He turned quickly, a black ski mask covering his face and black clothing concealing the rest of his body. I couldn't tell if he had a weapon in hand because Nick charged toward him, crashing into the killer and tackling him to the ground.

I screamed as the two of them fell, and a second scream echoed my own. It was Luis'. He was in the dining room.

"Luis, get out of here!" I yelled, forced to watch the men on the floor begin to struggle. They were blocking the only way out of the kitchen.

"Are you okay?" he yelled back.

"Get out! Now!"

He made no response, but he didn't leave. Seconds later, I heard his feet stomping up the stairs, taking two, maybe three steps at a time.

Nick handed the killer a few, swift and forceful punches across the face, keeping Bayer down for as long as he could. The killer was on his back and didn't have a chance to move as Nick jumped to his feet and kicked him in the ribs.

Mason squirmed but made no sound. Nick had the upper hand in the fight, but his luck ran short when the sound of Jo's scream suddenly filled the air. Instead of continuing his beating, Nick stopped for a look into the dining room.

"Who is that?" I heard Jo ask.

Mason moved, swinging his arm upward and out for Nick's leg. The butcher's knife in his hand glistened in the moonlight for a brief second, and I yelled for Nick to move.

It was too late. Nick screamed in agony after the knife pierced his left thigh. He reached for the injury and lost his balance as Mason withdrew the knife, a puddle of blood forming quickly once he hit the ground. He gasped in pain but wasted no time in trying to move away from the intruder.

Mason stood from the floor slowly, ignoring the sounds of our frantic screams. He had his eye on Nick, and though I wanted to find another knife in the kitchen and fight Mason myself, I couldn't. My fear wouldn't allow it.

Mason was tackled again, this time by Logan who dove into the kitchen unexpectedly. He managed to push the killer into a stumble, but failed to knock him to the ground. The moment Mason found his footing, he tossed Logan aside like a piece of trash.

Logan's feet came off the ground, slipping on the blood Nick left behind, and he fell. His head bounced on the floor like a basketball and afterwards, he didn't move. He remained on his back, his eyes closed, and his body still.

Mason took a step toward Nick who was still squirming on the ground, and that's when the first of the explosions came from the dining room.

I covered my head and dropped to my knees at the sound, screaming as though I was the one who was shot.

Mason tumbled backwards, but did not fall. The knife fell from his hand, followed by the sound of his dripping blood. He was hit in the shoulder.

The second shot came from a much closer range and it sent the killer backwards to the floor.

"Luis!" I heard Rebecca yell from the dining room.

Luis walked into the kitchen, the steaming gun in his hand holding it steady at the killer on the floor. The anger in my brother's face as he stared at Mason was an expression I had not seen in him before, and it was clear the he intended to defend the rest of us.

Mason was still breathing. I watched his stomach rise and fall quickly as he lifted his head to look directly at my brother's face.

Silence fell upon us all.

"Luis," I whispered to him, standing from the floor but not taking my eyes off the killer. "We'll call the cops. Let them finish it."

He didn't respond. Instead, he bent toward Mason and did something that stunned us all. While holding the gun in his right hand, Luis reached for Mason's face with his left. He grabbed the top of the killer's mask and stripped it off to reveal the face of Death. He tossed the mask aside and stood straight, grabbing the pistol with both hands.

Mason's pale face held steady. His black eyes were as stale as his expression. The blood that leaked from the corner of his mouth didn't even seem to bother him. He was unaffected by what was happening to him.

"Luis..." I said with a tremble.

Then, the killer spoke. His voice was deep and filled with anger, disgust even as his lips barely moved. Through clenched teeth, he looked at Luis and said, "Fucking pig."

He fired. The killer's head flew backwards as the bullet penetrated his skull.

A reflexive gag settled in the back of my throat as I tried to scream.

He fired again, then again. Luis didn't blink once as the gun exploded in his hands. He fired one more time, emptying the chamber, but continuing to pull the trigger.

Rebecca and Jo cried out for our Lord as I begged Luis to step away from the body. Nick was holding his leg, still crying in pain, and Logan was sprawled out on the floor.

Luis dropped the gun beside him and looked up at me. Something happened to him; I could see it in his face. It was expressionless. The raging anger I saw before was gone, and the emptiness that followed caught me by surprise. "They're dead," he said to me in a whisper. "All of them. They're dead."

My knees weakened, my mind randomly producing images of the slain bodies and the numbers painted on the walls above them. But Luis saw them all. It was the source of his rage, what gave him the power to kill the killer.

The sounds of everyone's cries, the blood now covering the kitchen floor, the nauseating smell of gun powder and the realization that our parents were dead were too much for me to take. My knees gave out, and I fell to the floor as my head began to pound with overwhelming fatigue. I looked up through the smoky air at my brother who was still staring at me with no expression, and every last ounce of that night settled in my stomach. I vomited violently in a fit of nerves, my ears ringing with the sounds of distant police sirens.

Help was on the way, and as though it was the gift of God Himself, I allowed the relief to loosen my finger tight grip on my sanity. Inviting the darkness to envelope me, I gave into the pain, and I passed out.

*

I woke up from the nightmare not having any indication of time or place. It wasn't my bed that I was lying on, it was the only thing I was certain of. There was a blue curtain following the edge of the bed left open enough for me to see a tired man resting on a chair less than three feet away, but preventing me from seeing the rest of the room.

A thousand noises filled my brain after pulling the curtain far enough to see directly in front of me. A traffic of doctors and nurses bustling hurriedly along the dank halls made my heart race as much as the atmosphere. As the realization that I was in the hospital settled, I wanted to scream, to cry for the others, but my dry throat wouldn't allow it.

"She's awake!" someone yelled from my right. It was a deep voice that frightened me, but I was too weak to jump. "Get a doctor! She's awake!"

It was the man on the chair, suddenly awakened. He jumped to his feet, exposing the khaki and brown colors of the county police, and a small trace of relief fell over me. I watched as he ordered a nurse to call for the physician, and she rushed away influenced by the uniform.

Within seconds, a large man appeared from behind the curtain dressed in fresh scrubs and equipped with a bright smile set against his black skin. "How are you feeling?" he asked me, his deep soothing voice relieving the headache more that any aspirin could. "Can you tell me your name?"

All I could think to tell him was the fact that my parents were dead, that my brother killed Mason Bayer.

"Where is Luis?" I asked him, the words barely audible.

The doctor was approaching my bed, but he stopped when my question was asked. He and the officer exchanged glances for a second before looking back at me.

"My name is Doctor Eugene Morrison," he said. Then, as he placed his massive hand on my forehead, he asked, "Can you tell me yours?"

I swallowed hard. "Cynthia Grazer."

"Do you know what day it is?"

I took a deep breath deciding I wasn't in the mood for twenty questions. "Where is my brother?"

"Your brother's here, Cynthia," the officer said then nodded toward Doctor Morrison. After checking the heart monitor and timing my breath, Morrison told me he would return to run more tests, and it was only after he left the room did the officer relax. He looked at me and offered a smile.

He was in his late twenties, early thirties; too old to be a rookie but too young to have worked directly with my father. Dad's team wore suits and had the tendency to grow overweight once behind a desk while this cop still had an athlete's build.

"My name is Officer William Kux," he said warmly. "I worked with your father and Detective Hector Corona on the Bayer case."

I acknowledged his presence, but I did not respond. I prayed he wasn't going to ask me questions.

"I wanted to ask you some questions about what happened last night."

"Last night?" I asked, not sounding nearly as surprised as I was. "How long have I been here?"

"Just over 12 hours."

I closed my eyes and my brain began to flash details of what happened like a picture slide show. I tried to stop them, and succeeded only when my eyes opened again. "Where's Luis?" I asked, feeling my breath just a bit shorter.

Officer Kux cleared his throat. "He's here."

"Can I see him?"

"In a second," he said with a nod. "There's something I need to tell you first. I know this will be difficult for you, but you will hear it eventually."

"I know about my parents. You don't have to say it." My voice was shaking as I found myself begging him *not* to say it. I knew they were no longer alive, but hearing it would only confirm it – and it would have destroyed me.

Officer Kux nodded and waited a second before continuing. "The man your brother shot is Mason Bayer. He was pronounced dead at the scene."

"Who are you?" I asked, my voice becoming stronger. The sound of the killer's name boiled my blood, giving me new life and energy. "Why are you telling me all this?"

Kux was surprised by my reaction, but he didn't turn and walk away like I hoped he would. Instead, he approached the bed slowly. "I worked with your father for over three months on this case. I looked up to him because he's the kind of detective I want to be someday." His voice kept even, soft yet steady. "I was watching over Bayer when he escaped the psychiatric facility, and on a gut feeling, I called Detective Grazer to warn him. The line was busy, so I called Detective Corona. Nobody was home. I rushed to your houses with back-up, but by the time I arrived…"

He tried to strip the emotion from his words, but I could read it. He felt guilty for not being able to catch the killer in time.

"I've been here ever since," he continued, "so when either of you had any questions about what happened, you would have someone to answer them."

"Where is everyone else?"

"Your Uncle George flew down from New York the moment he received word. Joanna and Rebecca are with him in the waiting area."

"The others?"

"Nick is still recovering. He's had some surgery done on his leg, twenty-six stitches on the back of his thigh and twelve on the front. He's doing well. Morrison said he's a quick healer. Logan suffered only a minor concussion, but he's awake now. It was a pretty hard hit he took."

"What about Luis?" I asked, noticing he hadn't mentioned the one person I asked about by name.

He sighed and wiped his forehead with the back of his hand. "Cynthia, your brother has fallen into a state of shock. He hasn't said a word since last night."

I closed my eyes, feeling my chin begin to quiver.

"The doctors here have a twenty-four hour watch on him and there's a specialist who will try and talk to him in a few hours. Morrison thinks this is natural for someone who saw what he did. Says it might not take much to snap him out of it."

I was crying, his words of encouragement of no use to me. I couldn't begin to imagine what my brother was thinking. He killed a man in rage, probably not realizing his actions until after they were completed.

Poor Luis…

"Cynthia, what he did was very courageous," Kux said. "He saved your lives, and he will be honored for that."

"When can I see him?"

"I'll see to it that it's as soon as possible." Kux straightened his back and turned to leave the curtained room. "I'll send the others in so they can see you, and I'll personally let you know when you can see your brother, okay?"

I nodded.

"One more thing. They'll probably want you to speak with the specialist that's coming to see your brother. I'll let you know when she arrives."

Again, I nodded, but the tears kept rolling. The realization of everything that was being said hit me like a sledge hammer, and I suddenly felt isolated.

"Cynthia, your father was a good man," Kux said. "I'm sure I don't need to tell you that. The station is prepared to give you anything you might need. I'll be here until you check out, so even if you want to just talk, call me."

He was sincere in his offer, and I thanked him quietly. But my world was split in two, now. The happiness and comfort of home seemed like nothing more than a memory, and no level of sincerity was going to bring it back. My parents, all of our parents, had been killed, and the one thing that no doctor or specialist would tell us, I already knew; a part of us was dead as well.

Aftermath

He broke into our house and robbed us of our parents, forever staining our lives with the stench of his presence. He destroyed the security we held within our own realms and eternally diminished our dreams, both in sleep and reality. A nightmare is what he gave us, and we had no choice but to face it. Only the nightmare truly began after the murders.

Six teenagers, mere children, forced to defend themselves against the man who killed their parents, and anyone in the given situation would have done the same. Only, there was no one to prepare us for what would follow, for the after effect was summed up in a term the six of us learned very well; Post-traumatic Stress Disorder.

We were diagnosed a day or so after "the incident," as we learned to call it. When just enough time passed and the realization settled in all of us, Doctor Morrison, Officer William Kux and Rebecca's father, Uncle George, were all at our side. One by one, we collapsed into their arms, and into a court appointed therapist who seemed more concerned about our recent celebrity status than our mental health.

He warned us that a traumatic experience, such as the one we had, brought on the possibilities of certain disorders that we would, more than likely, experience. Flashbacks, nightmares, hallucinations and anger were just some of the few I remember him mentioning, and he assured us they were all natural reactions. Despite his warnings, we were all terrified when the "disorders" fell upon us.

Sure, we all had trouble sleeping, and naturally, depression and denial loomed around us all. But amongst the feeling of detachment we briefly experienced, each of us were hit with the stages that promised to follow.

I became paranoid, unable to even sleep wondering if anyone had broken into the hospital for the rest of us. On two of the several nights that I did manage to rest, I woke in a puddle of my own urine. Embarrassed, I would mention it to no one, and the sour mood that befell me would be taken out on those whom I needed the most.

Officer William Kux, or Billy, as he preferred we call him, did as he said he would by remaining at our side for our stay at the hospital. Instead of being appreciative, I accused him of letting my parents die in one of my mood swings. It was an occasion for which I have apologized a thousand times, but he understood that it was all just a symptom.

Both Logan and Nick suffered the same effects as the other; it seemed the brothers dealt with things the Sheyer way. They secluded themselves from the rest of us, and from each other. They stopped talking, eating, and walked around for days in a stupor. Both Doctor Morrison and our therapist insisted that they were acting completely normal, then rambled off statistics on how many people feel detached from life after such a stressful situation.

"How many of them end up killing themselves?" Jo asked, sincerely concerned.

No one answered her then.

It didn't stop her from asking questions about our state of mind, and because of her thirst for knowledge, she filled her brain with information on stress disorders whenever she could. Though she voiced it to no one, I knew it was because her mother hadn't even bothered to put aside her carefree life in California to visit her daughter when she was needed the most. So, Jo kept busy so as to not delve in the depression of losing a parent and realizing the other didn't care. Though she loved her father very much, she never once cried over his loss, not in front of us. There were several nights during my insomnia in which I heard her crying alone. She was being strong, and she doing so for the rest of us.

Our therapist sat with her one evening and expressed his concern about the way she was bottling her emotions. She listened intently and nodded her head at his words without feeling, but she dealt with the situation the only way she knew how to; by not allowing herself to give into it. Through the roughest of our days, she remained our wall and our hope was that we could, one day, be like her.

There were some that had it a little easier than others. Rebecca, for example, had her father by her side. Uncle George flew to Florida from New York the moment he received word of the horrible tragedy, and though he had come to rescue us from delving into a darker world of intense and unpredictable feelings, it was to Rebecca that his presence gave the most comfort.

She went through a brief period of reoccurring and vivid nightmares from which she would wake screaming and sweating. After which, her new found fascination with death provoked countless questions and worries that every professional would assume was natural. Because of her father though, her disorders disappeared as quickly as they arrived.

And just as there were those who had it better than the others, there were those who had it worse – far worse. As Kux informed me, Luis, fell into a terrible state of shock immediately after the accident. He collapsed the moment Kux found him and the dead killer in the kitchen of our home and several different exams preformed by Doctor Morrison indicated his blood pressure rose to a very dangerous level. His blood shot eyes and dilated pupils remained open and glazed over as though he were dazed. He was not responsive to anything or anyone who came in contact with him, and his state did not improve for nearly three weeks.

One good morning, Luis sat up on his hospital bed and cried like a lost child. Though Morrison said it was probably the best thing for him, the worst was still to follow.

Something in Luis changed. He wasn't himself. He became jumpy, extremely sensitive to sounds that were loud and sudden, such as a ringing telephone. He spoke of the incident every day, repeating the story and the fashion in which the events took place as though he saw it in a movie. And amongst all this, a spell of defiant behavior fell over him, and there seemed to be no method in which he could be controlled.

The first occurrence took place with a nurse who was doing a routine check on his temperature and blood pressure late one evening. She woke him from his sleep, and in turn, he punched her in the stomach and spat on her face. Cursing her at the top of his lungs, the nurse ran out of the room and told Morrison to check on Luis himself. Our therapist issued several different drugs to help Luis' condition, but unfortunately, no sedatives helped the violence. Several days later, while my brother lied in a drugged trance, Morrison entered his room to draw blood for testing. Somehow, Luis managed to wrestle the syringe out of the good doctor's hands and stabbed Morrison twice in the right shoulder.

Because drugs would not calm my brother, our spineless therapist began drawing papers to have Luis committed despite Uncle George's wishes. The day the transfer to the mental hospital was to take place, all of us witnessed a side in Luis that terrified our very souls.

Three large men entered the hospital with a gurney complete with leather restraints. Upon a mere glance at the bed, Luis became extremely aggressive and cursed at them. They struggled to get him on the gurney as he kicked, screamed and yelled terrible things to them, calling them words I never before heard him use. Like a vicious beast, he growled and insulted their mothers as they restrained him, and the rest of us watched through wet eyes and broken hearts as they took him away.

And just outside the hospital's doors, a large crowd formed, all equipped with television cameras and microphones. The roughest days of our lives were to be the headlines of every news show and paper. We became celebrities, known as The Brave Six, but what made us even more popular was the fact that no one managed a snap shot of us with Mason Bayer's blood on our hands, or in our hospital gowns. For that, we had Billy Kux to thank.

He kept us away from the news articles and programs that were apparently overdone after the incident. We were forbidden, in fact, to watch the news or read anything on the murders or Mason Bayer. As a result, we learned nothing of the killer outside of what we already knew, and though everyone said that staying away from the media was vital to our recovery, it was Billy who enforced it the most.

Several months after the incident, Uncle George received a phone call from his superior at work claiming that his position would be filled unless he returned to New York immediately. Coincidentally, another call was received from a magazine show that offered us a few thousand dollars for an interview with The Brave Six, but Billy strongly advised Uncle George to turn them down. The truth was we were in no condition to do so.

Uncle George decided he was right, picked up the phone and called his office. After quitting his job, he dialed another number and set up an interview with the magazine program. Apparently, Uncle George had some plans of his own, no matter how much Billy objected to our interview session.

*

Uncle George promised the prime time news show an interview, and an interview is what they got. Only, it was not what they were expecting. They wanted to ask the questions everyone wanted to ask, to expose our fragile states and use it for ratings. After some heated negotiations, what they settled for was my uncle and the officer first on the scene of the incident; Billy. We weren't allowed to watch that program either.

Uncle George used the show to gain national support for rights to the adoption of The Brave Six, and it apparently worked. Churches, charities, and random kind people donated money for our well-being, and with the fifteen thousand dollars Billy and Uncle George earned from the network who aired the special, my uncle went before a county judge and was granted the rights to our adoption. He became our legal guardian in less than six months after the murders.

He purchased a house in Coral Gables, a prestigious suburban neighborhood just outside the Downtown area. It was a Victorian home, four bedrooms, three and a half baths, and all the room in the world for us to live comfortably. Each room was furnished with everything we could ask for, all thanks to the local charities and donations. Each bedroom was furnished with two twin sized beds, its own television set and ample closet room for a small town. The living room, dining room and kitchen were well equipped with sturdy furniture, some used, some new.

So much was missing though. Material items did not matter to us much after the incident; I would have rather had my parents returned to me as opposed to my diary or a ragged stuffed animal. But one morning, Uncle George and Billy surprised us with a truck load of our old possessions; clothing, pictures, and other personal trinkets that were removed from our old houses. Each item was as valuable as the other, holding sentiments we never even realized they could. The pictures were the hardest to go through without crying; seeing our parents in color made it more difficult to digest what happened.

"It seems like it was all a dream," Jo once said, and she was right.

Our therapist thought it wouldn't be a good idea to expose us to such vivid memories claiming that it would only interrupt our "healing," and the son of a bitch even forbade Uncle George from taking us to our parents' funeral service. Thankfully, Uncle George did not completely give into the quack's method of grieving and he brought us back the items that were rightfully ours. It helped us grieve more than anything else could.

Living in a house as opposed to the hospital helped us all heal. It gave us a sense that everything would be okay once we settled. And though it took us a while to figure it out, we soon realized that being together like a family was an enormous treatment of our healing, and it was to Uncle George that we owed our thanks. Only, there was still something missing…

Nick and Logan shared a bedroom, as did Rebecca and Jo. Uncle George kept the master room for himself while I was forced to spend the dark of each night on a bed that faced an empty one; it belonged to Luis.

His stay at the institution was indeed helpful. His improvement was phenomenal, or so we were told by the several doctors caring for him. Two months before the one year anniversary of our parents' deaths, he was discharged, and came home.

He adjusted well, much like the rest of us. We were all happy to have him back, now feeling complete, and each of us gaining a little more strength with his arrival. Together is how we needed to be, Uncle George told us. But Luis had not been cured completely of his symptoms as we hoped. There were still nights when he woke in sweats, sometimes screaming at a remnant of the nightmares. He was also inflicted with a strange disorder that no specialist could explain; mild dyslexia. At first, it showed in his writing with small words like "of" and "the." It progressively grew worse, showing in more and more words, but with time, like all the other symptoms, the dyslexia disappeared. The psychologist on staff at the hospital explained that it was expected he would suffer longer than the rest of us. After all, he pulled the trigger, and the guilt of killing a man is bound to last longer than the sorrow of losing a loved one.

Then, the calendar returned to the infamous date we would forever remember as the darkest day of our lives. June 6th returned, and there was nothing we could do to stop it or the feelings the day would bring.

That evening, Uncle George prepared a three course meal and served each of us a glass of wine. Billy joined us at the table and raised his glass as high as Uncle George did when he toasted in memory of our parents.

"I know that this past year has been the hardest we will probably ever see," he said, looking at each of us in the eye and settling a second or so before moving on to the next. "Though your parents are not here to watch and protect you, they will forever live in your hearts. No one can ever take that away. I assure you that they are watching, and they are just as proud of you as I am. Know that the bond you hold with each other is the most special ingredient in your lives, and that what you have been through has only made you stronger. Tonight, I toast your parents, and I toast to the six of you. May the days of the past be the roughest, and may what lie ahead be filled with blessings, and joy. You deserve it."

In tears, we chimed our glasses, and we hugged each other, promising to never part from the relationship we now held.

It began a tradition we kept for life. Every year, on June 6th, we held a memoriam dinner in loving memory of those lost on that fateful night. It was the hardest day of each year to wake to, but with all of us side by side, it was a little easier to cope with.

The next morning, Uncle George gave us the present that was forbidden to us before; he took us to the cemetery where our parents were buried. Our tears fell to the ground as we each took turns spending a moment with the grave plots. They were buried side by side, each name carved boldly on the headstone, and soon we realized that visiting our parents was exactly what we needed to finally put closure on the incident. We were emotionally drained when we left the site yet it gave us strength to face the coming day.

And when the summer was over that year, we found ourselves at a turning point. Come September, we were all ready to return to school and continue with our lives and dreams. In just one year, it was time for The Brave Six to head back out into the real world, each of us looking at our place on Earth a little differently.

Bring on your roughest situation, I remember thinking as I walked out of the house on a humid morning. There was nothing we couldn't handle now.

June 4th; Eighteen Years Later

Though the memories of our parents never subsided, there came a point when we learned to be happy again. Life began to work its course on us, and one by one, we began to form our new existence. It took us a long time, but the road to recovery was successful.

Some of us were married, then divorced. Some of us had children of our own, while others found their strength in helping children. Our tremendous recovery would not have happened had it not been for the people who surrounded us when we needed them the most; the strangers who became the foundation of support.

For me, Doctor Jennifer Simon was my largest form of support. After we each completed the required three years with the spineless therapist, I found Jennifer, a psychologist who came highly recommended. She did what no one else had the ability to do after only a few visits; she rid my mind of the plaguing nightmares.

Insisting I buy a journal to record my feelings for the purpose of reflection, I followed her orders only to realize that she inadvertently unlocked my talent. Nearly a year after the journal was purchased, its pages were filled with a story I wrote. By the time I was twenty-three, it was published and eventually, it became a best seller. I grew familiar with words like literary agents and publishing contracts, but most importantly, I found my own path. I owed it all to my friend and doctor, Jennifer.

My first book was dedicated to my parents, and it was published under my maiden name. After I was married, that never changed.

The journal on which I wrote my first novel was permanently resting on the bookshelf of her large, plush office. I gave it to her as a token of my appreciation.

My appointments were always on Thursdays, always at the same time. It became routine, and Jennifer suggested the only reason I continued the sessions were just that. She said I liked routines because it was the only way I knew that my life was controlled. I laughed when she told me that I was of complete sound and mind and that I didn't need her aid any longer.

The morning of Thursday, June fourth, two days before the eighteenth anniversary of the murders, she stood from her desk as I walked into her office, expecting me to break down as the door closed behind me. Much to her surprise, I didn't.

I took my seat on the opposite side of her glossy oak wood desk set just before the eleventh story view of the Downtown Miami skyline. She smiled and offered me a mug of coffee, which I gladly accepted. After taking her seat, she began with her usual line of questioning.

"How are you feeling?" was always the first.

I would immediately respond by delving into the problems generated since the week before; feelings of insecurities, arguments with my husband, but that particular week, "I'm feeling fine," I told her.

She was an older woman, in her early fifties, but she ran laps from her house to the moon every day. The wrinkles around her eyes were barely visible until she frowned. After so many years of seeing her react to my stories, I could read the expression on her face like a newspaper though she usually made attempts at hiding them. I was convinced that she didn't believe me.

"You're *fine*?" she asked, dropping her pen to the notepad on her desk. "It's two days before the anniversary of your parents' death and you're fine?"

I nodded. "It's no different than any other year. Tomorrow night, the six of us will get together, have dinner in their memory, and the day after, we will visit their graves, lay the flowers and cry. I'm okay, really."

"You say it like it's no big deal," she said, uncertain if it was the healthiest alternative.

Of course it was a big deal. The horrible fashion in which my parents were taken away scarred me for eternity. Sure the nightmares ended, but there wasn't a day that went by when I didn't think of them. I missed them terribly and each anniversary was as hard as the first. But those emotions became second nature to me.

"Every year I put myself through the same thing," I told her. "I have my own family now; my own husband and my own son. It's time I move on."

She sat back on her leather chair and took a deep breath, clasping her hands over her stomach. "No more nightmares, then?" she asked.

"None."

"Anxiety attacks?"

"Not since the last one." More than seven months before.

"Insecurities?"

"I can't be in the house on my own without checking to make sure all the windows and doors are locked, but that's more a habit than anything else."

Jennifer smiled, much like a proud parent. "Well, this is a momentous day. It only proves what I've said before. You don't need my services any longer."

I looked down to my hands fidgeting on my lap preparing myself for the next conversation. "That's the reason why I'm here."

Her head tilted slightly like a confused child. She was waiting for me to continue.

"What you said was right; I do like the routine in my life. I've reached a point where breaking some of them might be healthy. Namely, this one."

"Look at me," she said immediately. "What are you saying?"

I took a deep breath. "That I want to try things out on my own for a while, without a therapist."

I wanted her to pat me on the back, to tell me that I was doing the right thing, but all I received was another frown. "Cynthia, are you sure about this?"

she asked.

"I'm positive. There are a hundred other forms of therapy I can take part in, like my writing, my family, my friends. I just need to focus those energies onto something new. I learned that from you."

And there it was; the smile that I desperately needed to see. The approval in her brilliant white teeth always added to the comfort and support I required whenever making a life decision. "Good for you," she said with a nod. "Have you told your husband?"

"No, not yet. I wanted to tell you first, get your approval before making an official announ…"

"Cynthia, you don't need my approval. I would rather gossip with you over coffee on my lunch hour than sit in here, going over the same things every week."

"But I thought you might…"

"I nothing. Your time is up."

"What?" Here I was, making one of the biggest decisions in my life, and she wanted to throw me to the wolves! "But we still have…"

"No we don't. If we sit here and talk about it anymore, you'll find a reason to change your mind, and you'll be back in that chair next week. Now, go." She stood from her chair with her arms outstretched for a hug.

The embrace stirred emotions I wasn't expecting. A lump formed in my throat and my eyes watered as though I was never going to see my friend again. Life without her support promised a challenge, but like a bird leaving its nest, it was the natural thing to do.

"You're doing the right thing," she said to me. "You'll be just fine."

I left before I made a fool of myself in a crying frenzy but promising to take her up on the offer for coffee. I left the office without looking back. It was time to face the world with new eyes.

I stepped out of the building and directly into the humid summer air. Clouds were looming in the skies, covering the sun and promising rain, but my day couldn't be brighter. Normally, I would rush home, put my son to bed and slave over the computer, trying to hammer out the novel I promised my agent a month ago.

Not today…

I had more important things to attend to. That Thursday, I decided to spend the entire day with the person I loved the most; my son, Max.

*

Maxwell Todd was born when I was thirty-one years old, bringing with him one of the happiest chapters in my life. Even my writing improved with the inspiration his birth stirred in me. It was the year I realized that the road my life ventured on may have been troublesome, but triumphant. Suddenly, I had everything that I planned for; a successful career, a family of my own, even the husband of my dreams; Nick.

We were married when I was 25, and the others were thrilled to finally see it happen. They made bets amongst each other that Nick would never propose, but I knew he would. After seven years of a happy marriage, Max came into our lives, sealing the deal on our family.

I devoted most of my time to our son. Nick would spend his days working on a building contract for an architectural firm while I worked from my home office. Writing was no longer a priority after Max's birth, but when he was laid for his nap, it was my time to create characters in works of fiction. I refused to hire someone else to raise him so that I could work. I wasn't capable of it.

On Thursday mornings, Rebecca would watch over him during my sessions with Jennifer. I drove through the downtown traffic and into the suburban city to collect my son with thoughts of spending the day with him in my head. We'd do what he wanted to do, I told myself. If he wanted to spend the entire day at his favorite fast food restaurant, then so be it.

But when I arrived at Rebecca's, I couldn't get him to do much more than wave at me from the back yard of her house. It was an acre or so of plain grassland, and one of the reasons Max loved to visit. The second reason; a golden retriever named Buddy that ruled the yard. They would both play together endlessly, and there was no tearing them apart.

"I feel like I have to compete with your dog whenever I'm here," I said to Rebecca, walking out onto the terrace bordering the house.

She was seated at the lawn furniture set on the center of the terrace, underneath an umbrella for shade. She was reading the newspaper and hadn't noticed me until I spoke.

"Don't worry about it," she said with a smile. "Next time you visit, I'll lock him up in a cage so there's no arguing."

"I hope you mean Buddy and not my son."

She smiled. "Yeah, maybe that's a better idea."

I sat at the round table and served myself a glass of lemonade from the pitcher she put out.

"Where's Charlene?" I asked after looking across the yard and not seeing her daughter.

Charlene was born a year before Max to Rebecca and her second husband, Scott. They met working together in real estate and married three months later. Scott and Rebecca Brannon lasted longer than husband number one, and we all thought that she finally found her Mr. Right. Two years and one child later, the couple decided to end their relationship due to irreconcilable differences. It was a shame to see them split because they really did make a wonderful pair. Still, she had Charlene to be thankful for.

"She's asleep," Rebecca answered. "She was up all night with me."

"What were you doing?"

"Liquor shots, mostly. Although, I noticed she doesn't really like the hard liquor."

"More of a beer gal?" I asked, playing along for the cheap laugh.

"Yeah, I think so."

Buddy barked and Max laughed out joyously. It was amazing how much those two loved each other. Buddy didn't play with anyone as much as he played with Max.

"The truth is," Rebecca said after a moment of silence. "I had a really long night."

"Why's that?"

She folded the newspaper and laid it on the table reaching for the pack of cigarettes. She offered me one and I declined, not having smoked since the murders. She knew I quit the habit yet offered me a cigarette every time she reached for her pack.

"I had a nightmare last night," she said after lighting the smoke.

Rebecca's nightmares came and went throughout the years, each time taking longer to return. The last one was over a year before.

"A bad one?" I asked. "Like the others?"

She seemed hesitant to do so, but she nodded. "It felt so goddamn real."

A warm, thick breeze whirled between us and Rebecca weighed the newspaper down with the ashtray.

"It caught me off guard, is all," she continued.

"How so?"

"It's all in the timing, I'm sure. In two days, it's going to be eighteen years, can you believe it?"

"Sometimes I can. Sometimes it feels like it all happened yesterday, and other times it feels like it was a hundred years ago."

"Speaking of which, are we still on for tomorrow night?"

"My house, dinner at eight," I said.

"Good," she said with a smile, and I could tell it was forced. She seemed venerable, but was trying not to show it.

"I'm planning on spending the day with Max," I said to her. "Why don't you wake Charlene and come with us. Maybe it'll do you some good to get out of the house."

Before I finished my offer, she was shaking her head. "No, it's okay. Really, it's nothing."

I didn't believe her. "Well, come with us anyway. Let's get some lunch."

"It'll be impossible to wake Charlene. Besides, it looks like it'll rain soon and I'd rather stay in. Aren't you sick of this rain?"

I smiled and nodded, giving in to the subtle manner in which she changed the subject again.

She looked up to the clouds forming above and shook her head. "I'd be pissed if I was a tourist and found out that Florida really wasn't the Sunshine State."

"Tis the season, I guess. At least we can be thankful there isn't a threatening hurricane."

"Well, you better get going before the storm rolls in," she said, then called for Max and Buddy.

The golden retriever barked as the two broke into a race toward the house.

"Are you sure you don't want to come along?" I asked once more, giving my final offer.

"I'm sure," she said. "Really, I'll be okay."

I still didn't believe her. I gave her a hug, and she instructed me to call her if I needed help with the preparations for the anniversary dinner. I told her I would. After walking me to the car, I loaded Max in and instructed *her* to call me if she needed to talk. She said she would.

But I didn't believe her.

*

My extraordinary day was becoming rather ordinary after all. The rain fell sooner than I hoped, aiding Max to sleep before I could even ask him what he wanted to do. I should have known better; he was always exhausted after a few hours with Buddy.

I tucked him into his bed when we arrived home and kissed him on the forehead. Creeping out of the room so that not to wake him, I slowly closed the door behind me and stared out into the hall.

When Nick and I were married, we bought the modest house in the center of a suburban community. Three bedrooms, two baths, living room, dining room and a kitchen that we remodeled ourselves with glass cupboards and checkered tiles. It was an immaculate house, but a little intimidating when no one else was around. The storm outside was beginning to roll with thunder, stirring the unsettling feelings in the pit of my stomach.

I checked the picture window in the living room to make sure the lock was latched as it always was. After which, I slid to the main entrance of the house; a set of double doors standing seven feet tall. They were locked as well. Crossing the dining room, I moved directly to the sliding glass door leading to the back yard. Locked. So were the windows in the kitchen.

The alarm we installed upon buying the house was not armed, but it would indicate the opening of any door or window throughout the house with a high-pitched beep.

Every radio and television would remain off so that my ears could detect any noises through out any part of the house. As long as I was alone, I would be on guard for any or all of the ghosts that were a part of my daily life. I would never invite danger into my home, but if one day, danger managed to find its way in, I would be prepared.

There was nothing brilliant enough that Jennifer could say to strip me of the paranoia.

Rain

After Luis graduated from high school, he found his therapy working as a volunteer at a center for orphaned children. He helped kids of all ages cope with the stress of losing their loved ones to unusual circumstances. Fifteen years after he found the center, it was his. Ready to file for bankruptcy, the center found itself in need of serious repairs, and the local charities were no longer as charitable as they used to be. Uncle George co-signed for a loan from the bank, and Luis swept in to save the center from closing its doors for good. It was his proudest achievement, one that allowed him to make a difference in a dozen children's lives.

Jo jumped into the project with him. She graduated from the University of Miami and became a well-respected child psychologist. She worked full time along Luis' side, and before long, rumors of a blooming romance began to surface within the clan of six.

Of course, it was the first thing I asked them about when they arrived at my house for lunch that Thursday. After running into the foyer from the storm, I asked them both how they were doing, but with a certain glare in my eye indicating I wasn't asking about their health.

"We're fine," Jo said in protest of my suggestion. "How are you?"

"Hungry."

"Where's Max?" Luis asked, inspecting the living room.

"Asleep. He'll be up soon if the thunder gets any louder. I'm surprised he hasn't woken up already."

I led them into the dining room where the freshly made ham and turkey breast sandwiches awaited us. For the first few minutes while we ate, we made small talk about our day-to-day lives. It wasn't until Jo began reminiscing about a night with her father did we stop eating all together. It started out as a funny thought she had, but making mention of him inadvertently whirled unsettled emotions because of the coming anniversary.

"Will everyone be here tomorrow night?" Luis asked me, swallowing the last bite of his sandwich.

"No one has told me otherwise. It'll be the six of us."

"I think Logan wants to bring Angela this year," he said.

Logan and his girlfriend, Angela, were together for three years, and he didn't want her to be a part of the last two anniversary dinners. He said it wouldn't be appropriate.

"Good for him," I said. "I think Angela would be happy be a part of it."

"And what about Rebecca?" Jo asked. "Do you think she'll want to bring Scott again?"

"I doubt it. I think she's passed that stage in her life. Although, I don't know after this morning."

"What happened this morning?"

It was a complete accident. I wasn't sure if she wanted the others to know about the nightmare she mentioned. She wouldn't want to be overwhelmed by questions from everyone in the group.

"Cyn," Luis said, snapping me from my daze. "What happened?"

"She seemed upset is all," I answered, deciding not to mention the nightmare. "We're all a little stressed lately."

"I'll call her later to check up on her," Jo said.

"Why don't you go wake up Max," Luis said after taking a sip of his water. "I'd like to see him before we get going."

Normally, I would allow my son to sleep, but he was resting for two hours. If he didn't wake soon, he would never fall asleep come bedtime.

Leaving Jo and Luis in the dining room, I walked into the hall and towards my son's bedroom. Thunder echoed above, but not loud enough to over lap the voice that poured into the hall. I stopped, just at Max's door, the voice ringing in my ears as though someone were whispering into them.

I didn't hear it clearly enough to know what was said, but the voice was definitely a man's. I immediately ruled out the possibility that it came from a radio or television, and knowing that it wasn't my brother's voice, I tried to pin point its origin.

The voice spoke again, sounding just as elusive, but its source became clear. It was coming from Max's bedroom. Imagining the worse, I threw the door open, my heart pounding across my chest.

I was ready to fight any intruder I found with my bare hands, screaming for help as I beat whoever it was to a pulp, but I only found Max sleeping in the fetal position tucked underneath his *Star Wars* bed sheets, the same exact way I left him. The rest of his room remained undisturbed, and thankfully, so had the window. The vertical blinds were standing closed, swaying softly with the flow of the central air.

Trying to control my heart rate, I shot glances around the room, scanning every square inch before dismissing the voice as a figment of my imagination. Perhaps it was due to the thunder.

I shook Max gently, telling him that his Uncle Luis and Aunt Jo were in the dining room, and it didn't take much more to wake him. He bolted to his feet and ran out of the room to see them.

As he jumped into the arms of his uncle, I glanced back into the hall. The voice I forced myself to dismiss was ringing in my head, sending a nervous chill throughout my entire body. No matter how much I wanted to convince myself, I knew very well that it wasn't thunder that I heard.

*

Fifteen minutes after Luis and Jo said their good-bye's, I sat Max in the living room and tuned the television to the cartoon channel. Moments later, I stood at his bedroom doorway, inspecting the entire area before entering.

The room was the second largest in the house, large enough to store every last action figure and the hundreds of robot-thing-a-ma-jigs he owned. Every one of them were scattered along the plush blue carpet, just as they were for the past few days. I searched his closet, and underneath his bed, and found everything just as it should be; unsoiled by the hands of any intruder.

I stood in the center of his room, my hands on my hips and my brain trying to solve the mystery of the voice. Where did it come from? Whose voice was it?

I opened the blinds to the window and came in full view of the house's front lawn. The rain was still coming down, and the neighborhood street was deserted.

Maybe I did imagine the whole thing.

Maybe not. I froze after leaning against the windowsill for a further view of the street. It was wet, as though the window was open allowing the rain to form a puddle along the entire ledge. My heart accelerated again as I looked at the locking latch above the window. It was released.

"Max!" I called, locking the latch then rushing towards the living room. "Was your bedroom window open?"

He shook his head without looking from the television. I knelt before him for his undivided attention, forcing him to look back at me. "Did you open your bedroom window?" I asked. "You can tell me the truth, I won't get mad."

Again, he shook his head. "No, mommy. I promise I didn't."

His innocent face told me the truth, and I was at a loss for words. "And it wasn't open at all the whole time you were in there?"

He shook his head.

I felt unsafe; as though my house was being watched, as though *we* were being watched. I knew very well that the lock on his window was checked before I left the house that morning, and for some ungodly reason, it was unlocked in the afternoon.

"Do you want to go back to Rebecca's?" I asked him, deciding that if someone was going to break into the house, let them do it while we weren't there. They'll trip the alarm, the officials would rush to the house, and whoever it was that made the fatal mistake of vandalizing us would pay in jail.

He nodded excitedly, and I rushed to the dining room for my purse and the keys to the car.

*

Old-Man Brewer was the town's resident vagabond. He wandered the streets every morning at sun-up, wearing his light blue pajamas, and waving at everyone as they pulled from their driveway for a day at work. Some people said he was senile and all the children were afraid of his deathly pale face and large black eyes. He wasn't the most attractive man, but he lived a long life, and he was still smiling.

But it was only in the mornings when Old Man Brewer made his rounds, and it was surprising to see him when Max and I walked onto the porch that afternoon. He was standing at the foot of our walkway, wearing a black raincoat over his normal attire. The orthopedic shoes he wore were soaked, but he didn't seem to mind. He was smiling, staring at the front door as though he was waiting for us to leave the house.

Immediately, I thought of Max's window. Was the neighborhood's wanderer capable of such a thing?

"Is everything okay, Mr. Brewer?" I called to him, locking the door to my house in a hurry and keeping an eye on Max at the same time.

My son was staring at the old man, transfixed by his appearance. Normally, he would hide behind me whenever the old man was around, for which I would lecture him about how that wasn't a polite thing to do. That afternoon, I wanted him to hide, somewhere far away.

"It's a lovely day, isn't it?" he called back, waving his long thin hand at us.

Max waved back.

"You mean, besides the rain?" I asked. "It's gorgeous. Is there something I could do for you?"

Gripping Max by the hand and clutching my keys with the other, I was making it clear that we were on our way out. I wasn't going to step off the porch until the old man was gone.

"I don't mean to frighten you," he said, "but I wanted to know how your boy was feeling."

I glanced at Max, my body filling with heat suddenly. He was still staring at the old man.

"Why do you ask?" My voice was as firm as the look of suspicion on my face.

The old man looked at Max and smiled. Then, he nodded slowly at the boy as though he found something in Max's eyes, something he was searching for.

"He is fine," the man said with a light laugh, and then he looked at me. "It hasn't reached the children, yet."

"What are you talking about, Mr. Brewer?" I demanded, a drop of adrenaline soaring through my body.

"I think he told me June sixth. That's the day your parents died, right?"

My blood boiled, the volcano of emotions erupting within me, and I stepped off the porch, into the rain. "How do you know that?" I asked, charging toward the end of the walkway. "Have you been talking to my son?"

"No..."

"Mommy," Max called from the porch.

"You stay there!" I yelled back to him, reaching the old man and standing inches from his neutral face. "You listen to me," I growled through my teeth, "you stay away from my son, do you hear me? I will have you arrested faster than..."

"Nothing is as it seems," he said suddenly. "Listen to the boy, he'll tell you the truth."

"About what?" I asked, nearly yelling.

A shiny, new luxury car pulled up behind the old man, directly in front of my house. Neither Brewer nor my self paid it any mind, though.

"In time, you will know," he said.

A woman in a dark business suit hauled out of the driver's door and ran toward us. "Daddy!" she screamed. "What are you thinking?"

"Nothing is as it seems, Mrs. Sheyer. The boy will tell you."

"Daddy! Get in the car!" The woman was older than I was, and far more decorated. "I'm so sorry if he caused you any troubles," she said to me, taking her father by the shoulders and turning him toward the car. "This is my card. Call me if he broke anything." Without looking back, they both entered the vehicle and drove away.

And all I could do was watch.

He knew the date of my parents' death, and he knew my name. Standing alone in the rain, I looked back at my son on the porch and prayed there was another explanation.

*

Katherine Brewer Attorney at Law was printed in dark bold letters across the white business card. Her office and mobile numbers were just below her title, and I contemplated giving her a call. Only Max said Mr. Brewer did not open his bedroom window, not that morning, not ever.

I sat Max in the living room after Katherine collected her father. A dozen questions poured out of my mouth and he answered them immediately, each of his responses relieving me, but posing only new questions.

"Have you ever talked to that man?" I asked him.

"No," he answered.

"Has he ever been to your bedroom window?"

"No."

"And you've never told him anything about us at any time?"

"No, mommy."

Someone told the old man a few things about us, and *someone* opened Max's bedroom window. Nick knew better than to leave the window unlocked and Max was too short to even reach the shade's draw string.

Or maybe the old man was senile. Perhaps he had no idea what he was saying, or why he was saying it, and maybe it was pure coincidence that he was outside my house when I was in a panic.

"Mommy," Max said, sitting on the couch, kicking his legs in the air. "Can we go to Aunt 'Becca's house now? I want to play with Buddy."

"Yes," I told him. "Grab your raincoat, and we'll go."

He jumped off the couch, and I took Ms. Brewer's card off the coffee table, putting it in the pocket of my jeans. I would wait for Rebecca's opinion before I called the old man's daughter.

Nightfall

Nick graduated from Florida International University at the top of his class and went on to work at an architectural firm in Fort Lauderdale. His days were long, leaving the house at nearly seven in the morning and arriving twelve hours later, but he was never too tired to fill the void in Max's day. While I prepared dinner, he would spend an hour or so in Max's room, helping him construct massive Lego buildings. Max was thrilled, insisting that when he grew up, he would be an architect, just like his father.

I didn't mention any of the day's events; mainly because Rebecca convinced me that there was a good chance I overreacted then jokingly insisted I call Jennifer to reinstate my weekly appointments. I planned on telling Nick about everything, but I wanted to wait until Max was asleep. Our son didn't need to hear more than he already had, I probably scared him enough with all the questions.

Supper was served at a quarter to eight, and by nine, Nick tucked our son into bed, with orders from me to check his window's lock before leaving the room. Without question, he said he would.

After Max's time with his father, it was my turn to spend time with my husband. Like a young couple fresh at love, we shared the couch set strategically before the television set, cuddling to the warmth of our bodies. Arm in arm, we sat in silence, the light from the television cascading dancing shadows all around us.

He was just in time for the weather forecast, which was followed by the phrase any Floridian says when the weather reports; "Is the rain finally going to stop?"

"Not before this tropical depression brewing in the Gulf of Mexico begins to head toward us," the perky anchorwoman reported. The first actual depression of the season was closer to Texas, but its predicted path had southern Florida right smack in the middle of it. Its potential threat was worse; while crossing open bodies of water, tropical depressions usually picked up strength and morphed into tropical storms, the stage where they earn an actual name. The second stage, followed shortly thereafter was the ever-feared hurricane. Whether or not TD-1 would be named as a hurricane before hitting land was undetermined.

"Great," Nick sighed. "There goes the job contract."

"Funny, I just told Rebecca that at least we weren't threatened with a storm," I said. "I should just learn to keep my mouth shut."

"How is she?"

"Rebecca? She's fine."

"She'll be here tomorrow?"

"She offered to help."

"What else did you do today?"

"I quit therapy," I answered nonchalantly.

"Did you, really?" he asked in surprise. "How'd that come about?"

I shrugged casually. "I've been thinking about doing it for a while."

"We should celebrate."

"By any chance, did you open Max's window before you left?" I asked, sitting up to look at him. Now that everything else was out of the way, my tongue was burning to ask.

He frowned and shook his head. "What makes you think I would do that?"

"While Max was sleeping, I thought I heard a voice coming from his bedroom," I told him. "I checked the window to make sure it was locked, and it wasn't."

"Did you see who opened it?" he asked, anger filling his voice.

"No one," I answered. "But I'm not sure."

"What do you mean?"

I told him of my encounter with Old-Man Brewer, whispering in case Max walked into the room. Leaving out no detail, I told Nick all; even about Brewer's overly caffeinated daughter. "He said to listen to Max, that he would tell me the truth, then he told me that nothing is what it is, or something like that." I showed him the card Kathy gave me.

"And you think Old-Man Brewer's been talking to Max through his window?" he asked, skeptical of my conclusion.

"All I know is that I heard a voice in Max's bedroom, his window was open at some point, and Old-Man Brewer knows an awful lot about us. I call it a damned good possibility."

"Did you ask Max about it?"

"He says he's never spoken to him. That's where the trouble is. I believe Max, but the old man really pushed some buttons."

Nick sighed, shrugging his shoulders. "Maybe he's heard us before. I mean, this guy has been walking up and down the streets for years. He knows everybody's name, and maybe he knows a little more."

I nodded. "That's what Rebecca told me, but it doesn't explain the window, or the voice."

"Would it make you feel better if we called Billy and had him take a look around?"

"I don't know if we should bother him with that," I said, my gaze settling back on the television. "Maybe the window's cracked or something. I'll check it in the morning."

"I'll take Max to work with me," he insisted. "It'll be a short day at the office."

We watched the rest of the news in silence, a hundred thoughts whirling through my mind. Eventually, I took a deep breath, cleared my mind of the worries, and followed Nick to the bedroom. Max was tucked safely into his bed, and I, in the arms of my husband, found the security of my own home. All the doors and windows were locked, and the alarm was set. The sound of distant thunder filled the night's sky, and before long, I fell asleep. That night, we slept with the bedroom doors open.

*

The six of us lived within a five mile radius of Billy, now as great a Detective as the legendary Todd Grazer and Hector Corona. Throughout the eighteen years after the incident, he remained a large part of our lives and insisted we call upon him should any trouble befall us. When Nick suggested we call him, I told him not to bother. As I lied awake at a quarter passed midnight, I was kicking myself for stopping him. The thunder outside the window played nature's alarm, and when my eyes opened, I heard a dozen ghosts in my head.

"Nothing is what it seems," the old man told me. It was the first memory that popped in my brain, followed directly by the moment he called me by name.

I thought of him, standing at Max's window, tapping on the glass with his long, skinny finger while smiling. A chill rushed through my body, and so did the sudden urge to check on my son.

The long hallway was dark. Lacing my robe as I walked out of the room, I took the steps toward Max's door from memory. Darkness was one of the ailments that Jennifer was able to help me surpass, but not completely. I felt my pulse on my temples as I approached the door, praying that I wouldn't hear voices.

Peering into his room from the doorway, I listened carefully. Seconds passed, and the satisfying sound of silence was all I heard. Max's soft breath filled the air, a clear signal that his slumber was completely undisturbed.

As was the window.

After making sure the latch was still locked, I checked the alarm in the living room. It was armed, its green flashing light confirming that none of the entrances to the house were open. I ventured back into my bedroom, taking my steps slowly and quietly. Even a mere whisper uttered in the kitchen would sound loud enough for me to hear.

Before I carefully slithered back into my bed, careful not to wake Nick, I decided on calling Katherine Brewer first thing in the morning.

Friday, June 5th

The alarm clock erupted at half passed seven in the morning, nearly scaring me into full consciousness. Normally, I would smack the snooze button, allowing another slice of sleep to help me prepare for the coming day. Only, a day with plenty of important preparations was before me, and time was of the essence.

My room was dark and opening the shades to the window would not help brighten the house. It had not stopped raining. The music of raindrops crashing onto the window filled the room, but I wasn't surprised. It never failed to rain on the day of our memoriam dinner.

I dragged my feet to the bathroom Nick built into our bedroom years before. As big as the house was, the only bathroom was in the hall, and when Max was born, Nick constructed our own. It was a brilliant idea.

Washing my face and brushing my teeth, I thought of the day's plans; the dinner required a visit to the grocery store, preferably in the morning to avoid the crowd. Rebecca would probably help me cook, cutting the preparation time in half, which I would use to clean the house. First thing's first though, I needed to be fueled. Nick would normally leave Mr. Coffee with a carafe half filled, and that was an important part of my waking process; one large mug, three creams, two sugars.

I was alone in the house, Nick taking Max to work with him like he said he would. It wasn't a normal ritual, but it was becoming more habitual the older Max became. Nick's Fridays were spent at the office rather than a job site, so his days were always shorter. By three in the afternoon, both of them would arrive; Max excited to tell me stories of what he had done throughout the day.

I couldn't wait to see both of them.

Half way through the hall, I stopped at Max's closed bedroom door, and stared at it, sighing in frustration. I wondered how long it would be before I could pass his door without feeling the dire need to make sure his window was locked. The incident with Old Man Brewer is something Jennifer would have a field day over.

Analyze the situation. Knowing that was exactly what she would tell me, I heard her voice ring in my head. *There is no reason to be paranoid over something you are not certain about. Exhaust every option before making your conclusion.*

I took a deep breath and moved for the doorknob. However, before I walked into my son's room, I told myself that no matter what I saw behind that door, I would not panic.

And to my relief, there was no reason to.

I waltzed into the kitchen, my eyes moving directly to the coffee machine resting on the tiled counter. The kitchen was another room that Nick worked very hard on, but not to rebuild. He replaced the cupboards, counter, all the appliances and retiled the entire area all to my liking.

The cupboards were made of wood, polished every week and retouched once a year. They bordered the entire kitchen, the two largest set on either side of the window above the sink. The doors were made of glass, exposing their contents; dinner plates and matching bowls in one, and glasses, mugs and cups in the other.

I reached for a mug, leaving the cupboard door open as I poured the steaming brew. The rich scent that invaded the air was enough to wake me, but I couldn't wait for the first sip. I gripped the mug, careful not to spill anything on the floor, and closed the cabinet door.

I don't know why I didn't notice his reflection on the glass before, but I saw it clear as day then. He was standing beside the refrigerator on the other side of the kitchen, at least ten feet behind me.

And he was staring directly at me.

I turned quickly, a reflex action that almost produced a scream. The mug exploded on the floor; I hadn't noticed dropping it. The coffee splattered, a few drips burning my leg but gone unnoticed. The person I was facing kept me occupied as my eyes welded with tears, my mouth going dry, and my body frozen with fear.

How did he…

It was Old-Man Brewer. He stood motionless, watching my every move with his pale eyes. The wide smile that made him popular throughout the neighborhood was replaced by a slight, almost unnoticeable crooked sneer across his deathly thin face. His stare kept me paralyzed with dread, knowing his visit was not meant to be a kind one.

"What do you want?" I asked, my voice shaking and not at all firm.

He pushed himself off the corner and took a step toward me with a single movement so sudden, all I could do was take one step back in retaliation. I felt the cold sting of the counter behind me and I was trapped.

The thought of reaching for a knife at arm's length crossed my mind, but before I could, the old man was standing directly before me. My eyes locked with his, but only for a second. After just a glimpse of the clouded pupils, I looked away from him like a scolded child.

"What do you want?" I asked, my trembling voice almost a whisper.

He reached for my shoulder with his left hand, and my skin exploded with goose bumps. Through the cotton of my sleeping tee, I felt his ice-cold grip, and I hissed in surprise.

I smacked his arm in an attempt to unlock his grip, but failing as his hold tightened. He found a spot on my shoulder that paralyzed me with enough pressure, and as an electrifying jolt of pain spread, I fought to keep from collapsing.

"Let me go!" I ordered, my voice finally finding the firm tone.

But he didn't. Instead, his other arm flew up towards me, and in a split second, both hands were cupped around my neck, locking me in place.

I grabbed both his wrists, trying desperately to pull them apart. My eyes watered and my ears began to ring in seconds. My breath was restricted, and I tried to gasp a lungful of air. I couldn't.

Anger possessed the old man's face as I struggled to pull his hands away from me. His lips were curled, exposing his clenched teeth and his eyes were narrowed, filled with evil intentions.

An intense pressure fell over my head as the lack of oxygen set in. I began to hit Old-Man Brewer with what was left of my strength, my arms flailing about to hit him wherever they landed. Slamming into his arms, his face and torso, the old man didn't even blink. My fight seemed to fuel him, his grip on my neck becoming stronger as my flying fists grew weaker, and weaker still.

Suddenly, as the throbbing of my heart took hold of my face, I began to feel light-headed. My arms fell lifelessly to my side and I felt myself drifting. My entire body collapsed, my knees finally giving in. The old man's iced hands kept me from falling, and as I tried frantically to take one last breath…

*

…I began coughing at the amount of air I *did* take in. Drenched in my own sweat, clenching my chest, I sat up and gasped for air, my entire body trembling. My pounding heart prevented me from immediately realizing it was all just a nightmare. I was still on my bed, in my room, clear of any intruders.

But I felt as though the old man was still lingering.

I bolted from the bed, coughing, my chest still burning. My frantic eyes shot to and fro, searching the room for an existing threat; there was no one behind the closet door or tucked in the corner. Still, my nerves would not retire. After five minutes of heavy breathing, I felt my pulse residing to its normal pace, the uncontrollable shaking becoming small muscle spasms, and my breath falling into my control again.

It was just a dream, I told myself. Nothing else.

The alarm clock erupted, scaring the last scream out of me. Quickly turning it off, I looked around the room to see that Nick had already left for work, taking Max with him. I was alone in the house.

I tried to remain calm as I ventured through the hall, deciding not to check Max's bedroom window. My intention was to go directly to the kitchen, my nightmare flashing in my head as my bare feet slowly crept through the tiled floor, all the while reassuring myself that-

It was just a dream. Nothing else.

I cautiously stepped into the kitchen, my eyes moving directly to the coffee machine resting on the tiled counter. Half a carafe was waiting for me, as I expected it to be, but I wished it wasn't. Stepping in no further than the entrance of the room itself, I inspected the entire area, from top to bottom and left to right. There were no intruders hiding, ready to pounce the moment I walked in.

I was alone.

Because it was just a dream. Then, I told myself exactly what I told Rebecca about her nightmare; it was the stress of the coming day; one of the remnants that would forever remain with us due to that fateful night eighteen years before.

I shook my head, trying to ignore the vision replaying in my mind, but it was useless. I didn't give in to it. Despite my fear, I walked into the kitchen for my morning cup of coffee.

Closing the cupboard door before pouring, I looked into the glass to see the reflection of nothing more than the kitchen behind me. As the seconds passed, so had the fear. Little by little, I was beginning to find my paranoia a bit ludicrous.

It was no wonder I had the dream considering what happened the day before. My dream was nothing more than a display of fear that I had for the old man. Standing in the kitchen, holding the steaming mug, I questioned if the old man was capable of such things I feared him for, though it didn't seem likely.

Jennifer would have found the entire situation silly, and I thought about what she would say if…

A nauseous wave fell over me suddenly, erupting in my stomach, then flaring up toward my esophagus. A gag settled in my throat, and before I bolted toward the bathroom in the hall, the mug of coffee exploded on the kitchen floor. A few drops burned my leg, but I didn't react to them. I dashed into the bathroom, barely making it to the toilet before the eruption surfaced.

The irritation in my throat made my eyes water as I vomited, what seemed to be, pure acid. The violent cramps my stomach suffered kept my knees buckled to the floor, each spasm worse than the one before.

When they finally subsided, I struggled to stand, my head throbbing and my digestive track burning with no remorse. I took a deep breath as the pain finally settled, leaving behind the potential for a migraine.

Trying to avoid any kind of motion sickness, I slowly moved toward the sink and studied my blood shot eyes before turning on the faucet. I wouldn't have been surprised if I popped a few blood vessels with all the strain. I splashed my face with cold water before rinsing my mouth out repeatedly, then brushing my teeth to rid the sour taste. Patting my face with a towel, I glanced in the mirror again, and that's when I saw him.

The old man stood behind me, his long, frail arms extended toward me as though in greeting. His cold stare pierced my mind and sent my heart into another beating frenzy.

I yelled as I quickly turned to face him, this time, prepared to defend myself. But he wasn't there. I found nothing but a wall before me, to my left, to my right, then back to the mirror. He was gone.

I sighed, slapping my thighs and aggravated by not having control over my own imagination.

It was just a dream, I told myself again and again, training my brain to recognize it as that and nothing more.

It was just a dream, and almost unwillingly, a new thought followed.

But it was so goddamn real.

*

Normally, a trip to the local drug store took anywhere from ten to fifteen minutes, depending on traffic. That morning, I made it in less than five.

What could have caused the unexpected illness? I came to a conclusion that led me to the drugstore aisle I avoided for the past five years.

There were so many to choose from, making the selection an overwhelming process. Most of the home pregnancy tests claimed to be the quickest and cleanest, and all of them were doctor recommended for being the most accurate. I chose two, in case a second opinion was in order.

Intentionally, the drive home was not as quick. I thought of the last time I took a pregnancy test; my cycle was off by a few weeks, so Nick and I made the trip to the drugstore and took the test. It was positive, and nine months later, Max was born. I never suffered a moment's discomfort during the nine months, not even towards the end.

Nick and I spoke several times of giving Max a little brother or sister, but we never discussed it at length. Knowing Nick would be just as excited as I was if the test proved positive, I tried not to expect it to be. I didn't want to become upset if it was negative.

I pulled into the driveway and crossed the front lawn, trampling over the well-kept garden of grass to reach the front door. Rushing into the house, I threw my purse onto the couch and locked myself into the bathroom. Seconds later, the testing began.

After emptying the plastic bag on the counter, I read the instructions of each box carefully. The turn around time for the first test was only one minute, but it did not seem as easy as it claimed to be. Having to urinate into a tiny cup with an opening no larger than the circumference of a gumball was not what I considered simple. After the cup was filled, I dipped the cotton swabbed stick in, and according to the directions, the swab would turn blue if it was positive, and it would remain white if negative. From experience, I knew the test took a little longer than they claimed. After I followed the steps, I left the bathroom to occupy my mind.

Before I began pacing the kitchen, I served myself a tall glass of orange juice and drank most of it in one gulp. I glanced at the splattered mug pieces and drying coffee on the floor then decided to clean it after the test was complete.

Two minutes, I decided. *I'll give the test two minutes.*

The phone rang suddenly, and I picked up the receiver resting on the wall that was the entrance to the kitchen.

"Hello."

"Are you busy?" It was Logan, and no matter what time of day he called, he always asked the same question before his greeting.

"Not really," I lied. "What's up?"

"I just wanted to make sure we were still on for tonight."

"Of course we are."

"Good. Would you mind if I brought Angela along this time?"

"We'd be more than happy to have her, Logan," I said to him. "You know that."

"I just wanted to make sure. What's on the menu, anyway?"

"You'll see when you get here."

"I hope it's not filling. I want to save room for the beer."

I laughed. "I'll make a note."

"Okay, I'll see you tonight, then."

I hung up, finished the rest of the juice and glanced at my watch. Two minutes passed, and a touch of excitement filled my veins at the thought of inspecting the test's result. Keeping composed, I walked into the hall.

I opened the door to the bathroom, and there it was. Resting on the counter between the toilet and sink, I saw the swab stick resting inside the cup, but its color remained concealed until I picked it up. Before inspecting it, I closed my eyes and prepared myself for whatever the outcome was. If it was blue, I would have to confirm the pregnancy with my doctor before I made an announcement, and if it wasn't, then no one would have to know.

I took a deep breath then opened my eyes and inspected the entire stick.

It was blue.

Chapter Owt

Cynthia put the pen down and massaged her right hand carefully. It hadn't cramped yet, but her fingers began to stiffen, and given the wounds on her knuckles, she decided to rest. Only two hours passed since she began to write, and she deemed occasional breaks necessary if she wanted to complete her story by sun-up.

She stopped once before after only a few pages were filled, but it was on a technicality. Danny, the young check-in clerk delivered the first-aid kit himself, stating that because she didn't want anyone else to know her whereabouts, he thought it better than sending a bellboy for the delivery. It was a good idea and she was impressed by his thoughtfulness. Only his credibility was destroyed when he seemed eager for a peek into the room. Cynthia would not allow him past the room's foyer though, so he didn't see much at all.

She didn't trust him completely.

Immediately after his departure, she jumped right into her story, keeping the first-aid kit close, but unopened. She would make use of it once her story was completed, after she showered. No use in wasting the bandages and ointments beforehand, she figured.

The quaint hotel room did not seem as threatening to her anymore. Occupied by her writing, her claustrophobia drifted to make room for the emotions that stirred while telling her story. The thought of turning off a few of the lights crossed her mind, but-

Let's not push it, she told herself. *Little steps.*

She didn't feel completely safe, but that was expected.

She stood from the bed slowly; taking a deep breath to prepare for the pain her leg would inevitably produce. While lying still, her legs outstretched, the pain almost disappeared, and it was easy to forget the injury when she was wrapped up in her memory. Just as the sole of her right foot touched the floor however, the tear in her calf screamed with the burning reminder.

She limped into the bathroom, avoiding the glass door that led to the balcony. Throughout the night, the storm grew stronger, howling winds whipping through the shores of the beach and thunder rolling above the sea. The ghostly sounds weren't easy to ignore, but the constant reminder that her battle was over gave her all the strength to keep writing.

Without even a glance in the mirror, Cynthia turned on the faucet, cupping her hands underneath the cold water and splashing it onto her tired face. She was starting to feel exhausted, mentally and physically. Writing her story was not as easy as she thought it would be; especially when it came to writing of her parents' deaths. She whimpered softly as she wrote about it, tears falling onto the paper and smearing the black ink into the threads of the page.

And there was still so much more to tell.

She walked back toward the bed and assumed her position after fluffing up the pillows again. Quickly flipping through the pages she used; at least half of the first notebook, she estimated the rest of the story would take several more hours to write. She yawned again, knowing without the aid of caffeine, it would be nearly impossible to do.

Once her weakness became overwhelming, she would call Danny to order a large cup of coffee, cream and extra sugar. Hell, she'd tell him to bring up a gallon of boiling water and a pound of instant coffee if it would mean finishing her story.

She would stop at no lengths to complete it.

*

Danny thought about calling his friends at the book club. They would never believe that Cynthia Grazer herself checked into the hotel. And he actually *spoke* to her! But he didn't call them. It would betray her trust, and quite possibly impair the possibility of future interaction with the writer.

Instead, he sat behind the check-in desk of the hotel's lobby, hoping she would call soon. The phone didn't ring once since she went to her room, but he was optimistic nonetheless.

A man entered the lobby suddenly and looked around the small room before entering any further. Danny noticed him immediately because he was the only person to walk into the hotel in nearly two hours. After the storm gained force, business promised to be slow because no one was crazy enough to be out in such weather.

Except this guy. He was drenched completely. A black raincoat draped over his suit didn't help keep him dry. Then again, Danny didn't think anything could. His dark, thinning hair was combed backwards; water dripping onto his face but the man didn't bother wiping it off. As he charged toward the check-in desk, Danny noticed an urgency in the man's walk.

"What is your name?" the man asked Danny, his voice demanding an answer.

Danny frowned, crossing his arms across his chest. "Who are you?"

The man sighed impatiently, reaching into the inside pocket of his raincoat and extracting what looked like a wallet. He opened it and flashed a badge in Danny's face. "I'm a detective with the Dade County Police Department," he said, "and I'll be the one to ask the questions, understand? Now, tell me your name."

Danny's face went pale at the sight of the golden badge. He was never approached by any official before, and it was an unsettling event. "My name is Danny," he answered, his mouth suddenly dry.

"Has anyone checked in within the last two hours?" the detective asked, putting his badge away, then extracting a 3x5 photograph. "Namely, this woman?"

The picture was of Cynthia Grazer, and Danny's jaw nearly dropped to the floor. Suddenly, he was caught in a moral dilemma. He promised Cynthia that her stay would remain in secret; that he would tell no one where she was. But an official of the county police? How could he lie to him? All the while, Danny could only wonder what the writer had done to provoke the manhunt...

"Danny!" the detective called, snapping his fingers across the boy's dazed face. "Have you seen this woman or not? It's not a difficult question."

Danny sighed, feeling his honor fall to the floor faster than his jaw did. "Her name is Cynthia Grazer," he said, against his will. "She checked in a little over two hours ago."

Satisfied, the detective smiled, slipping the photo back into his raincoat. "What room is she in?" he asked.

"Seventy-seven. It's on the seventh floor."

"Have you been up there?"

Danny nodded. "A little after she checked in, I took a first-aid kit to her. She requested it."

"Did you see anything in her room or happen to see what she was up to?"

"No, sir. I didn't get a look inside the room, but it looked like she might have been writing or something. I saw a notebook at the foot of her bed. That's all."

The detective nodded, absorbing the information. "Has she asked for anything else?" he asked.

"No, sir."

"Any phone calls for her?"

"None as of yet."

"Did she seem strange when she checked in? Was she acting

suspicious in any way?"

Hell yeah she was acting suspicious, Danny thought to himself. But he shook his head. "No, not that I noticed. She seemed fine."

The detective nodded again, and for the first time since the man charged the desk flashing a badge and barking questions, Danny noticed he hadn't formally introduced himself by name. He had seen enough movies to know the detective should have at least given his last name.

"What time is your shift over?" the man asked.

Despite his doubts, Danny cooperated. "I need the over-time, so I'm working a double," he said. "I'll be here until sun-up."

"Good," the detective said, reaching over the counter for Danny's pen and the note pad resting directly next to it. "I'm going to need you to do me a favor, then."

Danny watched as the man scribbled onto the pad, upset that he took the liberty of obtaining the items without permission, but daring not to contest it.

Handing the notepad back to Danny, the detective recapped the pen and slipped it into his raincoat. "This is my number," he said. "If Ms. Shey…Grazer calls you for anything, you call me immediately and let me know. If anyone calls for her, you call me before transferring it to her. In the meantime, I want you to check in on her every hour or so. You don't need to knock, in fact, it's better that you don't. Listen in through her door, and if you hear anything suspicious, I mean *anything,* you call me. Understand?"

Danny nodded, studying the number written across the otherwise blank page. The detective didn't even write his name on the sheet. "Excuse me, detective," he said, waving the pad in the air. "But don't you have a business card or something?"

The detective glared at Danny, and the boy instantly read the "how dare you question me" look across his face.

Just as the detective expected, Danny looked away from him, defeated with a single glance. "Your cooperation in this matter will be greatly appreciated, son," he said then turned quickly and headed toward the lobby's doors.

Danny watched him leave the building, running into the storm towards the chariot from hell in which he must have rode in on.

"Who the hell does he think he is?" he said, almost to himself.

Danny was growing tired of being on the receiving end of demanding orders. He didn't even know why he was put in the situation on a night he thought would certainly be slow. One thing was certain; as he looked at the number scribbled on the pad once again, he grew determined to find out why Cynthia Grazer, the writer, was in trouble.

Somehow, he would find a way to help her.

The Memoriam Dinner

Everyone knew to be at my house by eight, and as usual, they were all late. Rebecca was on time, only because she was at my house by four to help me prepare. She helped liven up the house, bringing along her daughter Charlene, and Max's best friend, Buddy. Leaving the women in the kitchen, Nick and Max took Buddy to the yard and found a football. They were useless for the rest of the day.

Logan and his girlfriend, Angela arrived at eight thirty, each contributing to the meal. Angela handed me a covered dish and told me to hold it steady because the flan would drip. Logan brought the beer.

His relationship to Angela Ortega was the longest he'd ever had. Logan lived a free life for as long as he could; bedding as many women as humanly possible. One fine morning, he realized his charming smile and smoldering stares didn't impress as many women as they used to. Suddenly, the middle age crisis every man experiences at thirty-five fell upon him, nearly destroying "Logan the Legend" (self proclaimed). He met Angela shortly afterwards and she put a certain step in his walk we hadn't seen before. It's been true love ever since.

The rest of the clan arrived not five minutes later. Luis and Jo apologized for being late then contributed to the meal as well. Jo made her famous creamy pesto dip, and Luis brought more beer.

Within minutes, the dinner table was buzzing with countless conversations. Nick sat at the head of the table, talking with Rebecca to his left. The booster chair for Charlene separated her and Logan, and Angela took her place at the far left corner of the table. Luis and Jo cuddled together on the right corner, and Jo laughed at something silly he said. When I took my seat to Nick's right, I sighed, my legs feeling the wonderful relief of weightlessness.

"Tired, mommy?" Max asked. He was sitting on his booster chair to my right.

"Just hungry," I answered, then kissed his forehead.

The night had officially begun, and it was time for Rebecca and I to display the artwork we created for our supper.

The garden salad was served first along with a plate of grilled eggplant with sun-dried tomatoes as an appetizer. Baskets of sliced Italian bread, freshly toasted, were set out between each place setting, beside the crystal wine glasses set just above each plate. Before we dove into the food though, our tradition had to be carried out.

Nick delicately poured a finely aged Merlot into each glass, but no one dared touch it until the last was served. It was time for the ingredient that would set the mood for the entire evening. Before each memoriam meal, someone in the group raised his or her glass and gave a toast. There were no rules, and no one was ever forced to be the first to stand and talk, but every year, someone did.

Before anyone else could volunteer, Jo stood from her chair and lifted her glass off the table.

The rest of us followed.

"At any given time of day," she said after a brief moment of silence, "I think about how lucky we all are to have each other. I think of every important occasion in my life and you're all there, in every one of my memories."

"Not Angela," Logan said. "She's still new to this."

The rest of us laughed as the suddenly embarrassed Angela smacked Logan across the shoulder.

"For the past eighteen years," Jo continued, "we've had only each other to turn to when we needed guidance. Besides Uncle George and Billy, all we've had was us." Her emotional eyes danced across the table as they made contact with every individual in the room. "We do this every year in memory of our parents, but tonight, I want to celebrate us. Our families, God rest their souls, will forever be remembered and honored on 365 days of the year, not just on a single night. Tonight, I toast to us; the family that stuck together through the many highs and lows. We are lucky to have each other." She raised her glass high. "May the days we have come to know now be the roughest of what lies in the future."

The crystals chimed at Joanna's toast, followed by heartfelt hugs and kisses. Everyone moved around the table for an embrace on an emotional high. Even Angela was included.

After the first cup of the wine was gone, the main course was served; Chicken Parmesan, layered with melted mozzarella cheese and smothered in a homemade tomato sauce proved popular amongst the crowd years before, and ever since, it was the tradition. Accompanied by linguini in a creamy Alfredo, it was the perfect full course meal.

It was also the tribute meal to our mothers. Mom and Aunt Mayra were the cooks amongst their friends, and since they were both of Italian descent, an Italian meal was expected at any special occasion. Thankfully, they saved the ones they left behind by passing on their gifted genes to us.

And of course, the conversations kept flowing. As the plates emptied and glasses refilled, at least fifty conversations ended and fifty more were in full bloom. I took a moment to myself, watching the others interact with each other and the watching the manner in which their conversations went from point A to B. I smiled, thinking of the gatherings our parents had together. Though, as teenagers, we thought them unsophisticated with their empty plannings and senseless promises to each other, I realized that night we *became* our parents. Though they were dead eighteen years; they remained very much alive inside us all.

*

Near the midnight hour, the table was cleared and Angela's desert was devoured. We migrated to the living room, well lit by a chandelier hanging from the cathedral ceiling, and in the background, the stereo hummed with the sounds of a top ten countdown on the local radio station.

Bored out of their little minds, Max and Charlene fell asleep on the living room floor, and before eleven o'clock, they were carried into Max's room for peaceful rest. The rest of us were freed from the restrictions of watching our foul language.

The men cracked their beers open and the woman refilled their glasses of wine. I stuck to water, claiming I wasn't in the mood to drink.

As in every one of our gatherings, the men held a conversation about sports, their jobs, or something competitive enough to fuel their egos. The women remained on their side of the living room; even Angela joined us as we gossiped about life in general.

Throughout the entire night, I didn't mention Old-Man Brewer, nor did I speak of the pregnancy test I took earlier that afternoon. The topics danced in the back of my mind with every conversation, sometimes overwhelming me with the desire to tell them everything. While Jo gleefully updated us on her job at the orphan center, she caught me in a daydream, my mind involuntarily switching between the old man's attempt at killing me in my own kitchen and the mysterious voice I heard coming from Max's bedroom.

"Another one's over," Rebecca said, snapping me from my daze.

"Another what?" Jo asked.

"The memoriam dinner. Another year has come and gone."

I wasn't sure how everyone else felt, but I was happy it was over. It meant not having to deal with the torrid emotions, depression and nightmares for the next 365 days, and not a day sooner.

"Let's hope the next year brings better days," Luis said; a weak attempt at reprising Jo's toast. His tongue was swollen and his speech was slurred.

"Angela can tell you," Logan said after a sip of his beer.

Angela frowned. "Logan no," she shot back. Naturally, her reaction peaked our interest.

"Tell us what?" Rebecca asked.

"Don't tell them," she warned.

But Logan didn't listen. "Angela's psychic. Well, at least she claims she is."

All eyes were suddenly upon her. As though it had gone dark and a bright spotlight shined on Angela, our attention was diverted to her, and she blushed. "Don't ask me to prove it because I won't."

"You have to!" Rebecca insisted excitedly. "Are you really psychic?"

Again, she frowned at Logan, silently cursing him for letting her secret out. "My grandfather had the gift, and it was passed on to me. I don't use it very often, but..."

"Bullshit!" Logan shouted. "She has a list of clients that she reads for. You should see her in action!"

"You have to read for me!" Rebecca announced. She wanted to be impressed with Angela's gift, have her breath taken away as Angela reached into the future and told her what to expect.

We all did.

"I won't," Angela said. "It's not something that I can do at request. It takes time to prepare."

"Oh, come on," Rebecca whined.

Angela took a breath and let it out slowly. "I'll tell you what, come by my house, and I will read for you, but not here."

"Why not here?"

"Quite frankly because of Logan."

"She always finds a way to blame me for everything," Logan said to Nick.

"It's just that his energy won't allow me. He doesn't believe in it."

"You mean you've never read for him?" I asked.

She shook her head. "I can't. Because he doesn't believe, it won't work."

"You won't even tell me how it works," he argued.

"It's not something you can explain," she said to him. "My grandfather told me something when he found out I had the gift, and it's true. He told me that for those who believe, no explanation is necessary, and for those who do not, no explanation will suffice." She turned to Rebecca. "Do you believe?"

Rebecca nervously looked to Jo and I. "I don't know," she answered. "I've never had it done."

Angela's eyes narrowed at her. "I think you do," she said. "As a matter of fact, I see something immediate in your future."

Rebecca gasped as the rest of us leaned closer toward Angela, the spotlight growing heavier.

"What is it?" Rebecca asked.

"You're saying good-bye to Logan and I." She turned back to Logan. "It's time to go."

"Well, show's over," Logan said, finishing his beer. "Pack your magic bag and let's go home."

Angela stood from the floor and apologized for the disappointment.

"We better get going too," Luis told Jo, standing from the couch only to be greeted by a dizzy spell.

"No, you're not driving anywhere," Nick told him. "You and Jo stay here tonight. You're too drunk."

"You're drunk!" Luis said, falling back onto the couch.

"There's plenty of room," I told him. "That sofa turns into a bed so just settle in."

Before I had to convince him any further, his head fell to his shoulder and his light snoring began.

Rebecca tip-toed into Max's room and without waking either child, she carried Charlene out. She thanked us for the lovely night as Nick loaded Charlene into the safety seat attached to the car's back seat. We watched her drive off then thanked Logan and Angela for the lovely evening with heartfelt embraces. They promised to join us in the morning for breakfast, then Nick and I retired to the house for the rest of the night.

I closed the door after we entered, locking the bolt then arming the alarm, a short beep erupting with the push of every button.

Luis and Jo already made use of the sofa bed when we returned. Both were covered to their necks in bed sheets and lying back to back on the bed. Though Luis was in dreamland, Jo was not. She waved as Nick and I passed the living room and into the hallway.

We checked in on Max who was sleeping like a baby. Come sun-up, he would ask why no one said good-bye to him before they left, but his disappointment would vanish when we all grouped up together in the morning.

As Nick and I got ready for bed, I thought of the coming day. Another emotional journey would ensue because at eight thirty sharp, we would all meet at the funeral park in which all our parents were buried.

At least, that was the plan.

*

Thirst was the initial reason I woke. A dry itch in the back of my throat caused me to sit upright at nearly three that morning, but the moment my eyes opened, I took notice of something else.

Whispers. I could hear them bouncing off the walls of the hall, entering my room though the door was closed for the night. The muffled sound of someone speaking softly instantly stirred emotions in my stomach that worried me; my son was in his bedroom, and quite possibly, talking with the old man.

Without waking Nick, I ran toward the door of my room, praying, hoping I was wrong; that the whispers were the remnants of a dream I had brought out to reality. Only, by the time I opened the bedroom door, the whispers grew louder. Someone was definitely talking, and they were inside my house.

The hall was dark, but I didn't hesitate. No one would stop me from rescuing my son if the situation came to. I was determined to put an end to the old man's visits, if in fact, it was he who disturbed my sleep.

But my son's room was empty. Max slept undisturbed on his small bed, his tired face looking peaceful. The window remained untouched and its ledge dry.

Heading back into the hall, the whispers caught me again; the sound of a soft voice speaking in the air, and amongst them, simple words I could not understand, until I heard my name.

Cynthia...

I was being called, summoned to the place where the origin of the whispers stood. It was coming from the living room.

Jo was on the sofa bed where we left her. Only when we left, she was with Luis, and he was not by her side now.

"Cynthia," he whispered again.

I spun quickly, toward the dining room, and there he was, sitting at the head of the table in the darkness.

I could barely make out his silhouette amidst the shadowy room, but as I entered, I flipped on the soft light.

His face displayed no sign of awareness; his eyes wide yet glazed over with a hypnotic daze, and his body slumped on the chair as though he were exhausted. He didn't look at me when I entered the room, not even when I turned on the light. His eyes fell upon me only when I called back for him.

"Luis," I said, "who were you talking to?"

He didn't answer, and for a brief moment I wondered if in fact he was awake. He never walked in his sleep, much less talked, but the way he glared at me was drunk-like and unsettling.

"Are you okay?" I asked him.

He looked down at the table and barely smiled, but still he did not speak.

I took the seat next to him, his pale face unchanging. Was this the way he was dealing with the anniversary? Was he relapsing into the memory of our parents' death? A hundred more questions circled my mind as I took hold of his clammy hand.

"It's here," he said to me, still whispering.

I sighed. He was suffering. "I know it is," I told him, "but we'll get through it tog…"

"It'll kill us all."

My back stiffened at his words. "Honey, no one is going to…"

"You don't know because you haven't seen it," he said, finally looking to me, but with angry eyes and clenched teeth. Still his voice had not raised an octave higher than a mere whisper. "It's in me," he continued. "And it will kill us all." He looked down to the table again shaking his head ever so slightly then said, "Nothing is what it seems."

I stood from the table, the words pounding in my head like a jackhammer. I stared at my brother sitting at the table like a confused child, and though I wanted him to delve into an explanation at his choice of words, I told him to go to sleep.

"You're tired," I said to him. "We all are."

I turned my back to him and walked into the kitchen to serve us both a glass of water. He was drunk when he went to bed, less than three hours before, and there was no doubt in my mind the liquor had a big part in our conversation. He probably didn't even know what he was talking about.

I returned to the dining room with two tall, cold glasses in my hands, but I stopped. The room was empty.

"Luis," I called out softly, but there was no answer.

After putting the glasses on the table, I walked into the living room and crossed my arms in frustration.

He was asleep, resting comfortably next to the woman he loved. Both were snoring lightly as though neither were disturbed of their slumber from the moment they fell asleep; as though Luis never left her side.

I shook my head, deciding that Luis would have no recollection of the conversation we had because he, more than likely, wasn't even awake when it happened. He walked back to his bed and fell into a deep repose in mere seconds, and as I watched them sleep, I felt sorry for him. He suffered so much over the loss of our parents, more than the rest of us, and it still showed even eighteen years later.

As I walked back into my room, I decided not to ask him about the conversation come sun-up. If he brought it up, then we'd talk. It was nothing more than a combination of factors that brought the words out of his mouth; whether it was exhaustion, liquor, or the simple falling of the date, I was certain he would not remember, and my naïve thoughts told me to leave it untouched. The sixth day of June fell upon us, and there were more important things to attend to.

As I closed the door to my bedroom and slid back into the bed, the demons in my head would not allow me to dismiss the conversation. Something in Luis' eyes wasn't right, almost as though it wasn't him at all. As I tried desperately to ignore his words, I kept thinking of the one phrase I heard from two different people but delivered and received in the same menacing manner. What did it mean? Was it a warning? Repeating it in my mind, over and over again, I couldn't decide. Sleep was now slipping further and further from my grasp as Luis' words echoed in my head, his voice subtly changing into Old-Man Brewer's as they both repeated the words I grew to despise.

Nothing is what it seems.

Saturday, June 6th; A Day of Death

When the phone rang at nearly six thirty that morning, I prayed it wasn't a telemarketer. I finally fell asleep less than an hour before and the last thing I wanted to deal with was "Would you like to receive *The Miami Herald*?"

The night table where the telephone rested was directly next to my side of the bed, and as I rolled over to answer it, the thought of switching bedsides with Nick crossed my mind.

"Hello," I said, my eyes still closed.

"Cynthia, it's Billy. Are you up?"

Normally, I would have told him to call back at a more decent hour, but the urgency in his voice woke me completely. I sat up on the bed quickly, Nick waking from his sleep and asking the same question I asked Billy; "What's the matter?"

"There's - ah - been an accident."

A jolt in my chest sent my nerves to work. "Oh my God, are you okay?"

He hesitated, his filtered breath confirming that it wasn't good news. "Not me," he said. "It was Luis and Jo. I'm at the hospital…"

"Luis and Jo?" I asked, glancing at Nick who wanted to know what was happening. "That can't be, they're here."

After a brief moment of silence, his somber voice said, "No Cynthia. It was pretty bad."

Nausea fell over me like an unexpected storm. Without a word, I threw the phone onto the bed and sprinted into the hallway.

"What happened?" Nick asked from somewhere behind me, but I

didn't answer.

I ran into the living room, to the sofa bed Luis and Jo occupied the night before. I found exactly what I didn't want to see; the sheets hanging off the foot of the bed, and the worn pillows resting without anyone to use; it was empty.

Tears of desperation began to fall as I ran back into the hall and toward Max's room, praying that they hadn't taken my son with them. He was sleeping when I walked in, resting comfortably and unaware of what was going on.

Nick was sitting on the edge of the bed, hanging the receiver onto its unit as I walked in. His eyes met mine, and he sighed, his back losing support. "He says it's serious," he told me without looking up. "We should get to the hospital as soon as possible."

*

The parking at Miami Memorial Hospital was horrendous on any day of the week, at any time. With no actual knowledge of what had happened to my brother or Jo, Nick skipped the entire parking process and pulled along a curb at the emergency room entrance. He picked Max up from the back seat and we hurried into the hospital's lobby.

It was just as crowded as the parking lot. Our eyes scanned over the busy room for Billy, but all the faces we saw were strangers.

Where is he…

Nick suddenly dove into the crowd and worked his way toward the information desk where answers awaited us.

"Cynthia! Nick! Over here!" It came from behind us, but I didn't see where exactly, until Billy's hand shot up and waved above the crowd.

He was at the west side of the room, just before a set of double doors marked *Authorized Personnel Only.*

We approached him hurriedly, his face keeping tight and clear of any signals. I couldn't tell whether he was the bearer of good or bad news, and it scared me.

"What happened?" I asked still approaching nearly ten feet away. My nerves wouldn't allow me to keep from asking any longer.

He waited until we reached him, then turned and continued to walk with us, leading us toward the double doors. "They were brought in at about six fifteen this morning," he said, pushing the double doors apart and leading us into a surprisingly secluded hall. "The car accident happened at six."

"Oh my God," was all I could say while I tried to keep up with him. He walked quickly through another set of swinging doors and into another hall. "How did it happen?"

"Are they okay?" Nick asked. "Can we see them?"

"Someone wants to see you first," he said, then stopped at one of the doors on the right wall. It was to an office of sorts, but of whom, I wasn't sure.

Billy opened the door, and I was surprised to find Rebecca, Charlene and Logan seated on a small leather couch on the opposite wall of the room. The man who wanted to see us was sitting behind the desk just in front of them.

I hadn't seen him in nearly twenty years, but the moment my eyes fell upon his own, it felt like minutes. The familiar eyes brought back many emotions, some kind, some not.

Doctor Morrison stood to his feet and offered us a smile, then a seat on the fold out chairs he had put out for us.

As Billy crossed the room to sit by the doctor's side, I glanced at Logan and Rebecca. The worried look on their faces was a clear sign that they didn't know any details either.

That scared me, too.

"Can someone please tell us what's happened now?" Rebecca asked suddenly, her voice edgy and her hands trembling.

It was evident that Morrison was not going to speak first; he sat down and looked to Billy to answer our questions. With a sigh, Billy loosened his neck tie and undid the top buttons of his dress shirt, his tired eyes meeting each of ours before he spoke. "Early this morning, Luis and Jo were in a car accident while heading East on 88th street." He took a deep breath before he continued, leaving us in suspense another second longer. "An eye witness says that a black Ford Mustang, Luis' car, lost control in a puddle, and they ran into a street lamp post."

I covered my mouth and closed my eyes, visualizing the collision, hearing the exploding metal, and smelling the scent of burning tires. My heart nearly stopped when I pictured Luis and Jo being tossed inside the cabin on impact.

"Are they okay?" Logan asked, the fear in his voice making us all a bit weaker.

Billy looked to Dr. Morrison again, the same detail telling tag-team they displayed with me eighteen years before.

"Luis has suffered severe trauma to the head," Morrison started, and I held my breath. "When he was brought to me, he was not at all responsive to the environment or actions surrounding him."

Nick took hold of my hand and gripped it tightly. He knew that I was trying to keep calm when all I wanted to do was scream.

"What does that mean?" Nick asked the doctor, finding the strength amongst all of us to speak.

"It means he is comatose. His vitals have improved since he was brought here, nearly an hour ago. As of yet however, he is unresponsive."

"How long will he be like this?" I asked, my voice cracking.

"Luis will remain under my care while he is in this condition, and I have my best team of doctors and nurses attending to his every medical need. Unfortunately, the only thing I can tell you for certain is that your brother is being cared for."

"Can I see him?"

"I'm sorry, but I'm afraid not," Morrison said, rubbing his bald head with his enormous hands. "We're still conducting tests to see if metabolic and immune systems are coherent to determine the exact state that Mr. Grazer is in. Once we're done with those tests, and depending on their results, you will be free to visit him any time you like."

Picturing Luis in the accident, then the horrible shape he arrived in the hospital unnerved me, but the fact that I couldn't see him destroyed me. I buried by face on Nick's shoulder and cried for my brother.

"What about Jo?" Rebecca asked, wiping her face from the fallen tears then holding Charlene close.

"When the paramedics arrived at the scene, they attended Ms. Corona immediately. Her injuries were fat…"

"She wasn't wearing a seatbelt," Billy said, interrupting the doctor, his voice suddenly weak. "She was-ah…"

A tear escaped his eye, and he didn't have to say another word. The rest of us already felt the sharp edge of the knife pierce through our hearts.

He cleared his throat and wiped his face. "She was pronounced dead at the scene."

Rebecca stood from her chair, crying out loud and covering her stomach as though she were going to be sick. Logan rushed to her aid and while she struggled to breath, he put aside his own outburst to keep her breathing controlled.

Charlene began to ask questions, she and Max both confused as to what was happening. Max turned to his father, and asked why everyone was crying. Nick hugged him, his eyes filled with tears and his chin quivering.

All I could do was stare at Billy; shocked at the news he had given.

"I'm sorry," he said to me.

I watched Logan and Rebecca comfort each other in tears, embracing tightly and securing themselves in support. Nick put his hand on my shoulder, and when his sorrow-filled eyes met mine, I broke down.

Joanna was dead, and no matter how many times I told myself it wasn't true, I knew it was. We all did.

*

"I don't understand!" I told them. "The last time I saw them, they were sleeping in my living room."

After the tears fell and the nerves calmed, the anger settled. Doctor Morrison escorted us through the hospital to a secluded waiting room while he checked on Luis' progress. Promising he would inform us the moment we could see him, he left us nearly an hour before and we hadn't received word from him since.

Logan, Rebecca and Nick were seated on a small, plush couch resting against the pastel colored wall next to a candy vending machine. Charlene and Max fell asleep in between them, and as I paced the room, I demanded more answers from Billy. He decided on staying with us for the same reason he did eighteen years before; to answer any questions we might have.

"What on earth possessed them to leave the house?" I asked him. "Especially so early in the morning."

Billy shook his head. "I don't know, Cynthia. I'm so sorry."

"Who was driving?" Rebecca asked quietly to not wake her daughter.

Running his fingers through his graying hair, Billy took a breath and gnawed his jaw. "Luis was. Jo was in the passenger seat."

"How did it happen, exactly?" Logan asked, somewhat dazed. "I mean, how did it kill her?"

Billy shook his head. "All I know is that the car hit the light pole head on at, what is being guessed as, 65 miles per hour." He lowered his head. "As I said before, Jo wasn't wearing her seatbelt."

I looked away from him, feeling the tears build again.

"One of the officers at the scene called me after they were identified, and I arrived here at the same time the ambulance did. From the parking lot, I could see them bring Luis out on a gurney." He became dazed, reliving the moment and the emotions brought with it. "I could see the I.V. bag, I could hear the paramedics talking about him like he was alive, and I was relieved. I thought, 'Well hey, at least they're okay.'" He shook his head, and the rest of us listened to his every word. Our random sniffles and emotional sighs didn't distract him from continuing. "I introduced myself as Detective Kux so that I can get all the details, but that was a mistake. They told me everything I wasn't prepared to hear. First words out of their mouths were, 'The girl is dead, and this one barely made it.' I couldn't believe it."

I bit my bottom lip and offered another prayer to Jo, to Luis. To all of us.

"Did you see her?" Nick asked, wiping his face.

Slowly, Billy nodded. "Yes. Someone had to identify her, and I certainly wasn't going to make one of you do it."

Rebecca was in tears, and Logan began to pace the room as well while Billy spoke. Nick sat in a daze between the children, his elbows on his knees and his face in his hands.

Billy watched all of us for a second, and I admired him. His detective exterior stood long enough to inform us of the news, but it broke down when we were passed that. He was our friend, after all, and it was better to hear it from a friend than a persona.

"I know that last night was your anniversary dinner," he said after a moment of silence. "I want to ask you something because it will be known eventually anyway. Was Luis drinking?"

Each of us glanced at each other, wide-eyed and wondrous. But we all knew the truth.

"Yes," I answered. "He was."

Billy nodded slowly, the weight of the news proving it wasn't the answer he was hoping for. Whether it would cause us some trouble with the law remained his own conclusion. If it was bad news, he didn't want to add that to the day's events.

"I have to call my father," Rebecca said softly.

Calling Uncle George was not going to be easy. The news would break him.

"I already have," Billy said. "He should be on a flight to Miami International as we speak. I'll have a squad car escorting him here once he arrives."

"Thank you," Nick said to him, but not just for doing us the favor of calling Uncle George. The sincerity in his voice was for everything Billy had done for us; in the past and in the present. "For everything."

Billy crossed the room toward the door, insisting we spend a moment together. "I want to go to the station and review the file, talk to a few of the officers who were there, get some more answers. I'll be back later."

Rebecca thanked him again, and he left, leaving Nick, Logan, Rebecca and myself in silence. I looked to Max and Charlene as I realized that our clan of six, the family we built as our own, had been torn to five in a matter of seconds. It was supposed to be a day of reminiscing of the loved ones we lost, not the suffering over a terrible incident that brought us to where we now sat. Sad, frustrated, and confused, I couldn't help but think of something that stirred a dozen other emotions.

June 6th, it will forever remain the day of death.

Sleep

After Rebecca was married the first time, and after Nick and I announced our engagement, Uncle George decided to return to his life in New York. He rescued us from the narrow ledges of life we were thrown onto, and he won his place in our lives in an incredible way. He was our father.

He always made an effort to see us as often as he could. He flew down for my wedding, to be by Rebecca's side during her first divorce, even found the time to visit after my son's birth. The look on his face when he walked into the waiting room was completely different from when he's visited before. He looked the same as he did when he arrived eighteen years before.

His tired eyes met mine as he turned into the room. Nick stood immediately, surprised by the old man's presence. Logan looked at him and smiled, but Rebecca ran to him like she did when she was a little girl. Only her father could comfort her in times of distress.

They hugged silently for a while, Rebecca letting her emotions flow as she cried on his shoulder. He rubbed her back, holding his own tears to remain strong. His voice didn't crack as he assured her that everything would be okay. He didn't even flinch when the rest of the room joined his daughter in the display of emotions.

He embraced each of us individually before taking off his raincoat then greeted the two children. He was thrilled to see them. Showing no pain of the loss, he picked the children up in his arms and whole-heartedly laughed with them.

His beard had gone gray and his hairline began receding years before, but Uncle George was more fit than the rest of us. He stood at nearly six feet, five inches and kept his heart healthy by jogging five miles a day. We often joked that he would out live most of us, and now that the joke had become somewhat a reality, it wasn't that funny.

"Have you heard anything on Luis yet?" he asked us, taking his seat on the couch next to his daughter. She rested her head on his shoulder and pulled Charlene close to her.

"Nothing yet," I said, looking at my watch. Noon was approaching fast, and Doctor Morrison had come in only once, to see how we were doing nearly two hours before. I demanded to see Luis, he demanded I wait. He hadn't returned since.

"And how are you all holding up?"

"We're trying our best," Logan answered, rubbing his temples. "I just wish we had some answers."

"I still don't believe this is happening," Rebecca said. "I keep wishing it was a nightmare, or something."

Uncle George patted her arm and took a deep breath.

"Did you hear how…" I asked him, not able to finish the question.

Uncle George nodded. "The officer who drove me over filled me in. There's not much they know yet." He proceeded to tell us what he did know, speaking slowly and concentrating on not showing his emotion. He would close his bedroom door come nightfall and cry in privacy like he did eighteen years before. He knew nothing more than we did; just the details of the accident itself. "Has Billy told you anything else?"

"He's at the station looking over the details of the accident," Nick told him. "We've been here for hours waiting for him or Dr. Morrison to come with news, but neither of them have."

"Then go home," he said. "I'll stay here, and when we receive word, I'll call you."

"Absolutely not," I said immediately. There was no way I was leaving the hospital. "What if Luis woke up for one minute, and I'm at home? I'm not leaving."

"I think we'll all stay, dad," Rebecca said.

Uncle George slapped his thighs and stood from the couch. "Well then, let me take the kids home," he said. "No sense in having them see you all like this. I'll take them home, feed them, and keep them entertained. The moment you hear something, you call me."

"I'll call Angela and have her pick you up," Logan said.

"Have her drop him off at my house," Nick followed, handing Uncle George his set of keys, then took his hand in both of his. "I'm happy you're here."

Uncle George's eyes welded with tears for the first time that day, and though he tried to hide it, I think I saw his chin quiver. He gave Nick a hug, patting his back furiously like a proud father. "Me too, Nick," he said. "Me too."

He took hold of Charlene's and Max's hands then walked them out of the room. The rest of us watched our hero take our children, knowing that in his arms, they would be safe. Uncle George had returned, bringing with him the same security he provided years before. His mere presence equipped us with a layer of safety and reassurance, the way only a father could.

*

I hated Morrison for making us wait. By three that afternoon, we had been forced to live with our dire need for answers, and resort to patiently waiting for the moment when the good doctor reported with news. Logan and Nick had run out of their change for the vending machine, and I had found my own peace on the couch. Sleep was at my fingertips, teasing my tired mind with visions of the horrid occurrences of the past few days.

I sat up quickly, my heart accelerating when the door to the room opened and Dr. Morrison entered. He looked at me and offered a friendly smile. "Your brother has been moved into a private room. You can see him now, if you're ready."

I stood to my feet, the moment I waited for finally arriving only I wasn't certain if I *was* ready. For a moment, I hesitated.

"Can Nick come with me?" I asked him.

Morrison shook his head. "I'm sorry. I can only allow one person at a time."

"Go on," Nick said to me. "I'll call Uncle George."

I took a deep breath, trying my best to prepare for the worst. "Okay," I said in a breath. "I'm ready."

Morrison nodded and instructed me to follow him. He said nothing to me as we walked down another long hallway with dozens of doors, leaving me to study the bland walls. Through a set of double doors and into the east wing of the hospital, the air changed; it had grown thicker. I attempted to catch my breath, closing my eyes for a brief second, realizing I had lost control of my nerves.

Everything's fine, I told myself, *or I wouldn't be allowed to see him.*

The hallway seemed eternal, and I began to grow impatient. Staring at each of the closed doors as we passed, I hoped Morrison would turn suddenly and say, "Okay, this is it." Still, we continued to walk around this corner, down that hall, and through another set of double doors labeled *I.C.U.*

The Intensive Care Unit; a sudden explosion of activity displayed before us the moment we walked in. Nurses and doctors buzzed hurriedly to and from the hallways and doors surrounding the area. At least three of the seven or eight nurses looked up from the station as the doors flapped closed behind Morrison and myself. As quickly as we diverted their attention, they proceeded with their work. All the doors to the countless patients' rooms were open here though. I knew exactly why.

The ICU is where most patients are put when their condition is unstable. It was where Death was waiting patiently for its next victim, floating along the cold air ready to choose no matter what the doctors did to prevent it.

Morrison walked toward the station and turned the corner directly beside it. I followed, my eyes inspecting each room for a familiar face. Morrison finally stopped at the third door to the right. "Okay," he said. "This is it."

Though the door to Luis' room was less than a foot away, I couldn't look inside. Despite how much I tried to convince myself, I *wasn't* ready.

"Are you okay?" Morrison asked, detecting my hesitation.

"I need to know the truth," I said. "Is he going to be okay?"

Morrison looked away in thought. "Cynthia, it's hard to say for certain in these cases. He's under constant supervision…"

"Yeah, I know that, but I want you to be frank with me here. I mean, in your opinion, do you think he'll be okay?"

The doctor settled his black eyes on mine. "Cynthia, my opinion is based on what I've seen. I've seen people in worse conditions than your brother's live many years after they've been released from my care. I've also seen others that are not so fortunate. Your brother is stable at the moment, and right now, that's all I see."

I nodded and accepted his answer, not having a choice.

"I have other patients to attend to," he said softly. "If you need anything, if you have any questions, have someone look for me, okay?"

I smiled briefly and thanked him.

He disappeared through the hall, and I closed my eyes, praying that Luis would be okay. I prayed that his physical ailments would heal and that he would not fall into the same form of shock he did eighteen years before when he learned of Jo's death.

I prayed that Death wasn't lingering in his room.

*

The melancholy colors of the room suit its purpose. There were no windows to allow the sunlight to enter, not that the storm clouds would allow it. Soft bulbs built into the ceiling cascaded a minor glow illuminating just enough to see the person beneath it.

I heard his heartbeat echoing mechanically through the heart monitoring systems. Timed beeps and bleeps spilled into the air, ready to erupt into a single tone should his heart fail.

I didn't cry in case he could hear me, but the moment I saw him, it was what I felt like doing. He was lying still on the bed, a network of wires running to and from his body, a tube bound to his mouth to control his breathing. His stomach rose and fell under the bed sheet pulled just to his chest. He was living by artificial forms.

I covered my mouth, building the courage to take another step toward him for a closer inspection. His face was pale and decorated with numerous blue bruises. The swollen brows kept his eyes bound shut and his dry lips were just a shade away from purple. There was a contusion on his forehead, stitched to close the torn skin, and I wondered if it was the source of his coma.

No matter how many times I pictured his injuries, it didn't compare to actually seeing them.

"Luis," I whispered, hoping he would react at the sound of my voice. "Luis, it's me."

Of course, he didn't sit up and smile at me like I wanted him to. He didn't react at all.

I watched the heart monitor, the green neon line forming mountain peaks to correspond with the noises it belched, all the while keeping track of his beat. His heart seemed strong which should have encouraged me, but I could only think of one thing:

How the hell could this happen?

They were at my house, sleeping! Why would they wake up and leave at six in the morning? What made them decide to take a drive that early? There was so much I wanted to know and no one to provide a straight enough answer. For the first time that day, I thought of what Luis told me the night before; It's in me, he said. It will kill us all.

My mind was too weak to try and find a link as though it were all a puzzle. It had occurred to me, popping into my head the way Old-Man Brewer found his way into my head. Surely, one thing had nothing to do with the other.

Standing over my brother, nothing else mattered to me at that moment. Seeing him in so much pain weakened me no matter how strong I was trying to be and out of frustration, I cried like a child.

"God, what happened to you?" I asked him in a whisper through my cries. I wanted to know what happened; *needed* to know as though seeing it would ease my pain somehow. Luis drove everywhere everyday; he was a great driver, cautious and courteous. It just didn't make sense.

"Luis, can you hear me?" I asked, trying not to sound like a crying fool. I cleared my throat and asked again. "If you can, you're going to fight this, okay? Dr. Morrison is taking good care of you, and you'll get through this." I took a breath and wiped my tears. "I promise you I'm going to be right here until you wake up. We'll get through it together."

Taking hold of his lifeless hand in the hopes that he would grip back, I stared at his injured face and wept silently at his side. Before long, I was repeating an involuntary prayer over and over again, not realizing it was voiced out loud until the sixth or seventh time it was said;

"Please don't die on me, too."

*

A yawn fell upon my lips after the initial shock of seeing my brother had passed. A chair for visitors was set out on the east corner of the room, and I pulled it toward his bed to settle myself by his side.

I inspected the room through the same view Luis would have if he woke…

"*When* he woke up," Jennifer would say had she heard me. Not "if."

The daily reminders to be positive had escaped me, but I didn't care. It was hard to be optimistic when the world around you collided from one minute to the next.

I yawned again as my eyes fell upon the television set suspended from the ceiling and tilted down toward the bed. I thought of turning it on, hoping to find one of Luis' favorite shows. He couldn't see it, but maybe hearing it would make him more comfortable.

Or me.

The beeps from the heart monitor kept their rhythm,
becoming nearly hypnotic and less bothersome as the minutes ticked away. I slouched into the chair, my eyes growing dry and their lids becoming heavy at the tiring day. I fought them long enough to gaze upon my brother once more, then tuned my own breath with his.

I thought of Jo, and I fell asleep.

*

Visiting hours were over at 11:00, and Dr. Morrison refused to bend the rules as a favor to me. Luis was off limits at eleven sharp, without an extra five minutes to say good-bye. He did however, promise to keep the waiting room free from any other visitors should we decide to spend the night, and for that, I was grateful. Before leaving us for the evening, he promised to see us first thing in the morning.

Rebecca and Logan insisted on staying as well, but I told them to go home, giving my word to call them should any news befall us. I did appreciate their effort in support, we all needed it, but there was no use in them being there.

Nick and I stayed in the waiting room the entire night. Though there was enough furniture and space for both of us to sleep comfortably, we sat on the large couch, both of us wide awake. We made trips to the cafeteria for coffee and candy bars, but only one at a time. Someone had to stay behind in case the head nurse leaped at us with news.

Close to sun up, Nick went for more coffee, and I declined another cup. I was craving it, but I couldn't help but think of the life inside of me; the baby I hadn't even mentioned to Nick yet.

Sunday, June 7th; The Next Day

Morrison informed us that visiting hours resumed at eight, and by seven that morning, the entire entourage had arrived. Logan, Angela, Rebecca, Charlene, Uncle George, and my son Max walked into the room together, and by the looks of it, neither one of them had gotten much sleep either. With the exception of Angela, everyone else was even dressed in the same attire as the day before.

Dr. Morrison knocked on our door at a few minutes before eight wearing a fresh smile to match the fresh scrubs. "Are we ready to visit Luis?" he asked, his voice booming into the room like the chime of a bell tower heard across the city.

I was ready for round two. I waited for the moment that I could see Luis again, but it wasn't fair to the others. There was someone else I desperately wanted Luis to hear.

"I think you should go, Uncle George," I said. "I want you to talk to him."

I couldn't tell whether or not he was surprised by my suggestion because he didn't hesitate to stand to his feet.

Morrison nodded in his direction. "It's good to see you again, George."

My uncle nodded at the doctor, then breathed deeply before approaching the doorway.

"Nothing like a tragedy to reunite the family," Morrison said, shaking Uncle George's hand. "I'm sorry about your loss."

"Thank you, Eugene. It's good to see you, too."

They left the room together, and I prayed that his voice would help aid

Luis the way it always had. After a half hour or so, he returned with swollen eyes and a flushed face. His voice didn't make a difference after all.

I sent Nick in next, Morrison making an exception of the one-person rule so that Max could join. Afterwards, Logan took his turn followed by Rebecca and Charlene. Everyone returned looking as upset as Uncle George had.

I stood from the couch, thanking everyone for trying. I assured them that Luis appreciated it, though they didn't need the convincing.

Before I had the chance to dust myself off to visit my brother, Angela stood from the couch and asked if she could have a turn.

I wasn't surprised by her request, so I stepped aside and let her visit with him before me. If it helped wake Luis, I was willing to wait all day. She promised not to take long then left the room.

Seconds later, there was a brief knock before the door opened again. Billy stepped into the room, surprising us with his arrival. He closed the door behind him quickly and turned to face us.

"Good," he said, the urgency in his voice nearly startling me. "I'm glad you're all here."

"What's the matter?" I asked him.

"I need to talk to you," he told us. "It's about the accident."

By the look on his face, I could tell it wasn't good news.

"What about the accident?" Logan asked.

Billy ignored his question, removing his windbreaker then combing his wet hair back with his hand. Making use of the fold out chair on the other side of the room, he sat with a collective view of both couches. His shoulders didn't slump, and he didn't slouch. It was evident that he had not come to visit with Luis. In fact, Billy, our friend, had not come to visit us at all. The man sitting before us was Detective William Kux, and he had come on business.

"I was at the station all night reviewing the files for the accident," he began, looking at us, but at no one in particular. "Apparently, some questions have been raised regarding the situation, and there's going to be an investigation."

"What kind of investigation?" Nick asked.

Detective Kux cleared his throat to even his tone. "There's been some evidence found that suggests what we know about the accident is incorrect."

"Evidence?" I asked, somewhat afraid to.

He looked at me squarely for the first time since he arrived, but he didn't miss a beat in answering. "Evidence that suggests Joanna may have been dead before the accident."

"What?" Uncle George asked, nearly yelling.

The rest of us didn't know what to say.

Detective Kux nodded. "Joanna's autopsy report showed several injuries that do not coincide with what we thought happened."

"What injuries?" Logan demanded, Kux unfazed by his tone.

"I know you all have a lot of questions, believe me, I understand. But half of my time at the station was spent crawling through air ducts to find this information, so I don't know the answers to everything you're going to ask. Just bear with me, and I'll tell you everything I do know."

I was on the verge of losing my breath, and he was asking us to remain calm while he explained the horrible news he laid out before us with details he was uncertain of. And he wanted us to bear with *him*?

"Before I begin, though…" he said, trailing off looking to the children.

Without a pause, Uncle George jumped to his feet and told us he would take them to the cafeteria. Moments later, the three walked out of the room.

"Everything you've been told about the accident is true," he said once the door was closed. "Everything, except one detail."

"Which is?" Logan asked.

"Joanna *was* restrained in the car that morning, the exact opposite of what we thought. Also, the airbags had deployed for both she and Luis, which makes it difficult to believe the source of her death was directly related to the accident itself."

"What are you talking about?" Rebecca asked. "Of course someone would be killed in that kind of situation."

Kux sighed. "Not like this. The autopsy report showed something completely different..."

"So what was in it?" Logan barked.

His eyes told me he was hesitating, thinking of the way he should phrase his words to soften the blow. "There's no easy way to say this," he said after a long breath. "Her skull was cracked in seventeen different places, all along her forehead. That's only how many the coroner could count. When the inside of the car was examined, the dashboard on the passenger side of the car had been banged up pretty badly, and some pieces of flesh were found within its cracks. There's no official word yet, but some people already believe that Luis is responsible for her death, and the accident was made to cover it up."

I nearly vomited, my entire body convulsing with shock. The others remained in a spellbound silence.

"That's what this investigation is going to try and prove," Kux continued, his voice softened to let the news digest.

"So, it's a homicide investigation," Nick said with a nod.

"That's right."

"I don't understand," Rebecca said in somewhat of a daze. "How can they try and pin this on Luis?"

"If Joanna's airbag deployed, and her seatbelt was fastened, then it's doubtful she would have hit the dashboard at all, even in collision, and definitely not seventeen different times. It's being assumed her head was forced to hit the dashboard repeatedly."

Rebecca closed her eyes and covered her mouth near tears. Logan couldn't believe what he was hearing, and neither could I.

"Luis didn't kill her," I said to Billy, Nick taking my hand as my emotions began to peak. "You know that, don't you?"

"It doesn't matter what I think. They're going to investigate anyway."

"Can't you tell them to call it off? That you know he wouldn't do this?"

Billy shook his head. "I'm sorry, but I can't."

"Of course you can!" Logan said in outrage. "Tell them he's innocent, they'll listen to you!"

"I can't, Logan. They won't let me near this investigation because of my relationship with you all. If they knew I was talking to you now, they'd have my badge. Luis is in deep water here, and once this investigation is closed, the outcome will not be affected by my opinion."

"What does that mean?" Rebecca asked.

"If the investigation is conclusive, and the evidence is legitimate, Luis will be charged with manslaughter."

"Oh God, no..."

"So, let them investigate," Nick said. "There's no way Luis did what they think he did. He loved Jo, they'll see that."

"*If* he's innocent," Kux added almost as though it was against his will.

"What do you mean, if?" Logan asked. "You think he did this?"

"Don't get me wrong, I'm on your side," he said, as whole-heartedly as he could. "But I've seen the evidence myself, and it is conclusive."

"You think he did this." Logan stated, rather than asking this time.

He hesitated. "I know Luis loved Joanna more than life itself, and therefore I don't believe he's guilty. My hands are tied here, though. What I think won't make a difference."

"There's no chance that this is all a mistake?" Rebecca asked, hoping against the odds like the rest of us were.

He shook his head slowly. "I'm sorry, but no." After taking a deep breath, he stood from the chair and grabbed his jacket. "I know this is a lot for you to absorb right now. The reason I came to you today is because the two who have been assigned to this case are pretty ruthless, and it's important you're prepared."

"Who are they?" Nick asked.

"Detectives Maria Lopez and Raul Santiago. She's a pro and he's a rookie. Detective Lopez is known for being the queen of interrogation, so be prepared for anything she might have up her sleeve. They're already looking through Luis' psych files and detailing all the symptoms he went through after your parents' deaths. There's no doubt they'll use his violent streak against him."

"That was eighteen years ago," Rebecca protested.

"It doesn't matter. Just be sure to cooperate. Answer all of their questions, no matter how irrelevant they might seem. That's the only way to help Luis right now."

"When will they begin their investigation?"

"In a few days, most likely. Unfortunately, once it begins, I will not be able to contact you at all but I assure you, I will be doing everything I can to help." He apologized for the news and told us he'd come with more the moment he found anything new; so long as it was before the investigation, of course.

I watched him approach the door, ready to leave us behind when I stood from the couch and called for him.

He turned in surprise.

"If Luis is charged, what happens then?"

He took a deep breath, his chest rising and falling slowly as he thought about the answer. "If he is charged, then we'll fight it in court, depending on his health. But don't lose hope. There's always the chance the case will be dropped once you've all been questioned."

He was only trying to give us a false hope to live on. We knew that the case would not be dismissed so easily. We knew it as much as he did.

No one said a word after he left. As though we had taken part in group hypnosis, we dazed into the air, replaying the entire conversation in our heads. All the while, visions of Luis killing Joanna the way Billy described possessing my mind and lowering my defenses.

I knew none of us truly believed that Luis would do such a thing; kill the one precious thing that he loved most on Earth. None of it made any sense. Billy tried to answer each of our questions, but dozens more flowed in my already overworked mind and I found myself too confused to even cry.

Just keep focused, I reminded myself; a useful piece of advice I had paid thousands for.

But on what? On the fact that my brother is being accused of murder? Focus on the horrid reality that Jo was dead? I told myself to stop thinking about it all together, to take a walk instead.

I stood from the couch, my breath suddenly falling a bit short. Slowly, the claustrophobia was reaching me, and without a word I headed toward the door in a hurry.

"Where are you going?" Nick asked.

"To tell Uncle George what's happened," I answered without looking back. Nothing was stopping me from getting out.

"Want me to come with..."

"No, I'll be back."

I stumbled into the hall, taking a nose full of the sterilized air that reeked of medicine. I began to sweat, my temples throbbing to the beat of my racing heart. A nervous breakdown was upon me, its symptoms all exploding at once.

Deep breaths, Jennifer would say. *Long, deep breaths.*

I closed my eyes and did as she said, concentrating on my pulse for control.

Easy now...deep breaths.

There had been so many verges before; I was becoming a pro at control. Though there were fewer between the years, each one seemed worse than the one before.

As Jennifer's voice echoed in my head, I managed control of this episode, letting yet another breakdown pass. The voice was a little more difficult to get rid of. As I headed out of the ICU, I tried to block Jennifer's new comment.

You picked a hell of a week to quit therapy.

*

"You've got to be kidding me!" Uncle George said after I told him everything.

We took our time walking back from the cafeteria as I went over what Billy had told all of us. Our voices were low so the children walking by our sides didn't hear.

"He says the investigation might begin in a couple of days."

"Does he realize how ridiculous this all is?"

I told him how specific Billy was about not being able to get involved and Uncle George's reaction mirrored ours – he was shocked. How could they believe that Luis killed her, he had asked me. He loved her so much.

"What do the others have to say about this?" he asked as Max tugged at my hand. He wanted to be a part of the conversation.

"We don't know what to say. We're just so exhausted. It's bad enough what happened now we have to deal with some shit-heads who want to investigate."

"Mommy, that's a bad word," Max warned.

"I'm gonna tell!" Charlene followed.

I didn't care. *Shit-head* was the nicest thing I had to say at the moment.

Uncle George's eyes were filled with worry, and for a quick second, I silently wondered if telling him was the wisest thing to do. He had already planned on leaving the day after Jo's funeral service, and if we were lucky, the investigation would begin afterwards. I wondered if Uncle George needed to know anything at all.

"I'm going to take the kids," he said, suddenly stopping to face me.

I stopped as well. "What?"

"Back with me, to New York."

"Why would you do that?"

"Listen to me," he ordered, the way he used to when I was nineteen. "They don't need to be there when the investigation begins. They don't need to hear what they think Luis did, and they certainly don't need to see you all like this."

I appreciated his offer, but I needed my son with me. I needed family. "Uncle George, no..."

"Cynthia, I've taken care of the funeral preparations, okay? On Wednesday, the day after the ceremony, I'll take them back with me and I'll return in one week. Seven days, that's all. Hopefully, by then, this will all be over with."

"I don't know," I said after a moment's thought.

"It'll be good for all of us. Even for me. It'll be nice to hear the voices of children around the house again."

Despite my own doubts, I knew he was right. The kids would be better off with Uncle George. "Are you sure it's not an inconvenience?"

"Are you kidding me?" he asked, a smile growing on his face. "I was going to suggest it the moment I got here."

It managed to make me smile, too.

"One week," I said. "Then you bring them right back."

"You have my word," he said, then he hugged me.

Like Rebecca, I found comfort in his embrace. I thanked my luck that he was with us. Without him, we would have been destroyed.

A Warning

Nick insisted I go home. Uncle George left hours before, without the kids, and one by one the others attended to their day to day lives as well. When Nick and I were alone with Max, he told me that I should sleep in my own bed for the evening. I put up a fight at first but eventually gave in after he promised to call should Luis wake up.

Stepping out of the hospital, the humid night surprised me. I glanced at my watch amazed that the entire day had come and gone. It was 9:00 and that meant Nick and I hadn't slept for thirty-nine hours and more bad news falling upon us with each that passed.

And we hadn't even visited our parents' graves yet.

None of that mattered now. I told Nick that I would go home to rest, and that's exactly what I intended on doing. I would force myself to keep from thinking of Jo's death, the accident, and the investigation just so that sleep came easier. It didn't seem like it would be such a challenge. Walking towards the car, I felt myself growing weaker and more desperate for undisturbed rest.

Max begged me to let him sit in the front seat, and though I normally would not oblige, I did. His company was necessary if I was to stay awake for the drive home. I loaded him into the car as it began to rain and left the hospital's parking lot in a hurry. Heading out onto the main road, I prepared myself for the half hour drive home.

Max was asleep as soon as I shifted into drive.

Living in Miami where all the main streets and avenues are constantly traffic bound, one tends to venture in search of back roads for quicker routes. I had them all memorized. Down this neighborhood and around that corner, I made my way to a street just blocks from my house; a street known as Lover's Lane.

The two-lane road circled one of Miami's least known golf courses spanning six to seven miles in circumference. A fence of tall trees divided the course from the street, their branches stretching out over the road itself to protect passing cars from straying golf balls. During the day, the greenery was beautiful, but at night, the branches appeared more like black, fallen clouds hovering over the desolate street.

Nick and I conceived Max beneath those very branches. After a romantic dinner and one too many glasses of wine, we parked the car between an opening of trees and underneath the moonlight. The road was referred to as Lover's Lane ever since, and no one else knew why. It was our little secret. After making sure Max was asleep, I relaxed and thought about that night and it achieved the impossible; it replaced the thoughts of the accident, and it made me smile.

Something was moving between the trees at least a mile ahead, snapping me from my daze. Amidst the rain, at the point where the car's headlights were no longer focused, something disturbed the street's stillness, and I couldn't see what it was.

I pulled my foot from the accelerator and flipped on the high beams. Scanning the area with narrow eyes proved an unsuccessful search, whatever it was moved out of sight completely. It was probably a squirrel or a raccoon, I told myself. Or another figment of my overactive imagination.

I glanced at Max, sleeping on the passenger side, and I envied him.

The moment I refocused on the road, my grip on the wheel tightened as my foot slammed on the brakes. It wasn't a figment of my imagination after all. That something I saw moving now stood in front of my car, less than five feet away. It was Old Man Brewer.

My tires locked in the rainwater, and as I felt the back of the car begin to swerve, the noise of a hollow hit on the front bumper echoed inside the cabin. Watching in horror as the old man bounced from the hood and onto the windshield, I felt the car begin to spin along the wet road. He hit the roof of the car as the tires screeched along the pavement, and I began to scream, trying desperately to steer for control. Old Man Brewer rolled off the trunk when I realized my steering was taking us straight toward a tree trunk. Just before another fatal accident ensued, the car finally stopped.

That's when I heard Max's scream.

I undid my seatbelt and reached over for him to check his face, his arms, his entire body for a wound. "Are you okay?" I asked him, my mouth dry and my hands clammy.

His body was trembling and his little heart was pounding rapidly. Otherwise unharmed, I tried to calm him from the terrible fright that he witnessed.

"It's okay, baby," I said to him, caressing his face while looking out of the back window for a glimpse at the body.

The car's rear lights illuminated the area behind us a brilliant red, but not far enough for more than five feet. Old Man Brewer must have rolled off the asphalt and into the trees because he wasn't directly behind us.

I must have killed him.

My stomach went sour as I turned completely for a better view of the window. I couldn't see him at all.

"Mommy, can we go now?" Max asked between his cries. "I wanna go home."

So did I, but I couldn't just leave. My nerves were on a rampage, and I tried to not give into the idea that I just killed a man. Still, I couldn't help but assume that I had.

"Honey, I need you to do me a favor," I said, holding Max's face in my hands. "I need you to be a big boy and sit here while I check to see if he's alright, okay?"

He frowned. "Who?"

Oh my God, he was asleep when it happened.

"Just stay here, honey."

"No mommy, don't go out there!" he yelled as I reached for the door handle.

"I have to, Max."

He continued to beg, but I opened the door and stepped out into the rain, a thick gust of wind whipping at my face. Without moving an inch from the car, I turned, nausea falling over me as I anticipated seeing the old man's body twisted and contoured on the road.

But I didn't see anything at all; not form my viewpoint. Against my better judgment, I took one step toward the back of the car and stood on the balls of my feet for a better look. Still, I saw no one.

"Mr. Brewer," I called, my dry throat barely producing a sound.

There was no answer.

He wasn't on the curb, and the darkness of the trees that hid us from the rest of the world frightened me. It seemed he was never there to begin with, as though Old Man Brewer simply vanished.

"Mommy, get in," Max called. "Please!"

I wanted to further explore the area, find the old man in case he was alive. Max was in the car though, and I couldn't risk leaving him behind. There was someone else who could help me, I decided. Someone who looks for bodies on a daily basis.

*

I called Billy the moment I got home. I told him what happened, and without so much as faltering for a second, he said he would drive to the site and check it out.

"Where are you now?" he asked.

"At home, with Max," I answered nervously.

He told me he'd stop by after he investigated and hung up the phone in a hurry.

I sat with Max in the living room, impatiently checking the clock every five minutes. Max played with a pair of his action figures on the carpeted floor as though nothing happened.

It was better that he was asleep, I figured. For the rest of the ride home and after I spoke quietly with Billy, he didn't ask a question nor mention the incident at all. For that, I was thankful.

The doorbell rang, and I bolted to my feet, ordering Max to play in his room. Without protesting, he gathered his toys and walked into the hall.

After checking the peephole, I opened the door and allowed Billy in from the porch. He was soaked, dripping with rain, and he refused to enter beyond the doormat just inside the foyer.

"There's nothing out there," he said immediately. "There's no old man, no blood. Nothing."

"Are you sure?" I asked, remembering the sound of the body bouncing off the car. "Did you look everywhere?"

"Yes, I did. I'm telling you, there's nothing out there."

"Do you think he's alive, then?"

Billy sighed and shook his head. "How much sleep have you gotten lately, Cynthia?" he asked.

I frowned, knowing exactly what the question insinuated. "I didn't fall asleep at the wheel, and I didn't imagine it, Billy. I hit the old man with my car, I know I did."

"Did Max see it? Can I ask him?"

"No. He didn't see it because he was sleeping when it happened, not because I imagined it."

I don't know if he believed me or not, but he was convinced that my emotions were real. "Look," he said. "I'll go over to the Brewer house to see if anyone's seen him in the past half hour if that'll make you feel better."

"It would."

"But Cynthia, if he's there, unharmed, you have to promise you'll talk to someone."

"About what?" I asked.

"What with everything going on, you might want to think about talking to a doctor..."

"I just quit therapy, Billy. I don't need it because I know I didn't imagine it." He hit a nerve; I was truthfully upset that he would suggest such a thing.

"I'll check the Brewer house and let you know what I find," he said after I was done ranting. "Have a good night. And as a friend, I advise that you get some sleep."

He stepped out into the porch, the alarm chirping as he opened the front door. Without looking back, he walked to his black sedan parked in the driveway and pulled out onto the road.

I stood on the porch, lit by a hanging lamp above the door's entrance. As Billy's car headed in the direction of the Brewer house, I studied my car's bumper.

There wasn't even a scratch on my car. As I entered the house and closed the door, I remembered the way the car's headlights lit up the old man's terrified face a split second before I hit him. Then, I confused the image with the memory of my nightmare; when Old Man Brewer tried to kill me. As I punched in the access code to arm the alarm, the suspicion of the old man talking to Max in the window returned. Then, there was a feeling that overwhelmed me, an emotion that I didn't expect.

A small part of me felt relieved.

*

There are times when being a mother is not as instinctual as everyone assumes; especially when children ask questions that are rather difficult to answer. That night, as I tucked Max into his bed, he asked one of the most complicated questions ever posed.

"Mommy," he said, after I placed a kiss on his forehead. "What happens when you die?"

He took me by surprise. Everyone had been so careful to not let him overhear the conversations regarding the occurrence, but I knew that sooner or later, he would ask. I just didn't expect it to happen so soon.

I sat beside him on his bed and looked at his sweet face illuminated by the small lamp at his bedside table. Then, I hesitated for a mere second while pondering how to explain death to a five year old. "Death is something that happens to people when their time here on Earth is over," I said to him. "We go to Heaven where we can be with God."

"Where's Heaven?"

"Up in the sky, in the clouds."

"It sounds nice."

"It is. It's beautiful there. It's a place where people laugh and sing together during the day, and at night, the sounds of choir bells in the distance put you to sleep."

"Aunt Jo is in Heaven now?"

I nodded. He heard more than I thought. "Yes, she is. She's there with her mom, and your grandparents." I held back my own tears as I spoke. "She's happy there."

"I'll never see her again?" he asked, a look of sadness suddenly falling over his eyes.

"Whenever you want to see her, you look up at the skies, and she'll be there, among the stars, looking right at you."

"She will?"

"Aunt Jo is your guardian angel now. She will be with you forever."

"Can I talk to her?"

"Whenever you'd like."

His sad face was gone. Max sighed, seemingly content with the idea that he had a guardian angel now. "I'll talk to her tomorrow. Do you think she'll be mad if I just go to sleep tonight?"

I laughed. "Of course not, honey." He reached up and hugged me, and when he said he loved me, I let a tear escape.

After switching off the lamp, I kissed Max good night and headed toward the bedroom door.

"Will we be going to Heaven soon?" he asked from behind me.

I stopped and looked back at him, not thinking twice about how I should answer. "Not yet," I said. "Not any time soon."

He sat up on the bed again, folding his hands over his lap. "Aunt 'Becca's next."

My heart skipped a beat and my breath was suddenly robbed from my chest. I almost asked him to repeat what he said but I heard him loud and clear, and what scared me the most was how matter-of-factly he said it.

"Why would you say something like that?" I asked him.

He shrugged. "Because that's what I was told."

"By whom?"

He frowned, as though it were strange of me to ask such questions. "Uncle Luis told me when me and Daddy were in his room."

I frowned at him, now uncertain if he was telling the truth. "Max, your uncle couldn't have told you that."

"Yes, he did. When Daddy went to the bathroom, Uncle Luis talked to me. He said I shouldn't tell anyone."

"What else did he tell you, then?"

He shook his head. "Nothing. Daddy came back into the room, so he went back to sleep."

I was growing angry with him, frustrated with his lies. "Go to sleep, Max," I ordered.

"But, Mommy..."

"That's enough, Max," I shot back. "Go to sleep. We'll talk about it in the morning."

I walked out of the room and closed the door, trying to forget the last bit of the conversation. Max had a wild imagination; a trait Nick said was passed down from me. He wasn't known for lying, though. Of all things, I wondered why he would lie about something like that.

He couldn't have meant what he said, I thought to myself. It couldn't have been what it seemed.

Haunted

Luis forced Jo's head toward the dashboard and she bounced back into her chair, screaming in agony. I kept picturing it while the night progressed. Sleepless, weary, and unable to contact Nick or Morrison at the hospital, I stepped into the shower close to midnight hoping to relieve the stress, and the images.

Her forehead tore on the second hit, blood spilling from the wound, all over her dazed face. The images in my head flashed every time I closed my eyes; in yawn or in a mere blink, there they were.

I turned the shower on and stood in the stream of warm water hoping it would cleanse me of all my fears, worries and nightmares. I needed to concentrate on what was real. Luis *didn't* kill Jo; I knew it for a fact. There was no use in torturing myself with images I knew weren't possible. She was killed and he lies comatose because of the accident; that's the reality, and nothing else mattered.

It worked. As if the shower curtain stood to protect me from the demons outside, I bathed without another haunting vision. Taking advantage of the solitude, I stood in the center of the shower stream, my back straight and my chin slowly moving toward my chest to loosen my neck. I rolled my head onto my shoulder, first to the left, then to the right, then back down to the center. As the water rolled off my back, tickling the rest of my muscles, I found the perfect method for complete relaxation.

There was a change in the light suddenly. I opened my eyes as soon as the cold draft hit me, and what I saw paralyzed me.

The shower curtain was open, pulled completely to the far end of the curtain rod. Goose bumps erupted all over my body as I instinctively hid my private areas behind my arms, but no one else was in the room to see.

I stared into the empty bathroom, finding the courage behind the vulnerability to reach for the towel just outside the shower. Covering myself before turning the water off, I called out for Max, hoping he was playing little games. But he didn't answer.

My heart raced as I pondered the possibility someone had broken in. The alarm would erupt with blaring sirens, I tried to convince myself, but could I rely on electronics to save my life?

Slowly, I stepped out of the tub, my wet feet moving carefully across the tile. My eyes fell upon the door leading to my bedroom, cracked open just a bit; the way I left it. It didn't seem as though someone else had come into the room…

So who opened the shower curtain?

My bedroom was empty as well. Flipping the light switch on revealed everything untouched. Even the window. After replacing the towel with a terrycloth robe, I headed toward the hall, and straight for Max's room.

He was asleep, nestled in his bed, his soft breath whispering a sweet melody. He, like the room, had gone undisturbed. I closed the door, and moved on to the rest of the house.

The living room was dark, so I didn't move past the hall's end immediately.

I waited until my eyes adjusted for a clearer view before venturing, and when they did, they saw nothing out of the ordinary. No swaying shadows or silhouettes in the corner. No old men waiting to attack.

My teeth chattered and I realized then how cold the room was; I was too frightened to notice it before. I was too preoccupied to feel the overwhelming sensation that I *wasn't* alone.

I crossed the open space toward the alarm keypad in a hurry and found exactly what I hoped. It wasn't been triggered by any open doors or windows, and it was still armed.

No one had found their way into the house, so maybe it *was* Max playing games. Just as I decided on marching back into his room to ask, I was stopped.

In time to stop myself from screaming for help, I realized that the sudden explosion of noise was just the telephone. I reached for the portable unit on the coffee table and answered it quickly.

"Yeah," I said, between breaths.

"It's Billy," the filtered voice said.

The last time Billy called was with news of the accident. He didn't sound too thrilled about having to call again.

"Oh my God, is Luis okay?" I asked near frantic hearing a siren in the background.

"Are you watching the news?"

"What?"

"Turn on the news," he ordered. "Channel seven."

Without asking again, I reached for the remote on the couch and did as I was told. The television lit up the living room, and as I waited for the picture to focus, the voice of a news reporter filled the air.

She was standing in front of a Victorian house nestled in a community much like my own. Police cars lined the curb in the background as she rambled off details, and I tried to catch on.

"…in Miami where the well respected attorney Katherine Brewer has been charged with the murder of her father, Tomas."

"Oh my…"

"Listen!" Billy ordered through the phone.

"It's a gruesome story that has shocked this upper class neighborhood. Tomas Brewer was popular in the neighborhood for taking daily walks, and witnesses say his own daughter ran him down with her car earlier tonight on this very street, in front of their own house. There are reports that Ms. Brewer ran to him as he lied on the floor, seemingly dead, and instead of crying or asking for help, she allegedly washed her hands in his blood. Amazingly enough, Detective William Kux of the Miami Dade Police Department was passing by on routine, and stumbled upon this terrible sight."

The picture changed to pre-recorded video of Billy escorting Ms. Brewer to his car. She was handcuffed and did not appear as elegant as I remembered. She struggled with Billy, her eyes shooting in different directions, and her teeth clenched like a wild animal. She looked absolutely crazy.

The reporter was back. "It is a story that has shaken up many of the locals around here. Even the ones who witnessed it…"

"Billy," I said into the phone.

"I don't know how you knew it," he said. "You saw this man's death."

I closed my eyes, hearing and seeing him collide with my car.

"Cynthia, something's happening," he said softly, almost as if his present company prevented him from speaking louder.

"What do you mean?"

He hesitated, taking a deep breath. "I'm not sure, but I think I know…" There was silence suddenly, but the line didn't go dead. He stopped talking.

"Know what, Billy?" I asked. "What are you not sure of?"

He took another breath, sounding almost as though he were crying. "I feel like I'm going crazy… Go. All of you. Get out before the investigation starts." He *was* crying, and he wasn't making an effort to hide it. He sounded scared, desperate for help.

"Billy, what's the matter? Where are you?"

"I'm sorry," he said. "I can't talk. I have to go now."

"Where are you going, Billy?"

"To look for something."

"For what?"

He didn't answer.

"Billy? What is happening?" I was trying my hardest to keep him on the phone.

But the line went dead.

Shit. I tried to remember his mobile number as I nervously fumbled the phone in my hands but was distracted by the sudden high-pitched tone that filled the air.

I recognized it immediately. Turning toward the alarm unit resting on the wall, I prayed that it was a mistake. The alarm unit was flashing red, and the high pitched noise meant only one thing; a window open somewhere in the house.

Someone broke in.

Max.

I was ready to run toward his room and rescue him from the intruder but my knees nearly collapsed as another noise filled the air. Max's scream echoed through the walls of his bedroom; a scream rooted in his gullet and filled with more than just fear. It was filled with sheer terror.

The phone dropped from my hand and I darted into the hallway, barely slipping at the entrance. Desperation fell over me as I charged toward his door, but it did not match the determination I had to rescue my son.

He yelled again, and as my feet slid to a stop at his door, I screamed back, hurrying to open it.

But the door was locked.

"Mommy!" he cried.

It wouldn't budge! Deciding quickly that the door would have to be destroyed, I punched on the wood with both fists as hard as I possibly could. The adrenalin kept me from feeling any pain, even when the skin on my knuckles began to tear.

He continued yelling and I called out for him in tears, frustrated that a simple door stood between us. Then, a second voice echoed inside the room as well, smothering Max's scream.

I froze for just a second, chills soaring throughout my body as the man's voice rang in my ears like thunder. He called my name.

"Max!" I yelled, pounding on the door with my hands. "Open the door!"

"Mommy!"

I rushed the door, clenching my teeth as all my weight crashed into the wood. Failing to burst through, a blinding pain settled on my shoulder after I bounced off.

The voice called my name again, screaming louder this time, followed directly by my son's plea for help.

I tried again, prepared for the pain, but this time there was none. Splinters flew through the air into Max's bedroom as the door swung inward. Frantically reaching for the light switch inside, my eyes darted around the room for the intruder.

The lights flickered and failed to remain on. I caught a glimpse of Max sitting upright on his bed, his back against the wall and his knees to his chest. Shaking and crying, he seemed too scared to move toward me, even when I called for him.

No one else was in the room.

I rushed to him, taking him in my hands and pulling him toward me. He was sweating, his pulse pounding at an incredible speed, but otherwise unharmed. Untouched it seemed.

Like his bedroom window.

"What happened?" I asked him, trying anxiously to find an answer in his eyes.

He didn't speak.

I picked him up off the bed, and as he cried uncontrollably on my shoulder, I hauled him out of the bedroom.

"Was there someone in your room, Max?" I asked, sitting him on the couch and kneeling before him. "Who was in your room?"

He continued crying, too upset to answer my question.

"Max, listen to me," I commanded. "Was there someone in your room?"

He nodded.

I asked no more. Picking him up again, I grabbed the keys to my car, and took my son out of the house.

If there was an intruder, he entered into Max's room and disappeared the moment I entered with time to close the window behind him. If there wasn't, then either I was going crazy or my house was haunted. I wasn't taking my chances with either of the two.

I packed Max into the car, and in nothing more than a terrycloth robe, I fled my house without even locking the front door and drove cross town to Rebecca's.

*

Uncle George frowned when he opened the door and found Max and I standing on Rebecca's porch. Without asking why we weren't fully dressed, he stepped aside and invited us in from the rain.

"What's happened?" he asked, closing the door.

Rebecca was seated in the living room, but she stood immediately after seeing the concern on my face. Two cups of tea were set out on the coffee table, and I was thankful that they were still awake.

"What's happened to your hands?" she asked, walking toward us for a closer inspection.

My knuckles bled on the ride over, but the abrasions began to clot as I arrived. The injuries began to swell, and now that the adrenaline had worn off, the pain settled.

"Why are you wearing a robe? What's the matter?"

I looked at both Rebecca and Uncle George, tears welling in my eyes and a profound confusion residing in my mind keeping me from telling them all. I asked Rebecca for a glass of water and dry clothes, and as she nodded nervously, she ran into the kitchen.

There was so much to tell, I didn't know where to begin.

I used her bathroom to freshen up and clean my wounded hands. After changing into the loose-fitting jeans and tee shirt, I rejoined them in the living room, a third cup of tea waiting on the coffee table.

Max was asleep on Rebecca's lap.

In nearly a whisper, I told them everything, beginning with Old Man Brewer. From the way I suspected him of talking to Max, to the strange vision (if I can call it that) I had of his death. I told them of Billy's phone call, and finally, the intruder.

Both Uncle George and Rebecca listened with great intensity, their facial expressions fluctuating between shock and disbelief. As I told the story, I realized how ridiculous it all sounded, but it was all true. I swore to them.

"Have you tried to call Nick?" Uncle George asked.

"I can't get through to him at the hospital. I've been trying all night."

He stood from the couch and walked to the phone set atop a small table before the hall deciding to try himself. He dialed the number from memory then waited for an answer.

"Billy called us tonight, too," Rebecca said after sipping on her tea.

"What did he say to you?" I asked. "Did he sound okay?"

"He sounded fine. He called because he was worried about you."

"Me?"

She nodded. "He said he was on his way to the Brewer house to prove that you didn't kill him."

"He thought I was going crazy," I told her. "But it was a totally different story when he called me back."

"But you didn't kill the old man, Cynthia. His daughter did."

"I know. But what I saw…it was real."

She didn't respond. Instead, she drifted into a thought as she caressed Max's hair softly, aiding his rest.

"Nick," Uncle George said into the phone suddenly, and I looked up, amazed at how quickly he got a hold of him. "Listen, Cynthia and Max are here at Rebecca's, and I think you should get over here."

As he calmly told Nick that we were okay, just shaken up, I thought of the old man again. I thought of the mysterious warning he gave me outside my house just after he said that *it* hadn't reached the children yet. Though he wouldn't tell me exactly what It was, he did say that "nothing is what it seems."

I thought of the recent events, the open ended mysteries that surfaced suddenly, and I couldn't help if it was what he meant.

"Remember that nightmare I told you I had a few days ago?" Rebecca asked.

I did. She told me that it was one of the worst she'd had because it felt so real; like the one I had that very night.

"I didn't tell you about it because I thought it was silly," she continued, looking at Max as she spoke. "But hearing you tonight, I can't help but think there's something to all of this."

"All of what?"

"That night, I dreamt that Luis had killed Jo." She paused, waiting for my reaction.

I didn't respond.

"I know he wouldn't really do a thing like that, and I'm still not convinced that he would even with everything Billy told us. It's hard to explain, but in my dream, Luis wasn't himself. He was…it was like he was someone else that looked like Luis. That's why I told you it was silly."

"It was just a dream, Rebecca."

"I know. But now Luis is being accused of her death."

"Do you think your dream was some sort of prophetic warning?"

Fearing she would sound crazier than I was, she was hesitant to nod.

"Angela's the psychic one, not us."

She shook her head then glanced at her father. He was still on the phone, now trying to contact Billy. He had no luck.

"I dreamt Luis killed Jo, and a day later, the accident happened."

"I dreamt that the old man tried to kill me in my kitchen, but it never did."

"But you did see his death before it happened."

She had me there. I couldn't respond to that because it was true.

"I'm not saying it's what I believe. I just can't help but wonder of the possibility."

I sipped on the steaming tea slowly and watched as Uncle George tried once more to contact Billy. His frustration was beginning to show.

"I really hope there are no such things as premonitions," she continued.

"Why's that?"

She glanced at her father again then looked at me. "Because last night I dreamt Logan was trying to kill me."

Chapter Eeght

Three solid knocks on the room's door stopped Cynthia when her writing was on a roll. She had not stopped since her last break, and though her hand was beginning to grow tired, her motivation to complete the story was more powerful.

She looked at the door, the light above the foyer cascading a dimmed glow just against the solid wood. From the bed she could see the lock was set, still her nervous heart skipped a beat at the sound. Who could it be?

Definitely not anyone I know.

Three more knocks and Cynthia heard a distinct eagerness in each one. Whoever was on the other side of the door was not going to leave until they were told to.

"Who is it?" she demanded, taking the notebook off her lap and closing it.

"It's Danny, ma'am, from downstairs."

Carefully, she swung her legs to the left of the bed and pushed herself up. Nearly one hour past midnight and she had not called for anything since she arrived. She could not figure any possible reason for his visit.

She moved toward the entrance slowly, keeping as much of her weight as she could on her left leg. Until she reached the door, both legs began to burn with soreness from their recent state of rest.

She studied the plaque holding a map with a fire escape route before moving to the peephole set just above it. Holding her breath and squinting her eyes, she placed both hands flat on the door and looked out into the hall.

The distorted, enlarged face was that of the young man, but it gave Cynthia no comfort.

"Ms. Grazer," he called as she watched him knock again. "Are you there?"

"What can I do for you, Danny?" she asked, finding humor in the way he took a step back, surprised by how close her response came.

"I-ah, I've brought some coffee for you," he answered nervously. "I thought… maybe, that you would like some."

"Coffee?" She kept him pinned in her sight.

Danny's eyes darted up and down the door before settling on the peephole. She watched as his eyes squinted as well, and he leaned toward the door for a look in.

Instinctively, Cynthia stepped back, knowing he couldn't actually see inside her room.

"I thought you might like some," he repeated, his voice a bit more stable.

His visit was so unsettling because she did want the coffee. She wanted it bad. Was it coincidence? Was Danny just being nice, or did he actually *know* of her craving? A million more questions whirled in her head as she hesitated to reply.

"Leave it by the door," she finally ordered then looked through the peephole again.

Danny was confused by her response; she could see it in his face. "I beg your pardon," he returned.

She repeated her command, looking away from the hole and pressing her ear against the door. She heard the slight rattle of silverware on the floor outside the room after a brief moment of silence, followed by the descending hollow thumps of someone walking towards the elevator. It was only after hearing the elevator doors open then close did Cynthia look through the peephole again.

She found nothing more than the magnified vision of the wall before her room's door.

After unlocking the bolt, she cracked the door open and inspected the floor outside her room. A rather large mug of coffee and a silver spoon set atop a saucer and a bunched cloth napkin by its side. She opened the door a little further and poked her head out far enough to see the end of the hall. The number buttons above the elevator doors were lighting in a descending order towards the "L." Danny was gone, and she was relieved.

She locked the door quickly after picking up the gifts from the floor, immediately feeling contents of some sort inside the bunched napkin. Setting the coffee on the night table, she slowly sat back onto the bed and laid the napkin flat beside her.

Three cream shots and two packets of sugar; the exact way she preferred her java.

Cynthia sighed, staring at the napkin, wondering if the game was still in play. No, it couldn't be, she told herself. But how else would Danny know how she liked her coffee?

If he did know, then that would mean…

It would mean nothing, she decided. The war was over. She saw the end with her own two eyes. It was mere coincidence.

The second in one night.

*

Danny arrived at the lobby floor and glanced around the empty room before walking towards the door marked *Authorized Personnel Only* just behind the check-in desk. He found the detective exactly where he said he would be.

The room was small, posters of employee rules and regulations decorating the space. The detective was seated at the small computer desk resting just before the furthest wall. He seemed to be waiting patiently, his arms crossed over his chest, waiting for Danny's return.

He didn't like the detective too much. The man walked in from the storm fifteen minutes earlier, dripping wet as he crossed the lobby, requesting a place where they could speak in private. Confused, Danny glanced around the empty lobby then took him to the employee's room.

Shortly afterwards, Danny found himself taking the elevator to the seventh floor with a steaming mug of coffee, and a handful of instructions the detective had given him. Don't ask too many questions, don't say anything you don't have to, be friendly and get a glimpse of the room.

"She hasn't even called for coffee," Danny argued, but the detective didn't give. He was starting to wonder why the detective wasn't running his own errands.

In a sense, Danny was happy to report absolutely nothing when he returned to the employee's room. He only prayed the man would leave immediately afterwards.

"Did you see her?" the detective asked as Danny walked into the room.

Danny shook his head. "I'm sorry detective. Nothing happened."

The man frowned, his thick eyebrows falling low over his cold eyes. "What do you mean nothing happened?" he asked, bolting from his chair and taking a step toward the boy.

Danny took a step back from the intimidating man. "She didn't open the door. She refused."

"She didn't say anything to you at all?"

"No, sir. She made me leave the coffee by the door, so I left."

The detective slapped his thighs and shook his head in disappointment. Danny watched him rub his chin with his right hand, his left pushing his raincoat back to rest on his waist. Danny's heart skipped a beat after catching a glimpse of the gun holstered on the man's waist.

"No one's called for her?" he asked suddenly, his voice startling Danny away from the gun.

"No, sir."

"Are you sure? You wouldn't be lying?"

"I can show you the phone logs, if you'd like."

The detective shook his head. Without saying another word, he walked passed Danny and towards the room's exit.

Though a sense of relief fell over Danny suddenly, a certain emptiness did as well. The desperate need to know why Cynthia Grazer was being hunted still lingered, and he couldn't go another moment being ignorant to what was around him.

"Detective," he called, surprising himself.

The man just opened the door to leave, but he stopped, looking back at the boy.

"Why are you looking for her? I mean, what did she do?"

The detective smiled, probably expecting the question. "She's a suspect on a case I'm working on," he answered.

Danny took a deep breath, a neat line of sweat forming over his brow when he realized the detective wasn't going to make it easy. "But, what happened? Did she rob a bank or something?"

"No," the detective said immediately then stepped into the open doorway.

Danny sighed, cursing the detective for not answering his question.

Until the detective turned back, holding the door as it began to swing to a close. "She's the prime suspect in the murders of eight people."

Before Danny could respond, the detective was gone.

Monday, June 8th; the Pro and the Rookie

Nick and Uncle George left Rebecca's at nearly six in the morning. It was Nick's idea to get an early start after I told him everything that happened while he was at the hospital. He insisted on finding Billy. We were all worried; none of us could get in touch with him after his last phone call to me.

Rebecca and I watched as they left the house and into the rain. After loading into Rebecca's SUV, Uncle George at the wheel, they set out to find our friend.

Max and Charlene were sleeping, thankfully without a disturbance the entire night. They had no idea of what was happening around them, and we preferred it that way.

Rebecca filled a mug with coffee and sat in her living room, flipping through the television channels. Every station was broadcasting a weather forecast, each meteorologist standing before a computer image of the storm in the Gulf.

"Great," Rebecca said, almost with a sigh.

She raised the volume in time to hear the most important of news; overnight, the tropical depression grew into a hurricane. It picked up speed along the Gulf, moving East at ten miles per hour toward central-southern Florida. With winds of eighty-five to ninety-five miles per hour, it was labeled a category one; a baby storm to those with hurricane experience. By the time it hit Florida, it was expected to be a category three; winds reaching up to 130 mph. Alida was her name, and the warning was out; she would whip through our town by the week's end.

"It seems there's one every year," Rebecca said.

I ignored the news, sleepless and tired of what was already plaguing my mind.

Max woke at eight; Charlene was a half hour behind. By nine, they were outside playing with Buddy underneath the overcast skies. Rebecca and I sat in the dining room, waiting to hear from Nick and Uncle George. They hadn't called with news about Billy since they left, and it was starting to take its toll on us both.

"I'm sure Billy's okay," Rebecca said to me. "He's a good detective."

He really was one of the best.

They finally arrived at a quarter past noon. After Uncle George and Nick walked into the house, a third person followed them in, but it wasn't Billy.

Logan appeared distraught, almost dazed. His eyes were filled with such a profound sorrow I nearly bolted to my feet when I looked at him.

"What happened?" I asked, worried that their news of Billy was not good.

"We couldn't find him," Uncle George said.

"We went to his house, the hospital, and the police station," Nick followed. "No one's heard from him since last night."

Logan threw himself onto the couch and sighed. Though we were very close with Billy, his sorrow seemed to originate from something else.

"What's wrong with Logan?" I asked Nick quietly.

"Angela left him this morning," he said.

I was shocked. "Why?"

Nick shrugged. "He says she seemed bothered by what was happening, the accident and all. He thinks she couldn't handle the pressure."

"Poor Logan."

"Don't mention it to him," Nick said. "I don't think he wants anyone to know."

I nodded then looked to Logan with sympathetic eyes. He was

wounded, but too numb to realize it. His barrier would break with time though.

Before another word could be said, the doorbell rang throughout the house, each of us trading glances immediately afterwards.

Rebecca moved toward the door first, the rest of us watching in silence as she opened it.

A dark skinned, middle-aged woman stood on the porch dressed in professional business attire and tight-pinned hair. The man standing behind her was fairer and younger, his dark eyes matching the black raincoat he wore over his suit. Each held a suitcase as if they were salesmen, yet the smiles missing from their faces proved they were not.

"Rebecca Joules," the woman said after the door opened.

"Who are you?" Rebecca asked.

The rest of us crept toward the door for a closer look.

Like robots, they simultaneously reached into their coats and flashed golden badges. "My name is Detective Maria Lopez, and this is my partner Raul Santiago. May we please come in and ask you all some questions?"

*

After they were seated in the living room, declining any offer to a drink, Uncle George excused himself to watch over the kids in the yard. Detectives Lopez and Santiago had no objection.

Billy told us that she was ruthless, and it was evident when she proceeded to name us all by face without the aid of any notes. Her partner, the rookie, seemed less brutal, apologizing for their unannounced visit then asking we cooperate with the questions they needed to ask.

The rest of us nodded. Billy warned us of the investigation, and he did so as a favor. We weren't supposed to know what they had up their sleeves and acting like it promised a challenge.

Maria set her suitcase on the coffee table and opened it, extracting a small notebook and pen. Flipping to a blank page, she quickly glanced at her partner sitting upright and at attention.

The interrogation began.

"The accident that took place on June sixth of the past week involved Joanna Corona and Luis Grazer. As a result, Ms. Corona is deceased and Mr. Grazer lies in critical condition at Miami Memorial..."

"I'm sorry, Detective," Logan said suddenly. "We know what happened. What is it that you'd like to ask us?"

Rebecca frowned at Logan, echoing Billy's advice to cooperate with the team.

"Mr. Grazer lies in critical condition at Miami Memorial Hospital," Detective Lopez continued without acknowledging Logan's words. "Some test results provided to us by Doctor Morrison indicate that Mr. Grazer was not intoxicated at the time of the accident." She looked directly to Logan. "What I'm here to ask you is if there is any reason he would want to kill her."

Logan gnawed his jaw, but didn't respond. He was boiling to.

"We know what the assumption is, Detective Lopez," I said to her. "But I can assure you that my brother did not kill her."

"The autopsy report indicates otherwise," Det. Santiago followed.

I sat back on the couch and closed my eyes as he rambled off the same information Billy did; the seventeen cracks on her skull, the beaten dashboard, "and there was a piece of torn skin that we obtained from the vehicle's dashboard. The DNA is an exact match to Ms. Corona's." He opened his suitcase and held a file folder toward me, the words *Autopsy Report* stamped in bold red letters across the front. Nick accepted the file after I didn't.

"Were they romantically involved?" Det. Lopez asked.

"Yes," Rebecca answered after no one else opted to.

"Have they had any arguments lately?" Raul followed.

"None."

From there, it was like a tennis match. First, Maria would ask a question then it was Raul's turn. They were quick on questioning everything from their financial status to their plans of marriage, but so were our answers. Rebecca did most of the talking, but she didn't elaborate beyond a simple "yes" or "no" if she didn't have to.

"Has Luis suffered any traumatic events recently?" Santiago asked me, evidently tired of Rebecca's answers.

"No," I replied with a frown.

"Nothing that would trigger the same effect he had eighteen years ago?"

"What are you talking about?" I asked, and though Billy warned us of their tricks, my blood pressure rose at the question.

Maria cleared her throat. "We know that your brother suffered from extremely violent outbursts and traumatic stress after your parents were murdered. In Luis' file, Dr. Morrison stressed his concern after Luis attacked him. It takes almost nothing to have people sink back into those syndromes under any number of given circumstances. We're wondering if, because of the anniversary, the accident was caused in an outburst. Had he given any signs to indicate that he was under any kind of pressure that would..."

"No." Her theory disgusted me, and I wasn't hiding it. "That's the most ridiculous thing..."

"He didn't go crazy and kill her," Logan said, sounding as offended as I was. "You're wasting your time."

"We're not so sure of that," Maria said, reaching into her briefcase. "Do any one you know what the letters E-N-O stand for?"

My back stiffened at the question as the events that changed my life eighteen years before suddenly came screaming back to me. E-N-O. It was the signature left by the dyslexic killer to number his first victim; the same killer that murdered our parents.

Nick caught it just after I did, Rebecca and Logan not lagging too far behind. We had been stunned by her question, and I don't think any of us were prepared to answer it.

"I take it by your silence that you do know what it means," Raul said as his partner moved her briefcase off the table.

She laid out three Polaroid pictures before us, making sure we all had a clear view of them. They were of the car's interior, the passenger side to be exact; Jo's place in the car. The leather seat was empty, and the full color photograph had not been edited for our viewing. The head rest of the seat was covered in blood. I looked away from the photos for a second, glancing at the others' faces as they, too, saw the horrid picture. And though it was the most prominent feature of the shot, a second look proved that it was not what the detectives intended for us to see.

The seatbelt was fastened across the empty chair. The entire picture was taken for what was on the belt, seemingly left as some sort of signature. The letters E-N-O were written in blood in a descending order on the belt's chest level.

"That blood proved to be Joanna's," Raul said.

"You think Luis wrote this?" Nick asked.

"There was blood found on the index finger of his right hand..."

"Luis is left-handed," I said quickly. "Like me."

"His fingerprint was traced in the letters," Maria said. "We know for a fact that he wrote this, the same exact way Mason Bayer numbered his victims."

"Bullshit!" Logan shouted in outrage. "You're saying Luis thinks he's Mason Bayer? That's bullshit!"

"Under the right kind of stress, and with Mr. Grazer's mental history, I'd say that it is very possible," Maria answered keeping her cool.

It was a name I had not heard in years, then suddenly twice in less than a minute. Mason Bayer, a name that stood for all things both grotesque and wicked, rang in my ears and boiled my blood. That they suspected Luis of having obtained a trait, the signature of the murderer, enraged me even more. Who the hell did they think they were?

"My brother did not go crazy," I said to them through my teeth. "My brother killed Mason Bayer eighteen years ago, and it took a long time for him to get over that. He loved Jo. He would never do anything to hurt her, especially number her the way that son of a bitch did our parents."

It wasn't until I was done that I realized I was screaming. Nick gripped my knee in an attempt to calm me as both Detectives shifted in their seats.

"Unfortunately, with the evidence we have, Luis is a prime suspect. Unless you can tell me that those letters across the seatbelt are initials, then he will remain a prime suspect. Can you tell me that, Mrs. Sheyer?"

I tried to think of someone with those same initials, but I couldn't. I couldn't even make one up.

"Then this investigation will proceed," she snarled.

"I want you to leave," I told them.

Without hesitation, they began packing their pictures and files. "That's all we have for now anyway, but we'll be in touch," she said, standing from the sofa.

Raul followed directly afterwards.

Nick led them to the door and the rest of us watched from the living room.

"By the way," Maria called to us as she approached the door. "I have to ask you all to stay in town while this investigation is pending in case we need to ask you some more questions. No one is to leave unless Detective Santiago or myself are notified first, understand?"

"Good day, Detective," I told her.

She smiled at me, amused with my anger. "Tell me, Mrs. Sheyer, I mean Grazer," she said. "Will you sign a copy of your book for me? I'm a big fan."

I didn't know if she was being sarcastic or not, but I held my ground and didn't respond.

She shrugged. "I guess not."

They stepped onto the porch and Nick eyed them closely as they passed him. Just as soon as they were out, he motioned to close the door and Maria turned. "Have a good day everyone," she said, dripping with sarcasm.

Nick slammed the door in her face.

The Visit

No one knew what to think of the evidence the detectives brought with them. After they left, we filled Uncle George in on the details of their visit, and again, his reaction was much like our own.

I wanted to visit him. Hearing all the accusations and theories hurt me; no one had the right to accuse him of such nonsense. I longed to be with him suddenly, as though I could protect him from the people who wanted to put him behind bars. No matter what they thought, he was still my brother, and he certainly couldn't defend himself.

Rebecca offered to watch Max while Nick and I went to the hospital. The rain was falling and Nick drove through the streets at his own pace, both of us in silence. The thoughts buzzing through our heads were easier to sort out in the peace.

When we arrived at the hospital Nick found a parking space mere paces from the entrance. I had not seen my brother in, what felt like, an eternity, but a sudden thought nearly made me hesitate from getting out of the car.

"Nick," I said as he killed the engine. "The last time we were here, when you visited with Luis, did you leave Max alone with him?"

Nick frowned at the question but humored me by thinking about it. Max told me that Luis woke up when Nick went to the bathroom. He told Max that Rebecca was to die next, and though I dismissed it as a lie earlier, the recent events made me think again. It was my mind trying desperately to make sense of the accusations.

"Not that I can remember," he answered.

I knew it. Of course Max made it up. How on Earth could Luis wake up and talk to…

"I did go to the bathroom, but that's it."

My heart skipped a beat.

"Why do you ask?"

"Max told me something before I heard the voice in his room last night," I told him, finding it hard to believe that I was telling him even as the words left my mouth.

"What?"

I told him of Max's warning, watching his face as I spoke. But he was stumped; he didn't know what to say.

I sat back in the seat and sighed. "Nick, I think something else is happening here."

"What do you mean?"

"The voices I'm hearing, Old Man Brewer's death, the accident, I can't help but think that there's something else at work in all this."

"You think our house is haunted?"

"In all the years that we have lived in that house, it never once crossed my mind. I don't even know if I believe in ghosts. Until recently."

"By what then?"

I shrugged, looking out the passenger side window. Raindrops rolled on the glass in a hypnotizing pattern, and I nearly fell into a daze. "The ghosts of our past," I answered, and I wasn't being poetic. "When Billy told us Jo was dead, I got the same feeling of emptiness I had when I realized Mom and Dad were dead. Everything that has happened brought up feelings that I haven't had in eighteen years."

Nick nodded slowly. He may have not agreed with me on the haunted house, but he agreed with me on at least that. He'd been feeling the same way.

"And now, these assholes think Luis wrote E-N-O on Jo's seatbelt. Somehow, it isn't enough that waste of a human killed our parents, he's got to find a way to drag his name into this as well."

"You think Mason Bayer's doing all this?"

I took a deep breath. "I could very well live the rest of my life without hearing that name again." I didn't believe he was to blame, how would that be possible?

"He's not doing this, Cynthia. I'm sure Rebecca won't die next, Max was just imagining things with all this talk about death. No matter how much we're trying to protect him from all of this, he's probably confused. We'll get through this, you'll see."

"Luis told me we were all going to die."

Nick frowned. "While he was in a coma?"

"No. The night before the accident, I found him in the dining room. He was whispering to himself, then he told me that *It* was in him, and that we were all going to die."

Nick shook his head, not knowing what to do with the information I was giving him.

"Then he told me the same thing that Old Man Brewer said just a day before; nothing is what it seems."

"Why didn't you say anything about this before?"

I shook my head and shrugged. "How was I supposed to know what it meant?"

"What does it mean?"

"I still don't know, but I'm starting to think something other than the obvious is happening to us."

"Whatever it is, it's not Mason Bayer. I don't want to believe that your brother did kill Jo, but have you considered the possibility?"

"Nick..."

"Listen to me. We all know what happened to Luis after our parents died. From what you're telling me now, what he said to you in the dining room, it sounds like he wasn't in the right frame of mind."

"There's no doubt that he could have snapped, I've pondered the possibility myself," I told him. "But I know he wouldn't kill Jo. Not like they think he did. Those violent outbursts happened almost twenty years ago, and they were all brought on by something that triggered them, he wasn't just attacking random people. Besides, his snapping doesn't explain what I heard in Max's bedroom, nor does it explain..."

"If you think our house is haunted, fine," Nick said. "We'll stay at Rebecca's from now on. We'll get through this. But I don't think you should jump to some outrageous conclusion. Mason Bayer is dead, he died eighteen years ago, and we killed him. What's happening here has nothing to do with him."

I forced a smile and nodded, but he hadn't convinced me. There was too much happening at once, too many incidents all beginning on June 6th. And somehow, they were all connected. I could feel it.

*

Nick said he wanted to talk to Doctor Morrison when we reached the ICU. He told me to go on in without him and promised to meet me shortly.

The room was cold and dark, the only noise filling the air was that of the machines; the heart monitor, the breathing pump all beeping and hissing to keep my brother alive.

I left the door to his room open as I approached the bed, preparing myself for the sight. His face, now covered behind the shadow of a three-day beard, was healing. The abrasions were still visible because his color had not returned, and his lips were cracked now. I cried when I saw him; I couldn't stand looking at him in such a condition.

"How are you, Luis?" I asked softly, taking his hand then sitting on the chair that I left at his bedside.

I closed my eyes, resting my head beside him. Reveling in the fact that he had no idea of what was happening around him, I was more at ease. My visit with him had nothing to do with the outside world. It was my time with him alone.

I told him that everyone was waiting for him to wake up, and that we missed him so much.

Despite Morrison's request that we visit Luis one at a time, Nick stepped into the room. He held my hand while we watched my brother in silence. Luis knew we were there, I could sense it. Talking to him the entire time wasn't necessary, so long as we were with him.

Nick left shortly afterwards, assuring me to take my time with him. He said he'd be in the waiting room so that I could be as long as I needed. When the door closed and Luis and I were alone again, I grabbed the television's remote control and began flipping through the channels.

The selection was limited; three news stations covering Hurricane Alida, an old crime-drama rerun, and a home shopping channel. After settling into the chair and taking a long look at my brother by my side, I tuned to the drama show and sighed in relaxation.

The television's volume remained loud enough for me to hear, but low enough to not disturb my brother's peace…or mine. I wasn't able to forget the trouble that befell us, but the drama show was a distraction; it took my mind to a different place where there was nothing to be worried-

The television turned off. The screen went black and silence filled the room suddenly.

Confused, I looked to my hand, the remote control resting in my palm, my fingers far from the power button. Keeping the shrug to myself, I outstretched my hand, my finger hammered the control and I watched the television click on again.

Seconds later, it turned off.

It was unfair. All I wanted was to relax my brain and drown it in the hour show but an electrical surge or an old television was keeping me from doing just that. Frustrated, I stood from the chair and walked across the room to the foot of Luis' bed.

Suspended from the ceiling, the television stared back at me, its black screen menacingly still. More menacing was the fact that the power button on the television was at the upper right hand corner of the set; completely out of reach.

I had half a mind to demand a working television set, but just as I turned toward the door, I stopped. The timed beeps of my brother's heart monitor machine changed. It was now a single toned high-pitched scream indicating Luis' heart stopped.

I turned to the monitor to witness the flat line myself, but before I could panic, before I could scream for help, I was filled with paralyzing confusion. When I looked to the bed, Luis was sitting up, staring right back at me.

There was no emotion in his face, his cracked lips exposing no smile and his wide eyes as pale as his skin. He didn't look alive, but when he blinked, I knew he wasn't dead.

"Luis," I whispered to him, hopeful that the heart monitor was mistaken.

But he didn't answer. His empty eyes stared back at me, and I couldn't help but wonder if this was some sort of side effect from the medication or trauma. I rushed to the door, determined to bring whatever nurse or doctor I found to my brother's aid. He had come to, and he needed help. But the door was locked and I fought to open it, struggling with the door knob in frustration…until it hit me. A doctor should have run into the room the moment the heart monitor's alarm erupted.

His gaze suddenly burned my back, sending a chill up my spine and settling on my neck. Slowly, I turned back to the bed and found Luis' stare had followed me to the door.

His lips parted, a wheezing breath spilling from his mouth as though he were trying to speak.

I called his name again, covering my mouth to not cry out loud. I was scared of him because what I was witnessing was not a phenomenon that occurs during comas. I felt threatened knowing very well that it was unnatural.

"I killed her," he said, almost in a whisper.

My knees nearly gave in at his words, my brain registering his message.

Jo...

His face began to fill with emotion suddenly. His eyebrows angled low over his wide eyes and his lips curled to expose his gritting teeth. "I killed her," he repeated his voice louder and deeper than usual.

"What's wrong with you?" I asked, my own voice quivering as I took a step away from the bed.

He called to me, saying my name slowly, his voice chiming in my ears and my heart nearly stopped. The voice was not Luis' own, but I recognized it. It was the same voice I heard in Max's bedroom the night before.

The heart monitor's alarm continued, but it suddenly became obsolete. There was no explanation for what I was witnessing, and I wanted to get out of the room. The door was still locked though, and somehow, I knew it would remain that way so long as Luis wanted.

My brother was not conscious, of that I was certain. The thing that spoke before me stirred every fear in my bones. It was not my brother.

"Who are you?" I asked between breaths.

A slight, almost undetectable smile fell upon his lips as he watched me cower with fear. "Look for me in Logan," he said, "then I will look for you."

His eyes turned away from mine and settled on my stomach and he smiled wickedly as though he were a vicious animal looking for young to feed on. Instinctively, I covered my belly with both arms suspecting he smelled my baby.

"It will never live to breath its own air," he warned with the smile.

"Leave us alone!" I yelled, finally resorting to the idea that what was now before me was the reason for everything that happened in the past week.

"Leave us all alone!"

I screamed so that not to hear his voice if he spoke again. He threatened my unborn child, the child I told no one about, and all I could do was scream.

But I did hear his voice again. Above my scream, his words reached me, though he didn't speak an octave higher than before.

"I've already reached Max," he said.

*

The heart monitor's alarm died and the timed beeps returned. As though I was magically transported, I was back on the chair at my brother's bedside, the television running the credits for the drama-cop show. Luis was fast asleep on the bed appearing as he had never woken at all.

It was all a dream.

I stood from the chair, keeping my eyes on my brother. My rapidly beating heart told me that what I witnessed was real, and though I had every reason to believe otherwise, I couldn't help but flee the room quickly.

It was just an accumulation of everything that's happened, Jennifer's voice said. *The pregnancy, Jo's death, the investigation, it all gathered in a dream.* Far be it from her to suggest that all those events had one thing in common; one greater force that caused all of it.

As I ran passed the nurses' station, I wondered if the *It* Old Man Brewer referred to was talking through Luis; if the It made Luis kill Jo, and if Max's warning was not a fib at all.

Of course not, Jennifer said as I hurried to the waiting room. *It was nothing more than a simple dream.*

I ignored her.

Nick stood from the couch when he saw me. "Are you okay?" he asked.

"I'm ready to go," I told him, showing no fear. I would tell him everything on the way home.

"Are you sure?"

I looked back over my shoulder toward Luis' room. Half expecting to find him standing in the hall waving at me with the same wicked smile, I turned back to Nick and nodded. "I'm sure."

*

"It was just a dream," Nick told me, my own thoughts echoing through his words. Uncle George and Logan tried to convince me of the same thing, which I expected them to. When Rebecca told me that I was just under too much pressure lately, I was somewhat disappointed. I thought at least she would share my concern over the nightmares.

"We're all having a hard time understanding what has happened," Uncle George said. Then, like Jennifer, he suggested my dreams were nothing more than an accumulation of everything that occurred.

I thanked him for his advice half-heartedly and stood from the couch. Frustrated that they weren't taking me seriously, I walked away from the group to take a breath. Their refusal to deviate from reality to ponder other possibilities was easier to deal with if I wasn't looking directly at them.

Max and Charlene were in one of the spare rooms Rebecca turned into a toy ground after the second divorce. Charlene's personal playing temple; a white vanity table and matching dresser set against lavender walls, a bookshelf filled top to bottom with her favorite bed time stories and coloring books, and three chests filled with toys. Many toys. One for her dolls and their accessories, another for board games, and a third for the random toys left behind by her friends, the one Max could find something that appealed to him.

As usual, they were both seated on the floor in the center of the room. The carpeting was plush and comfortable enough to sleep on.

"Hi Aunt Cyn," Charlene said to me as I rested against the doorway. Besides Luis, she was the only other person to call me "Cyn."

I smiled back, but I did not enter. I stood in the doorway and watched them play together like we had all done many years before. Those innocent times were gone for us, and as I watched it in the children, I prayed that my dream was wrong. If there was indeed a force at work, I would do anything to keep it away from the children. They had nothing to do with what was happening, they didn't even understand most of it.

Jo's funeral was the very next day, and the day afterwards, Uncle George was flying to New York and taking them with him. Though I didn't want to part with my son, I was now convinced that it was the best thing to do.

I walked back into the living room nearly ten minutes later and found the others exactly where I left them. They were discussing the issue at hand, and even though I brought it up, I was tired of the revolving conversation.

"Look, I know it sounds crazy to you all," I said to them without taking my seat and deciding to end the conversation for good. "I was just considering the possibility that maybe something else was happening, something bigger. What exactly? I don't know. I just think this dream was telling me something, that's all."

"How much have you slept these past few days?" Uncle George asked me, stroking his gray beard.

I shrugged thinking back. "Not much." *Because every time I close my eyes I have another damned nightmare.*

"I think that's what you need. Some undisturbed sleep might do you some good."

"That's beside the point," I told him. "Rebecca's had a couple nightmares recently that even she thought were prophetic." I looked at her. "Didn't you?"

She hesitated, but she nodded and I took a deep breath.

"You see? Maybe I'm not crazy."

"I still think you need some sleep," he said. "All of you. Why don't you all stay here tonight and we'll go to the funeral together in the morning."

"I'll have to run home to get a couple of things," Logan said.

"I'll take you," Nick told him. "Then we'll stop by my place."

"Cynthia will stay here," Uncle George demanded, then turned to me. "I'll fix up something to eat quickly, and straight to bed with you."

"No, Uncle Geor..."

"I'll give you a wonderful pill my doctor prescribed. It's quite strong, but you're guaranteed a peaceful night's sleep."

"I won't take a pill."

"One won't harm you," he said. "I'll mix into some juice so it's easy on the stomach."

"No, I can't..."

"That's enough, Cynthia. You will have..."

"Uncle George, thank you but no. It's not that I don't want it, believe me, I would gladly take it. I just *can't*."

Both he and Nick frowned.

"Why?" Rebecca asked.

I looked to Nick and sighed "Because," I said, "I'm pregnant."

Farewell

Joanna Corona, Beloved Daughter and Friend is what was engraved on the marble tombstone for those she left behind. We all agreed on it, but looking at the bold words during the ceremony, it didn't seem like enough.

Rebecca, Logan, Uncle George, Nick and I stood side by side amongst the dozens of others who dressed in black and paid their respects. Even though the clouds began to roll in over Miami Memorial Park early that morning, everyone stayed throughout the entire ceremony.

And what a beautiful ceremony it was, though the celestial sight of Joanna's coffin hovering above a bed of rose bushes to conceal the plot underneath gave us no comfort. The reverend who guided us in prayer spoke meaningless words of the works of our Lord and His mysterious ways. It is said that we are not to question who is taken from our lives for their time on Earth is over, and their presence in Heaven will help us overcome all our doubts and sorrows. Yet as we watched the coffin begin to descend into the unseen abyss, I knew that it wasn't the work of our Lord that had taken her. There was still so much Jo wanted to accomplish, so many children that she wanted to reach out to and help. There had to have been a foil in God's plan, someone or something that intervened and robbed her of her life before her time on Earth was over. Though no one else shared my theory, I knew it to be true.

Joanna Corona, beloved daughter and friend, was now a part of the earth; gone from our lives forever, but waiting for us in the next.

When the service was over, Uncle George privately thanked every individual for attending as everyone began to disperse toward their cars. Nick and I remained seated with Max between us. A few people hugged as they passed each other, but seemed hurried to return back to their own lives. Rebecca held Charlene close as she sat silently, staring at the roses that were now a part of Jo's home. It seemed that it took only minutes before everyone else left the park entirely. Uncle George returned, taking his seat by Logan, and joined us all in our silence.

There were two people who didn't leave immediately. They stood outside the barrier gates of the park, fifty yards away, and they were looking at us. A man and a woman, both resting on a black sedan and armed with umbrellas for the coming storm. I recognized them immediately. Detectives Maria Lopez and Raul Santiago were following us.

"What are they doing here?" Logan asked. He spotted them as well.

"Ignore them, and they'll go away," Uncle George said.

Not another word was spoken of their presence, our attention turning back to the neat row of tombstones before us.

Amongst the sea of graves, it was the row I could spot out a mile away. We visited the row many times before, but there were usually only four graves; one for Nick and Logan's parents, one for Jo's father, one for Aunt Mayra, and the final one was for my parents. Now, a fifth tombstone was erected directly next to Hector Corona's; his own daughter's.

When Max asked me about death, I told him all about heaven. In Jo's case, I hoped it to be true. If Jo was in heaven with her father and our parents, then I knew she was looking down on us, guiding us through the horrible times. In that, I had solace.

We left the park at noon that Tuesday. We didn't look to see if the detectives were following us. I don't think any of us really cared.

*

Come Wednesday morning, there was another farewell we concentrated on. Uncle George's flight was due to depart at ten that morning, and by nine o'clock, we were at the airport.

Before we arrived, Nick and I spent an hour preparing Max for the trip. At no time however, did we anticipate the emotional roller coaster brought on when we arrived at the terminal gate. Beyond that point, only ticketed passengers were allowed, so that meant my son was minutes away from his first plane ride - and it was without me.

Rebecca was crying as much as I was the moment we arrived at the gate, Uncle George assuring us our children would be okay. There was no doubt in our minds that both Charlene and Max would be safe with him, but parting with them was difficult nonetheless.

Nick and Logan took their time wishing the children a safe trip as Uncle George embraced Rebecca, then me. He told us that we had nothing to worry about as far as the children were concerned. "Be with Luis," he advised. "He needs you more than the children do." I cried uncontrollably as he embraced us both one more time. "One week," he said. "We'll be back in seven days."

His whole reason for taking the kids was because of the investigation that had started just days before. He was right in his reasoning, and I prayed that by the time they returned, it would all be over with.

When Uncle George turned to Logan and Nick, Rebecca and I threw ourselves at our children for a long hug. Max and Charlene were oblivious to the tears, the excitement of riding in an airplane glazed over in their eyes. We told our children to behave while they were with Uncle George, and they both promised they would.

I knelt before my son and kissed him good-bye, assuring him that I would see him again in a matter of days. He smiled.

"We better get going," Uncle George said from somewhere behind me. "The plane will start boarding soon."

I kissed Max again and told him that I loved him. Before I stood and allowed Uncle George to whisk the children away, Max tugged my arm, keeping me before him.

There was a concerned look on his face suddenly, a sadness in his eyes that made me wonder if he did know what the reason for his departure was.

"What's the matter, baby?" I asked him, wiping my cheeks.

He hesitated to say anything, glancing at the others as though he didn't want them to hear.

"You can tell me, honey," I whispered to him, letting him know he could whisper back.

"Mommy, can you promise me something?" he asked.

I smiled. "Anything."

"Will you take care of Buddy while I'm gone?"

I wanted to laugh. Of all things, he was concerned of the golden retriever that was his best friend. "Of course I will, baby," I told him.

Uncle George took both of the children by the hand and the rest of us watched as they walked through the gate until they vanished into the crowded terminal. Within minutes, they would be in the air and far, far away from the rest of us.

We watched in silence as Uncle George, the angel that had rescued us eighteen years before, rescued our children from the situation around us.

...In Logan

Rebecca insisted we stay with her after we left the airport. She told us she couldn't bear the silence of an empty house, and considering the events that took place the last time I was home, I was happy to oblige.

Still, Nick and I had to stop by our home to collect several days' worth of clothing amongst other items. The moment we stepped through the door and into the foyer, I was immediately reminded of the voice I heard in Max's room and later through Luis' mouth. I told Nick that I didn't want to be long, and he understood.

I went directly to my room and quickly began to throw clothes into a duffel bag as Nick headed into the home office to check the answering machine. There were three messages that echoed into my bedroom as Nick listened to them.

The first was of dead air, the sound of a phone hanging up just after the prompt to leave a message. I nearly laughed when I heard the second message; Jennifer had called to check up on my therapy-free progress. The third distracted me from packing any further. I broke into a light sweat the moment I heard his voice.

"Cynthia, Nick, it's me."

It was nearly four days since we heard from Billy, and he didn't sound any better than his last phone call. I walked into the hall and towards the office as the message continued to play through.

"I'm...ah, I wanted to go to Jo's funeral, but I couldn't. I know you want an explanation for the last time we spoke, but I can't do that, either. You'll understand with time if you don't already know."

"Already know what?" Nick asked me.

I shrugged.

"Anyway, I've tried to call the others, but I didn't get in touch with them, either. If I'm not mistaken, the two detectives should have already contacted you, and they're trying to get a hold of me. Don't let them know I called. I hope everything is okay. We'll talk soon."

And just like that, the line went dead.

Nick replayed the message and we listened as though through fresh ears. When it was done, he turned the machine off and looked to me with a blank face. "What do you think is happening to him?" he asked me.

"I don't know. He's been as elusive since the last time we spoke."

Nick nodded, staring at the machine while trying to sort it out in his head. "Maybe he's working on a case and he doesn't want us to know about it, the way your father used to do."

"Maybe," I said, but it wasn't what I believed.

Both Rebecca and Logan had a message on their answering machines as well, and both of them were as concerned about Billy as Nick and I were. Logan even tried to reach our friend directly after hearing the message, but of course, to no avail.

"At least we've heard from him," Rebecca said, and though that much was true, we didn't know if he was in any kind of trouble, or if he was safe. "He'll call again."

I nodded to not bring up the feeling that there must have been another reason Billy was acting the way he was. Something else had to have happened.

Something bigger.

*

Hurricane Alida was less than a hundred miles from Tampa on the west coast of Florida. It had not picked up strength since its last upgrade, but it was still headed our way. The forecasters predicted that by Saturday night, it would beat through Florida so they advised everyone to plan for the storm with anticipation.

We had done nothing to prepare. Nick said we should board the windows, but beyond that, nothing else was mentioned. It seemed there was too much on our minds already.

The phone rang at nearly six that evening. Rebecca shot to her feet and hurried to the phone as though she were waiting for a phone call. Truth is, we all were. Several people could have been on the other end of that line, and I held my breath as I wondered who it could be. Billy, Doctor Morrison…

Rebecca picked up the receiver and we all watched her anxiously until she revealed the caller.

"Hi, daddy," she said, a smile brightening her face.

Uncle George arrived to New York safely, and for that much, I was thankful. She spoke with him briefly then asked to speak with her daughter.

"So when did you find out?" Logan asked me, giving Rebecca privacy.

"Find what out?" I asked.

"That you're pregnant?"

We hadn't spoken much about it since the announcement, and though I knew his mind was on not much else since Angela left, I humored him with the small talk. "Just a few days ago. I want to confirm it with my doctor first, though."

"Have you called her?" Nick asked.

"I will," I answered, not having to give an excuse as to why I hadn't already.

"Cynthia," Rebecca called to me, holding the receiver in my direction. "Max wants to say hi."

I grabbed the phone quickly, my heart longing to hear my son's voice. I missed him terribly, and he was gone only eight hours.

I didn't let my emotions seep through my voice. I spoke with my son as though he were at a neighbor's house and I would see him before sundown. He told me of an exciting pizzeria Uncle George took them to when they landed and described the tall buildings of the city. I smiled and told him that I loved him.

He asked about Buddy, and as I heard the dog's bark echoing from the backyard, I assured him that the dog missed him as much as I did.

After handing the phone to Nick, I took my seat in the living room and let it all out. I cried for my son, foolishly feeling as though I would never see him again.

Logan walked towards the entrance of the kitchen before the sliding glass door that led into the backyard. He asked if anyone wanted a drink, but we all declined.

"Uncle George says he'll call us tomorrow," Nick said, hanging the phone up. "He says not to worry about the kids, they're having the time of their lives."

"Charlene sounded happy," Rebecca said.

Buddy's bark bellowed viciously into the house. Almost immediately, Rebecca, Nick and I ran into the dining room, to the sliding glass door to find the golden retriever on the porch, inches from the glass and peering into the empty room. His fierce growl breathed through a snarl, and he barked again, jumping onto the glass as though trying to break through it.

"What's the matter, boy?" Rebecca asked, as though the dog could actually answer.

Buddy barked uncontrollably as his eyes frantically searched the room we stood in. He jumped at the glass again, growling at the air.

"Buddy!" Rebecca called. "Calm down!" But it seemed her order fell upon deaf ears. The dog continued to howl, growl and bark.

Until Logan walked into the room from the kitchen.

The dog looked at Logan, a slight cry replacing the unvarying bark. Almost immediately, the retriever's tail fell between its legs and it turned back toward the yard.

"What was that all about?" Logan asked after sipping on the water.

"I don't know what got into him," Rebecca said. "He went crazy."

"I'll go check on him," Logan said, approaching the glass stained with muddied paw prints.

"Be careful, Logan," Nick advised.

But Logan sucked his teeth, insisting there was no reason to be scared of Buddy. He slid the door open and stepped out onto the porch calling for Buddy.

The three of us followed, finding Buddy in the center of the yard. He definitely calmed since his barking attack, and as Logan approached him slowly holding out his hands, the dog licked its snout as though anticipating Logan's arrival.

The rest of us watched from the patio, Nick and Rebecca both lighting cigarettes.

Buddy still motionless as Logan knelt before him, taking the dog's head in his hands. They stared at each other for a while, neither of them moving outside taking a breath.

"What is he doing?" I asked, barely loud enough for the others to hear.

The clouds were rolling in and Nick's eyes squinted as he looked up. "I don't know, but they'll both be soaked if he doesn't hurry and get in here."

"Logan, get inside!" Rebecca called. "Bring Buddy with you!"

He didn't answer, didn't even move. He remained on his knees, holding the dog, and staring into its eyes.

"They're bonding," Nick said. "Maybe we should leave them alone."

He and Rebecca laughed, but I didn't. I watched Logan's new found intrigue with the dog, my mind telling me that everything was okay, but my heart screaming otherwise. Something wasn't right.

Buddy seemed hypnotized, his tail barely wagging while he stood uncharacteristically still. Neither one of them moved when we called for them, and it brought on an unsettling feeling.

A gust of wind whipped around the three of us standing on the patio.

The storm was coming in fast, but neither the dog nor Logan seemed to care.

"Logan, what are you doing?" I asked. "Get inside."

He looked at us, taking his eyes away from the dog for just a second so that we could see the smile upon his face. His hands had not moved off Buddy, and just as Rebecca and Nick decided on heading back into the house, he turned back to the dog.

"Wait a minute," I told them.

He forced Buddy's head upward, nearly lifting his front paws off the ground.

"Logan!" Rebecca yelled. "You're gonna hurt him!"

The smile on Logan's lips curled, his teeth gritting underneath as he twisted the animal's face backwards. Though thunder clapped in the skies above, we heard the distinct sound of cracking bone, then watched as the dog's body convulsed for a mere second before Logan let it drop to the ground.

Rebecca screamed in horror and I turned away from the sight as Logan stood from his knees. He turned to face us, the smile on his face returning as though he were proud of the fact that he just killed Buddy.

*

Nick jumped off the porch and sprinted toward the center of the yard, Logan standing over the dead dog as though admiring his work. After shoving Logan aside, nearly knocking him to the ground, Nick knelt on the wet grass and inspected Buddy.

Logan simply watched as though nothing happened. His face was not marked with the slightest hint of remorse.

Rebecca lost control. She too jumped off the porch and charged toward the animal killer. However, instead of simply shoving him aside, she yelled at him, throwing punches in his direction.

"Goddamn killer!" she yelled, slapping his face before pushing him back, then slapping him again.

Nick did not try to stop her.

Looking suddenly confused, Logan cowered away as he turned his shoulder toward her while she continued her beating. He ordered her to stop, but she didn't listen.

Nick stood from the grass then carefully picked Buddy up in his arms. Leaving Rebecca to beat Logan to a pulp, he crossed the yard toward me, and I stared at the dog's lifeless head bobbing up and down with every step.

"Stop it!" Logan yelled to Rebecca.

Much to my surprise, she listened. She took a step back to catch her breath then moved back in for one final slap across his face.

"What the hell is wrong with you?" he asked.

She didn't answer. Instead, she dropped to her knees, buried her face in her hands and cried for the loss of her dog.

Nick put Buddy down on the porch to face me and the sight of the animal's face formed a knot in my throat. His pale tongue drooped out of his mouth and rested sideways on the porch much like the animal it was attached to. His golden fur moved only with the breeze, destroying all hope that maybe he survived. The animal wasn't breathing at all. But the image that will forever remain burned in my memory was of his eyes. They were open, filled with death, and looking directly back at me.

I turned away, swallowing vomit.

Logan stepped onto the porch and approached me suddenly. He left Rebecca to mourn on her own in the yard.

"What happened?" he asked me, rubbing his sore cheek in utter confusion.

I stepped away from him, disgusted by the question. Though it begun to rain, I joined Rebecca in the yard. She cried helplessly, and all I could do was rub her back to console her.

Nick was bent over the dog, shaking his head in frustration. Logan turned and approached them slowly. "What happened?" he asked again.

"Get the hell out of here!" Nick yelled to him, his anger much more forceful than Rebecca's.

Logan shook his head. "Will someone tell me what the *fuck* is happening?"

In a swift motion, Nick moved inches away from his face. A single punch across the jaw sent Logan to the floor. "You killed Buddy!" he yelled as Logan tried to stand up again. "You broke his neck, you son of a bitch!"

He looked at the dog on the porch, his face expressing nothing but shock. He looked to Rebecca and I, then Logan's eyes settled back on Nick.

"I did what?"

*

"We saw you do it!" Nick yelled.

I led Rebecca into the house and out of the rain. Most importantly, I took her away from the sight of Buddy, and away from the arguing taking place between Logan and Nick on the porch. They could still be heard through the sliding glass door, though.

"I'm telling you, I didn't fucking do it!" Logan returned. There were only two circumstances in which Logan ever cursed; if he was drunk or upset.

"Are you okay?" I asked Rebecca, trying to distract her from the voices.

I took her to the kitchen where she grabbed a kitchen towel to weep into as I served her a glass of cold water. She wasn't okay, but the crying was fading.

"What am I going to tell Charlene and Max?" she asked, slapping her thighs. "Especially Max?"

Instantly, I wondered why I didn't think of it before. Only, when Max's plea for me to look after the dog echoed in my head, I wished I hadn't thought of it at all.

"You're coming with me," Nick ordered Logan as he threw the sliding glass door open.

"Where?" Logan asked directly behind him as they stepped into the house.

"To take Buddy to the animal hospital."

As Nick stomped into the living room, Logan closed the sliding glass door slowly then he looked up at Rebecca and I. There was shame in his eyes and sorrow across his face.

"I didn't do it," he said to us nearly whispering. "I swear."

Rebecca didn't look up from her glass of water, and I silently instructed Logan to not continue.

"Rebecca, you have to believe me," he said, approaching her. "I didn't kill Buddy, I wouldn't do…"

Without saying a word, she stood from the table and stared Logan in the face for a few seconds. The anger in her eyes told him that she wasn't going to listen, that she wasn't going to believe him no matter what he said.

Logan closed his eyes and shook his head, a tear rolling down his flushed cheek.

She walked out of the kitchen and out of sight. Seconds later, the door to her room slammed shut, and that's when Logan opened his eyes.

"Let's go, Logan!" Nick called from the living room.

He met my eyes, and I saw the wall of tears that formed. "I didn't do it," he told me then walked towards the living room; his shoulders slumped and his head hung low.

And at that moment, as I watched him walk away, something unexplainable filled my heart. Maybe it was the sorrow in his eyes, or the innocent way he pleaded for us to believe him. As they left the house that afternoon, Buddy in Nick's arms and distress in Logan's eyes, I took a deep breath as his words repeated in my mind. "I didn't do it," he said.

And I believed him.

Revelation

Logan and Nick were gone for over an hour, and as the sun began to set behind the clouds of the west, the rain fell harder.

Rebecca and I sat in her living room, barely making small talk as the time passed. The television was tuned into more news on Hurricane Alida, but neither of us paid much attention to it. Our thoughts were elsewhere.

Rebecca asked a question that I'm sure was meant rhetorically; "What could have possessed Logan to do such a thing?" Considering the recent events, possession just may have been the answer.

I read enough dark fantasy books and seen plenty of horror movies to delve so deep into the unknown. What if Logan *was* possessed by something that made him kill the dog? It would give reason to the brutality in the fashion of which Buddy was killed, and why he didn't remember afterwards. But if he was possessed, then by what?

The same thing that possessed Luis in the hospital room. I argued the thought, knowing the incident with Luis was just a dream.

Nightmares, voices, warnings, and death were all a constant in the past few days. Why not throw possession in the mix and explain over half the incidents?

Rebecca dreamt that Luis was going to kill Jo. A day later, the accident took place, and Jo was dead. Then, she dreamt that Logan was trying to kill *her*. Though it was Buddy he killed, maybe her dream was some kind of premonition, but it was misread.

If her dreams were premonitions, then what of my nightmares? It felt as though it were all connected somehow, but there was something missing; a piece of the puzzle that had yet to be revealed.

I stood from the couch when the news went to commercial and asked Rebecca if she wanted something to drink. She asked for her glass to be refilled with water and I made my way to the kitchen avoiding a glance into the back yard. Still, the thoughts lingered.

He swore he didn't do it, I could clearly remember the look on his face when Rebecca walked away from him and he turned to me. He was confused, frustrated, and most of all, ashamed. There was no killer instinct in his eyes like there was when he killed Buddy.

That force, that undeniable feeling that something else was at work…I couldn't help but wonder if it was the same power that made Logan kill Buddy. If it did, was it still a part of Logan? Was it still inside of him, ready to strike again?

I looked out into the rain and prayed that it wasn't. If so, Nick was in danger.

I tried to ignore my thoughts all together as I filled Rebecca's glass, then a glass of my own. I drank the water in a single gulp, the thirst I hadn't even noticed diminishing completely.

The skies lit up, cascading beams of light through the windows of the house, followed by thunder that shook the ground beneath us. Hurricane Alida may have been a little less than one hundred miles away, but the outskirts of the storm was looming over us for the past week, and it was only going to get worse.

Nothing is what it seems.

The old man's voice suddenly echoed in my head, and for the first time, I realized I heard the voice before. In Max's room? Through Luis? I rubbed my temples at the familiar voice, unable to pinpoint the exact time and place I heard it. I repeated the phrase in my head;

Nothing it what it seems.

Forcefully blending it to the voice that called for me in Max's room, it sounded the same though I could not be certain for my mind was desperate for answers and quite possibly forcing their pitch. I could not muster the trust of my own brain at such a venerable moment; not even when I blended the voice with the tone my brother took in my dream.

But then, as I walked back toward the living room, I heard it as though a ghost whispered it into my ear. As the glass of water I held for Rebecca slipped out of my hand and exploded into a hundred shards on the floor, the voice echoed in my head, and I was certain I knew its origin.

Nothing is what it seems…it whispered, then it said, *Fucking pigs.*

"Cynthia, are you okay?" Rebecca asked, walking into the dining room, finding me shaking uncontrollably. "What's the matter?"

My brain flashed with a hundred pictures in a second, beginning with the memory of the night our parents died, the night Mason Bayer was killed in our kitchen. The only words he said before Luis fired the shot that killed him pounded my head relentlessly; *Fucking pigs.* ENO. It was written in Jo's blood across the seatbelt, and the detectives insisted my brother wrote it. Buddy was killed, and Logan didn't remember his own actions that took place seconds before.

"Cynthia," Rebecca called again, stepping closer to me as my head grew light and as my knees grew weak. "What's the matter?"

"I think Nick's in danger," I said between breaths. "He's in Logan." As I spoke, the words Luis told me in my dream replayed themselves. *Look for me in Logan,* he said. At that moment, I knew I was right. About everything.

"What do you mean?" she asked.

"It's why Luis wrote E-N-O after he killed Jo."

She frowned. "You think your brother killed her?" she asked. I didn't even notice my choice of words until then.

"My brother didn't kill Jo," I said. "But something made him do it. We need to find Logan and Nick because that something is in Logan now."

"Cynthia, I think you need to relax…"

My pulse was rising and I was beginning to sweat. "Listen to me," I said to her nervously. "Nick is in danger because Mason Bayer is in Logan. We need to find them!"

Her reaction was as I expected it to be. Her eyes widened at my words as concern fell upon her face. "Mason Bayer?" she asked. "Cynthia, Mason Bayer is dead."

Though I just figured it in my head, I couldn't explain it to her. The sudden urgency had me at a loss for words. If she didn't understand what I was trying to tell her, she would once we found them. Without wasting another second, I ran into the living room and grabbed Rebecca's car keys off the coffee table.

"Where are you going?" she asked, following me.

"To find them."

"Don't you think you might be over reacting?" she asked. "Give me my car keys!"

I ignored her order and opened the front door. I took one step out onto the porch and stopped. A black sedan was parked on the curb across the street, a sedan much like the one Detectives Lopez and Santiago were resting against at the funeral. Though I couldn't see if it was them in the car, a silhouette in the driver's seat was clearly visible.

I turned and went back into the house. If it was them, then they were following us, watching our every move like they somewhat promised to. I couldn't lead them to the source of our predicament and inadvertently bring more trouble to us.

"Cynthia, this isn't healthy for you," Rebecca said, taking the keys from my hand. "You're pregnant, and this kind of stress will cause a mis..."

"You said yourself that the reason your dreams scared you so much was because neither Luis nor Logan seemed to be themselves. What if they're not? You told me you dreamt Logan was trying to kill you..."

She shook her head. "He didn't kill me. He killed Buddy, Cynthia."

"What if whatever made him kill the dog is what will try and kill you next? Maybe your dreams were some kind of warning and…"

"That doesn't happen in real life," she argued.

"I'm telling you that Nick is in danger as long as he's with Logan!" I shot back, nearly yelling at her. "It's six miles to the animal hospital, Rebecca! They've taken over an hour already and all they were going to do was drop Buddy off! What would be taking them so long?"

"The storm, car trouble, traffic. There are a hundred reasons they would be running late, but you don't see me jumping on the phone calling an exorcist."

I walked away from her and headed back toward the living room. She followed.

"Look, Cynthia. We've all been freaked out about what's happened. Have you talked to Jennifer about any of this?"

"Spare me the psycho-babble, Rebecca. I'm not crazy."

"That's not…"

The phone rang, and I was happy to answer it. It was my ticket out of the conversation that would have inevitably ended in an argument.

"Cynthia?" came the filtered response, and though I recognized the voice, I was hesitant to respond.

"Angela?" I asked after detecting the concern in her voice.

"Is Rebecca with you?"

I glanced at Rebecca. "Yes."

"Can you two come over?"

"No, it's a bad time. We're waiting for…"

"Nick and Logan are here. They're okay, but you need to come over right away. There's something we need to talk about."

Rebecca was trying to get my attention by waving her hands at me, but I ignored her. "Okay," I said into the phone. "We'll be right over."

"Hurry," she added. "I don't know how much time we have."

Angela Ortega: The Psychic

The rain continued. Nick and Logan were driving back from the animal hospital, both in silence; Nick at the wheel concentrating on the slippery road. He told us that was the reason he didn't see the attack coming.

When we arrived at Angela's, Rebecca making the twenty minute trek in nearly half the time, she invited us in immediately then asked us to follow her to the living room. As we walked through the house, my eyes ventured into every room, across every wall and over every piece of furniture. Nick and Logan were somewhere in the house, and I was desperate to see them.

The living room was small, its space cut in half to include the kitchen. With barely enough room for a center table, two mismatched couches lined opposite walls. Nick sat on the one to the left, holding an ice pack to his bruised right eye.

He looked up at me and smiled, and I ran to his aid. "Are you okay?" I asked, throwing myself next to him to inspect the eye myself.

"*Shh,*" he ordered then pointed to the couch across from us.

I didn't noticed Logan lying on his back. His hands were folded across his stomach that rose and fell with every breath. A folded washcloth covered his eyes, and I was certain they were closed.

"What happened?" Rebecca asked Angela, both of them standing at the entrance to the room.

That's when Nick told us about the attack. He mentioned that Logan was silent during their entire journey to and from the animal hospital, but he thought it was due to his brother's guilt. He thought Logan was contemplating the actions his hands took upon themselves to carry out on the defenseless dog.

Within seconds though, Logan's hands were flying toward Nick in a rage; a swift punch landing above his right brow. Stunned, Nick managed to keep the car under control even when Logan threw another blow. It was then that Nick found himself capable of fighting back. He pushed Logan toward the passenger side door, his head slamming into the window and inadvertently knocking him out. Ever since then, he told us, Logan had not woken up.

"And how did you end up here?" Rebecca asked him.

"Take a seat," Angela replied. "I'll put on a pot of coffee. We may be here for a while."

*

After distributing the steaming mugs, she sat on the floor; her back resting against the couch Logan slept on so to face us. We watched her as she pulled her hair back into a pony-tail and taking a deep breath before settling her attention on us.

She told us that there was something she needed to talk to us about; something that was troubling her for a few days. Her nervous hands indicated that whatever it was she was planning to say wasn't going to be easy, and she asked us be patient with her. She warned us that it would be difficult for us to understand, and requested that we put our disbeliefs aside.

Rebecca glanced at me, frowning as though she didn't understand Angela's request, but I did. I had a feeling I already knew what she wanted to tell us.

She began by reminding us of the day after the accident, the day she wanted to visit with Luis in the hospital after each of us had our chance. She explained that there was no real particular reason why she wanted to visit with him other than say a few words in the hopes that it would help him, and to pray over his unconscious mind. But there, she said, she became overwhelmed with a feeling that something was not quite right; something was happening *inside* Luis that alarmed her. She thought it a simple struggle of Luis' soul trying desperately to wake up, but his physical body wasn't allowing it.

However, the compelling discomfort she felt being around him told her otherwise, and she took it upon herself to grasp his dead hand and use her gift to pinpoint the struggle.

"You did a psychic reading for him?" Rebecca asked, "while he was in a coma?"

The night we discovered Angela had the gift, Rebecca was eager to see her perform. The tone in her voice was different now; she was skeptical.

Angela explained that her gift gave her the power to, amongst other things, read energy. It was how she read futures. Her mind wasn't filled with pictures of things yet to be nor was she blessed with the ability to peek into the coming year rather, she analyzed the state in which the path of life seemed to be headed based upon several factors. The most important factor, she said, was energy she received from whom she was reading. Though she said she wasn't sure if she would receive a clear signal from Luis before she began, she did find something rather quickly, and very powerful.

"What did you see?" I asked, knowing that her answer could possibly confirm my suspicion.

Angela hesitated at first, looking at us individually, possibly weighing out who would believe her and who wouldn't. She took a breath and said, "There was something inside of him that was keeping him in his coma."

"What exactly does that mean?" Rebecca asked.

"It means that an outside force, some sort of entity, was harboring inside his body."

"He was possessed?"

"Not exactly," Angela answered. In possession, she explained, an entity would take over a body or place for a short amount of time to carry out a specific goal. Though this entity had the power to possess, she felt what it was doing to Luis was something completely different. Luis is weak, she told us. The entity was fighting Luis' soul to achieve its ultimate purpose; to take over Luis' body completely.

Rebecca shook her head in disbelief, nearly laughing at Angela while she spoke. The psychic ignored her, though. I, on the other hand, believed every word she was saying and not because of what I already discovered on my own. The certainty in her voice was enough to turn my stomach and send electrifying chills throughout my entire body.

"Who is it?" I asked her, though I was certain I already knew.

"Something or someone that's been with him for a very long time."

I closed my eyes, visions of the dream I had of Luis flashing in my head.

"This thing that was inside Luis," she continued, "I felt nothing but horrible intentions coming from it, and it scared me because all of you were included in its plans."

"All of us?"

"That's what I saw. That's why I broke up with Logan. I wasn't sure what it was capable of, so I figured the only way to be safe was to leave."

I didn't blame her. "Did it make Luis kill Jo?" I asked.

She looked to Nick before answering, but a second later, she nodded.

"Why Luis?" Rebecca asked, still cynical.

Angela shook her head. "I'm not certain of that. Something unexpected has happened recently, and I'm still trying to figure it out. "

"What is it?" I asked.

Angela looked over her shoulder to the couch behind her. Logan was still resting, comfortably it seemed. "It left Luis," she answered.

"So that's it? It's gone?"

"No," Angela answered. "It's just moved."

"Moved?" Rebecca asked as though it was the dumbest thing she'd ever heard. "Where?"

"Into Logan," I answered before Angela could.

She looked at me and nodded, not at all surprised that I knew the answer. "Whatever this energy is has probably already reached all of you by now. If not physically, then in dreams or even in your thoughts."

"I'm sorry," Rebecca said, nearly laughing. "This is just too weird for me. I mean, listen to yourselves. You sound like you belong in a nuthouse."

"It's all true, Rebecca," Angela said.

"I don't believe it! Look, maybe Luis did kill Jo, but it's possible he snapped just like any of us can at any moment. You're talking possession! First you said this thing was in Luis, now it's in Logan? That's ludicrous!"

"Nick can tell you," Angela said, and Rebecca nearly froze. Slowly, she turned to Nick, and so did the rest of us.

He told us again of the attack Logan sprung on him on the ride home from the animal hospital, his eyes holding steady on the ice pack he was playing with in his hands. He revealed a detail that he left out before, stuttering as he spoke as though he couldn't believe the words coming from his own mouth. During the attack, Logan spoke to him, in anger it appeared, and what he said made Nick convinced that his brother had either gone crazy or was under the influence of someone or something else.

"What did he say?" I asked.

Nick looked at me and swallowed hard. He didn't want to say, I read it in his face. But he took a breath, "He said he fucked my mother and made my father watch before killing them both."

I gasped, my eyes welling with tears while goose bumps ran throughout my entire body.

"That's when I pushed him into the window," Nick continued.

"That's how you ended up here?" I asked.

He nodded. "With everything that happened, I figured Angela might have some answers."

I looked to Logan, still sleeping on the couch, resting comfortably and I wondered if the evil was still in him. Would it attack us if it woke up at that very moment?

"Don't worry," Angela said. "It left Logan now."

"So, this spirit," Rebecca said, "Who is it? I mean, why is it after us?"

Angela took a breath. "I can tell you what my theory is, but based on the evidence shown to you of Jo's seatbelt, and what it said to Nick through Logan, I'm sure your answer is the same as mine."

A profound silence fell upon all of us suddenly, allowing our own minds to reveal the horrible truth.

Mason Bayer.

"Bullshit!" Rebecca said, standing from the couch. "Look, I'll go along with a psychic reading any day of the week, but this is getting out of hand!"

Angela stood from the floor quickly to meet Rebecca's eyes. "Please, let me finish. There's so much more you need..."

"No, Angela. I won't listen to this any more. It sounds like something Cynthia could write as a novel, it's not real!"

"Rebecca, please..."

"Logan needs to get to the hospital and you're talking ghosts!"

"No!" Nick said, standing from the couch. "We can't take him there."

"Why the hell not?" Rebecca fired back.

Nick looked at me nervously for only a second then looked back to Rebecca. "Because it's crowded there." He glanced at Logan on the couch. "What if it comes back?"

Rebecca rolled her eyes and slapped her thighs in disbelief. "So what, we're supposed to seclude ourselves now? Is that how this works?"

"Unfortunately, yes," Angela answered.

"Why?" I asked.

"There's an order to the way things are going to happen, and as far as I can tell, you're already far enough into its game that this really shouldn't shock any of you." She looked back to Rebecca. "First, you'll think you're going crazy. There are things you hear, but you're not certain of them, things you see just out of the corner of your eye, but they're not really there. Then, things become more apparent; solid objects move right in front of you with no help from anyone. You'll hear voices call your name in the halls of your house in the middle of the night, but there's no one there to account for them."

My heart sunk just as fast as my soul did. It was as though she reached into my thoughts and was explaining everything that occurred in the past week.

"The stage in between," she continued, "is the most critical. It's when you've suddenly lost the ability to differentiate what's real and what's not. Even your dreams are so vivid, you don't know they're dreams until you wake up." She glanced at Logan, then looked back to Nick and I with concern slapped on her face. "No matter who it is that's doing this to you, it's not like your ordinary haunted house. This thing messes with your mind until it has completed what it's here for."

It became clear that Angela tore through the wall Rebecca built with a sledgehammer. Slowly, Rebecca took her seat and no longer contested the psychic. It was as though she knew it all along but refused to give into the belief, and I understood. How does one learn to accept what they thought was never possible? She covered her face with her hands and took a deep breath, her mind, body and soul digesting everything at once.

"What exactly are we dealing with then?" Nick asked, though I'm not sure he really wanted to know.

"Evil," Angela answered, situating herself on the floor again. "The purest of all that is evil and wicked. If this is, in fact, Mason Bayer, it knows your every weakness and fear, and it will inevitably use it against you to weaken your defenses."

The way she phrased her words made it appear as though there was a possibility that the entity was something other than Mason Bayer, but none of us considered it a possibility. Mason Bayer was a killer driven by revenge, and in death it appeared to be no different. He returned to make us pay for what was done to him many years before. The only question that any of us could think to ask was thrown at Angela by Nick.

"Why now?" he asked. "Why eighteen years later?"

"What you don't know is that it's been with you for those eighteen years. It always has. It appears as though it waited patiently for the right moment to strike. It waited until your lives were perfect, when you no longer lived in the shadow of that night."

Suddenly, it hit me. I found the answer to what dozens of specialists and Doctor Morrison himself couldn't eighteen years before. After the murders, Luis fell into shock then suffered strange stages that no one could explain. I wondered if Mason Bayer was the cause of his violent outbursts, and dyslexia.

"You say he was in Luis before he was in Logan," Nick said. "Why's he doing that?"

Her answer was quite simple; to get to the rest of us. Since Luis was immobile, it used whatever means necessary to get to the rest of us, but Angela believed that whenever we were free from its presence, it was back in Luis, fighting for control.

"He can take over any of us?" I asked. "At any time?"

"Yes. It does not have a body of its own and can't physically harm you without one. It needs a vehicle to carry out its business, and to make you weaker, it'll more than likely use one of you."

I glanced at Nick, then to Rebecca. "You mean he could be in one of us right now?"

"It's not here," she said, certain of her words.

I looked at the others again as though I could confirm Angela's answer by simply looking at their eyes.

"How will we know?" Nick asked. "I mean, are there any signs, or anything?"

"You mean, besides what you saw in Logan?"

He nodded.

"Physical attributes are what you'll want to keep an eye out for. It can conceivably lie dormant in your body without exposing itself, but the one thing it cannot hide are its own physical attributes. For example, if it had a limp in life and one of you suddenly walks with a limp then odds are you've been invaded. Anything from the voice to..."

"Writing backwards?" I asked, Jo's seatbelt in my head.

Angela nodded. "If that was one of its traits, then absolutely."

I noticed her referral to "it" as opposed to "he." She knew exactly what we were up against, and I was thankful she was around to tell us as much as she had.

"So, let's just say that you're right," Rebecca said, her first words since she was silenced with the truth but obviously still having trouble with it. "Let's say Mason Bayer is in fact trying to get his revenge. How do we stop him?"

Angela sighed and glanced at the three of us. She took a sip of her coffee, and my back stiffened. She was hesitating. "There are several options you can take to avoid confronting It," she said.

"An exorcist?" Nick asked.

Angela shook her head. "This is religion failed. It's not a demon, and it may not have religious beliefs of its own rendering an exorcism useless. Forget everything you know, or think you know, about the unknown."

"Then how?"

Through actual documented events that Angela studied before, she explained that the haunting spirit usually picks a single person to attack. Many believe that the safest way to avoid being "singled out" by an entity was to stay in groups making an attack less likely. Our situation however was a different story. Since Mason needed a body to carry out an attack, an option we had was to seclude ourselves from one another. She advised that we forget we ever met and move miles away. Still, it would not guarantee our safety since Mason would eventually catch up with us. She explained that the only way to be certain was to trap the spirit.

"And how do we do that, exactly?" I asked.

"Destroy the vehicle It's in. Kill the body, and you trap the soul."

Silence fell over us again as what she suggested set in. Each of us exchanged glances, all of us looking as scared as the other, and all of us were at a sudden loss for words.

"This is all too much to take in right now, I know…"

"We have to kill each other?" Rebecca asked, somewhat dazed.

Angela nodded.

"There has to be another way."

"There's not."

My heart began racing. How could all this be possible? Jennifer would keel over and die if she ever got wind of this.

"Damn it!" Rebecca said, her voice cracking under the pressure. "What the hell gives him the power to do this?"

Angela shook her head. "That I cannot answer, but that's not important. Don't lose focus here and listen to me because without fully understanding what I'm about to tell you, there will be no winning. Once It has taken over a body, the soul of that person is lost in conflict much like Luis is now. If you choose to take action, listen very carefully, you are not killing the person. You have to understand that. Yes, they will die, but as nothing more than a casualty of war. What you kill is the thing that has invaded…"

"That doesn't make it easier," Rebecca said.

"I know, but at least you'll be certain."

Rebecca did what all of us felt like doing. She covered her face with both hands and cried. "I don't believe this," she whispered, but it was said differently from when she said the same thing before.

I looked at Logan sleeping on the couch. He had absolutely no idea of what was happening, and explaining it all to him promised a challenge.

"If you do decide to take action," Angela said, "then it must be quick. If It sees a blow coming at him or considers the situation a threat, It will jump out before the attack."

That's why It left Logan. It probably jumped out just before Nick fought back.

"Have you seen how this ends?" Nick asked her after a brief pause.

"I have," she nodded. "But I won't tell you what I saw because it can change. The future is nothing more than a place where your road is headed, and the slightest event can change everything. There's no need to fill your head with what I saw.

"Understand that each of you are powerful enough to beat this. The signs are there. Simply look for them, and you will know when It is around."

"What about Uncle George and the kids?" I asked. "Are they safe from all this?"

"For now, maybe. But if It succeeds and you don't, there's no telling who It will target next. Hell, I'm not even sure I'm safe..." She continued to talk, but the rest of us tuned out. She didn't see what we saw because her back was turned toward the couch. Logan's hand went from his stomach to the towel over his eyes.

He was waking.

A Decision for Life

Logan was disoriented, it took a while for his eyes to adjust to the light when he finally removed the towel. Confused, he inspected his surroundings and found us all staring at him as though we never saw him before. He quickly grew uneasy, especially when he saw Angela.

"What happened?" he asked, sitting up rapidly, but the sudden pain in his head took him back down.

"It's okay," Angela said, kneeling before him. "Just take it easy."

"How did we get here?" he asked through gritted teeth.

"Relax," she ordered softly, caressing his blond hair. "I'll explain everything."

Logan took a deep breath, shutting his eyes tightly to cope with the pain of his injury. The rest of us watched him, left wondering what he remembered, and if he was, in fact, himself.

"I'm thirsty," he said, almost in a whisper.

Angela stood from the floor. "I'll get you some water."

"Is he okay?" Rebecca asked so that Logan wouldn't hear.

Angela didn't answer in front of him. She walked into the kitchen, signaling us to follow, and we did just that.

The four of us crammed in the small room as Angela turned to us, her arms folded across her chest. "He'll be okay," she said. "It's probably going to take him some time to recover."

"I really didn't think he hit his head that hard," Nick said.

"It's not the injury he needs to recover from."

The three of us stared at Angela for a second. She didn't need to explain any further; we knew what she meant.

"It's going to be tough explaining it to him," she said, pouring the water into the glass. "With any luck, he would have already put some of it together like you all had."

"He'll need convincing," Rebecca said. "Even more so than me."

"Would you mind giving us some privacy while I tell him?" she asked. "There are some things I need to say that wouldn't be appropriate if other people were around."

"We'll be outside," Nick said. "I need a cigarette, anyway."

For the first time in years, I wanted one. As quickly as the thought entered my mind though, I dismissed it. By no means would I light a cigarette as long as I was pregnant. I couldn't do that to my unborn child.

Angela thanked us, and we headed toward the front door. There was a discussion that needed to be held amongst the three of us as well; a conversation I never thought would take place.

*

We sat underneath the canopy over the front door of Angela's house. As though the psychic knew we would need it, a small patio table and three chairs were set out just before the canopy broke. The night's rain fell less than an inch away, its mist brought in by the thick, gusty air.

"Did any of you know it?" I asked them. "Suspect it at least?"

They both thought about it before answering.

"I had my suspicions after Detectives Lopez and Santiago showed us those pictures," Nick admitted. "I just never said anything because I was afraid everyone would think I was crazy."

"What Angela said was right," Rebecca said. "I thought I heard voices in my house, but I honestly thought it was my imagination." She looked at me. "But then you came over the night you heard someone in Max's room and I knew something was happening. Never, in my wildest dreams, did I think it would be...well, this."

"None of us did," I said.

"I think you should get on a plane and leave," Rebecca returned. "Go to New York and be with Uncle George and the kids."

"Why would I do that?" I asked.

"Because you're pregnant."

"Rebecca, no…"

"She's right," Nick said. "If what Angela just told us in there is true, then you should leave. You can't risk the stress, or worse."

I shook my head. "I'm not leaving. Angela said that hiding is only a temporary solution."

"Just for the time being," Nick said.

"I can't, I won't. Besides, Detectives Lopez and Santiago said that we are forbidden from leaving town."

"You heard what she said in there, Cynthia," Nick answered. "The only way we can stop him is to…" His words drifted as he couldn't bring himself to say it; the horrible truth of the situation; to kill the person It's invaded to save the others.

I looked across the table to my husband then to the cousin I considered a sister and imagined the worst. Could I bring myself to do it? Could I kill either of them to save myself or the children? If push came to shove, I would certainly let them take my life to save the rest; somewhere in the back of my mind it's been the same way for decades, with or without the spirit of Mason Bayer. But could I shoot my husband or break the neck of my best friend to save myself? In turn, could they kill me if I was invaded? I couldn't even stand thinking about it, so what did that mean for when the time to act came around?

They both lit cigarettes and I watched them puff away as a moment of silence fell amongst us. They, no doubt, were lost in the same thoughts as I, and almost unwillingly, I said the words that was on both their minds.

"If it happens to be me, then do it."

They froze.

"I mean it. If it was meant to save everyone else, I would want you to do it."

"Me too," Rebecca said suddenly, her chin quivering with emotion. She wanted to continue, giving us permission to take her life if the situation were to arise, but her emotions prevented her from speaking any further.

Nick took both our hands into his and sighed. "If it came to that," he said, "then me too."

One week ago, my life was perfect; I was convinced nothing could make the path of my life deviate. If Angela told me that my husband and best friend would be sitting on her patio, plotting to kill one another to save the rest, I would have called her crazy.

"Let's just get it right the first time," Nick said, a failed attempt at trying to lighten the situation.

I sat back on the chair and watched as both Rebecca and Nick puffed away in silence. Could we really do it? From words to actions, there was a large stretch and it was much easier to be on the receiving end of a bullet than being the one to pull the trigger. One thing was certain, though; all of us, no matter how scared we were of dying, or how much we feared the unknown, we wanted Mason Bayer out of our lives for good. Would it be enough to fuel a killing hand? I assumed only time would tell.

Nick stood from the table and headed toward the front door of the house suddenly, flicking the butt of his cigarette onto the lawn.

"Where are you going?" I asked him.

He said he'd be right back and entered the house, closing the door behind him. Seconds later, he returned with a pen and a spiral bound notebook.

"What's that for?" Rebecca asked.

"Angela said one way to know if Mason is…inside one of us, we'd write backwards," he said, taking his seat. "We take a test right now."

"What?"

"To know for sure. We each write something just to make sure he isn't..."

"Angela said he wasn't around," I told him. "Do we really need to put ourselves through this right now?"

No matter how much we said we were ready to "stop" It, it became evident at that moment we weren't. Nick proposed a test, write something down and if it's backwards, you're possessed. "Then what?" I asked. "We kill each other right here on Angela's porch?"

"Maybe not," he said. "But it's better that we know."

"Wait a minute," Rebecca said. "Shouldn't we wait? I mean, maybe there are other ways."

"I think we should weigh out all our options," I followed.

"But you just said that if the situation arose..."

"We know what we said, Nick. The truth is I don't want to have to kill you if there might be another way."

"And how do you expect to find that other way?"

"The same way you'd fight any other opponent. We find out about Mason Bayer."

Rebecca put her cigarette out and sighed. "But how?"

"We don't know anything about him," I answered. "We never did. I think if we found out his weaknesses, his strong points, his entire life the way he knows ours, we may find another way."

Nick thought about it for a second, then nodded. "There's one man who knows more about Mason than anyone else alive," he said, almost to himself.

"Billy?" Rebecca asked.

He nodded.

But Billy was nowhere to be found. In the moment we needed him the most, he disappeared. None of us heard from him since...well, since he called me; hysterical. Stumbling upon the murder of Old Man Brewer did something to him; something that none of us could guess. Despite my better thoughts, I couldn't help but wonder…

"Do you think he knew what Mason was capable of?" Rebecca asked, pulling the words from my throat.

It didn't matter, really. Billy was MIA, and as long as he was missing, he couldn't help. Nick said we'd search for him come sun up, then he opened the notebook.

"We deal with the threat right now," he said, then without saying another word, he began to scribble on the page.

Rebecca and I exchanged glances as my heart began to accelerate.

He finished quickly then studied the paper. We watched his face in suspense, hoping the slightest flicker of dread didn't fall upon him. But he seemed satisfied with whatever it was he wrote then slid the notebook and pen to his right, toward Rebecca.

Nervously, she accepted the tools and inspected the page. Taking the pen in her hands, she looked to both of us and said, "Whatever happens, if it turns out there is no other way, promise me Charlene will be taken care of."

Before we could say anything, before she could see the weakness that fell over me, she began to write. Seconds later, she was done, inspecting the page the same way Nick did.

She took a breath then slid the notebook and pen toward me.

So far, both of them passed. Their signatures were on two consecutive lines, beginning at the top of the page. Both were written from left to right, and completely legible.

Nick Sheyer

Rebecca Joules

The third line was for me. I did it quickly, without giving it much thought, and as I wrote each letter, I began to feel more and more relieved about the entire situation.

Cynthia Sheyer

We were safe for now; Mason wasn't inside any of us. But that only left one question that followed immediately. If he's not inside one of us, then where could he be? Inside Luis?

*

It didn't take long for Angela to explain everything to Logan. By the look on his face when he stepped out onto the porch, he was just as terrified as we were.

Angela followed him out and the rest of us stood from the table.

"We should get out of here," Logan said.

He was right. As far as I was concerned, we should stay away from everyone we cared about until it was over.

He turned to Nick, his jaws clenched as he hung his head low. "I'm sorry," he said. "I didn't…"

"It wasn't you," Nick told him. "I know it wasn't you."

Logan was trembling, his concern for hurting Nick far more apparent than the anxiety of what was really happening.

"I probably won't be here if you have any more questions," Angela said softly. "I think it'd be best if I left for right now."

We nodded.

"Before you go, I want to say that from here on out, things will probably be different."

"Different how?" Nick asked her.

"It won't make it easier now that you know. Rest assured, It knows that you're no longer ignorant to what's happening."

"We'll be okay," Rebecca said, though it was only to calm Angela's worries. We didn't know the outcome, and the psychic supposedly saw the path in which it was directed.

"Just remember," she said, "that nothing is what it seems. It will use your own eyes to make you weak and to cloud your judgment."

Each of us took our turn in thanking her for her help. She hugged the four of us individually, her tears falling faster with each embrace. Nick, Rebecca and I walked toward the cars as her final embrace went to Logan.

They kissed and held each other quietly as Nick and I piled into our car and Rebecca stepped into her SUV. Before long, Logan loaded into the passenger side of her car, and we left Angela's house together.

She stood on the porch and waved as we drove off, Nick and I following Rebecca. We didn't know where we were headed. Home was the safest place to be; away from the public and locked away on our own.

As we approached the intersection for the main road, Nick cursed, then shook his head. "This is just what we needed," he said.

"What is it?" I asked, then I saw what concerned him.

A car drove right passed us, but it drove slow enough for a full inspection. I wondered if Rebecca and Logan saw it as well.

It was a black sedan, and it was headed toward Angela's.

CHAPTER RUOF

It was hours since Danny heard from the detective, and his frustration was beginning to show. He waited for the phone to ring while praying the main door of the lobby would open, waiting desperately to hear from the man he grew to hate. Cynthia Grazer, his favorite writer, was just seven floors away, wanted for murder, and the detective was the only one who held the answers. Danny was *dying* to find out more.

But nothing for the past two and a half hours! Danny thought to himself, glancing at his watch. It was 3:37 A.M.

A few times throughout the early morning, he toyed with the idea of running up the stairs to the seventh floor to reach Cynthia. He wanted to tell her that she was being watched, warn her that the detective was on her trail. Hell, maybe she would even kiss him passionately in return for the warning. In the end, Danny knew it wouldn't be a good idea. With his luck, he and the detective would cross on the way back down the stairs. Though he wasn't absolutely sure there was a law against it, he was certain he would go to jail for interfering with an investigation.

There was no way Danny was stupid enough to try it. At least, not without checking on the detective's car first.

It took him about an hour to build the courage to do it the first time, walking to the plate glass door and peeking out through the storm. Had it not been for the light poles illuminating the nearly empty parking lot, he would have not seen the car at all. It was black, four doors, its windows tinted to match. It was parked in the second row from the building, in a space with a direct view of the front door…

And right behind Cynthia's car!

Danny also realized that they had a clear view of the balcony to Cynthia's room.

On his second trip to the window, nearly fifteen minutes later, he was lucky enough to catch a glimpse *inside* the car. The interior light was on, and Danny nearly pressed his nose to the glass for a look. But the downpour proved too much of an obstacle. All he saw were mere silhouettes, shadows of the people inside…

People?

The detective was sitting in the driver's seat; Danny recognized the intimidating build immediately. In the passenger side, there was another shadow, someone he hadn't seen before. It was definitely a female, her body appearing much more slender than the detective's. Danny could even spot the shadow of a ponytail when she turned her head quickly.

"Probably his partner," Danny said to himself after wondering who in their right mind would stay in their car on a night like the one before him.

He froze, suddenly realizing that he stood in their direct view. One of them, or both, cold be looking right at him as he stared foolishly, and because of the brightly lit entrance to the hotel, Danny was certain that what they saw wasn't just his shadow.

His face flushed as he turned away quickly, realizing his chances of running up the stairs to live happily ever after were stomped. He rushed back to his desk, hoping the detectives couldn't see him. But again he froze, his heart pounding in his throat instantly. The lights inside the building went out.

*

Cynthia stopped writing and frantically looked around the room. It became dark in a blink; all the lights turned off, all the power down. She took a breath and tried to calm her nerves, but she failed.

Her breath ran short as she felt the pulse of her beating heart on the temples of her aching head. Was this the work of evil? she asked herself, all the while Jennifer's voice telling her to remain calm. A thousand whispers and crawling shadows called to her amidst the darkness of the room, bringing Cynthia to near panic. Every wound and abrasion she lost in the concentration of her story began screaming with pain as a terrible thought crossed her mind;

I'm not alone…

Then, the lights flickered. The darkness strobed into light, until finally, the power was restored. The shadows held still once again, and the voices died. Cynthia took a deep breath and closed her eyes.

Maybe it wasn't such a good idea to write this story.

She closed the notebook on her lap immediately and struggled to stand up from the bed. She was tired. The coffee helped, but only for about twenty minutes or so. The cigarettes were great company, but on their own, they weren't enough to keep her awake. Her eyes grew heavy and her body grew limp; and slowly, it was defeating the determination to stay awake and write the entire story.

She stretched her cramped right hand as she moved toward the sliding glass door that led to the balcony. It was her first trip to the window since she arrived, and though she vowed not to look at the storm, she needed the change in scenery.

The storm was incredible. She could see the traffic lights on the deserted main road just outside the hotel's parking lot. They were swinging violently on the cables from which they hung, the wind proving too strong for even the surrounding palm trees. After just a few seconds, Cynthia counted two branches dancing across the road like tumbleweed.

Lightning cracked a few feet away, bringing the sky to life with a ground-shaking explosion of thunder.

Cynthia screamed out of surprise, quickly turning away from the window. It was no wonder the lights were unstable; the storm seemed to be hovering right over the building.

As she moved back toward the bed, she thought of calling Danny and asking for a flashlight in case the power surged again. But she didn't.

She didn't need it. As she sat down on the bed and slowly repositioned herself against the headboard, she realized there was no reason for her to be scared of the dark. She lit a cigarette, and like every cigarette before, she puffed it slowly, convincing herself that there was no reason for her to be scared of even the storm. After she picked up the pen and studied the last few words she wrote, she knew that, when it came down to writing her story, there was no reason for her to be scared at all.

Thursday, June 11th

Once reality escaped us and we accepted Angela's warning as the truth, sleep was out of the question. On the transitional night between Wednesday and Thursday, a long conversation took place between us all where we decided that we would stay together until…well, until death did us part. It was Nick who said that the more we stuck together, the quicker the problem could be resolved.

After talking about our situation until sun up over Rebecca's dinner table, I wanted to leave her house. I felt imprisoned, waiting for whoever or whatever was haunting us to strike, waiting for the moment that we would be forced to act upon each other. I needed to do something, something that could help our situation. I wanted to do what I had in mind since we found out what was happening.

"Where are you going?" Nick asked as I stood from the table and excused myself.

"To the library," I said. "I'm going to find out everything I can about Mason Bayer."

"I'll go with you."

"No," I said, turning to him. "I'd rather go…"

"Absolutely not, Cynthia," Rebecca said, standing from the table. "Either we all go, or we don't go at all."

There were a few reasons I wanted to go on my own, mainly to think things through in silence. Other factors were directly related to the situation; because we didn't know where It was, I felt more secure behind the wheel of a vehicle on my own.

Still, we piled into the SUV and what I planned as a short getaway turned into a group field trip. I asked Rebecca if I could drive, and she told me she'd rather drive.

I made her write her name first.

When we reached the library, I told the others to wait in the car, that I wouldn't be long. That didn't work either. Nick insisted on coming with me.

We entered the building which was nearly as empty as the streets during the storm. I could only count half a dozen people immediately, and the second floor was just as desolate.

Against the south wall of the second floor, buried behind the countless shelves of books, a row of public access computers among private desks awaited us. Each workstation had internet access, and I told Nick to find everything he could on Mason Bayer and print it out.

"Where will you be?" he asked.

"I'm going to look for something else."

Down the stairs and around the corner, tucked deep in the labyrinth of rows was a section I rarely stepped into. The words *Horror & Occult* hung from a sign just above the only two rows that carried books of that nature.

There were hundreds to choose from; books on famous haunted houses, tales of psychic phenomenon and the unexplainable. Sandwiched between a reference book on legendary phantoms and an encyclopedia of monsters, there was a book simply titled *Ghosts.*

Flipping through its pages, several key words jumped out at me; words like, *poltergeists…unexplained phenomenon…* and*…possession.* I read no further. Instead, I tucked the book under my arm and headed upstairs to join Nick.

He already printed up a few newspaper articles, and when I jumped onto the workstation beside him, I found more. Together, we printed nearly everything we could find on the killer; from cradle to grave.

Within ten minutes, we were back downstairs and on our way out.

Halfway through the front door of the buildings, a high-pitched alarm erupted, nearly frightening me to death. I forgot to check the book out.

"It's okay," I told Nick. "Go and check on Rebecca and Logan. I'll be right out."

He hesitated, taking a look inside the library behind me. Concern was in his eyes when he looked back to me; he didn't want to leave.

"I'll be fine," I said. "Go on, I'll only be a minute."

"If you're not in that car in five minutes, I'm coming back."

"That's fine."

He kissed me, and I turned back into the library. The check-out desk was just to the right, and luckily, it was free of other patrons. A kind elderly woman waited to help me with a warm smile.

Her name was Edna, it was hand written on the name tag sticker pasted to her pink silk blouse to match her cheeks. She greeted me with a, "Hello dear," accepting the book and asking for my library card.

She swiped it like a credit card then stared at her monitor. She readjusted her paisley-framed glasses for a better read, then looked up at me.

By the look on her face, I knew I was identified.

"You're not *the* Cynthia Grazer, are you?" she asked.

I couldn't help but look over my shoulder as her words echoed through the library. Thankfully, no one heard her. "Yes I am."

Edna laughed, a loud belly jiggling laugh interrupted by a snort. "I've never met a writer! Oh, this is so exciting! Gosh, I just love your books!"

I forced a smile to be polite and thanked her for her compliment. Hoping she would detect I was in a hurry, I glanced at my watch, then looked toward the entrance of the building.

"Ghosts?" she asked, inspecting the book. "What's the matter, honey? Is your house haunted or something?" She laughed again, and I forced another smile.

"It's research," I told her, "for a book I'm working on."

"Oh you must tell me about it! Is it a horror? Wait a minute; you writers call it 'Dark Fantasies,' not horror. Is that what it is?"

"It's a work in progress," I answered, looking at my watch again. "I'm not exactly sure where it's going."

She scanned the bar code on the book and pecked away at her keyboard happily.

"I really admire you for what you did," she said.

I wasn't sure she was talking to me since the statement practically came from nowhere, but no one else was around…

"Excuse me?"

She looked up, taking her hands off the keyboard. "When you killed the man that killed your parents," she answered. "What was his name…Jason Majors or something wasn't it?"

Reluctantly, I answered. "Mason Bayer."

"That's right. Mason Bayer. What an evil, evil man."

Most of my fans knew of the incident, but no one ever questioned me about it at random. It was unsettling, and not only because of the current situation.

"Tell me something, did you look into his eyes?"

I frowned. "I beg your pardon."

The smile was gone from her face. "When you killed him, did you look into his eyes?"

My palms began to sweat, as I suddenly grew uncomfortable with the old woman and her strange questions. My mind was suddenly ordering me to run, but I couldn't.

"They say that the eyes are the window to the soul," she continued. "If you look into the eyes of a dying man, it's said his soul never reaches its destination. It goes right into you."

Run, stupid! It *is in her!*

"Then again, I haven't killed anyone to know for sure," she said then blurting out her laughter followed by another snort. "Maybe that's what your book should be about," she said. "It'll make a great story."

Though her smile returned, my relief didn't. "I'm sorry, but I have people waiting for me, and…"

"Sure, honey. I didn't mean to hold you up. The due date is on the back of the book." She handed it to me. "Good luck with your new story, dear. It was a pleasure to meet you."

I smiled. "Thank you."

I turned toward the automatic doors set just before freedom and quickly approached them. I was convinced that she would say something to push me over the edge completely; to convince me that It was inside of her.

But I made it out. Without looking back, I ran to the SUV and told Rebecca to drive quickly.

*

Back at Rebecca's we sat around the dinner table once again, the newspaper articles, freshly printed, scattered amongst all of us. We each took turns blurting out facts on the man who killed our parents.

To my surprise, the oldest newspaper article about Mason Bayer was dated thirty-six years before, and it was about his parents.

He was born into a family farm in Homestead, Florida; a pig farm to be exact. Owned by his father, James, and his mother, June, the farm supplied many of the local supermarkets with fresh pig meat, and the meat was in high demand. The Bayer farm was booming with success.

An outbreak of semolina suddenly killed dozens of people across the city, and it was all linked to the Bayer meat. The Department of Health declared the pig meat hygiene both poor and unsafe, and in a board of seven members, they forced the Bayer farm to close its doors and the animals were confiscated.

Two agents working for the DOH served James Bayer with the papers. They warned him that they would return in one week, at which point, he would have to surrender his farm. Adding insult to injury, just days afterwards, more than ten lawsuits were filed against the Bayer family farm.

Paula Carmona and Richard Decocq, the two DOH agents, returned in a week as they promised. What they found was something the newspaper described as "straight out of a horror movie."

Twenty to thirty pigs were scattered amongst the field, all disemboweled and rotting to the earth. Blood and intestines soaked the grass, the entire ranch, and the two farming vehicles owned by the family.

The inside of the farmhouse was in the same condition. The wooden floors were painted in blood, as were the walls and some of the ceiling. A pig was found slaughtered on the dining table, its underside sliced open, its intestines on the floor beside it. The tool used to slaughter the pig was a dull steak knife found next to the carcass, bound to the table in a drying puddle of blood.

Naturally, Agents Paula Carmona and Richard Decocq were shocked by what they saw, and before they could call on the help of the local police, they stumbled upon a more terrifying sight.

James Bayer hanged himself at the top of the staircase that led to the second floor. His body hung from a thick rope tied to an exposed ceiling truss, a chair on its side directly underneath him.

The authorities arrived shortly afterwards and the sickened agents were escorted out. Afterwards, James Bayer's body was cut down immediately, leaving the rest of the second floor to be discovered.

June Bayer was dead as well. They found her in the master bedroom, its walls a pure white and untouched with any blood at all. She was strangled with her own bed sheets.

It was immediately assumed that the seizure of his farm was too much for James Bayer to deal with. Finding no other way out of the trouble he was in, he killed himself after he killed his wife. By the advanced stages of decay in their skin, it was estimated that they were dead for more than five days. A mystery remained, though. Some experts said that the Bayers died before the pigs were slaughtered. The blood was fresh, and each of the carcasses had only begun to rot.

The second article, dated a few days later, told of a whole new chapter in the Bayer case. There was another room in the house that wasn't mentioned in the previous article. A second bedroom in the Bayer farm was found, its walls marked with blood, but not like the rest of the house was. There was illegible writing on the walls, senseless words incorrectly spelled were randomly smeared across the wooden walls. It was later discovered that the Bayers had a son. Mason. The bedroom was his, the blood was the pigs' and the writing was backwards English.

Suddenly, the authorities realized that James did not kill the pigs himself. Instead, they were slaughtered by his son. Enraged with the death of his parents, he killed each pig, taking his time to make sure they were dead, and he fled.

While the farm grounds were being cleaned up, a statewide manhunt was under way. But their efforts in searching for the boy proved more difficult than they anticipated. No one knew what Mason Bayer looked like, he had not been registered in any of the county's schools, it seemed almost as though there was no evidence to prove he even existed. Had it not been for the few pictures and his birth certificate later found at the barn, the authorities would never have made the conclusion. Mason Bayer was only ten years old at the time, and it was assumed he was not of sound and mind. In fact, the only other thing anyone knew about the boy other than his age was that he was capable of slaughtering pigs all on his own – with a dulled knife.

Months passed, the mess at the Bayer farm was cleaned up, and the manhunt was called off with no trace of the boy. It was assumed he was dead. For a while, the Bayer name slipped into silence until eventually, the neighboring people forgot them all together.

On a summer morning, eighteen years later, two bodies were found dead in their homes, one clear across town from the other. A woman sleeping alone in her bed was slain in the middle of the night, and an old man was murdered in his kitchen. Both were killed in the same fashion; sliced across the belly and disemboweled. Words were found at each of the sights; on the wall above the woman's bed, and on the floor next to the man's body. The words: *ENO* and *OWT*. Their names: Paula Carmona and Richard Decocq.

Before the authorities could make the connection, a third body was found. Mark Shaw was murdered in his bed, his wife sleeping directly beside him. She claimed she heard nothing throughout the entire night, even when the murderer wrote the word *EERHT* beside the body.

All three victims were retired board members of the DOH. All of them were on the board of seven that forced the Bayer farm to close.

The chief of police, aided by a pair of highly qualified detectives, put a task force together, issuing the remaining four retired board members round the clock protection. The two men in charge of the team were Detective Todd Grazer and Hector Corona and both of them knew that this was probably the work of the missing boy, now twenty-eight years old, and with a taste for vengeance.

One by one, the remaining members were killed mysteriously; right under their noses.

Mercedes Rodic - *ROUF* - killed while showering.

Michael O'Neill - *EVIF* - killed while napping in his living room.

Patricia Greer - *XIS* - killed while working late in her office at Florida International University.

All of them were disemboweled over the course of a week, but the killer was never even seen.

With only one board member left, the team of officials were in a frenzy to catch Mason Bayer. While trying to break into the second story window of the seventh board member's house, he was shot in the leg, but not by my father or any of the cops. The man, remaining unnamed, was aware of Mason's plans and protected himself and his family by purchasing a gun and waiting patiently for Mason to come. He was successful, and Mason was arrested.

Escorted by my father and Hector, Mason was given a psyche evaluation then sent to a high security mental facility for observation. It was there that specialists discovered there was no real hidden meaning behind the backwards writing. Mason Bayer suffered from severe dyslexia.

The doctor in charge of his care at the facility was under pressure by the officials to make Mason talk. The eighteen years he was missing remained a mystery, and everyone wanted to know what he was up to; where he was hiding, what he learned. Nothing was discovered about him, though. Mason escaped the institution before they had a chance to question him on anything.

None of the articles went into exact detail of how Mason made his escape from the maximum-security institution. I don't think anyone knew how he simply walked out without being detected.

The next article picked up right where the preceding left off. Upon learning of Mason's escape, the county officials set up surveillance crews and snipers all around the seventh board member's house. They assumed that Mason would return to the unnamed Department of Health agent's house late that night. None of them had any idea that the killer now had new plans. None of them knew that Mason Bayer, one of the most elusive killers in Miami's history, was on his way to kill the man who put him away. None of them knew.

Except one man.

"Lieutenant William Kux arrived to find Detective Todd Grazer and Detective Hector Corona dead, alongside their family and friends," Rebecca read. "To his surprise, he found Mason Bayer dead as well, killed by the six children the murderer left as orphans."

The last few articles were mostly about us. We read through only the first two, each chronologically detailing our recovery process and health status. They proved too difficult to get through, and we stopped reading when a list of victims Mason Bayer killed was found at the end of an article. Among the names, twelve all together, six were of our parents. They were listed as such:

Detective Hector Corona - *NEVES*

Detective Todd Grazer - *THGIE*

Mary Grazer - *ENIN*

Mayra Joules - *NET*

Samuel Sheyer - *NEVELE*

Tamara Sheyer - *EVLEWT*

Nothing is As it Seems

By six that evening, I showered and found my self growing increasingly exhausted by the minute. Rebecca insisted I sleep, claiming my body needed the rest, and she allowed me the use of her daughter's room. Leaving her, Nick and Logan in the dining room, I did as I was told and laid on Charlene's twin sized bed after I locked the door to her room.

I smuggled the book on ghosts in with me; not my usual bedside reading, but it was bound to be helpful. With the aid of the soft light from the lamp on her night table, I flipped through the pages and filled my brain with facts of the unknown.

The first thing I learned was the difference between a spirit and a ghost. A spirit is the essence of a person who has passed, but has found their way to their final destination. They may pop in every now and then to say "Hello," or to give visual comfort to those left behind, but they always return to where they're from. A ghost has not found their way to the afterlife. Ghosts haunt houses, linger in the areas they were most attracted to when they were alive. Most ghosts may not realize they are dead, therefore have no clue as to where they should be going. In the world of the occult, it almost made perfect sense. Ghosts exist because their life, more than likely, was cut short by murder, an accident, or any other number of unnatural deaths. Most of them can communicate with the living in some fashion, and nearly all of them had some unfinished business that kept them bound to Earth, and until their business was completed, they would not leave.

The first few pages of the book explained methods in which to rid a house of ghosts; comply with its needs. Ask what it wants, and do it. In the end, the ghost will more than likely leave.

But what if the ghost wanted to kill you? How do you stop it then?

Of course, I didn't read the book from cover to cover, but it didn't appear as though the pages held an answer for our situation.

Ghosts can gain power while they exist, the book explained in the chapter labeled *POSSESSION.* Taking over a human body to perform its own tasks was common amongst the community of poltergeists, and it could happen without anyone's knowledge. It was possible that the invader lie dormant inside a human with no traces until it chose to expose itself. There were two downsides for a ghost to take over a body, though. The first, it takes much of the entity's energy to take over a body, leaving it weak and venerable. It needs a place to rest; an immobile body that it can recuperate in if it chose to possess another active being.

Luis… He was in a coma, and as I read the book, I feared that Mason was using his body to recoup. According to the book, a ghost like Mason would take over one of us, do what it needed to do, then use Luis' body to rest. I prayed it wasn't true because the "side-effect" of a resting place was explained right afterwards.

It was the second downside of possession. A stage called transmogrification can take place if a ghost has invaded a body for too long. Like Angela explained, the soul of the person of whom the ghost has invaded is lost in conflict during possession. If the conflict is too grand or too long, the ghost can become one with the body, forever controlling it as though it were its own. In this case, physical characteristics of the ghost will begin to show in the body. In short the person's face and body will completely change to resemble the ghost itself. Though the book explained that it wasn't likely to happen, there were several documented cases in which it did.

I stopped reading, the facts too much for me to digest all at once. There seemed to be so many possibilities in the war we found ourselves in, and none of them made me hopeful.

The sun began to set, and I tried my hardest to forget about Mason, possession and transmogrification. I thought about my son, Max, and my niece, Charlene. They were safe in New York, and that was the only thought that gave me comfort. I thought of the unborn child I carried in my uterus, and I knew, I was certain, I would end this war myself if it meant protecting the lives of the children. They had nothing to do with this, and over my dead body would Mason reach them.

Eventually, I managed to fall asleep. My senses were altered, though. I heard every noise in the room, felt the glow of the light that shined beside me, and I was ready to defend myself should Mason find his way into the room while I slept.

*

There was darkness when I opened my eyes; night had fallen, and the lamp was turned off while I slept. There was no time to question who cut the light though, I heard a breath coming from somewhere inside the room the moment I woke.

It was a soft breath, whimpering with the slightest sound of a voice.

I held my own breath, suddenly feeling venerable and exposed. Somewhere in the abyss of darkness, someone was watching me while I slept, watching me as I tried to lie still hoping that whoever it was wouldn't detect my fear. But my body began to tremble, and my heartbeat was loud enough for anyone to hear.

The noise of someone taking in a soft breath filled the room again, followed by a heavy exhale masked with a long, sighing moan.

Then, my bed moved. At the end of the bed, by my exposed feet, the bed angled downward as though it were being pressed. Whoever was in the room just sat down next to me.

That was when I heard the whisper that seared through my very soul and into the pit of my very stomach. Concealed in the darkness, behind the shadows of the room, the voice touched me, causing a reflexive movement no matter how much I tried to remain still.

"Cynthia," it called.

I sat up, a scream forming in my throat and nearly escaping from my lips as the adrenaline took hold of my body. The urgency in which I moved caused my visitor alarm, and it was then that I saw his face.

"It's just me," Nick said quickly and quietly. His hands were on my shoulders as he spoke, but I didn't feel his grasp. My fear wouldn't allow me. "It's just me."

And it was just him. I knew it simply by looking into his eyes. The warmth of his hands on me covered me with a blanket of comfort so suddenly, it was nothing more than reassuring that it was *just* him. There were no ghosts at that moment, no death, nothing more than just him. Just us.

I cried, finding I could do nothing more. One by one, all my fears came together in a bundle of emotions, and as I confessed each one to Nick; my fear of death, my fear for the life inside me, my fear of the entire, unbelievable situation, he did nothing but listen. He didn't fill me with hopes that everything was going to be okay, nor did he tell me lies simply to calm the plague of fright; he simply listened. Partly allowing me to exorcise the thoughts that were circling my head, and partly because he was just as scared as I was.

He brought my head to his shoulder, holding me in his arms the way he used to when we were first married. The security he offered was more than enough to sooth my anger, to wash my pain away, but I wanted more. I wanted to *be* with my husband as though it would make me feel everything was right with the world.

I took hold of his face in my hands and forced his lips to mine. He was caught off guard, not expecting the advance, but it excited him - and me.

All the petty things I didn't care for were of no worries to me at that moment; his beard stubble, the cigarette still lingering in his breath, it was all obsolete as he gently pushed me down onto the bed. My arms were around him and his around mine in a tangle so gripping, I swore I would never let him go.

The situation at hand brought us to this. All the talk of death, of losing another loved one, it lead to one explosive moment where all our worries and needs combined in an emotional mess – the result of which was intoxicating.

I wrapped my legs around his as he kissed my forehead, my cheeks, my chin, then moved in toward my ear. It was my weak spot, and he knew it. Whenever the moment rose, he went straight for my ear, knowing that, not only would it entice me, but all foreplay was unnecessary afterwards. On nights I claimed to have a headache, he went for the ear.

I arched my back, my breast rubbing against his chest as he breathed into my ear – his breath reaching my spinal cord and settling around my waist. He inhaled rapidly, his breath growing heavier with every second, and I knew he was ready.

I reached for him, his lips still in my ear as he said;

"You smell just like your fucking mother did."

*

I pushed him off and jumped off the bed, moving to the night table, and switching on the light in a single, swift, movement.

But there was no one. Nick wasn't with me, but I knew what I experienced was not a dream. It appeared as though I was alone, but I wasn't. Mason was with me; I could feel him.

I ran to the door and panicked when the knob didn't move. After realizing that I myself locked it before going to bed, I quickly opened it and hurried into the hallway. It was just as dark as the room was, but I didn't care. Just outside the door though, someone was waiting for me.

I nearly collapsed to the floor after we collided into each other, the fear robbing me of the voice to scream. Logan caught me just as I fell toward him.

"Cynthia," he said, sounding as scared as I was.

His voice gave me the strength to stand on my own, and I could have hugged him at that moment. "He's here," I said, between breaths. "He's in the room."

"I know," he whispered. "I felt him."

"Where's Nick and Rebecca?" I wanted to wake them up and run out of the house.

"Rebecca's in her room and Nick is in the guest…"

I didn't give him time to finish. Rebecca's room was at the end of the hall and Nick was in the room directly next to it. Both doors were open, and I ran toward them.

The door to Rebecca's room slammed shut just before me, inches from my face, and completely on its own. The guest room's door did the same directly afterwards.

I screamed for them, a cry escaping as I beat on both doors with my already injured hands. I called for Nick and Rebecca, but the voice that called for me electrified my body and filled my veins with terror.

It was the voice of a demon, and it came from behind me. When I turned to face It, my back against Rebecca's door, I saw that it came from Logan.

He stood in the center of the hall, the soft light from Charlene's room lighting only the right side of his face. Its cold stare was the same one I saw in Luis.

"Cynthia!" I heard Rebecca yell from behind the door. She was awake and trying to get out of the room.

Nick followed shortly afterwards.

But I didn't answer either of them. My eyes remained securely on Logan.

"No matter what you read or learn of me," It said through grit teeth, "you won't win."

"Cynthia, are you alright?" Nick called, pounding on his door.

"He's here!" I yelled back.

"When you conceived your rotten baby," It continued, "it was me you were fucking. Not Nick."

It was trying to scare me, weaken my defenses by hitting the soft spots. It only angered me instead.

There was a loud bang on Nick's door as though he were trying to break his way out.

"You and your mother both taste the same," It said, "like the whores you are."

"Fuck you," I said to It. "We know how to stop you."

Another bang on Nick's door.

It smiled at me, amused with my strength. "You think you can stop me? Go ahead."

Another bang.

Its smile turned into a snarl. "Kill Logan right now and save me trouble of killing this pathetic, cock-sucking pig the way I killed your parents."

Another bang and I heard the wood crack.

It took a step toward me. "Did you know that a pig lives for five minutes after its been disemboweled? It's the same with humans, gives them the privilege of seeing my work before they die."

Another crash, and the door swung open. Nick ran out of the room with an aluminum baseball bat in his hands, and he charged Logan immediately.

It took a step back, surprise falling over his face. I watched as Nick swung the bat upwards, and like eighteen years before, I screamed for him to be careful as he approached the killer.

Logan fell back, screaming for help as the bat came down at him. He covered his face with his arms, his body immediately cramping into the fetal position on the floor.

"Nick, stop!" I yelled, running toward them.

Behind me, Rebecca opened her door and ran out of the room.

The bat came inches from Logan before Nick stopped his swing. He took a breath, holding the bat close to his side as he took a step back.

The three of us watched Logan tremble on the floor, looking up at us as confused as he was when he woke at Angela's.

"What the hell are you doing?" he asked Nick.

"He's gone," Rebecca said.

"Who's gone?" Logan asked. "Mason? He was here?"

I turned to Rebecca. "Are you sure?"

Nick walked into the dining room, turning on the living room light as he passed. He returned with paper and a pen. Without a word, he put the bat down long enough to write on the paper, using the coffee table for support. After inspecting it, he handed it to Rebecca.

Logan stood from the floor nervously. "Was he in me?"

Rebecca inspected her signature, then handed the paper to me.

"Was he in me?" Logan repeated. Still, no one answered.

Cynthia Sheyer

It was not in any of the three of us, but one person remained to be tested. I handed the pen and paper to Logan.

He accepted them with a shaking hand and slowly walked to the coffee table. He was sweating, his breath short and uneven. Hesitating to write, he looked to the bat in Nick's hand before glancing up at the rest of us. "Was he in me?" he asked again.

"Just write, Logan," Nick demanded. "It doesn't matter."

He nearly cried as his concentration fell to the paper before him. He wrote quickly, desperately wanting to close his eyes to not see the results.

I think we all felt the same way.

His back stiffened as he frowned at his signature and my heart skipped a beat. Suddenly, Logan stood from the couch, pushing the coffee table over with anger, the page falling to the floor and sliding across the living room.

"Kill me!" he yelled to Nick.

Rebecca and I locked arms with each other and moved away from

Logan as Nick held the bat ready to swing again.

"Kill me, now!" He was crying, but desperate to rid himself of the demon inside. "It's not me! Do it!"

But Nick couldn't. He took a step back as Logan approached him, screaming at the top of his breath to be killed.

Rebecca cried out and turned her head from the sight, realizing the paper was at our feet and turned up to see the signatures herself.

"Kill me, please!"

Nick clenched his jaw and swung upwards again. He was prepared to kill his own brother.

"Wait!" Rebecca yelled suddenly, picking the page up to show it to Nick. "It's not in him. Look!"

Nick took the paper then glanced at Logan.

"What do you mean?" Logan asked, trembling. "It's backwards."

"No, it's not," Nick said.

Logan Sheyer was written directly underneath my name. It was a fact that Logan was possessed, but not at that moment. Mason used his power to confuse Logan, like we were warned he would.

Logan fell to the couch, weeping helplessly as Nick threw the bat to the floor with anger. Somewhere, Mason was laughing at us. He brought us to the point of killing one another without his even being around, and that only left the wonder of what else he could do to us to make us suffer more that we already had. But he wasn't around. He was probably resting inside Luis, recouping for his next possession…

"Look for me in Logan," he told me through Luis. "Then I will look for you."

Friday, June 12th; A Long Day

Hurricane Alida picked up strength. Now a category two, it was brewing stronger in the gulf, heading toward Florida at seven miles an hour promising severe damage once it hit land in less than two days.

But the real storm was taking place inside Rebecca's house. Logan separated himself from the rest of us. He claimed he was frightened that Mason wasn't done with him yet, but I think it was because he couldn't stand to look at Nick, embarrassed by what happened.

The somber attitudes were all around. There was no conversation sprouting, nor was there a smile on any of our faces. Nick kept the bat by his side, waiting for Mason to appear again so that we could make our next move.

It was clear that, at least, Nick was ready for him.

At almost five in the morning, Rebecca found the courage to walk back into her bedroom on her own. It was two hours since Mason graced us with his presence, and she finally decided to change out of her nightwear and into a pair of jeans and a tee shirt. Afterwards, she put on a pot of coffee and made us all buttered toast. She apologized for her lack of hospitality by admitting she was in no mood for cooking a full breakfast.

It didn't matter. None of us had much of an appetite.

"I'm sorry," Logan said, almost to himself. He was seated on the love seat, and it was the first thing he said since he asked Nick tried to kill him.

"For what?" Nick asked.

He shrugged. "For whatever it was he made me do or say…"

"It wasn't you," I told him, a phrase that was becoming all too familiar.

"Still," he said, "I'm sorry."

The telephone rang, suddenly. Rebecca answered it quickly, frowning for just a second when she glanced at her watch. It was barely six in the morning, and an early call was never good news.

It was a quick conversation, one that consisted of two "yes's," and a single "okay." She hung the phone up and told us that it was Doctor Morrison.

"What did he want?" Nick asked.

"For us to get to the hospital as soon as we can," she said then looked at me. "He said it's about Luis."

*

Morrison was in the hospital's lobby. He was talking to a nurse, reviewing a file of some sort, and the moment we saw him, his conversation ended.

"Let's talk in my office," he said, then led us through the corridors until we reached the place he first told us of Luis' and Jo's condition earlier in the week.

I didn't realize how much I despised the room until we walked back in.

He closed the door as we took our seats on the couches, and we watched him as he walked behind the desk. "How are you all?" he asked.

"Holding up, I guess," Nick answered.

"What's wrong with Luis?" I asked him. I wasn't in the mood for the formality of small talk. He called us to talk about my brother, and naturally, I was anxious to hear his news.

He cleared his throat and readjusted his glasses. Opening a file folder that was sitting atop his desk, no doubt Luis', he revised it before beginning. "When your brother was brought in, his chances of surviving the coma were fifty-fifty. That was six days ago. I'm afraid his condition has not improved. In fact, it's getting worse."

"How so?" Rebecca asked.

He looked at the file again. "His breathing is regulated, but his heart beat has slowed and his brain waves have nearly depleted. The only thing that's keeping Mr. Grazer alive is the life support machines he's hooked up to."

I didn't lose control of my emotions the way the good doctor probably expected me to, but I was biting my lip to prevent doing so. "Is there anything else you could do for him?"

He shook his head clasping his hands on top of the file. "We've tried everything, Cynthia. The reason I called you here today is because you might want to consider cutting off the life support..."

"No," I said immediately.

But he was prepared for my response. I'm sure he heard it many times before.

"Cynthia, I'm sorry to have to tell you this, but frankly, your brother is already dead. His chances of coming out of this coma are..."

"I don't care. He stays on the machines until I say so."

"Maybe you should think about this," Rebecca said softly.

"Not now," I told her.

"His insurance will no longer pay for the cost of keeping him alive," Morrison said.

"I don't care. I have enough money to pay for it myself."

Morrison took a breath before continuing. "I understand your position, believe me, I do. But Luis hardly has his own thoughts anymore, and..."

"Can I see him?" I asked.

Morrison sighed, taking off his glasses and tossing them onto the desk. "I'll take you to him, but I have to warn you, he doesn't look healthy."

"I don't care. I want to see him."

He told the others to stay in his office, that he would return once he walked me to Luis' room.

"There's something I think you should know," he said to me once we were in the hall. "There are a couple of detectives who've come to ask me some questions recently."

"I know," I answered. "Detectives Lopez and Santiago. They've been following us all around town."

"They're saying that once Luis wakes up, they plan to arrest him for murder."

"I know all this, Morrison. They think Luis killed her, but he didn't."

We entered the ICU and walked through the traffic without notice. It was understandable that the doctor didn't take much notice in the crowd anymore, but neither did I.

"It's another reason I think you should cut the machines," he said, stopping me in my tracks.

"What do you mean?"

Morrison turned to me, his face appearing somewhat sympathetic. "Given his medical condition, Luis will not survive the pressure of a trial or going to jail."

"I can't cut the machines, Morrison."

We reached Luis' room.

"Think about it," he said. "It may be the best thing for him…for all of you."

I didn't want to do it, but my reason was not what he thought. What with everything we've been through and learned in the past week, I began to grow comfortable with death. I wasn't afraid of it, and I thought I was prepared for losing another person close to me. My reasons in not cutting the life support were my own.

*

Morrison was right. Luis didn't look healthy at all. His face lost the fullness it once held; his cheeks caved, the area around his eyes grew dark, and though the bruises began to fade, they were still detectable amongst the paling skin.

Still, I didn't grow emotional over his sight. My reason in requesting the visit was not to see him one last time before I decided on flipping the switch. In fact, I had no intention on visiting Luis at all.

I came to visit Mason.

He was in there somewhere, resting. I was certain of it.

I closed the door to his room, keeping an eye on the body in case Mason decided to show himself. Slowly approaching the bed, I looked at my brother through different eyes; there was no memory of the good times we had, of his smile or of his voice that I missed so much. My brother was lost somewhere beneath the exterior, Mason made that clear the last time I visited.

Flipping the switch would kill them both. I knew I could end it right then, but what if it didn't work? Angela said the kill had to be quick, and I didn't think Luis' heart would stop the moment the machines turned off. Mason would jump out before he was trapped. Then what? I just saved him the trouble of killing the second victim.

I wasn't going to play his game. I was smarter than that.

My anger was beginning to boil. Watching Luis' body and knowing what Mason was doing fueled the fire in my veins. There was no fear to be found in me at that moment. Only rage.

"Leave him alone, you son of a bitch," I said through my teeth, inches from Luis' face.

I waited for It to respond, to sit up on the bed and lash out with more grotesque words. But nothing happened. Amongst the silence, the only noise heard was that of the heart monitor, and I took a deep breath.

Maybe I was wrong. Maybe Mason wasn't there at all. Why would Mason hide inside a body that was dying, anyway? Would it be too risky? He could inadvertently trap himself.

The anger subsided and I felt the sorrow begin to build. In a mixture of frustration and distress, I nearly began to cry.

That was when I decided to leave the room. I turned and headed toward the door, contemplating the idea of telling Morrison to kill my brother.

Flip the switch, I would tell him, and end my brother's suffering.

Halfway out of the room though, something happened that made me reconsider once again. The television suspended from the ceiling turned on suddenly, the sound blaring loud enough to wake the dead.

I glanced back at the bed. Luis was still asleep, the remote control on the chair by his side. Mason *was* inside of him, mocking me with his power and begging me to do something about it.

I planned to, but cutting off the machines was not the answer. It couldn't have been that easy.

*

I told the others that I wanted to leave, and it didn't appear as though they had an objection. We walked through the building's lobby, quickly approaching the automatic doors, but on our way out, we had the privilege of running into the people who were watching us.

Detectives Maria Lopez and Raul Santiago were on their way in as we walked out of the hospital. There was no way to avoid them, they spotted us at the same time that we spotted them.

"Good morning," Maria said, stopping us just outside the building.

"You're up to no good early today," Logan returned.

"I'd watch myself if I were you," Raul warned.

"Is there something you need with us?"

Maria and Raul exchanged amused glances. "We thought we'd see what you were up to," Maria explained. "You all left the house in a hurry this morning, so we figured we'd stop in and ask Morrison a few questions about your visit, if you must know."

"My brother is dying, Detective," I said as thunder echoed above. "We're here discussing whether or not we should terminate his life…if you must know."

"Did you?"

"That's none of your business."

"We'll find out right now through Morrison," Raul sneered, combing his thick hair with his hand. "He's been very cooperative with our investigation."

"Is there anything else we can do for you?" Rebecca asked.

"As a matter of fact, there is," Maria answered. "Until this investigation is over, or until Mr. Grazer wakes up, I'm going to issue round the clock observation on him. From now on, before you visit, you will need to let us know…"

"Give me a break!" Logan said, slapping his thighs. "You think he's just going to get up and walk out of here? We just told you he's dying."

"He's still the prime suspect in the murder of Joanna Corona, and until we get some answers, the investigation will proceed as such."

"Why don't you go look for some real murderers," Logan growled. "For your own sake, leave us alone."

"Logan…" Rebecca said, fearing he would leak the truth of our situation. If he did, there was no telling what the detectives would do.

Raul frowned and stepped closer to Logan. "I'm sorry, Mr. Sheyer. Was that a threat?"

He gnawed his jaw, his face flushing with anger. "Take it any way you want. I'm telling you that you should leave it alone. You don't want to get mixed up in what is really happening."

"Logan, that's enough."

"Tell me what's happening, then," Maria said. "Tell me why we should leave it alone."

"Look, we're all under a lot of pressure right now," Nick said before Logan could bury us any further. "My brother has not gotten much rest and we just found out that Luis is dying. We can play this game later."

Maria and Raul looked at each other again. We watched as she nodded to him, ordering him to release the stare he placed on Logan.

"I'm not sure I believe you," she told Nick. "But rest assured, we'll get to the bottom of whatever it is you think is really happening."

They turned and proceeded inside the hospital. Rebecca and Nick both looked to Logan angrily.

"Don't say we didn't warn you!" he yelled to them before they were out of hearing range.

Nick shoved Logan back, "Shut the hell up! You want to get us all arrested?"

Logan didn't answer. He looked to the rain falling over the parking lot. Rebecca and Nick were clearly angry with him for saying what said, but I wasn't. If I had half the nerve he did, I would have told them myself.

Jump

"Maybe you should reconsider," Rebecca said. "At least for Luis' sake."

Hunger had not yet struck, but going back home was not something the four of us looked forward to. Instead, we jumped to a small diner across the street from the hospital after our run in with the detectives. I knew forgetting our problems was not possible, but I thought we could have a cup of coffee and hang out the way we used to when we were all alive. It seemed, however, the only thing we could talk about was Luis' life, or lack thereof. Both Logan and Rebecca sided with Morrison, they thought I should kill the machines, but Nick, being the faithful husband, supported my decision.

"I won't reconsider," I told her, not bothering to explain any further.

We figured the diner was a safe place to seek refuge for the time being. It didn't appear as though the small restaurant was a favorite amongst the community; bright red booths lined the walls, and small circular tables ran down the center of the room, and all were empty. There was no one else in sight, and it was better that way.

We were seated at the booth furthest from the entrance in the far left corner of the room. After Dolly, our extremely robust waitress, served a round of water, she jiggled away beneath her tight uniform, leaving us with the menus. They remained untouched.

"Why?" Logan asked me. He couldn't comprehend my decision to keep Luis alive. "I know it hurts, but if it were Nick, I'd end his suffering."

"It's not that simple," I told him, watching as Dolly sat a young couple in love in the booth behind us. They walked in arm in arm, smiles across their worry free faces, and I wanted so much to feel like they did.

"Why isn't it that simple?" Rebecca asked.

I sighed. "Because I'm not so sure Luis is dying." Naturally, they were confused by my response, so I continued by explaining what I learned in the book. A ghost needs to rest between possessions, and Luis just may have been the resting place for the ghoul that was after us.

"More of a reason to do it," Logan said.

But I shook my head.

"Ya'll ready to order?" Dolly asked, suddenly stepping to our table and snapping us back into reality.

"What's your special?" Nick asked without meeting her mascara caked eyes.

She snapped her gum between her blood red lips then dryly responded, "The Monster Mash. That's a monster burger with American and Swiss cheeses, two strips of bacon, lettuce, tomato, onion, pickle on the side and an order of mashed potatoes."

"We'll have four of those."

"How would you like your burgers?"

Nick sighed. "Well done. All of them."

"Something to…"

"No!" He looked up at her, and as the young couple frowned in his direction, he took a deep breath. He didn't mean to snap at her, but we wanted the privacy. It was the reason why we came to the desolate diner in the first place. "That'll be all," he said, much calmer this time.

Dolly roller her eyes, collected the menus and bounced away.

"All I'm saying is, if you're right, if Mason is hiding in Luis, wouldn't cutting the life support kill them both?"

I shook my head again. "What if Mason is making it seem as though Luis is dying? Angela said the soul is lost in conflict during possession, and I don't want to risk losing Luis if I don't have to. Luis lives until this is over. I don't care if it takes a year."

As though Rebecca finally realized my mind was not going to be changed, she said, "I still think you should leave town."

I sighed, watching Dolly reappear with two waters for the booth behind us. "Rebecca, that's not going to solve anything, you know that."

"Besides," Nick added. "Those detectives won't allow it."

"Screw those sons of bitches!" Logan said, his voice filled with anger. "They're a couple of dumbasses who have no clue as to what's going on!"

"Excuse me," Dolly said from behind him.

Logan turned, surprised to see her standing so close.

"I'm going to ask you to lower your voice, or ya'll will have to leave."

Logan nodded, his face flushing. "I'm sorry."

The waitress nodded.

"If those detectives keep digging," Logan continued, "they may get in Mason Bayer's way. They'll..."

"Mason Bayer?" Dolly asked, crossing her arms over her large chest. Logan didn't realize that she hadn't left. "Why, that's a name I haven't heard in such a long..." She stopped, frowning as her eyes suddenly dashed back and forth. Her face turned somewhere between excitement and shock when she realized... "Oh my God. Ya'll are those people, aren't ya? Those kids who killed him like twenty years ago, I remember!"

Now, that never happened, not after the first three years. The four of us looked at each other, recognized by a fan and trying to find the proper way to handle it. Since I had some experience with that sort of situation, they turned to me.

"Yes," I answered with a smile.

Then Dolly smiled, exposing her pearly white teeth. "This is so exciting! Can I ask you something stupid?"

"Sure."

"How did ya'll do it?"

I smiled again, not quite sure that I wanted to answer her.

But before I even had a chance… "Never mind that. Tell me something' else," she said. "Did you look into his eyes?"

I locked onto hers, my pulse rising.

"What?" Rebecca asked.

And just as I wished she hadn't asked anything at all, the waitress spoke again. Though in merely a whisper, it was easy to tell that her voice was not her own. It was the demon's.

"Fucking pigs," It said.

*

The four of us scrambled from the booth. Nick and Logan both jumping away from the waitress as Rebecca and I followed directly behind them.

But it was Nick that It had its eye on. It glared at him, ignoring Rebecca and I as we ran from the booth swiftly moving toward the front of the restaurant. We called for Nick and Logan to do the same.

The young couple turned to watch the commotion and Rebecca told them to move as well.

Finally, Logan took hold of Nick and led him in our direction; toward the front door. But he didn't succeed because Mason intervened.

It pushed Logan, a blow with both arms straight to his chest. Logan flew backwards onto the table, crushing the glasses of water underneath his back. Rebecca and I screamed for him as he slid off the table and onto the floor.

"Someone do something!" I yelled as Logan clutched his chest, gasping for air.

The only cook in the diner emerged from the kitchen to join the three busboys who were already watching the fight. They did nothing. The young couple ran from their booth and made it to the front door before us and suddenly, we were alone.

Dolly smiled and turned to Nick.

Thankfully, he wasn't frozen by Its stare like the rest of us were. He acted quickly and stepped between It and Logan.

It watched Nick pull Logan off the floor, and I screamed for him to hurry. The demon stood close enough to whisper in his ear, and I couldn't bear to think it would make a move.

But It didn't. While Logan struggled to stand, doubling over in pain, It simply watched with a crooked smile.

Nick forced Logan into a run, and the four of us headed toward the door in a hurry. Glancing over my shoulder, it didn't appear as though Dolly was following us, but we continued running anyway.

Spilling into the parking lot, our pace continued toward Rebecca's car. She was already digging for her keys.

The young couple stared at us as we passed them, their faces filled with curiosity. It occurred to me then that they would probably call the cops, and if Detectives Lopez and Santiago received word of this…

"Open the door!" Nick ordered, Logan still slumped on his shoulders.

Rebecca did as she was ordered and held the back door open wide. As Nick shoved Logan into the back seat, I glanced back at the diner in case Dolly worked her way toward us.

"Get in!" Rebecca ordered, opening the driver's seat door. Before the rest of us could move though, before any of us had a chance to smell safety, someone called us from directly behind.

"Excuse me," the voice said.

We turned quickly. It was the young man from the couple, his girlfriend approaching him from behind. She looked confused by her boyfriend's actions.

Nick stepped before him, "What?"

The young man grabbed Rebecca suddenly, twisting her arm. In a single second, the keys dropped from her hand, the young man's girlfriend screamed for him to stop, and he turned to Nick with the same crooked smile.

"Where you headed," It asked.

Nick punched him in the face, sending him to the ground.

I grabbed the keys when Rebecca was released. As the young woman cursed us for breaking her lover's nose, we piled into the car; Rebecca in the back seat, Nick in the passenger's and I at the wheel.

Without looking back, I peeled out of the parking lot and sped onto the main road, leaving the diner and Mason far behind.

*

"My God, he's everywhere!" Rebecca cried nervously.

Logan coughed more, his breath finally returning, as did the color in his face.

"He can be in anyone at any time," Nick followed, somewhat dazed.

I only prayed the police weren't called. Luckily, everyone escaped unharmed, except for the young man. They probably memorized our license plate and could give a detailed description of each of us.

Nick opened the glove box and quickly rummaged through it. "Does anyone have a pen?" he asked when his search turned up nothing.

"Why?" Rebecca asked.

"We're taking the test."

"Now?"

"Yes, now."

"Maybe I should pull over," I said, but I was quickly shot down.

"No. He could be in one of us right now!"

Logan coughed again then took a deep breath.

"And if he is, what would you do, Nick?" Rebecca asked. "You're gonna kill one of us here? In the car?"

He found a pen, forfeiting an answer to her question. He scribbled his name on the palm of his hand just as we came to a stoplight. As soon as he wrote the first letter of his name, the rest of us were relieved on at least one aspect of our fear. There were three more to go.

He handed the pen to me.

The anxiety from the pressure of the test didn't settle well with my stomach. Nausea fell upon me the several times we already took the damned thing.

"Nick, I don't think this…"

"Take the fucking pen, Cynthia!" He wasn't playing games – and it was evident he wasn't going to let it slide. Taking a breath, then holding the pen out for me once more, he said, "Please."

I looked at his incredibly steady hand, then to the others. Their neutral looks left me with no choice. I took a breath, then accepted the pen.

The test. It was such a ridiculous notion. Write backwards and we'll kill you. I couldn't help but wonder what would have happened if I *did* write backwards. But I never did see what happened. Before I even wrote the first letter, I blacked out.

*

I was closed out of my outside world and enveloped in an abyss of black. I wasn't scared, nor did I panic. With the sudden change came a euphoric feeling as though I were floating amongst the darkness rather than walking within it.

I could hear sounds like voices, though in mere whispers like thoughts echoing through the mind. Only, it wasn't simply words I heard. The voices were screaming.

Suddenly, the darkness gave way to an abandoned field. An ocean of tall grass stretched out before me, and the night's sky filled the air with a gentle, calming breeze. I stood before this field, amazed by the serenity and hypnotized by the glimmering stars in the sky. I didn't question how I got there, nor did I fear for my life at any given moment. Not even when I turned to see the barn behind me.

Then I realized that the screaming voices were not human at all. They were coming from somewhere inside the farmhouse. They were coming from *pigs.*

The wooden two-story house rested just yards away from a pigpen; it was empty.

Without taking a step or without even thinking about it, I was inside. I could see stairs, but not much else. The house was dark, only the moon to illuminate what its beams would reach.

I heard the pig again, somewhere behind me. It squealed; a high-pitched noise that seemed to be a cry from pain or joy, I couldn't tell which. Until I turned and saw it.

Blood spilled across the floor from the dinner table. I watched the large pig squeal again as the naked man wrestled with it. Struggling to keep the pig still, he didn't notice my presence, and since his backside was toward me, I was conscious to remain absolutely quiet.

He cursed at the pig, his arms jabbing at it, though I couldn't see with what. More blood spilled, and finally, the swine let out its final squeal.

"Fucking pig," Mason said then took a deep breath. He stared at his kill, admiring the open belly of the pig. His back tightened suddenly, and his breath grew rapid as the sound of slapping skin filled the room.

I wanted to close my eyes, disgusted by the sight, but I couldn't. I was being forced to watch.

More screams filled the air suddenly. They were louder now, and they were human. Three different voices all hollering together, but each as recognizable as the one echoing with it. Rebecca's scream was the loudest.

Mason's arm continued to thrust at his pelvis, his breath becoming even shorter as he grunted viciously over the pig. He let out his final grunt, finishing his repulsive ceremony, then Mason turned to me, his hand on his groin. It was engorged with pig's blood and semen.

I heard Nick scream my name. He sounded desperate, even scared.

"This is for you," It told me, extending It's soiled hand toward me. "Open your eyes."

*

The screams came into full audio suddenly, and as my eyes refocused on reality, I screamed as well.

I was at the wheel and the car was speeding on the interstate, on the wrong side of the road.

Three cars simultaneously swerved to avoid us, and I let go of the wheel in utter panic.

Nick threw himself onto it from the passenger's side before the car lost control. "Take your foot off the gas!" he yelled.

"He's in her!" I heard Rebecca yell from the back seat.

I slammed on the breaks, not knowing the car's turbulence was coming from a flat rear tire. By the time I realized it, the car began to fishtail.

Two more cars sped passed us.

Logan and Rebecca screamed as Nick ordered me to release the breaks. "Turn the wheel!" he yelled.

But it was too late. The SUV was on its way over to its side. I looked out of the driver's window and saw the ground rushing at me through the glass.

The metal crashed, jerking us all to the left. Rebecca and Logan were tossed to the same side of the car, their screams ending in unison when they collided into each other. Nick remained tied to his chair, and my head bounced off the door's glass that shattered as we slid across the asphalt.

I heard the sound of screeching tires from another car, and I braced for impact. The safety of my baby was the last thing I thought about before the metallic crash rattled the entire car and brought the darkness for all of us.

Trapped

The light hurt my eyes when I came to, though the room wasn't brightly lit. Before I could focus on anything, the smell of the air and the noise surrounding me hit with a realization that both relieved me, and scared me. I was in the hospital.

I tried to sit up on the bed, but the throbbing in my temples kept me down. My dry throat could barely produce a sound as the memory of what brought me to the medical center revived in my mind. Be it mental or not, I felt a sudden emptiness within me, and I suddenly grew restless.

The curtain around my bed came into focus as I tried to sit up again, the same curtain I saw when I woke in the hospital the night my parents died. I was praying I wouldn't wake up with the same news regarding the other three that were in the car at the time of the accident.

"She's awake!" I heard someone yell, just like Billy did eighteen years before. "Someone get Doctor Morrison!"

Nick's face came into view, and instead of relieving me like it normally would, I grew more anxious. His arm was in a sling; it didn't appear to be broken since it was free of a cast. His left cheek was badly bruised, swollen around the three stitches that was holding the torn skin closed, but all of that wasn't what concerned me. It was the look in his blood-shot eyes.

"Nick…" I said softly, wanting to ask so many questions, but my throat wouldn't allow it.

He ordered me to lie still, softly combing my hair with his fingers. "You're okay," he whispered to me. "Everyone is okay."

Morrison pulled the curtain back in a hurry, moving Nick aside to inspect me. He took my wrist and timed my heartbeat. "How do you feel?" he asked.

Like a truck ran me over, pulled back and ran me over once again. As I was slowly coming back to full consciousness, the pain that was dormant in my every muscle was waking.

"It was a pretty bad accident," he said. "All of you are lucky have walked out of it the way you did."

"How's my baby?" I asked him, fighting to produce the words. I had to ask, and a dry throat was not going to keep me from doing so.

Nick's head hung low suddenly and Morrison appeared to be fighting the urge to look back at him for a glance.

I was wide-awake now. Something happened to my unborn child, and before hearing any news, the tears began to conjure. "What is it?" I asked.

Morrison took a deep breath. "Cynthia, I'm sorry to have to tell you this," he said.

I braced myself for yet another impact, trying desperately to not let my sorrow get the best of me.

I knew it.

"Nick told us about your pregnancy when you were brought in here, and we immediately did everything we could to help you out. But there was nothing to do," he said.

I frowned. "What?"

"I'm sorry, Cynthia," he said, "but you were never pregnant."

I sat up, the pain oblivious to me now. Nick hesitated to look at me, but when he did, I knew that Morrison was telling the truth.

"But the test..."

"I know you're confused," Morrison said. "But we've run several tests ourselves, and none of them proved positive. Those home pregnancy tests are not one hundred percent accurate, and Nick tells me you never confirmed it with your doctor."

I shook my head.

"This isn't the first time something like this happens," he said. "I'm sorry to have to be the one to tell you."

How could that be? The test was positive, and I even *felt* pregnant. There was morning sickness and…

Then it hit. There wasn't a single doubt in my mind that there was an underlying reason that I thought I was pregnant. Nothing is what it seems. I discovered my pregnancy just before Luis and Jo's accident, on the very same day I dreamt about Old Man Brewer. Mason Bayer was responsible for making me believe all along that I was pregnant.

The overwhelming sorrow that fell over me turned into a raging anger.

"We need to go," I told Nick suddenly.

His back straightened, and he nodded. "I'll go get the others."

"Hold on a second," Morrison said as I threw the blanket aside. "We're not done with you."

"I feel okay," I lied to him. "I want to go home."

"That's not a good idea, Cynthia. You banged your head pretty bad, and you need to stay here for the night so that we can observe you."

"Morrison, I…"

"No one is going anywhere," Detective Lopez said as she entered the curtained area. "I've been waiting for hours for you to wake up, and I have a couple of questions to ask you."

I rolled my eyes at her sight. Of course she had some questions, why wouldn't she? She probably already talked to the others, and after she asked Morrison and Nick to give us some privacy, I grew worried that I would tell her something the others did not.

"We'll be right outside," Nick said to me as Morrison escorted him out.

"And you'll be here until tomorrow," the doctor added.

And just like that, they were gone, leaving the detective and me on our own.

Her hair was pulled back into a ponytail, and she was in a pair of jeans and a tee shirt marked with the initials D.C.P.D.; Dade County Police Department.

I watched her as she sat on the chair opposite the bed, and for a while, she said nothing. She didn't have a notebook, nor did she seem as determined to find answers like before.

"I don't like having to work on my day off," she told me.

So why are you here? I didn't respond.

"Do you want to tell me what happened?"

"We were in a car accident," I told her, matter of factly.

"I know that," she said. "Your car flipped on its side while you were speeding on the wrong side of the road, but that's not what I'm asking. I want to know what happened at the diner."

Shit! I didn't know what to tell her. Someone called the cops, and I knew she would receive word one way or another. Unfortunately, I didn't think of an alibi while I was comatose, so she caught me off guard.

"I don't remember," I said, hoping she would believe me. "I hit my head pretty hard and…"

"Selective amnesia," she said with a nod. "How convenient."

I wasn't in the mood for her questions, and I was trying my hardest to gain her sympathy before she asked for any more information. "I just lost my baby," I told her. "Do you mind if we do this later?"

She stood from the chair. "Morrison tells me you never were pregnant."

I decided then to keep my mouth shut before I dug myself deeper into a hole I would never be able to get out of.

"Now, I'll ask you again. What happened at the diner?"

"I told you, I don't remember."

Maria shook her head. "There was a young man a few doors down earlier who says Nick was responsible for his broken nose."

"Did he say he attacked Rebecca?" I fired back. "He tried to wrestle her to the ground and Nick saved her, that's..."

"I thought you didn't remember."

I shook my head, and looked away from her, wanting desperately for her to leave.

"He and his girlfriend didn't want to press charges, and you should consider yourself lucky for that," she said. "But from now on, I suggest you all keep your hands to yourself and call the authorities to deal with the situation."

"Can you please leave me alone?" I said to her. "We can talk later."

She nodded, but before she left, she crossed her arms and said, "I'll tell you this, Cynthia. You, your husband, Logan and Rebecca are being watched closely. I suggest you watch yourself and be careful of your actions."

She disappeared behind the curtain, and instead of falling back onto the bed and surrendering to the frustration she brought, I slowly stood, and began searching for my clothes.

There was no time to be trapped in a hospital when there was so much that needed to be done.

*

Logan and Rebecca suffered only minor scrapes and bruises. They too had been questioned by Detective Lopez while at the hospital, but they weren't extensively warned like I was.

While I was unconscious, they took a cab to Rebecca's to retrieve my car. After they helped smuggle me out of the hospital, we quickly sped out of the parking lot and headed back toward Rebecca's.

Logan was at the wheel this time.

"I'm sorry to hear about the baby," he said to me after a moment of silence.

I appreciated his condolence, but the truth was, the loss of my child was not an issue with me at the moment. I chose to block it out of my mind for one reason only; it was never real. It was the work of a demon, and I wasn't going to allow myself to give into his game. It's the only way we would win.

"Tell me what happened," I said to no one in particular. The morbid curiosity got the best of me, and I felt the need to know how and why we ended up on the wrong side of the road, leading to the accident that slowed us down.

It was explained rather quickly, Nick confirming Logan and Rebecca's version of events. Quite simply, I sped through the red light at the intersection we were stopped at just after Nick handed me the pen to take the test. Shortly afterwards, I jumped the median, and sped through oncoming traffic. Moments later, the car flipped. They all said that they were convinced it was Mason the moment I sped through the intersection.

A unanimous decision was made shortly there afterwards. We would travel as little as possible by car, considering it seemed to be Mason's weapon of choice.

The rest of the ride was spent in silence. I wanted to ask if any of them tried to "stop" me while Mason trapped my soul somewhere in the darkness, but I thought the better of it. Why ask if I was still alive? In severe pain, but alive nonetheless.

I hit my head on the glass during the collision, and the mark it left across my forehead was an unpleasant sight. Until I got into the back seat of the car, I didn't notice a gauze bandage was taped across my forehead to cover the long scratch caused by the shattered glass, and though it was a mere flesh wound, the pain that ensued deep within my head was something I couldn't bear. I needed aspirin. Now that I knew I wasn't pregnant, I longed for a cup of coffee; maybe even a hard drink to help sooth the pain.

It was nearing eight in the evening as we turned onto Rebecca's neighborhood street, and I could already taste the vodka.

Logan stopped the car suddenly, letting out a curse word at something he saw ahead of us.

The rest of us saw it immediately afterwards. Rebecca's house, nestled at the end of the street yards away, suddenly became threatening. The black sedan was parked on the curb of her front yard. Someone was waiting for us.

"Who could that be?" Logan asked.

"It's probably Detective Santiago," Nick answered from behind him. "Lopez was by herself and she told me that her partner was still investigating."

"Let's go," Rebecca said hurriedly. "Let's get outta here."

"Where to?"

"Somewhere, anywhere, before he sees us."

Without any thought at all, Logan turned onto a neighboring street and found his way onto the main road.

Nick and I kept our eyes on the back window in case Santiago followed us, but it appeared as though he hadn't seen us at all.

"How the hell are we supposed to get through this with them on our tail like that?" Logan asked.

No one answered because none of us knew how we would get through anything in the public eye. We needed to be isolated, somewhere the detectives wouldn't find us, but close enough to society in case we needed help.

"I have an idea," I said. I knew the perfect place to hide out; at least for the time being.

*

Luis and Jo's apartment was empty for nearly a week. The time passed so quickly that none of us ever thought about the possessions she left behind, didn't even consider the possibility that we should put them in a box so it wasn't as painful for Luis if…when he returned.

It was a single story apartment resting on the second and final floor of a small duplex just outside Downtown. Built for a single couple in mind, it was one bedroom, one bath, kitchen and living area. Small, but cozy and often the place we would all gather for a night of board games and drinks.

But it was haunting to us that night. The light to the kitchen at the entrance of the apartment was turned on, and a pile of dirty dishes rested in the sink. Even the smell of Jo's perfume still lingered in the air.

The light to the living room was also on. They left for the memoriam dinner as nightfall began, and leaving the lights on in their apartment was their way of repelling intruders.

A knot formed in my throat when my eyes fell upon a picture they took days before the accident. They went to the Keys the weekend before, taking a break from everyday life to enjoy time to themselves. It was framed and placed on top of the entertainment center with half a dozen other pictures of the six of us on several different occasions.

It was a different time back then, and I knew that the same feelings of comfort and love that took so long to build would probably never return. For so many years, we fought to put the past behind us, to retrain our minds to have positive outlooks, and it would be even longer before we would recover from our present. Especially when it seemed as though each attack Mason brought was worse than the one before.

The book stated that after possession, the entity was technically exhausted, and that it needed to regroup. Mason took hold of three different people in a matter of minutes, and nearly killed us every step of the way. Most of the emotions that soared throughout my body in the past week boiled into anger, fueling me for the battle. But the anger never fully replaced the fear. I was scared to face the ghost, and as I looked at the faces of the others, I knew they were too.

They walked through the apartment in the same dazed state I did. We were slowly deteriorating with fatigue, frustration, and lack of sleep. Each of us had bruises, scratches and bandages; clear signs of war, but what did we have to show for it? Absolutely nothing. If it was a war, we were losing.

"We should probably stay here throughout the hurricane tomorrow night," Logan said. "There's only one window in the living room, it's easier to board up, and I don't think any of us would be found here."

What he really meant was that we should keep ourselves trapped in the apartment until it was over. Sure the hurricane was a threat, but I read it in his face. Maybe Lopez and Santiago would eventually discover where we were hiding, of that I had no doubt. However, they had to realize we were missing first, and that could take days, maybe even more since Hurricane Alida promised...

The phone rang suddenly, and the four of us froze. Maybe we weren't as lucky as we thought. Everyone who knew Jo and Luis knew of the accident, there wasn't even a message on their machine for the past week. Who would call just as we arrived?

"Should we get that?" Logan asked, the phone ringing for the third time.

Nick adjusted the sling on his shoulder after he shrugged.

And since no one else made a move, I walked to the phone resting on the side table beside the couch. With a sweaty palm, I answered it.

"Hello," I said in merely a whisper.

"Cynthia! Are you all okay?"

"Billy?" His voice filled me with comfort, and the sound of his name surprised the others. "Where are you?"

"Are you all there?" he asked me.

I looked at the others. "The four of us are, yeah."

"I'm on my way over," he said. "I'll be there in about an hour or so."

The line went dead, and I hung up the phone, telling the others that Billy was on his way. Truthfully, I didn't know how I felt about that.

"Why not?" Nick asked.

"Because," I answered, "I don't want Billy involved in this."

The Guest

An hour and a half passed and Billy had not yet arrived. The four of us sat around the dinner table, Rebecca willing to make coffee. But my wish for liquor was answered when Logan reached in the refrigerator for a beer. The four of us worked through two bottles each in less than half an hour.

"Does anyone have any weed?" Logan asked in a cheap attempt at humor.

It worked. The rest of us smiled.

We decided on not telling Billy about what was happening. It was best if he knew nothing; it was the only way to keep him safe – my father wasn't all wrong in not telling us about his cases for a reason. Besides, Billy wasn't the type of person to believe in ghosts and the supernatural. He'd probably call the psychiatric hospital if we told him a dead man was trying to kill us.

We would have to convince him to forget about us for the time being; until it was over. But the great Detective Kux would not comply with any requests until he knew what was happening himself. It would be difficult to keep such a secret from him, but it had to be done.

Nick asked if anyone wanted another beer, and I declined his offer. The two beers already began working its magic on my mind, and on my bladder.

I excused myself from the table and walked into the hall as Nick headed toward the kitchen. I closed the door and locked it.

It took less than a minute to relieve my bladder, but I was in the bathroom for more than five. As I washed my hands, I looked at my face in the mirror for the first time in days, and naturally, I didn't like what I saw.

The bags that grew underneath my eyes were beginning to weigh down, and my skin was pale next to the fresh bruises. My forehead was not healing yet, but the scratch was not as bad as it appeared when I first saw it. It was easily concealed underneath my bangs, but it would take more than make up to cover the years that suddenly fell upon my face. I needed to rest.

I splashed my face with water instead. As I reached for the soft towel folded neatly beside the sink, I recalled Jo's voice specifically asking me not to use it. "Those are for decoration!" she would scold about the towel in my hands and the other two that matched. I laughed at her silly quirk, but beyond the laugh was a terrible sadness. I missed her like I missed my parents.

A soft rumble filled the room, and I sighed. I was growing sick of the storm and its thunder, day after day and night after night of just rain. But when the soft rumble echoed again, I second-guessed myself. It didn't sound like thunder suddenly.

The noise was hollow, coming through the walls and into the bathroom. Something on the other side was running against the wall repeatedly, dragging back and forth, back and forth.

I stood still for a moment, concentrating on the noise and trying my best to identify it. But then it stopped, and I heard nothing, not even when I pressed my ear against the wall.

Slowly, I walked out of the bathroom. The light from the living room poured into the hallway, but the room wasn't visible until the hall's end. I didn't move though, becoming extremely uncomfortable the moment I stepped out of the bathroom because the silence was too prominent.

"Nick," I called out.

There was no answer, and I began to sweat.

"Rebecca, Logan."

Nothing.

My heart was racing and my legs were beginning to grow weak, but I took a step toward the hall's end. Slowly, I approached the living room, my eyes dashing upon every inch of the view that was growing with every step.

I saw Nick's arm sling on the floor, then lost my breath just as the lights went out.

I couldn't see anything. The darkness returned, but nothing took over me this time. I heard the switch of the lamp seconds before, and I was still in the hall. This time, the abyss was real.

I threw myself against the wall, hoping to blend into the darkness and trying my hardest to not make a sound. My breathing was uncontrollable though, and I knew that It would find me.

"Who's there!" I called out against my will, hoping against all odds that someone would answer.

But still, there was nothing. For what felt like an eternity, there was nothing. The room was dead silent, feeling a few degrees cooler than before.

I slid further along the wall, towards the living room, but my eyes would not adjust.

"Cynthia," a voice whispered from somewhere in the darkness.

I stopped, nearly collapsing because it was the voice of the demon, and it was coming from somewhere close; somewhere in the living room.

My knees were growing weak, and I tried to find the anger that fueled me so much. Only fear was found within me at that moment, stripping me of all my defenses.

"Cynthia," It whispered again. "Look at what I did."

The light flipped back on.

I gagged on impulse when I saw the bodies. Both Rebecca and Logan were sprawled on the living room floor, side by side in a pool of blood; too much of it to assume they were alive.

I couldn't scream, I couldn't breath, I couldn't move when I turned to the lamp in the corner of the room. Nick was standing just beside it. He saw the bodies as well, and was staring at them in shock. He didn't notice his shirt, stained with as much blood as a butcher's apron. He didn't notice the equally bloodied knife in his trembling hand. He didn't notice the word he wrote on the wall directly behind him.

EERHT it read.

"Nick!" I yelled in tears, my knees finally collapsing.

He watched me fall to the floor, but he did not move to help me up. As he looked to his right hand and found the knife, he realized It used him to do the job.

I cried out half way through a scream and I watched Nick's face, the horror in his eyes as he stared at the bodies not knowing what to do. He wanted to scream, to cry, to collapse like I did.

He dropped the knife on the floor then fell to his knees, and just as he let out a cry of confusion, Billy entered the room.

*

He stopped, just as he discovered the sight. He looked to Nick, to the word on the wall behind him, then to me, but his face wasn't asking for answers. He crossed the room, stepped over the bodies and helped me off the ground. Keeping his eye on Nick, still kneeling in the corner of the room and staring at the bodies in shock, he told me to stop crying. Then he told me that everything would be okay. "Go outside and get some air," he ordered.

I shook my head furiously. "They're dead!" I cried, feeling my sanity slipping from my fingers. I tried to pry myself from his grasp. I wanted to run to Nick and help him snap out of his shock, but I couldn't. Billy's grip was too tight.

"Cynthia, listen to me!" he said. "Go outside, now. I'll take care of Nick."

"They're dead…" Nick said, almost to himself.

Billy turned to him quickly, releasing me and asking Nick to look at him. But when Nick didn't respond, Billy stepped before him. "Nick, talk to me," he said, shaking Nick gently then helping him off the ground.

Nick's focus finally went to Billy. "I didn't do it," he said, a tear escaping.

"Listen to me, Nick. I need you to take a shower and change out of your clothes."

Nick looked to the bodies again.

"Don't look over there, Nick," Billy ordered. "Look at me."

Nick did as he was told.

"Go take a shower and change into some of Luis' clothes, can you do that for me?"

It took a while, but Nick nodded.

Billy turned to me. "Cynthia, I told you to go outside and get some air. You don't need to be here."

I looked at the bodies of Rebecca and Logan, both turned downward to cover their faces and the wounds that killed them. My entire body trembled with fear, disgust and most of all sorrow.

"Get out, now!" Billy screamed.

"Billy, I…"

"We'll talk later," he said then took Nick by the arm and led him into the hall.

My husband couldn't even look at me as they passed.

I decided to take Billy's order when I was left alone in the living room. I certainly was not going to stay in the room when the bodies of my two friends…

Logan coughed, and my heart stopped. I looked at the bodies for the second time and watched as his arm moved slightly to the left.

"Logan's alive!" I screamed into the hall. "He coughed! He's alive!"

Billy ran into the living room and knelt beside Logan, feeling for a pulse on his neck. He looked up at me suddenly, and once again, told me to leave the apartment.

"Should I call an ambulance?" I asked him

"No!" he barked. "Just leave. I'll take care of this."

*

When I saw the word *EERHT*, I thought both Rebecca and Logan were dead. It would only make sense since Jo was *ENO*. But Logan lived. There was so much blood though, completely drenching the carpet in the apartment. If he was attacked, I feared he wouldn't survive unless he received medical attention. And if he did survive, did Rebecca?

A million more thoughts ran through my mind as I nervously paced the balcony outside the apartment. I wanted to see what was happening inside, what Billy and Nick were doing to help Logan and Rebecca. Feeling useless on my own, all I could do was pray that everyone was alive.

But It left Its signature; It made a kill.

Nick walked out of the apartment wearing a fresh pair of jeans and a tee shirt. The blood was cleaned from his hands, but the truth still showed in his face. Without saying a word to each other, we cried and hugged one another immediately.

"Rebecca's dead," he said, crying on my shoulder. "I killed her."

"No you didn't," I said. "It wasn't you."

Billy stepped onto the balcony but didn't interrupt us. It was the first time Nick released his emotions, and he waited for us to finish.

"Logan is okay," Billy told me. "Completely unharmed."

"I thought he was dead," I told him, wiping my face.

"From what I could get, he was hit on the head. He was knocked out."

"Where is he?"

"Showering. It took him a while to stop vomiting after he saw…sorry. I'm used to sharing information like that."

"Look, Billy, I think we should explain what's happened," I said. The agreement we made earlier about not letting Billy know anything was nullified since he walked into the middle of a murder. He had to know.

But he shook his head and held an index finger up at me, ordering me not to explain anything at all. "Not now," he said. "We have to get you all out of here. Detectives Lopez and Santiago are on your butts, and it'll only be a matter of time before they find you."

"But what about the apartment and Reb…"

"Don't worry about the apartment," he said. "I'll take care of it."

Though we were uncertain of what he had planned, he left us no choice but to cooperate. The three of us waited outside the apartment until a very dismal Logan walked out, also wearing some of Luis' clothes. He held a plastic bag of ice up to the back of his head, which still appeared to be spotting with blood.

"Whose car did you come in?" Billy asked us.

"Mine," I answered.

"Lock up here then you're going to follow me."

"Where are we going?" Logan asked.

Billy turned and descended the stairs, ignoring Logan's question.

We followed, trailing Billy by only a few paces. It seemed Billy knew exactly what he was doing, so we had no choice but to trust him. Without giving us a second to mourn the loss of our friend, he laid out a handful of rules to keep us focused and in control.

But I didn't understand why.

Mason Bayer

We drove for miles, heading west on 88th Street. The wet roads weren't completely free of other cars that night, but the further west we traveled, the less traffic appeared.

We turned south once we reached Krome Avenue, a street dubbed The Avenue of Death. It was a desolate, two-lane road tucked far enough away from society that people often forgot it even existed. There were no street lamps, and the forest of trees surrounding the road prevented even the moon's light to penetrate come nighttime. Drivers often sped through the road since even the officials stayed clear of the area, and when automobile accidents occurred on Krome, they were usually fatal.

Billy's car remained less than ten feet ahead of us throughout the entire journey. We continued driving further and further away from the city lights, heading south for miles.

"Where's he taking us?" Logan asked, but he didn't receive a response from any of us. Beside the fact that we didn't know, all we could think about was Rebecca.

Billy turned right, onto a side road off Krome I never even knew existed. Still we followed, and the road suddenly became unstable.

Ditches and hills the size of speed bumps made the ride turbulent, dust and grime kicking up behind both cars as we proceeded.

The sound of the tires crunching rocks beneath filled the car, but the three of us remained silent. We were glancing out the windows to the left and to the right as our speed dipped below twenty miles per hour.

"What is that?" Logan asked from the back seat, pointing out the window to his left.

A wooden fence ran alongside the road, barricading some sort of field behind it. It seemed to stretch for acres, the darkness of night preventing us from seeing further than a few feet.

"It looks like some kind of park," Nick said, bobbing his head up and down from the passenger side.

We traveled along side the fence for nearly two miles, but still, we had no idea what Billy had in mind. His car finally came to a stop when the wooden fence gave way to two aluminum panel gate doors. They were shut, but not locked.

Billy stepped out of his car, and without looking back to us, he pushed both doors open. One at a time, he locked them down, then got back into his car and drove through.

We followed him in, the headlights of our car suddenly illuminating a house.

It was a two story, made of wood, and chillingly familiar. I saw the house before. I saw it in a dream.

"What is this place?" Logan asked, his head suddenly between Nick's and mine.

"It's the Bayer farm," I answered.

Both of them looked at me, probably wondering how I knew.

Billy parked in front of the house and we parked beside him. Within seconds, the three of us jumped out of the car.

"What are we doing here, Billy?" Logan asked, approaching him.

Billy looked over his shoulder, to the house behind him. "This is where it all began," he said.

The farmhouse was not as dark as I remembered it, but it was just as unsettling. The windows of the second floor were boarded with plywood, as were a few of the windows on the first floor. The unkempt grass surrounding the house stretched upwards toward the stairs that led to the porch. It was obviously been abandoned for years, left untouched and forgotten about completely.

I looked to the right of the house and found a pigpen just yards away. It was empty.

"This is where I've been for the past week," Billy told us.

"Why?" Nick asked.

"Preparing it."

"For what?"

He walked up the stairs and onto the porch, the wood squeaking beneath his every step. "Come inside," he said. "I'll explain everything."

*

The house was smaller than I envisioned it. We entered into a rectangular room, the ceiling less than seven feet above us. The stairs leading to the second floor lined the right wall, and on the opposite side was a large, empty room. It was the room I saw Mason killing his swine.

Logan stared up at the second floor, looking at the spot where James Bayer hanged himself nearly four decades before, but the floor remained masked in darkness.

Billy clicked on a machine that made a terrible rattling noise, much like a lawn mower. Suddenly, there was light. Wires ran along the dampened walls, a high-powered bulb dangling from it in the center of the room.

"There's enough gas in this generator for about four days," Billy yelled above the noise, then signaled us to follow him.

He walked into the empty room, also lit by the generator. Once we all entered, he closed two wooden sliding doors that surprisingly drowned enough of the noise to not cause a migraine.

A new, fairly large cooler was lined with the south wall, and before I could question what it was-

"What's through that door?" Logan asked, pointing to the east of the room.

The door practically blended with the wooden walls, and had it not been for the rusted knob and hinges, I would have missed it completely.

"That leads to the barn," he said. "You won't need to use it."

"What the hell are we doing here, Billy?" Nick asked, inspecting the room.

"I brought you here because this is where you all are going to stay," he said. "At least until it's over."

"What do you mean?" I asked him. *Does he know?*

"No one will find you here," he said. "No one even remembers this place."

"Billy," Logan said before he could continue. "Do you know what's..."

He didn't proceed with his question because Billy was already nodding. "I've known for years that something like this might happen."

I was shocked. We all were.

"How...why didn't you say anything?" Nick asked him.

He sighed, rubbing his forehead. "Those newspaper articles you read, there was one thing none of them could tell you; how Mason escaped the institution the night your parents were killed. None of them gave any detail because it couldn't be explained; no one even saw it happen. Except me."

Nick and I exchanged glances as Billy sat on the cooler, his back against the wall.

"What did you see?" Logan asked.

Billy shook his head, recalling the night. "I was amazed at how simple it was for him. He simply walked out. There were three security gates he passed to reach the front door, dozens of security cameras and clearance codes along the way. He made it through every single one."

"He walked *through* them?" Nick asked.

Billy shook his head. "That would have been more believable. It was like he connected with every single guard on that ward. They willingly opened the doors for him. How he connected with them, I still don't know. It was like they were caught in a spell in his presence, and they did as he wished. I followed him the whole way out, and he never even knew.

"You see, Mason Bayer was missing for eighteen years, and all of us were desperate to know what he had been up to. Who knows what he learned in those two decades? No one. But he must have learned something because how does a low-class farming boy with no education learn to control someone else's mind and have them at his will? It was then that I realized we weren't dealing with a human. This man was some sort of walking ghost.

"After the murders, and after he was killed, I tried my hardest to keep you all away from him in any way I could. That's why I wouldn't let you read the newspapers or see the news for years. In the back of my mind, I had a nagging suspicion that Mason had more power than we would ever understand. It seems I was right."

"So, you've known about this since the night our parents were murdered?" Nick asked in disbelief.

Slowly, Billy nodded. "I didn't know exactly what to expect, but I knew that something was possible."

"Why didn't you tell us?" I asked.

"Because I wasn't certain. Why bring it up? I became suspicious after news of the accident and the supposed murder of Jo. I mean, why would Luis kill her, right?"

The three of us nodded.

"Since then, Mason has killed two more people, and…"

"Wait a minute," I said. "Back at the apartment, he wrote 'three,' but he's only killed two. Jo and Rebecca."

Billy gnawed his jaw. "There's another," he said. "The only other person to survive an attack from Mason Bayer was the seventh board member of the DOH."

"He was still alive?" Nick asked.

"Yes. I happened to stumble right onto his murder just after it took place."

My heart skipped a beat as I remembered seeing Billy on the news the night he called frantically. "Old Man Brewer," I said.

"Otherwise known as Tomas, yes."

I closed my eyes in disbelief. His poor daughter sat in jail for the murder of her father, and she more than likely had no idea of what happened.

"After that, I came here. I knew that if this was the way Mason was working, then it had to be done in isolation, away from crowded areas. I've boarded up most of the windows, there's a few you'll have to do before tomorrow night, before the hurricane." He tapped on the cooler between his legs. "In here there's plenty of water and canned foods for about a week, so you should be…"

"You can't expect us to stay here!" Logan said. "This is where he grew up. This is his home!"

"You don't have a choice, Logan. Anywhere you go in Miami, Detectives Lopez and Santiago will find you. God forbid they walk in on a sight I've walked into twice already."

"What if we need help?" I asked.

"No one can get involved without risking their own life. I've gone too far myself, that's why I have to get going." He stood from the cooler and took a deep breath.

"Where will you be?" I asked, a knot forming in my throat.

He shrugged. "I don't know. Somewhere. Anywhere."

He bid us farewell individually, keeping a poker face at play. Before he opened the door to let the sound of the generator pour in, he said, "Everything I've done, I did it to protect you. Leaving you here hurts me more than you will ever know." Before he allowed a tear to show, he walked through the door.

Nick, Logan and I watched him leave. Billy Kux was our father, our brother, our friend for all our lives and he was leaving us behind to kill each other in a battle even we couldn't understand. I found myself praying that it wouldn't be the last time we saw him, then I knew I had to see him once more before he left.

I threw the doors open and ran through the house toward the door. I called for him as I stepped out onto the porch, my voice echoing in the night's sky.

He had just opened the door to his car when he turned, exposing his flushed face.

I ran off the porch and met him on the rocky road. "I need to ask you something," I said, fighting my own tears.

He nodded briefly.

"Before Rebecca died, she asked that if anything should happen to her, she wanted to make certain that Charlene would be looked after. Charlene has a father to take care of her, but Max..." I stopped, choking on my own words. "If anything happens to us, if we don't walk out of this alive, will you – I mean, would you..."

"Watch over Max?" he asked.

I nodded, letting the floodgates open.

"It would be my honor," he said then took me into his arms.

We cried together, but only for a brief moment. Detective Kux was not used to the sentiments.

"Before I go," he said, reaching into his car, "I want you to have this."

I accepted what he handed to me without looking at it. Surprised by its weight, I nearly dropped it when I realized what it was.

"What is this?"

"It's a gun," he answered.

"I know what it is," I said, holding the gun out as far from me as I could. "Why are you giving it to me?"

"There's no weapons in there, Cynthia. This is your only defense."

"I don't know, Billy. I mean, I've never fired a gun before."

"It's fully automatic. Just point and shoot. There's six bullets in there."

"Billy, I…"

"Take it, Cynthia," he ordered, then kissed me on the cheek. "I'll see you soon."

He got into his car and started it as I stared at the pistol in my hand. I didn't know much about guns, but this was a 9mm I held. It said so in an engraved insignia on the handle.

I watched as Billy's car drove off onto the road outside the barrier fence and vanished behind a thick cloud of dust.

I walked to the passenger side of my car and hid the gun inside the glove box. Neither Nick nor Logan would know of the weapon, as I was certain it would only cause trouble.

Heading back toward the house, the clouds above began to sing with thunder. The wind howled somewhere in the distance, and as the sounds of the chirping crickets slowly died out, I was certain of one thing alone.

The storm was headed our way.

CHAPTER EVIF

Cynthia's hand was downright hurting, and her neck didn't linger too far behind. Not once did she find it difficult to concentrate on her story, but the need to move her body, loosen all her muscles, was becoming a necessity.

She finished her cigarette first, then slid off the bed in the same careful manner she had before. Standing still, she took a deep breath then stretched. Her hands reached for the ceiling, and she would have touched it if only she could have stood on the balls of her feet to stretch her legs. The wound on her calf prevented any such movement.

But they were able enough to walk or run, and that was fine for her.

For the second time that night, she went for a view out her window, only there wasn't anything new to see. Rain. It was still nighttime and still raining. Cynthia sighed tiredly, her longing to see the sun growing stronger. She wanted to feel its warmth on her aching body, to bask in the light knowing it would be there for her the next day. She *needed* the sunlight.

What with there being not even a moon, she settled for the lamppost in the parking lot…

Oh my God.

She did see something new after all. Two parking spaces away from the lamppost, directly behind her car, she saw a black sedan.

Shit!

"They're on to me," she said, turning away from the window suddenly.

In seconds, she was glancing around the room, wondering if she should pack up and leave, lose them in a car chase if she had to. But where would she go? Home was out of the question, and her strength would only hold until the next hotel. Besides, it was raining.

She took a deep breath, reaching for another cigarette while praying she was wrong.

A lot of people drive black sedans. And if it is them, screw 'em!

She wasn't going to run. She grew viciously tired of the running and hiding. She came to write her story, to birth the one thing that would tell it completely. Less than a day ago, she was warned that no one would believe it, but she didn't care.

So, she picked up the third notebook having worked through the first two completely. Cracking the fingers of her right hand, she picked up the pen, kissed the foam finger grip, and puffed on her cigarette.

She would prove it was all real somehow. She needed to as much as she needed the sun.

*

Danny stared at the golden 77 on the door of her room, his heart racing in his neck. He decided to warn her, tell her that two detectives were on her trail. He would help her pack, help her dress, and in a sign of her gratefulness, she would ask him to run away with her…

Stop it!

He almost knocked twice before, but in the ten minutes he stood there, he only stared at the door. He even listened in, but there was nothing; not even the sound of the television. The only thing stopping him from telling her was knowing the detective could walk into the hotel at any given moment.

But he hasn't for the past five hours, so do it!

He clenched his fist, and as a neat line of sweat formed above his brow, he brought his arm up. He was going to do it!

But the elevator's bell rang throughout the hall.

*

Cynthia stopped, her instincts catlike as the sound of the elevator's indicator echoed into her room. Someone had come to her floor, and though she thought it may have been the driver of the black sedan, she hoped it was Danny.

*

The elevator doors slid open and Danny nearly collapsed when he saw the detective. Already, he was picturing his jail cell as the detective stepped off the lift, eyeing him with a burning stare.

Danny clenched his jaw to not blurt out anything stupid. He stared back at the detective innocently planning on lying should the detective begin questioning.

He was going to jail for sure.

The detective placed an index finger over his lips, ordering Danny to remain completely silent, and he complied. He swallowed hard when the detective signaled him toward the elevator.

*

Cynthia looked out the door's peephole, but no one was in the hall. She didn't know if to be relieved or frightened, so she listened closely. Nothing. Almost as though the doors opened on their own.

Maybe it's another power glitch, she thought.

As she left the door behind, making her way to the bed, she shook her head. She knew better than to think the doors would open on their own.

*

"So, what were you doing up there?" the detective asked as the elevator began its descent toward the lobby.

He was dripping wet. Danny listened to the muffled sounds of water drops falling off the detective's raincoat and onto the elevator's carpeting, all the while feeling the detective's eyes still burning. He wouldn't dare look at the detective, though.

"Checking in on her like you asked me to," he answered dryly.

"Tell me something, Danny. Are you a fan of hers?"

He nodded.

"Have you read about what happened to her when she was young?"

He had, but dismissed it as mere rumors. "She killed the man who did her parents in," he said, surprised he didn't realize it before.

"That's right," the detective said. "Do you want to know what's happening to her right now?"

Danny didn't respond, didn't move, finally on the verge of knowing more.

"She's gone nuts, Danny," he said. "She killed eight people in the same fashion Mason Bayer did. She thinks she's him."

He looked up at the detective, surprise on his face. He remembered the way she was asking him to follow the orders she laid out for him, he remembered her torn hands and bruised face. She didn't seem like a killer.

"Don't listen to anything she tells you, Danny," the detective continued. "She's great liar and will come up with the most incredible stories you've ever heard to prove her innocence. She's a dangerous woman."

The elevator stopped and the doors opened finally. Danny walked off quickly, headed toward the check-in counter but the detective followed him closely.

"Do you know what the consequences of interfering with an investigation is, Danny?" the detective asked.

"I wasn't interfering."

"It's prison, two years minimum. Do you know what happens to boys like you in prison?"

"Look!" Danny shouted, turning to the detective quickly. "You're the one who came in here, mouthing off orders. I told you, all I was doing was what you asked me to do."

The detective glared at Danny, making him second-guess his sudden outburst. The performance didn't amuse the detective at all. "I'm just letting you know that she is not the type of person you want to befriend," he said.

Danny looked at his shoes, hearing the wonderful sound of the detective walking away. He looked up at the man suddenly, finding himself sick of the games.

"Detective," he called out, loud enough to echo throughout the lobby.

He stopped and turned, surprised.

"Can I see your badge again?" he asked.

"I beg your pardon," the detective followed, crossing his arms over his chest.

"Your badge, can I see it?"

"What for?"

"This has been going on for hours already, and I don't even know your name."

The detective smiled, and turning back toward the door, he said, "Don't get smart with me, kid."

Danny nodded to himself as the detective walked back into the rain. There was only one reason the detective would deny him credentials. As Danny watched the man disappear into the outside world, he began to wonder if the detective was even a detective at all.

Isolation

We couldn't sleep. Midnight was approaching, Billy left us in the farm nearly an hour before, and not one of us had even yawned. At this strange new place, I figured we wouldn't sleep at all.

We sat in the same area, what we figured was the living room. The doors were closed to drown the sound of the generator that gave power to light the room, and after five minutes of silence, Logan began to panic.

"We're not really staying here, are we?" he asked.

Both Nick and I looked at each other, knowing that neither of us wanted to stay. The house alone was haunted by more ghosts than my own, but we also knew that Billy was right. We had to stay secluded from society, away from the detectives, doctors, and any one else who might step in the path of our war. Quite simply, we had to stay away from absolutely everyone.

Being isolated to the farm limited the people Mason would possess. The battle promised to be shorter there.

Logan knew there was no other choice; he was just asking the question burning on everyone else's mind.

Everything seemed to happen so quickly and there wasn't even time to mourn the loss of Rebecca. Though every moment of discovering Rebecca's death felt like an eternity, the minutes flew by after arriving at the farm. I don't know if it was the silence of the outside, but an emptiness fell over me when I watched Nick take a seat on the cooler, rubbing his right shoulder in pain. The sadness sunk in as I turned to Logan when he settled on the floor by the opposite wall. I realized then that it was just us left. Three.

"How are we going to tell Uncle George?" I asked, my chin quivering suddenly. The mere mention of his name was difficult enough, I couldn't bear the thought of having to tell him his only daughter was dead.

Nick's arms fell lifelessly on his lap, and he sighed, looking up at the ceiling. It was as though he forgot about Uncle George, and for a minute or so, we all did.

No one ever answered the question, but I didn't expect them to. The three of us remained silent, crying like lost children. We didn't pat each other on the back and fill the air with lies like "Everything's gonna be okay." We remained silent; showing our pure, raw emotions to each other without care.

There was nothing we needed more.

Just a week ago, there were six of us who were willing to defend each other at any time of day, given any situation. Six soldiers that were faced with an unforeseen war, a battle no one was prepared for. Seven counting Tomas Brewer. But one by one, Mason already got to four of us. Sure, one was still alive, but artificially. The rest of us stayed alive long enough to figure what was going on, how to save ourselves, and just like that, one more was stripped away.

And one more still had to die.

What chance did the three of us have?

Nick stood from the cooler suddenly, claiming the house was too humid for him to bear. He headed toward the door at the back of the room; the door Billy claimed led to the barn. He opened it, letting in air that was twice as humid, and he stepped out into the night.

"Go with him," Logan said. He was slouched on the wall across from me, his head turned to look at the door.

"What?"

His gaze locked onto me. "You should be with him as much as you can. Who knows how much longer we have?"

"Logan, don't say..."

"I don't want to hear it, Cynthia," he said, calmly. "Just go outside and be with him."

*

The stars were clear when I saw the farm before in the vision Mason fed me. But Alida's clouds were coming in, and there were no stars to be seen that night. As I stepped out of the house and onto the field, I instantly realized how detailed the vision was.

A wooden boundary fence circled the field, it was part of the same fence we saw just off the main road. The field was an ocean of overgrown grass and weeds stretching over ten acres of land. Behind the house, there was an opening; the fence broke apart, giving way to a concrete path that led to the barn just meters from us.

It was tall; nearly twice the size of the house and nestled completely in darkness. From our standpoint, I couldn't see its condition.

Nick was staring at it too from the gate's opening. He lit a cigarette, and though I toyed with the idea of having one, I wiped it from my mind. Instead, I approached him quietly.

Just before I reached him, he turned suddenly, jumped in fact, when he felt my presence.

"You scared me," he said when he realized it was me.

"I'm sorry." I stood by his side and studied the entire field. There were more structures covered in the night, and I would have to wait for morning to inspect them fully. From my view, they appeared to be more pens scattered aimlessly amongst the field.

"Are you scared?" he asked, after a puff of his cigarette.

"I'm terrified."

"Of dying?"

I thought about it for a second. "No. I don't want to die, but I'm not scared of it. I'd just like to see mom and dad again."

"You believe all that, don't you?"

"I do. You can't blame me for that."

He took another puff and nodded. "I'm scared, too."

"I know."

We stayed silent for a while, in each other's company. I realized that Logan was absolutely right. I did need time with Nick because either one of us could be dead come the next day, and if it were him, I would have solace that we had this moment. But if it was me who was to die next...

"I want you to quit smoking," I said to him.

He frowned.

"Not right this minute or anything, but when you're ready, I want you to stop it. It could kill you."

He nodded slowly, looking at the cigarette between his fingers. "When it's over, I'll quit," he said. "You can't blame me for *that*."

I smiled and threw my arms around him. I told him that I loved him and we kissed each other passionately, only to have the moment ruined by a sudden downpour.

We were soaked in less than a second, and together, we ran back into the house for the night.

But not once while the sun was down, did any of us manage to get any sleep.

Saturday, June 13th; The Last Day

The sun fought to break through the clouds come seven that morning, and Nick and Logan decided to get an early start. Billy said that a few of the windows still needed to be boarded before the hurricane was over us, and we had less than fifteen hours to do so.

After turning the generator off, Nick ordered me to move the car to the back of the house. He said it was better to keep it clear of any wanderers coming off Krome Avenue. He and Logan were going to inspect the barn since it didn't seem as though Billy left any equipment behind.

They found a ladder, a stack of plywood, and a plastic bag filled with boxes of nails. There were two hammers indicating that quite possibly, Billy had some help while preparing the house, but from whom? Who could he trust with such an outrageous secret?

After Rebecca's murder, he convinced us that the apartment would be cleaned with just eno phone call. As I watched Logan and Nick move the equipment toward the house, I wondered if more people knew about the situation than we realized.

It didn't matter who else knew. It was our war; no one else's.

So, the work began. Nick and Logan hammered boards to the house, covering the windows and several panels of wood that seemed to have weakened with time. By eight that evening, the storm's torrential downpours would begin, and one hour later, its full force was to be upon us. The question burning in my head was if the old farmhouse could stand through 130 mile per hour winds.

Though the farm was abandoned for years, the wooden house seemed to be in mint condition. The rain had not rotted through the panels yet, and there were only a few areas that needed to be reinforced. Still, I would have much rather spent the storm in a concrete building.

They took a break at noon, hunger striking them more than the humidity. Using one of the hammers, they opened two cans of soup and two cans of ravioli…each. After splitting a gallon of lukewarm water, they went back to work. I begged them to let me help, but they insisted I get some sleep.

"I'm not tired," I told them. "We can get a lot more done if I help."

"We're almost finished, honey," Nick said, a cigarette dangling from his lips.

"We're out of nails," Logan said while hammering. "There's another bag filled with boxes in the barn. You can help by getting them for us."

*

The door to the barn was missing, and unlike the house, the windows were not boarded. There were more than a dozen throughout the building, and most were completely broken through to allow the sunlight in. At the very least, I was thankful it wasn't as dark as the house, and like every memory I had of the past week.

The large opening entered into a narrow hall that ran the entire length of the barn. At the end of the hall, a wooden door was halfway open leading to a room that was unseen from my viewpoint. Since none of the equipment rested in the hall, I began to approach it slowly.

The entire facility was made of lumber, and the smell of wet, rotting wood filled the surrounding air. Its walls were dark and murky, rainwater dropping from cracks in the high ceiling and landing in echoing puddles that formed on the ground. Every inch of that ground was moist, and soaking in some areas, so I was careful to watch my footing.

My senses were on full alert; my ears altered and my eyes scanning everything as I walked through the hall. Upon hearing the slightest noise or seeing a moving shadow, I would bolt out of the barn leaving a trail of fire.

When I reached the door, I peered into the room careful not to push it open. If there was someone or something in the barn, I didn't want my presence to be announced by a squealing hinge. I didn't want to be announced at all.

It was a kitchen, and it was larger than the farmhouse itself. An industrial sized stove lined the furthest wall from corner to corner, and countless cabinets and cupboards hung loosely on the wall to its left. There was a door on the east wall, and it was left half way open. Still, none of the equipment was in the kitchen, so I entered, approaching the door swiftly and silently.

It was another hall, running parallel with the one from which I entered, and much wider. Its walls were not made of solid wood, rather wooden gates standing nearly four feet tall. There were four on either side, all open and all leading to small rooms parted by broken walls. They looked like small jail cells, but I knew they weren't intended for human use.

The holding pens… It was the area in which the swine were kept, probably from birth until they were transferred to the outside pens.

And there, in the center of the hall between both walls of gates, I could see the equipment. A dozen more wood panels were laid out and there were a few plastic bags marked with the name of a hardware store resting directly beside them.

One bag was filled with boxes of ten-inch nails, and the others contained other items Billy used while he was here; among them were two flashlights and two pairs of working gloves.

Two pairs...

Something moved, somewhere behind me, inside one of the pens. I heard a soft shuffle on the ground and spun in time to see the door slowly closing until it latched all on its own.

The bag fell to the floor as I found myself praying that it was just the wind, but I was tucked far enough in the barn that the outside wind didn't reach. The overwhelming feeling that I wasn't alone fell over me and I stood absolutely still.

I didn't hear another noise amongst the echoing puddles, but the desire to run out of the barn still gripped me. The door did not lock before my very eyes, and just as I was resorting to the idea that I may have been over reacting, I felt It.

My hair, tied in a ponytail, moved as though someone pressed it up against the back of my neck and caressed it in a downward motion. Chills erupted throughout my entire body just a second later when the soft breath of a whisper landed upon my right ear. I spun, letting out a scream on reflex, and as I feared, I was alone.

I broke into a run for the door, taking each step as fast as I could. I almost made it, too. Before I could grip the doorknob though, the darkness settled over me once again.

The Deaths

There was no intoxicating euphoria, nor was there any confusion as to what happened. I knew that what I was seeing was being fed to me by the demon.

I saw Hector. He was sleeping on the couch in the living room; the same place he was murdered eighteen years before. But he wasn't dead here…I could hear his snore; the animal like sounds Nick told me about before we entered the house for the beer.

The room was dark and the house was silent; but when I saw the moonlight cascade into the living room after the distinct sound of the window opening filled the house, I knew it was being invaded.

I watched as Mason silently crept into the house, quietly landing on his feet like a ghost, as Billy referred to him. He studied his surroundings, and through his black ski mask, I saw his gaze settle upon Hector.

Carefully, he passed me, not detecting my presence. He made his way to the kitchen as though he knew exactly where it was, and he found a steak knife resting upon the counter top. Crossing back toward the living room, he stopped, his instincts telling him to do so. Mason quickly glanced around the dining room, in search of something, but I wasn't sure what, until his gaze fell upon the sliding glass door that led to the back yard.

He saw the pool house, and he studied it for a moment, then he walked away to complete what he came to do. He didn't think the pool house was a threat; he didn't know that it was housing six teenagers. He didn't know that those six would be the death of his physical life, consequentially giving birth to his more powerful side. He didn't know…

Or maybe he did.

He walked to Hector, slowly gliding across the floor, making no sounds and careful to remain amongst the shadows. Hector continued snoring as he approached, unsuspecting, and venerable to the knife in the killer's hands.

Mason watched him sleep for a while, standing at the foot of the couch and studying the victim before making the kill. He raised his right arm slowly; the knife in his hand glistening in a ray of moonlight and reflecting on Hector's face, and it woke him.

He was confused, uncertain as to why he was awake, and before his eyes even settled on the killer standing just before him, Mason swung the knife down toward him, piercing his stomach.

*

I screamed, and it echoed through the barn. My head was throbbing with the vision It showed me, and as I fought to keep my footing in a dizzy spell, the darkness returned.

*

Hector was dead, covered in the same blood Mason was using to leave his signature. The right handed killer painted the word on the wall just above the couch, then pulled the knife out of his back pocket before heading up the stairs for the rest.

I stared at the word like I did when I discovered it on that night. *NEVES*, it read.

*

I fell to the dampened floor of the barn, unable to fight the demon. It was in me, and I kept conscious enough in my vision to try and fight him out. Though he eluded my mind with the memories in his head, I actually kicked him out of my body by force.

But I was too short of breath and weakened by his powers to revel in the discovery. I felt my heart beat viciously at my temples and suddenly felt a new sensation, a weakness, in my eyes. He returned; taking hold of me through the windows of the soul, and bringing the vision back with him.

*

I saw my mother and father sleeping in each other's arms as the killer slowly opened the door to their room. He was at their bedside, watching them sleep, tilting his head at them as his grip on the knife tightened. Swiftly, he sliced my father across the gut first, then another swift swing went to his neck.

My mother wouldn't have woken had my father not sat up in a convulsion of agonizing pain. She watched in horror as he tried to gasp for air, but his sliced throat wouldn't allow it. And just when she took notice of the blood pouring from the gash in his neck, she nearly began to scream.

She hadn't noticed the killer crossing the room to her side of the bed. Despite his injuries, my father tried to warn my mother of the intruder as the colors drained from his face. In his last breath, he watched as Mason shoved the knife into the back of my mother's neck.

THGIE and *ENIN* appeared on the wall above their bed, the corresponding bodies resting underneath their numbers.

*

I wanted to vomit, my body trembling with fear and my stomach clenching with disgust. I screamed again, but still, there was no one inside the barn to hear me, and Nick and Logan were far from hearing range.

I managed to get Mason out of me once more, and the moment I realized he no longer held me captive, I tried to stand and run back to the house to tell the others.

Just as I took my footing, I was shoved back to the ground, and back into the darkness.

*

He opened the door to Luis' room and entered, carefully closing the door behind him. Aunt Mayra was sleeping on the twin sized bed, and Mason was drawn to her like a magnet. His face came inches from hers, taking in every breath she released. He smelled the fair skin of her face before rolling out his tongue through the opening of his mask, and toward her lips. He didn't touch her, but he wanted to.

He slowly pulled back her sheets and watched her chest rise and fall with every breath. Her breasts were barely exposed beneath the light sleepwear, and Mason held his groin tight to fight the urge to mount her. It was as though he knew there more people in the house, and his work had to be done quickly.

The knife danced across the center of her lingerie, cutting the threads each time the tip passed until a hole was made, completely unbeknownst to my sleeping aunt.

He sliced the cloth then stripped his left hand of the glove he wore. Sliding his hand into my Aunt's sleepwear, he cupped her breast.

My Aunt gasped at the icy sting of his skin and kicked when she saw the assailant. Before she could make another sound, Mason withdrew his hand from her breast and covered her mouth. By that time, the knife was already in her stomach.

He gave into his temptation, after all. Lying in a pool of her own blood, Aunt Mayra watched as the killer joined her on the bed, mounting her and thrusting his pelvis at hers. When she died, Mason finished using her, then numbered her victim *NET.*

*

My chest ached as I fell short of breath, lying on the barn floor crippled with the images. I screamed again, crying for someone to help, but no one came. I was alone, but Mason was still with me.

Though I managed to evict him from my body once again, the barn grew unnaturally cold. Mason was not done with me yet.

I cried for help once more, hoping, praying that Logan or Nick would hear. However, it seemed the only one who heard was my enemy for the darkness had returned to me again.

*

The Sheyers slept in my bedroom that night, and they did so with the door opened which made Mason's entry that much easier. Without the aid of light, he crossed the room without fumbling over the stranded luggage left by Rebecca the night before. He stood next to their bed, ready to make his kill.

But something happened. He heard voices suddenly; a slight giggle of a girl and the soft voice of a boy coming from somewhere outside the house.

Mason crossed the room toward the window in a hurry; the direction in which the voices were lingering in the air. Taking the sheer curtains apart only an inch or so, he looked to the back yard and found the source of the noise.

It was Nick and I, walking toward the house for our beer run.

He turned back to the bed and stood still as Mrs. Sheyer shifted her position on the bed and moaned slightly. She was turning toward the window.

Mason slid along the wall, away from the direct moonlight, and blending into the shadows of the room.

She sat up. She heard something, or felt the presence of someone else in the room. She looked to her right where Mr. Sheyer slept peacefully, then scanned the room suspiciously once more. Deciding to put her mind to rest, she laid her head back onto the pillow, and never saw the knife coming straight for her throat.

Mason twisted the knife full circle in her throat and pulled it out quickly. She fell off the bed, pulled to the ground and landing with a lifeless *thump* on the floor.

Mr. Sheyer sat up and immediately saw the killer walking around to his side of the bed. He jumped off and swung at Mason in defense.

Mason ducked, extended his right arm, and swung it around at Mr. Sheyer's stomach. The knife pierced him, crippling Mr. Sheyer instantly. Mason stood against his body and forced the knife upward toward Mr. Sheyer's gullet. Without a sound, without even breaking a sweat, he killed Nick and Logan's father.

Victims *NEVELE* and *EVLEWT* were numbered shortly afterwards.

*

I freed myself of the demon again, finally becoming fully conscious of the method in which to do it. I screamed for help again, my voice traveling no further than the rotting wood of the barn, but I was not discouraged.

There's another way…

I pushed myself off the floor keeping a steady eye on the door of the barn. I wanted to get out before Mason caught me again, before the darkness returned for me. Though I was still drunk with the invading spirit, my determination to break out of the barn was far more powerful.

And just as I reached the hall of the barn, just as the exit was mere paces away, the darkness returned one final time.

*

The first shot went to his chest, but it didn't knock him down. Luis held the gun steadily as he entered the kitchen, approaching the killer as the rest of us were forced to watch. The anger in my brother's face as he stared at Mason was an expression I had not seen in him before, and it was clear that he intended to defend the rest of us.

A second shot sent the killer to the floor.

Mason was still breathing. I watched his stomach rise and fall quickly as he slowly lifted his head up to look directly at my brother's face.

Silence fell upon us all.

"Luis," I whispered to him, standing from the floor but not taking my eyes off the killer. "We'll call the cops. Let them finish it."

He didn't respond. Instead, he bent toward Mason and did something that stunned me completely. While holding the gun in his right hand, Luis reached for Mason's face with his left. He grabbed the top of the killer's head and stripped off his mask to reveal the face of Death.

The face belonged to Logan.

*

The barn's door was just paces away, and the last vision did not floor me like the others. Mason was gone; I could feel it. The temperature in the barn returned to normal, and the chills electrifying my body diminished.

I hauled out of the barn, replaying the last vision in my head. Knowing why Logan appeared as the face of the demon, I ran as fast as I could toward the house, my energy rebuilding with every step. I had to reach the others before Mason reached Logan; I had to tell them there was another way to stop It.

Desperate Measures

Nick and Logan were nowhere to be seen outside the farmhouse where I left them, and as I ran across the field, it made me nervous. Then, a more terrifying sight stopped me from running all together, and all I could do was stare.

The car's passenger side door was open, and from a few feet away, I noticed that the glove box was as well. The gun Billy gave me was discovered.

I continued my sprint toward the house; the vision playing itself in my mind again as I prayed I wasn't too late. Just feet away from the door though, I heard a loud explosion that shook every bone in my body. It was a gunshot, and it came from inside the house.

I didn't think of my own safety as I threw the door open and entered the farmhouse near panic as I looked for Nick and Logan. The cooler was turned to its side, several of the cans had rolled out, and a puddle of water had formed around it. The men were nowhere to be seen.

I took a breath to scream for my husband, but I didn't because he called for me first.

"Cynthia," he whispered from just outside the room in the hall. "Be quiet."

He was standing along the wall just beside the generator, and I nearly melted at his sight. I was relieved to see he was alive, but there was no sign of relief coming from him.

He waved at me, signaling me to stand beside him, and I did as I was told.

"It's Logan," he said, his eyes wondering toward the staircase. "It's in him."

My heart dropped to my feet as his words registered. Like the vision prophesized, Logan was possessed by Mason.

"Where is he?" I asked him, whispering as well.

"He went up the stairs. I tried to leave, but he shot at me from up there." He pointed to the door, and though I didn't see it before, it was clear as day then.

The outside light beamed its way in from a hole in the door. It was about 9mm in diameter.

"There's another way to stop him," I said between my breaths.

"Why didn't you tell me Billy gave you a gun?" Nick asked, ignoring my words.

"I kept it hidden so that..."

"Cynthia!" Logan called from the second floor. "Is that you?"

Nick hushed me, ordering me not to respond then moved me back toward the room from which I entered.

It didn't sound like Mason Bayer, but because of the look on Nick's face when he heard Logan call for me, I didn't question anything. Seconds later, we heard the sound of Logan running down the stairs, and both of us ran into the room.

Nick was right; Logan was holding the gun in his hands. I saw it the second he turned the corner and entered the hall. He approached us quickly, a look of anger on his face, but before he reached us, Nick closed the doors to the room and locked them. Logan was locked out, and we were sealed in.

Nick and I stepped away from the doors as Logan began pounding on them. "Let me in!" he ordered. "Cynthia, open the door!"

"Don't listen to him," Nick said.

But it was hard not to. He was screaming as loud as he could, begging for us to let him in. The doors trembled with every blow received and it didn't appear as though Logan would give up trying soon.

"Fight him Logan!" I yelled through the door. "You can fight him out!"

Nick pushed me away from the doors in the event Logan broke through. I didn't care, though. No one else had to die, and I was determined to make the others understand that there was a way to fight Mason out. Though the new determination stripped me of my fear, my heart accelerated when I heard what Logan screamed at me through the door.

"It's not me!" he shouted. "He's in Nick! Get out of that room!"

Nick looked at me blankly, and as Logan's words rang in my ears, my heart sunk with fear. He did nothing to deny what Logan said, and I stepped away from him, toward the door that led to the barn.

The doors bounced open and Logan entered, stumbling over himself. He gained his footing as Nick turned to face him casually; unfazed by the gun that was now pointed to his head.

I screamed when the shot was fired, but not for Nick. Logan was tackled and the gun discharged when Nick attacked him. Both men fell to the ground, Logan underneath Nick struggling to get away. His arm fell flat and bounced on the floor, the gun sliding to my feet inadvertently. Before I thought of picking it up, I watched Logan take a forceful swing at my husband.

Nick's face merely flinched before he returned a swing at Logan that nearly knocked him out.

Both men stopped when they heard me pull the gun's hammer back. Nick looked at me, then Logan, both as surprised as the other when they discovered the barrel of the gun pointed directly at them.

Nick stood from the floor first, his hands in surrender. His face was bloodied up, but not as badly as Logan's. He struggled to stand from the floor, his eyes locked on either me or the gun, I couldn't tell which.

"It's him," Nick said between breaths, pointing to Logan frantically.

I aimed the barrel at Logan.

"It's not!" Logan returned. "It's in *him*!"

Nick shook his head as I aimed the gun at him. "He found the gun,

Cynthia! How would he know where it was if you never told us about it?"

The gun went back to Logan, and he didn't react. He seemed to be lost in a thought, suddenly.

"How did you find the gun, Logan?" I asked, my hands beginning to tremble.

He frowned, thinking to himself, but not finding an answer. "I don't know," he said. "But I swear, it's in Nick. Not me."

Before Nick could respond, I walked to the back door of the room, taking my steps easy and keeping my eyes on both men.

"Outside, both of you," I ordered, opening the door.

The only one who hesitated was Nick. Logan walked directly to the door without looking back. After several seconds, Nick followed.

I walked behind them, holding the gun steady between both of them.

"Inside the glove compartment of the car, there's a pen," I told both of them. "One of you get it."

"For what?" Logan asked.

I pointed the gun at him. "Do it."

He sighed then walked to the open door while I held my aim steady at Nick. Logan found the pen quickly and showed it to me.

"What do you want me to do, write my name?"

I didn't answer. He uncapped the pen and scribbled on his hand. Without even inspecting it first, he held his left palm up to me.

Logan.

"You see?" he asked.

Another tremble fell over my hand as Nick accepted the pen and took the test. He showed his left palm to me.

Nick.

The men exchanged glances as I sighed, my arms finally falling to my side. It was gone.

A thick gust of humid air whipped between us as Nick approached, extending his arm toward me. In his hand, he held the pen.

"Your turn," he said. "I'll hold the gun this time."

My heart skipped a beat at what he was insisting. But it was only fair since I had just done the same to them. I took the pen, and though I was reluctant to give him the gun, I did. My left hand trembled terribly as I tried to write my name on the palm of my right hand. Out of the corner of my eye, I saw Nick hold the gun up at me as I wrote. His hand was incredibly steady.

What if I just handed the gun to the killer? What if he shoots while I'm writing, haven proven once again that nothing is what it seems? He could have very well written his own name backwards and made it appear normal.

Cynthia.

I showed it to them before the ink smeared with the sweat. Nick's arm dropped to his side and Logan's shoulders slumped. None of us were possessed.

Maybe It was back with Luis, having caused enough confusion between us. It could have very well left the dirty work to us seeing as we were seconds away from pulling the trigger.

It was an attack of a different kind. Mason was playing off our own emotions, and the exhausted state it left us in convinced me it was the worst attack of all.

*

"There's another way to stop him," I told them both.

We made our way back into the house after I secured the gun in the glove box of the car. The three of us were somber and empty, but they had to know what I discovered.

"What do you mean?" Nick asked.

I told them of the vision Mason fed me in the barn, then told them how I managed to kick the demon out of my body at will. I exorcised the spirit by remaining conscious enough after he invaded me, therefore we didn't need to kill anyone else to stop It. We just needed the will power.

"I don't know," Logan said after a brief moment of silence. He sat on the cooler and wiped the sweat from his forehead. "Angela said the only way to be certain was to kill the body. She said anything else would just be a temporary measure, like separating."

"She also said that it wasn't likely Mason would attack anyone who wasn't directly involved, and she's been proven wrong."

"What if you're wrong?" Nick asked me. "What if he left on his own? Maybe he wanted you to believe that we can make him leave at will."

I remained silent at first, contemplating his suggestion. If Mason did leave on his own accord, convincing me we held a certain power over him, what would it mean for us? He would kill us all, then what? Go after our kids and Uncle George? It wasn't a circumstance I wanted to think about.

"I want to go to the hospital," I told them.

"Why?" Logan asked.

"To see Luis. Maybe we can end this right now."

"You mean kill him?"

"To test my theory. I'll tell Luis to fight him, and if, for any reason I suspect Mason is in him, then I will tell Morrison to flip the switch."

"I thought you wanted to keep Luis alive," Logan said.

I did, but, "What other choice has Mason given us?"

"What if it doesn't work?" Nick asked.

"It'll leave Mason without a resting ground," Logan said. "He'll be forced to come after us."

"We should go together, then," I suggested, but Nick quickly shook his head.

"No. We should separate. Cynthia, you go to the hospital, Logan and I will go our own ways."

"There isn't any where to go for miles, Nick," Logan said.

"It doesn't matter," Nick responded, turning to Logan. "Until Cynthia returns, you and I can separate and if Mason comes after us, he can't kill either one."

"There's no way to guarantee that, Nick," I told him.

But he nodded. "Yes, there is."

*

He had an idea. It was an idea that seemed outrageous enough to work, and it only took another hour or so of our time.

He insisted they lock themselves in two different rooms of the house then reinforce the doors with what was left of the plywood. "We trap ourselves in," he said, "making it impossible for anyone to break in or out of the rooms."

And just like that, the work began. There was more work that needed to be done on the outside of the house so we started there; sealing the last of the windows and reinforcing the rest of the weak wood. Then, for the first time during our stay in the house, we made our way to the second floor together.

It was a narrow hallway that had two doors to different rooms, one cornered to the other. Quickly reflecting on the news articles we read, I knew the first door was to the master bedroom, and it was the room Logan would stay in. He stepped in, and without so much as giving him a supportive nod, Nick and I closed the door and hammered it up. The room was completely sealed, Logan trapped inside.

Without taking a break, Nick and I ran toward Mason's bedroom. This time, I had to seal the room on my own. I wanted to cry for them as I hammered up the wood across the door frame, but there was no time. The threatening clouds were already beginning to brew, and I still had to make my way to the hospital.

By one that afternoon, neither one of them could walk outside the place they now were. Each was equipped with flashlights to help aid their view inside the darkness they resided in, with no way to even communicate with each other. It seemed to be a fool proof plan, and as I was left alone outside and with no time to worry about the men I was leaving behind, I prayed it would work.

I had a mission to carry out; it was now up to me to save the rest of us. I started the car and checked the glove compartment to make certain the gun had not been moved. Slowly, I drove out of the farm grounds and back onto the main road without glancing at the rearview mirror. I had less than seven hours to reach the hospital and tell Luis to fight Mason, or tell Morrison to kill the machines and return before the hurricane.

The plan seemed simple, and I was hopeful that Luis was strong enough to fight Mason on his own. If not, I hoped to rid ourselves of Mason Bayer once and for all.

Deluded

I kept my mind only on the road as I sped toward the hospital. Hurricane Alida still had not shown a sign of winds nor rain, but her threat had already affected the city streets. The gas stations were filled with lines of frustrated drivers who waited until the last minute to fill their tanks once more before the storm, and the supermarket parking lots were filled though the rows of canned foods and water gallons was empty for days. To my advantage, it left the streets empty.

I made it to the hospital in under an hour, just as the newsbreak erupted through the radio. The update on the storm reminded us to remain indoors after 8:30 that evening. I turned off the car and glanced at my watch; 2:43 P.M.

I had plenty of time.

It would all end today, I thought to myself as I entered the hospital. If not for others or myself then for the children. There was no telling what Mason would do to them if we lost, and I wouldn't stand for it.

While walking to the ICU, I was certain that Luis would volunteer his life if it meant the children's safety. He would go to a good place for it, of that, there was no question.

I approached the nurse's station and had Doctor Morrison paged. Seconds later, he walked through the double doors, fresh lab coat and clipboard equipped.

He seemed relieved to see me and asked for the others as he approached.

"I came alone," I told him. "There's something I need to talk to you about…in private."

"Sure," he said without missing a beat. "My office?"

I nodded, and he asked for a second to make a quick phone call. With his back turned toward me, he reached over the nurse's station, grabbed the phone and punched a few numbers. He whispered into the receiver for a few seconds, then smiled at me when he was done.

We walked through the hospital toward his office with him in the lead. "Are you prepared for the storm?" he asked over his shoulder.

"We're getting there," I told him, not caring for the small talk.

But he continued. "I'll be here all night. Hurricanes promise a busy night, every doctor on staff is here tonight."

His pace was fast as though he were in a hurry, as though he didn't want to be stopped by anyone. I was hoping he wouldn't rush me through what I had to say; I would take as long as I needed to give the order.

"How are the kids?" he asked.

He chose the worst of moments to make conversation.

"Fine," I answered dryly.

Once we passed through the double doors leading to the desolate hall, his pace didn't slow. After dodging the doors swinging my way as I entered, I watched him dig through the pockets of his coat frantically. He was definitely in a hurry, and knowing how difficult it would be to ask him to terminate Luis' life, I nearly thought of forgetting the whole thing.

He found his keys and unlocked the door, leaving it open for me to enter behind him.

"Shut the door," he ordered, switching the lights on.

I did as I was told then saw Morrison taking off his coat to throw it forcefully on the couch by his desk. His attitude changed suddenly, an anger fell over him, and I felt it directed toward me.

"Is everything okay?" I asked him, frowning.

"Sit down," he said then walked around his desk toward his leather chair.

"No, this won't take long, actually."

"Cynthia, sit down!" His angry eyes were beaming at me over his glasses.

But I glared back. This was my moment; I didn't care what Morrison had to say.

"Morrison, I need you to…"

"Those detectives were here again today, Cynthia," he said, crossing his arms. "They've been looking for you all. Where have you been?" He was ordering his questions, demanding answers and I was taken aback.

"None of that matters. I need you to cut…"

"It matters, Cynthia, because I can't have them running my hospital like this. They want to put a man outside Luis' door to watch him."

"Morrison, listen to me. None of that matters," I repeated.

"Do you know what the consequences are for obstruction of justice?"

I frowned at his question. "They're not going to arrest you. They can't."

He took a deep breath. "I'm not talking about me," he said.

Then, as if on cue, the door to his office opened, and in walked the one reason that made me believe good ol' Doctor Morrison led me right into a trap.

Detective Raul Santiago walked into the room and glared at me.

Suddenly, Morrison's fast walk, the secret phone call and subtle small talk all made sense. He intended on turning me in from the start. I looked upon him for the truth, and he met my gaze with satisfied eyes.

Santiago closed the door and took a step toward me, reaching for something at the back of his waist. When he retrieved a pair of handcuffs, I took a step back in shock, my heart instantly beginning to pound.

"What the hell is this?" I yelled at them, backing into a wall.

"Mrs. Sheyer," Santiago said, opening one of the cuffs. "I'm going to have to ask you to turn around, please."

"You're arresting me? For what?"

"You're charged with obstruction of justice," he said. "You have the right to remain…"

"No! Wait!" I begged. "We've cooperated in every way!"

"Where are your friends?" he asked me.

I didn't answer. I couldn't tell them.

"You have the right to an attorney." He took one more step toward me.

"But…"

"Mrs. Sheyer, I will use force if you don't cooperate!" he warned. "Now, turn around. That's the last time I will ask you."

I couldn't believe what was happening. Feeling desperate and betrayed, I wanted to wake up – realize it was all just another nightmare brought on by Mason Bayer. Though it was, I was awake for this one.

"Now!" he barked.

Defeated, I did as I was told. Slowly, I turned, to face the wall and before my feet were settled, Santiago was already pulling on my arms. As he recited my rights from memory, I felt the cold metal slapping against my wrists.

I shot a final glance at Morrison as Detective Santiago pulled me off the wall and forced me toward the office door.

The son of a bitch didn't even look at me.

I wanted Mason to take me; to prove to the imbeciles that we were all innocent. It was clearly the only way to make them believe. But I was alone. No one would rescue me. Not even Mason Bayer.

*

Detective Santiago drove me to the station in the back seat of his black sedan. My hands were restrained and my back was twisted for comfort. Kind enough to remove the cuffs when we arrived, he led me through the building and into an interrogation room I had been to once before while researching for a book. Only I was on the opposite side of the viewing glass to study the suspect's actions. This time, it was me who was being watched…and for a very long time.

Santiago left me in the room after ordering me to take my seat at the single table. The son of a bitch left me in the room for an hour and a half, waiting.

The psychological game played with almost every suspect brought into the room was not working with me. Most would become scared and intimidated by the solitude, but it was only making me angrier. There was no time to play games.

When he finally showed up, I stood from the chair and cursed at him for leaving me locked in the room for such a long time.

"I had to take care of some preliminaries," he said with a shrug, then ordered me to sit back down.

Cursing again, I threw myself onto the chair and closed my eyes, trying to compose myself. The anger broke into sweat the moment he walked in, and if I wanted out, I had to calm myself before he began his interrogation.

I watched Santiago keep his own cool as I refused to answer his first few questions. I did want to cooperate, but not when he asked questions regarding the others. He wanted me to tell him where they were, and I wouldn't say.

"You may as well tell me, Mrs. Sheyer," he said pacing the room. He had been pacing since he entered. "We'll find them either way."

"For what?" I asked. "So you can arrest them for something they didn't do as well?" I waited for his response, but he simply continued pacing. "I won't tell you where they are, so don't ask me again."

He nodded, accepting my answer. His technique was evident to me, but to half the suspects he brought in, he was a pro. The wet behind the ears attitude he had alongside Maria Lopez was gone now. Detective Santiago knew how to handle his questions, knew when to accept the answer to gain the suspect's trust.

"Fine," he said. "We'll move on, then." He stopped pacing and looked at me in the eye long enough to ask his next question. "Why have you denied your right to an attorney?"

"Because I have nothing to hide," I shrugged.

"Except your friends." He knew exactly where the question would lead me, and again, I walked into it. "Are they dead?"

They might be now that you stopped me from ending it. "No."

"Well, you need to convince me, Cynthia, because right now, we're not so sure."

"You think Luis killed them too?"

"Why have they been hiding?

I sighed in frustration. "I can't tell you why they do what they do, detective, because I'm not them."

"Fine," he said. "We won't talk about your friends."

Finally!

"Why don't you tell me what you know about Tomas Brewer?"

The name struck me like a hammer on my toe, but I managed to keep my face from reacting. "I don't know about Tomas Brewer," I said as nonchalantly as I could.

"You don't?"

"No."

He took the seat across from me. "You've never met Tomas Brewer?"

"I didn't say that. He lives in my neighborhood."

"And I'm sure you know about his connection with Mason Bayer, right?"

I didn't answer.

"He was the seventh member of the team assembled by the DOH to issue the closing of the Bayer farm," he said.

I listened as though it were new information.

"Of course you know that already, don't you? You and Nick both signed onto public computers at the library and downloaded virtually everything on Mason Bayer. Why'd you do that?"

I bit my bottom lip to not tell him everything in a desperate plea for help.

"I know about your relationship with Detective William Kux," he said, "and I know he contacted you after walking onto the scene of Mr. Brewer's murder. Here's the funny thing, though. Joanna Corona was numbered the same way Mason Bayer numbered his victims when he was alive, and Brewer's daughter, Katherine almost did the same. The only reason she didn't was because Detective Kux came onto the scene."

He waited for it to sink in before continuing. I was beginning to sweat as the thought they would blame me for the murders somehow and keep me jailed for life.

"These people were murdered with the signature of a serial killer that died almost twenty years ago, both by different people. We think you know why."

"I don't," I said, clearing my throat.

"Detective Kux quit the force after he found Katherine Brewer went crazy. Do you know why?"

"No. He hasn't contacted us ever since that night."

"It seems everyone has a secret, Mrs. Sheyer. The rumor is you might know them all. Tell me something to prove them wrong," he said, leaning over the table. "I need something to go on here. Help me out."

I sighed, looking away from him. "I don't know anything, detective. Believe me, if I did, I would tell you."

"Then why can't you tell me where your friends are?" he asked. "Would they be in danger if you did."

No, you would. "That's ridiculous."

He fell back onto the chair and took a deep breath. "Fine," he said.

"You're free to go, then."

"What?" I yelled, standing to my feet in disbelief.

He shrugged. "Unless you want to stay here the night."

"I haven't been arrested?"

He shook his head as innocently as he stood. "Truthfully, Mrs. Sheyer, we have nothing to hold you for. I still think you're hiding something but until I hear it from you, there are no charges."

I could have beaten him to a pulp, and I grit my teeth in anger. The time wasted with him was vital to our survival, and all I could do was turn toward the door before an involuntary punch escaped.

"If you are hiding something," he said as I opened the door, "or if any of your other friends are dead, we'll find them."

I wanted to ignore his words, but the boiling blood in my veins wouldn't allow it. "Thanks to you," I said over my shoulder, "we may already be dead." I opened the door to the room and demanded a ride back to the hospital.

*

"What did you mean by that?" Detective Santiago asked.

We drove in silence for more than half the journey back to the hospital. Riding in the front seat this time, seatbelt fastened, I was thinking of the quickest route back to the farm. Nick and Logan were probably concerned by now. Terminating Luis was not going to happen right away, I decided. I would have to collect the others first, and together, we'd think of another way…

"Mrs. Sheyer," Santiago called, snapping me form my daze. "What did you mean when you said you were all dead thanks to me?"

I sucked my teeth and sighed. "I meant nothing. Forget I said it."

He remained silent, but this time, he wasn't satisfied with my answer. Still, he kept his eyes on the road, and not to provoke another conversation, I did the same.

Night came early. It was barely half past five and heavy clouds along the desolate highway covered the sun completely. The winds already picked up, and the air's smell indicated that rain was shortly approaching.

I watched the rows of trees speed by, knowing that by sunrise, they would have all been destroyed with the storm. The deep river tucked safely behind the trees would be contaminated with thousands of leaves and large branches, no doubt. All of Miami would feel the wrath of the storm.

"It won't take me much to believe," Santiago said suddenly.

I glared at him, uncertain of what he meant, and afraid to ask.

"If there's something else happening here, you can tell me," he continued. "I won't think you're crazy."

My heart jumped as I wondered exactly what he was getting at. I kept my mouth shut and looked out my window, praying he didn't make me explain anything.

"You see, I'd almost say that it was Mason Bayer who's doing this," he said, looking at me.

"Keep your eyes on the road," I ordered.

"It would make perfect sense. The motive is there, and it's his trademark we're finding. Only, he's dead, so it's impossible, right?"

"Anything is possible," I said, under my breath. I couldn't tell if his questions were genuine or if he was mocking me for anything he might have overheard. He and his sidekick probably bugged our cars.

"Billy told me something about Mason Bayer once," he said.

I tried my hardest to not show my interest.

"He was telling me about the night Mason escaped that institution, and he said something that was really strange. He said, 'When Mason Bayer is angered, and the floodgates of his rage opens, prepare yourself for Hell on Earth.' Actually, he told me those were your father's words. He used it as a pep-talk before he sent his crew after the killer."

"What are you getting at, detective?"

"Could Mason Bayer's anger fuel him enough to come back from the dead?"

Though I laughed, it was just for show. Really, my nerves were shocked that he hit the situation right on. I shook my head at him. "You watch too many movies."

Again, he was unsatisfied, and for a second, the questions stopped.

We weren't far from the hospital now. Two, maybe three miles.

Then, Santiago's right arm fell over the back of my headrest, and I adjusted in my chair, startled. When he frowned at me, and I realized he was just resting his arm, I almost apologized. But he grabbed the back of my head suddenly, and before I could react, he shoved.

The dashboard raced toward my face, Santiago's hand guiding my head downward with extreme force. A blinding pain beat on my forehead as the dashboard cracked against it. My body flew back into the chair, my head whirling with dense pain. My vision blurred and my thoughts were jumbled, but I held fast to the idea that Santiago was not himself.

The car swerved on the streets as Its hand took hold of my head again, and I reacted. I threw my arms in front of me as It shoved me toward the dashboard again. Quickly knocking his arm from my head, I tried to open the car door.

It grunted and called me a bitch as I realized the squad car wouldn't open from the inside.

The car began to speed on the road, and though I didn't noticed, Mason was laughing.

Terrified, I looked at the speedometer as we approached a sharp turn. Quickly passing sixty miles per hour, I thought of throwing myself onto the wheel, but it would only cause an accident.

It reached for me again, cursing at me as I tried my hardest to fight him off. Then he turned the car against the sharp curve suddenly, and my body was thrown onto the car door. My head bounced off the window, dazing my senses again.

The sedan nearly fishtailed, the backside slamming into a tree as Mason took control of the turn. Again, I was thrown around in my seat, pulled back by the restraints. My vision began to clear when I noticed my door swung open with the impact.

The car picked up more speed and another curve was just before us, lined with even more trees.

Its knuckles turned white around the steering wheel as it eyed the row of trees with great anticipation. It was going to kill us both by crashing into the forest.

I jumped out of the car and onto the speeding pavement, rolling against the rough ground and tearing every exposed part of my body in the process. I stopped along the curb of the road and looked up just in time to see the car head straight for the trees.

It missed, crashing through the shrubbery of two nearby bushes, the car sped straight toward the river. Seconds later, there was a muffled splash, and I swear I heard the car sink.

I lied still, but not because of the pain. Fearful It would walk through the bushes and chase after me, I watched the line of trees for a minute or two.

I struggled to stand, a nauseous wave falling over me as I did. I fought the bile from spewing as I regained my footing. It took a while to collect my thoughts, and when I did, I turned to the road.

Detective Raul Santiago was dead, and I felt no remorse for him. Not at the time. I was too hopeful that Mason was dead as well, and the fact that I didn't see a mysterious number appear on the road only made me more encouraged. Then again, Santiago probably hadn't earned his number; he wasn't part of the equation.

I had no choice but to make the remainder of my journey to the hospital by foot. There wasn't time to attend to my wounds for the storm was due in a few hours, nor was there time to cry in desperation. It would be a short while before Santiago was discovered missing, so I had to be quick. Get to the hospital, kill Luis and save the others.

There was a plan, and I had to stick to it.

Only the adrenaline that prevented me from feeling the searing pain began to weaken. After a mile of dragging my feet, my head began to throb and my weakened mind was growing frail. The hits to my head proved dangerous when I had my first dizzy spell on the side of the road. The second was worse.

I cursed Mason's name as I trekked on. But in doing so, I began to wonder if It had taken over me. I was the closest living thing around had he jumped out of Santiago. I tried not to think about it too much as it began to distract me from the determination of the road ahead.

As I walked into the hospital's lobby, nearly forty-five minutes later, I shuffled my way to the information desk, catching stares from everyone as I passed.

Doctor Morrison was paged to the ICU on the speakers above, and the sound of his name made me cringe.

"Can I help you?" an older nurse asked me as I reached over the information counter and snatched the pen from her hands.

I ignored her and focused on the palm of my right hand. I already wrote my name across it, and because it had begun to fade, I traced over the same area.

Cynthia. I wasn't possessed.

I turned to the crowded lobby and, in a stupor, I looked at the ocean of people. Unable to catch my breath from the long walk, I felt the last few ounces of energy drain itself through my feet. As my vision blurred again, I caught sight of the person I didn't care to see. Detective Maria Lopez spotted me across the lobby, and she was approaching.

I didn't see much more of her though. Before she even reached me, my body simply gave in to the exhaustion, and I passed out.

Transition

Maria Lopez was the first person I saw when my eyes opened. I was bound to virtually the same bed I was in when Morrison told me I was never pregnant, and Maria was seated in the same chair across from me.

She was happy to see me awake.

"What time is it?" I asked her, suddenly eager to get to Nick and Logan.

"It's ten minutes to seven," she answered, looking at her watch. "You've been asleep for a little over an hour."

Though my heart settled over the fact that I hadn't slept through an entire day, I was suddenly wakened by the fact that I still had a mission to carry out.

"Where's Morrison?"

She shook her head and shrugged. "He's gone MIA."

"What?"

"Missing in action. I've had him paged several times since you've arrived, but he hasn't shown and no one has seen him."

I figured it was better that way as I quickly stood from the bed, pulling the IV needle off my right hand.

"What are you doing?" Maria asked, standing from her chair and rushing toward me. "You can't go anywhere."

"Don't worry, I feel fine," I told her, frantically pacing the room in search for my clothes.

"Just like that?" she asked. "I think you should get checked out, especially after the way you collapsed out there."

I found my clothes folded neatly on another chair. I thanked Maria for her concern then slid my shorts on underneath the hospital gown. Turning my back toward her, I removed the gown and replaced it with the cotton tee shirt, still wet with my own perspiration.

"You can't just leave," Detective Lopez told me as I sat on the chair to lace my sneakers.

Watch me.

"I have some questions to ask you," she added.

I stood from the chair and frowned at her. "You've wasted enough of my time with that little stunt you and your partner organized," I told her. "I'm through answering your questions."

"Where is Santiago?" she asked.

I couldn't believe that I forgot. He was dead, and she had absolutely no idea.

"I don't know," I told her. "He dropped me off here and he left."

"Did he say where he was off to?"

I shook my head to not voice another lie. Then, before she could ask me another question, I headed toward the curtain divider.

"I don't want to ask you where your friends are, Cynthia," she said from behind me. "I don't want to ask you any questions about Luis or Jo, either."

I turned to her. "Then, why are you here?"

She took a breath. "I'm here because since the accident that killed your friend and wounded your brother, you have all checked into this hospital at least once. This is your second visit in two days. I want to know what's happening."

"We're just stressed," I said, without looking directly at her. "Some people handle it better than others."

"Are you kidding me?" she asked, almost laughing. "Look at you. You look like shit!"

I gnawed my jaw. Detective Maria Lopez bugged me from the day she entered my life, but with the aid of her sarcasm, she pushed me over the edge.

I turned to her, cold faced and certain of myself. Standing just a few feet away from her, I asked, "You want to know what's happening?"

She crossed her arms, smiling to finally have me at the point she wanted.

So I told her…everything.

"Eighteen years ago, we killed the man who killed our parents," I said without blinking. "Now, believe it or not, he wants us dead, and he is using every method possible to make sure he gets us there. If you don't believe me, ask Katherine Brewer. Ask her if she remembers running her father down, and ask her why she numbered him in a backwards 'two' the way you think my brother did Jo. She'll tell you she didn't do it, and do you know why she'd say that? Because she didn't. She didn't kill her father, and Luis didn't kill Jo. Mason Bayer did."

It was out; I didn't hold back once I started, and like a deflating balloon, I let all the air out – and it felt great.

Maria didn't flinch at my story. She didn't even blink when I told her that Mason Bayer killed them, and for a second, I thought maybe she believed me.

But then she laughed. "I'm sorry," she said, "you can do better than that."

"I beg your pardon."

"I thought you were a writer," she said, still laughing. "Aren't writers supposed to be great liars?"

I didn't respond. I could only grit my teeth in anger.

"I'll tell you something Cynthia," she continued. "You go to anyone with that story, and they'll throw you in a psychiatric hospital faster than you can imagine. No one will believe you, so I suggest you keep that story for a book and save yourself the embarrassment."

She walked passed me toward the curtain divider and I let her go…

For those who do not believe, no explanation will suffice.

"Your father would turn over in his grave if he heard you," she said. "Don't even think about leaving this hospital yet."

And before I could retaliate, a horrid scream filled the air.

It was woman's voice on the other side of the curtain, and as though we were working together, Maria and I ran far enough to see what the commotion was about.

From the nurse's station, we heard the scream again and pinpointed it to a young nurse standing at the door to a patient's room. She was trembling, her mouth covered with her hands as she backed away from the room, letting out another shriek.

Two other nurses and a doctor ran to her aid, and when they caught a glimpse of what troubled the young woman, they joined her to form a chorus of yells.

My heart nearly stopped when I realized they were standing at the door to Luis' room.

*

I ran to the room, my mind considering a hundred scenarios that would cause the nurse to react the way she had. After pushing her aside for a clear view I wished I hadn't stepped into the room without preparing myself first.

There was blood everywhere; on the floor, some on the walls, and even on the ceiling. I turned away, catching a glimpse of the bed sheets, also soiled with blood. There was too much of it to assume that Luis was still…

He was breathing. Barely, but breathing nonetheless. The sheets covered his body completely, but the rise and fall of the blankets told me he was still alive. The heart monitor still detected a small, faint beat, and when I saw a bloodied scalpel on the floor beside the bed, I screamed for help.

Maria pushed me aside as she ran into the room and toward the bed.

Two nurses followed her in to attend to my brother, ordering everyone to leave, but no one did.

They pulled the sheet back and everyone in sight of the bed gasped in shock.

Doctor Morrison was barely recognizable behind the blood painted on his face. He was comatose, and his stomach was torn open to expose his intestines.

And Luis was gone.

"Who could have done this?" one of the nurses asked.

As I watched the horror unfold before me, I thought of Mason. I thought of everything I learned in the past week and immediately came up with the answer. The transition between the possessing spirit and its host was complete; Mason was reborn in Luis' body. There was no other explanation.

I kept my nerves in control as Maria retrieved a mobile phone from her pocket and began barking orders. With all the attention off of me, I slipped away from the crowd and toward the all-access staircase.

Mason Bayer now had a body to call his own, and he was more than likely on his way to the farm; on his way home.

*

There is a difference between being scared and being terrified. When someone is scared, their hearts pound uncontrollably, their body trembles and, at best, one might lose control of their bodily functions. Being terrified takes fear to an entirely different level. People have died from being terrified, their faces frozen with fear from whatever it was that stopped their hearts. Being terrified is when the fear erupts from the core of the soul, paralyzing the body and thoughts, even takes it as far as settling on your tongue so the terror can be tasted.

When I reached the farmhouse, I was terrified.

There was a car parked in front of the house when I arrived; a white four-door luxury car that I didn't recognize. One single glance at the car's license plate confirmed my fear. *DR-MRSN;* Doctor Morrison. Mason Bayer arrived before I did.

I opened the glove box and retrieved the gun, quickly estimating how many rounds were left. Billy told me there were six, and two shots were fired. There was plenty left for the kill.

The air grew restless, and it began to rain as I slowly stepped out of the car. There was silence; the sickening sound of absolutely nothing haunted my mind with thoughts that Nick and Logan were already dead. As my eyes examined the front of the farmhouse, I prayed I would hear either one of them, even if they were calling for help.

Morrison's car was empty, the keys still in the ignition, and the hood still warm. Mason may have arrived before I did, but I wasn't too far behind him.

The front door to the farmhouse was sealed shut and locked. Nick barricaded it from the inside, and from the looks of it, the panels he hammered up were still intact. Mason had not worked his way through, so it was possible that neither Nick nor Logan knew of Its arrival.

I looked out into the dark field wondering if It was watching me from a distance.

I heard a noise, a shuffle of sorts, coming from behind the house. In a single, swift movement, I jumped off the house's porch and carefully stood against the east wall holding the gun with both trembling, sweaty hands.

Sliding easily against the wall, I made it around the corner. The rain slammed on my face and body, but I didn't care; my concern was taken completely by the sight of the door that led to the barn.

It was dark inside the house, the generator silent and resting from powering the lights, yet there was a glow in the center of the room.

A single flashlight was powered and left on the floor as though it was dropped. Its light shined into the hall that led to the stair case, and I worked up my courage to enter the house and pick it up. It was one of the flashlights that

Nick and Logan had before they were barricaded.

Taking careful, slow steps, I kept my eyes locked onto the object until I obtained it and made the fatal mistake of inspecting the room.

I gasped when I discovered the writing all over the wooden walls. In no particular order, words were scribbled, and though they weren't in plain English, it didn't take long for me to figure what they meant.

ENO, OWT, EERHT, ROUF, EVIF, XIS, NEVES

They were all written in blood and repeated countless times.

Mason numbered us all.

There was another shuffle and I nearly screamed on instinct alone. It came from somewhere on the second floor, and as I spun to face the hall, I knew I had no choice but to enter further.

The flashlight's beam bounced with my trembling hand, but I kept my focus ahead of me as I walked into the hall. The smell of gasoline hit me after the first several steps, and when a puddle splashed beneath my feet, I turned to the generator. It was demolished.

A yell erupted from the second floor, stripping me of my courage. I nearly collapsed when I heard the deep, rumbling voice holler in pleasure. Its voice was stronger, more alive than I remembered it, almost as though two voices were screaming at once.

My entire body trembled and I lacked the courage to continue. Looking back at the door from which I entered, I thought of running out, calling for help from someone, anyone who would listen. But then I thought of Nick and Logan.

My grip on the gun fastened, and I headed toward the stairs.

Taking one step at a time, I kept both the flashlight and the gun pointed upwards toward the second floor. There was nothing to see except the plain walls and desolate entry until I reached the top of the stair case; the place where James Bayer hanged himself.

The wood we used to barricade both doors were torn to splinters, and

I heard nothing coming from either room. It was as though they were empty and I fought the urge to call out for Nick and Logan, but I didn't want to announce my visit to the enemy. I was convinced though, that my heavy, uncontrolled breathing had done that already.

I continued toward the first room, and standing against the outside wall, I peered in.

Nick was lying on the floor in the center of the empty room, and I fought to keep my knees from buckling. His arms were outstretched as though he was crucified, and when I shined the light on him from the entrance, he didn't move.

I ran into the room and held the light directly at his face. His eyes were closed, his mouth partially open, and after I noticed the word sprawled on the floor above his head, I realized he might have been dead.

RUOF, it read.

I knelt beside him, dropping the gun next to me to feel his entire body. There was no wound, no source of blood, and he was still warm. I leaned into him and felt the glorious wave of his breath and immediately began patting him gently on the face, begging him to wake up.

Then, a hand entered the flashlight's beam from within the darkness, and slowly reached for the gun.

I pushed myself away, falling backwards onto the floor, screaming. Fumbling with the flashlight, I managed to shine it directly on whoever was in the room with me.

Logan appeared unfazed by the fact that I was in the house. With the gun in his hands, he stood from the floor and aimed it across the room.

"Move out of the way, Cynthia," he said, keeping his eyes locked above me.

It was then that I realized It was in the room with us.

I stood to my feet and bolted to the other side of the room, by the entrance where Logan stood. Then, I shined the light on our killer.

Transmogrification; the state in which the possessing spirit has begun to physically show through the host's body, was what I saw.

I wanted to scream, I wanted to cry, to vomit at what Mason turned my brother into.

His eyes were sunken into their sockets, barely visible through the shadows of his brows. His cheeks caved, taking the fullness of Luis' face, and his lips, cracked and torn, were filled with blood.

It smiled at my reaction, then twisted Its elbow outward toward the light to expose the chunks missing from his forearm. It bit through the skin several times causing an extreme loss of blood.

"Logan, put the gun down!" she yelled from the door way to the room.

Maria Lopez appeared just as It hid back in the shadows, and for the first time ever, I was happy that she followed us throughout our entire journey. She came in at a very critical time; a time to save our lives.

But Logan didn't listen; he kept his aim steady at the darkness.

"Put the gun down, now!" she yelled, then her eyes looked passed Logan, and directly at Nick.

She frowned in shock, looking to me for an answer then stepping into the room for a closer inspection of my husband.

"It's not what you think," I told her nearly yelling. "Mason is..."

"Bull-shit!" she said, still holding the gun toward Logan. "I don't want to hear about Mason." She bent her knees to check the pulse on Nick's neck, but her aim did not move from Logan. "He's still alive," she said, almost to herself.

"Maria, please..."

"Not another word!" She stood from the ground. "Logan, put the gun down or I will shoot!"

In an attempt to explain what was happening, Logan turned, and involuntarily pointed the gun at her.

Maria fired.

He flew back, his right shoulder exploding with blood as he fell to the ground. The gun bounced from his hand and I screamed.

He whined in pain as Maria quickly crossed the room to collect the gun without hesitation, but as she bent for the weapon, the weapon moved away from her.

As though it was pushed or kicked, the gun slid across the floor, completely on its own. Both Maria and I watched as it stopped directly before the killer.

With surprise painted across her face, Maria turned to me, then turned back to see the monster before her.

It was holding the gun up to her, a few feet away from her face, and without warning, It fired as well.

I didn't scream this time as Maria fell to the floor, convulsing because of the bullet wound in the center of her forehead. Within seconds, her body died, and I was left alone with the killer.

It smiled at me again, holding the gun in Its bloodied hands.

Logan squirmed on the floor toward Maria, leaving a trail of blood as he tried to lift himself off the ground but failing. His breath was short, and I could see him falling weak from his injured shoulder.

"*Psst,*" It called to me.

It moved, without my noticing, toward Nick. I begged It to leave him alone as It stepped on my husband's neck and pointed the gun right at his head.

"You son of a bitch!" Logan yelled.

But It didn't listen to him. Instead, It looked up at me.

"Who should I kill?" It asked, Its voice making me tremble. "Nick, or Logan?"

Logan froze as Mason aimed the gun toward him.

"No!" I cried, begging It to stop as though I could reason with him – as though it were still Luis.

"It's your choice," It said.

"Me!" Logan yelled to him. "Kill me!"

But It didn't want an answer from Logan. It was waiting for an answer from me.

"Who will it be?"

"Me!" Logan yelled again.

And I could only cry, begging it not to kill anyone.

It pulled the hammer back and brought the gun closer to Nick's head. "Nick it is," It said, and I watched as Its index finger hugged the trigger.

"Stop!" I yelled, taking a step toward him.

I was relieved when It looked up to me, surprised. He stood straight but kept his foot on Nick's neck. "Then Logan?"

"Yes!" Logan yelled, inches from Maria's body. "Kill me!"

It smiled when I didn't respond. Logan answered for me.

But instead of lifting the gun toward Logan, instead of pulling the trigger and killing another one of my best friends, Mason looked back to my husband and grit his teeth.

The sound of Nick's neck crunching underneath the killer's foot echoed louder than my scream which followed directly afterwards. Mason laughed as I fell to floor with the realization that my husband was dead.

Mason killed Nick and robbed me of my will to fight at the same time.

A gun discharged, and I screamed again. I thought Logan was killed as well, and that I was sure to follow. But I saw Mason looking down to his chest, blood drenching the hospital gown as it poured out of the bullet hole.

Logan reached for Maria's gun and fired.

It fell backwards, Its eyes filled with surprise, and Its face filled with death.

Logan dropped Maria's gun and took a deep breath.

The smell of gunpowder took me back eighteen years, to the night Mason Bayer was reborn inside of Luis. As Logan struggled to push himself toward me, I stared at Luis' body through my tears.

Luis was dead, but he had been for the past week. It was Mason who was number *EVIF*. Mason was finally dead, trapped in Luis' body for eternity.

The End

"Let's get out of here," Logan said.

Though I felt too weak to move, I stood from the ground, then helped Logan do the same. Together, we walked to the doorway of the room, all the while making a conscious effort to not look at the bodies behind us.

But I couldn't help it.

There were three all together; Nick, Luis and Maria. All dead, all covered in blood. It was truly a ghastly sight.

A dizzy spell fell over me as my sight blurred again. My legs began to give out beneath me, and as I fell to my knees, the emotions whirled in my stomach all at once.

"Cynthia, no!" Logan yelled, trying to hold me up but proving too weak to do so.

"I ca…I can't breathe," I whispered, my body falling cold as though Death came for me too.

Logan knelt in front of me and took hold of my shoulder with his one good arm. "Relax, Cynthia," he said softly. "Just relax. Take it easy."

"They…they're all dead," I gasped. "They…"

"Look at me," he ordered. When I didn't, he demanded it. "Look at me, Cynthia!"

I looked into his familiar green eyes, finding just as much fear as I felt.

"There is nothing we could have done to save them, you know that," he said. "Now come on, I can't make the rest of it on my own. The storm is coming and Maria probably called for back up. We have to go."

My head hung between my shoulders as I concentrated on his words and my breathing. He was right; we did have to go, but despite his words, I could not gather the strength to stand after I looked up and saw Luis standing directly behind him.

It grabbed Logan's head with both hands as the fury took over Its face, and in a second, before Logan even had the chance to realize what was happening, another crack filled the air.

I pushed myself away from It as Logan fell to the floor, face first and still.

It stepped over his body and approached me.

By a stroke of luck or a gift from God, I found one of the guns at my side, picked it up, and aimed it at Mason.

It stepped back, a new expression on Its face; an expression of fear.

I stood from the floor quickly and watched as Mason's eyes widened and his lip actually quivered.

"What are you doing, Cyn?" he asked; the voice of the demon gone, and the voice of my brother speaking through. "Put the gun down."

My eyes welded with tears at the sound of his voice, and the gun became unstable. "Luis…"

"It's me, Cyn."

I wanted so much to run into his arms and hold him in mine forever, tell him everything I wanted to say for the past week. I wanted so much to believe that it *was* him.

"What are you doing with that gun?" he asked, taking a step toward me with a confused look upon his distorted face. "It's me," he continued. "It's Luis."

No matter how hard I tried to convince myself that my brother was long dead, the sound of his voice weakened me. His tone, the pronunciation of his words, it *was* Luis. I began to believe his presence, looking beyond the battered face and mutilated arms, I saw Luis in his eyes. That is until he paid no mind to Nick's body as he stepped over it as though Nick, my husband and his best friend, was merely a piece of trash on the floor between us.

The gun fell steady in my hands, and I pulled the trigger.

My arms jerked upwards as the gun exploded in my hands sending a jolt throughout my entire body.

The bullet pierced Mason in the left side of his chest, very near the heart. I watched as he took the bullet, nearly falling back while covering the wound with both hands.

He cried out for me, still using my brother's voice.

It's not Luis…

I fired again, shooting him in the stomach.

He took gasping breaths, blood trailing from the three holes in his torso. Tears began to run down my face as I watched the body that was once Luis struggle to breath.

"Fucking pig," It whispered to me.

It's not Luis…

The gun exploded again, sending him back with another blow to the chest.

Mason fell back, inches from Nick's body, still gasping for air, wheezing with the voice of the demon.

I stepped over him and stared at his face for a moment, looking into the eyes of the killer. I hated him for all he had done, for all he had taken away from me, for the deaths of my own life. I would never recover from the emptiness he had forced me to endure.

It's not Luis…

I fired the last bullet in the chamber of the gun, knocking Mason's skull to the floor with a shot to his forehead. He didn't move again.

I watched him for several minutes, hearing the winds howl outside the house as Hurricane Alida began her wrath. Mason Bayer died in his very own farmhouse that night; of that I am certain. I killed him myself; stripped him of his life the way he stripped me of mine.

*

The winds outside proved too strong as I walked toward the stairs. The ceiling above began to crackle and splinter seconds before it caved in, my right leg caught in some of the debris. The broken wood tore the flesh of my calf rather severely, but I didn't pay any mind to it. The pain in my soul was far greater.

I braced myself for the walk into the night's storm; rain began to fall over the entire city, promising more destruction than the simple farmhouse.

I opened the car door and sat in the driver's seat, my legs still settled on the dirt road. Exhausted and in nauseating pain, I cried until I vomited, letting the fear take hold of me as I realized the hardest part of the journey was still ahead. I thought of Uncle George, Max and Charlene, and the questions they would inevitably ask; questions that deserved answers.

I looked up at the two cars that would be left behind; Morrison's and Maria's. I was certain the house would be destroyed by the storm, but eventually, the cars would be found, and so would the bodies. I had to get away, I decided, before my name was linked to the mess I just witnessed.

As I left the farm that night, making my way ot the main road, the emptiness inside became overbearing. I cried, understanding that they were gone, and I missed them so. But I didn't look back. I couldn't.

Why was I the only one to survive? I wanted to die, to join all the ones I lost and hold their hands in the comfort of the same distant choir bells I told Max of. But I couldn't. Max alone was reason to live for. It was then that I my survival would not go unnoticed. I decided to tell my story for all those who required answers, for all those who would listen.

For all those who would believe.

Though the road ahead was dark only one thing was certain; my life was important to at least one other person. Max was waiting for me, and I needed him more than ever.

Chapter Xis

She closed the notebook and wiped her cheeks from the fallen tears. The memories, the scars, the taste of death still fresh in her mind, she couldn't help but cry as she recreated the most difficult part of her story.

But Cynthia Grazer, the writer, was finally finished. Ten hours and twice as many cigarettes after she began, her story was complete. As she intended, she did so just as the sun rose over the shores of Miami Beach, Hurricane Alida dissolving into nothing but a pitiful drizzle of rain. Sunday, June 14th arrived, and with it came new hope. She forced herself to believe it.

It was now time to indulge in what she promised herself after her seventh novel was written; a shower. She slowly stood from the bed, stretching her right hand and massaging the new writing callus that formed on her middle finger.

As she walked into the bathroom and closed the door behind her, she locked it and thought briefly of the others in her life that were still alive. She had yet to make the phone calls she dreaded, but she decided not to think of it just yet. This was her time now. Stripping from her clothes, she resolved to call everyone after her shower. She wouldn't prepare a speech, and though she knew they would have plenty of questions, she would hand over her story to answer them.

Without much more thought of anything else, she stepped into the tub and prayed that pain and emptiness in her stomach would wash away with the water.

*

"Should we just go upstairs now?" Billy asked.

His butt grew beyond numb in the car seat while waiting out the storm, and he was eager to let Cynthia know that he was there, waiting for her, and that he knew everything. But...

"Not yet," Angela answered. "She's not ready."

Both got on each other's nerves long before the sun began to rise in the East, but now that the storm was over and Alida caused all the damage she would do, Billy was ready for something else. He looked up at Cynthia's window having a clear view from where they were parked, and he was even growing tired of the same sight. He wanted to get out, run a mile, take a walk, do something to get his body moving.

"I can't imagine how scared she must be right now," he said, "what she must be thinking."

"She's a strong woman," Angela replied. "She would have killed herself for her friends if that's what it came to."

Billy nodded, looking through the windshield and at the entrance to the hotel.

He saw Danny look out toward the parking lot several times throughout the night, and though he didn't want to tell the boy that Cynthia went crazy and killed her friends, he had to. He had to tell Danny something to keep him away from her. No one was to go near her before Billy.

He was worried sick about her, wondering what she was doing locked in her room the entire night. Because of the information Danny gave him, he knew she hadn't called Uncle George. In fact, she hadn't called anyone at all. He also knew that she hadn't slept at all the entire night. Twice, he saw her at the glass door to the balcony, and she even spotted them once. He was certain when she turned from the window quickly and concealed herself behind the blinds again. Though it was his black sedan she saw, he was also certain that he was the last person she thought it would be.

Still, he couldn't wait to see her again. The familiar face would only do her good, and letting her know that he watched over her the entire time would relieve her. He would let her know that he could confirm every event to the authorities, make her story public to those who needed the answers.

But until that point, until he could embrace Cynthia with all the comfort she needed, he remained worried.

"Have you seen how it ends?" Billy asked, looking up at her window again. "For her, I mean."

Angela sighed slowly, collecting her thoughts before answering. "I have," she said with a nod. "But I won't tell you."

Despite himself, he nodded. She told him that several times throughout the night, and it downright pissed him off.

He looked out his window and watched as the storm clouds drifted, breaking apart to expose the beams of the rising sun.

And for the first time in nearly a week, he felt relief.

Chapter Пeves

She cleaned each wound, but the pain didn't wash away as she hoped. Stepping out of the tub and into the steamed bathroom, she patted herself dry and wrapped her body in a complimentary robe provided by the hotel.

She was happy to see the mirror covered in steam to avoid her reflection. Maria was right the night before when she told her she looked like shit, and Cynthia wasn't prepared to face it. Standing before the fogged reflection, she played with the mist on the glass. Almost dazed, she carved into it with her index finger, watching as her hand moved helplessly across the glass.

Then she turned and walked out, closing the door behind her to not let the steam escape into the ventilated room.

She walked slowly to her bedside toward the night table. As she sat, she stared at the phone wondering who she would call first. Billy? Uncle George? Jennifer? There were so many…

One of the notebooks slid off the bed and landed at her feet. It was the first of the three notebooks she used to tell her story, and when it hit the floor, the front cover opened, revealing the page that Cynthia used to take the test.

When she settled into the bed, before she began to write, she wrote her name three times on consecutive lines. She needed to convince herself that, despite all her fears, it really was over. And to her, it appeared that it was because her signature was her own.

What she saw before her now was different. She frowned at the notebook, picked it up, and inspected the page herself.

AIHTNYC REZARG

*

Angela froze, a terrible feeling falling over her as her heart suddenly dropped to her feet, and she gasped on reflex.

Billy turned to her, surprised by her dazed look. "Is everything okay?" he asked.

She didn't reply. Her eyes wondered left and right as though she were searching the air, inspecting it for the answer. "No," she whispered anxiously. "We have to get up there. Now!"

*

She couldn't believe what she was seeing. Cynthia closed her eyes, closed the book, praying that it was all her imagination. She took a breath, trying to control her heart, but it didn't work.

She opened the notebook again, to a random page this time. Then, she opened her eyes.

No!

Pure gibberish was spilled across the pages; words she couldn't understand unless she read them backwards. Frantically, she flipped through the pages of the other notebooks, only to find the same dyslexic cursive.

*

Danny jumped to his feet when Billy and Angela ran into the lobby, both of them yelling at him.

"Get the keys to her room!" one of them yelled.

"Hurry, he's up there!" the other followed.

As they rushed to the check-in desk, nearly crashing into each other, Danny stepped back. "What's going on?" he asked them.

"We need to get into her room!" Billy ordered.

Danny looked at both of them and smiled at their urgency. Finally, the chance came where they needed *his* help, and he had the chance to prove he's not a kid to mess with.

"No," he said simply.

Billy frowned in shock. "Listen to me! You will get the keys to her room, and you will..."

Danny crossed his arms over his chest. "No. I won't do it." And before he could deny any further request, he was suddenly staring at the barrel of a gun.

The detective wasn't playing games.

*

Cynthia was happy to see the clouds drifted when she stepped onto the balcony. The sun was rising, and as far as her eye could see, temperate, unfiltered rays of sunlight lit the horizon of the city. She let the sun caress her skin for a moment, then closed her eyes as she walked toward the ledge and took a deep breath of the salty air.

She heard the waves crashing onto the distant shores and smiled when she thought about Max playing amongst them.

*

Danny nervously fumbled with the key when they arrived at her door. With the detective still holding the gun at him, he couldn't concentrate on getting the damned lock opened.

There!

With a click of the bolt, Danny pushed against the door, but it didn't budge beyond an inch.

She utilized the chain lock.

"Move aside," Billy ordered.

Both Angela and Danny did as they were told.

He kicked the door, but it sprang back; the chain proving too strong.

*

She heard the banging on her door, but she paid it no mind. She didn't think of anything at that moment, not her son, not her friends, not her question as to how It survived. She didn't think about the fact that It was inside of her, nor of how she needed to make the kill; swift enough to keep him in. That morning, as the sun grew stronger, Cynthia concentrated only on its warmth.

Keeping her eyes tightly closed, she controlled her thoughts long enough to not open them and let Mason see the ground of the parking lot below rushing toward them.

*

Billy and Angela ran in when the door swung open, and Danny slowly crept in behind them.

"Where is she?" Danny asked, watching as they inspected the room frantically, both appearing uncertain as to what they should find.

Angela was the first to notice the empty balcony. She peered over the ledge, and as though she saw it before, she simply closed her eyes and said a prayer for her.

Then Billy looked over the ledge and saw her broken body on the asphalt. Her eyes were still open and looking up at the clear skies, though Billy thought that she was looking at him.

"Did she…" Danny said from behind them, finding himself unable to actually ask.

When Angela walked into the room, her eyes filled with tears, he knew the answer. She walked directly to the phone, and he watched as she dialed 911.

Shocked, Danny looked around the room unsure how to react from the news and disappointed in himself. He could have saved her, gone to the room when she was alive and talked her out of doing it. But how could he have known?

He sat on the bed, wanting to cry. But he found a notebook on the floor, then quickly saw the other two on the bed.

"Why," Billy whispered, tears flowing through the air toward the pavement. "Why, Cynthia?" He wanted answers, he wanted to know what pushed her, if It pushed her. "You had Max. Why?"

"Look at this!" Danny excitedly called from inside the room.

Billy entered from the balcony and saw Angela and Danny hovered over a notebook, flipping through the pages.

"What is it?" he asked, wiping his face.

"I don't know," Angela said, handing him one of the three.

He flipped through the pages, glancing at words, but not reading them. Then, he stopped, perplexed by something he found.

"She wrote the story," he said, reading of his last meeting with Cynthia. It was exactly how he remembered it, down to the last detail, and all completely legible.

Angela collected the other two and handed them to Billy. With tears still fresh in her eyes, she told him, "They're yours now." Then, she walked toward the bathroom, continuing her inspection.

"She wrote a story then killed herself?" Danny asked. "Why?"

Billy ignored his question and flipped through the rest of the notebooks, amazed that she wrote so much in one night. Beginning with Mason Bayer's death eighteen years before to the moment she left the barn, she wrote *everything.*

Angela called for Billy, standing at the door to the bathroom. She saw it when she turned on the light just as she thought she would; just like her vision told her she would.

Billy entered the humid bathroom and saw it almost as quickly as she did.

Across the center of the mirror, engraved in the mist of her shower, the word reflected brilliantly.

NEVES it read.

It didn't take long for Billy to realize what must have happened. As Angela told him before, Mason had powers to fool even the eyes. Nothing is as it seems, she said, and as he stood in the room, his eyes locked onto the word, he knew Cynthia fell victim to one of Mason's games.

He felt it.

"That's it, right?" Billy asked her, suddenly falling short of breath. "It's over, right?"

Angela looked upon the mirror and breathed in slowly. She felt the evil that Cynthia felt many times before, and as goose bumps erupted throughout her entire body, she felt the evil with them still.

"No," she answered. "There are two children."